BOLD AS LOVE

Also by Gwyneth Jones in Gollancz

Divine Endurance
Escape Plans
Kairos
White Queen
North Wind
Phoenix Café

BOLD AS LOVE

A Near Future Fantasy

GWYNETH JONES

GOLLANCZ

LONDON

This edition first published in Great Britain in 2001 by
Gollancz
An imprint of Orion Books Ltd
Orion House, 5 Upper St Martin's Lane, London WC2H 9EA

A CIP record for this book is available
from the British Library

Typeset at The Spartan Press Ltd,
Lymington, Hants

Printed in Great Britain by
Clays Ltd, St Ives plc

Visit the official Insanitude Website: http://www.boldaslove.co.uk
for more information plus acknowledgements, outtakes,
lyrics, tour dates, merchandising, trivia, discography.

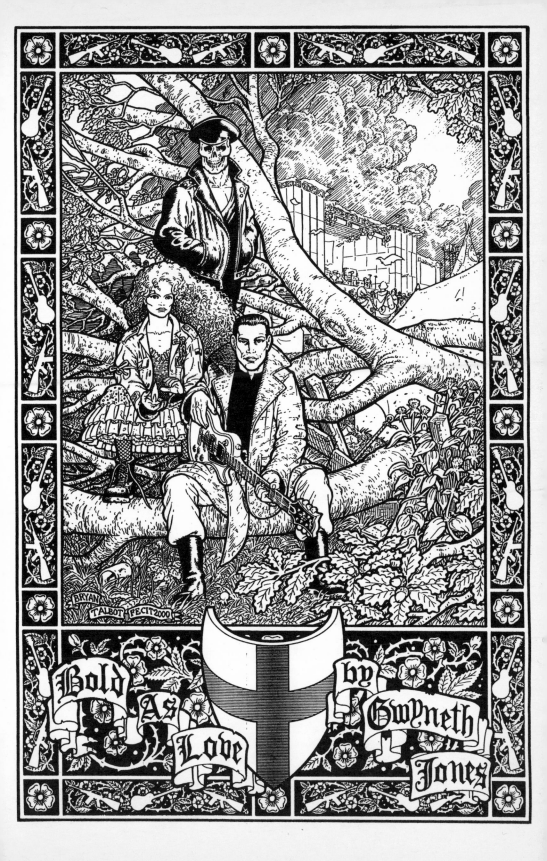

'All Mythology masters and dominates and shapes the forces of nature in and through the imagination; hence it disappears as soon as man gains mastery over the forces of nature . . .'

KARL MARX

But, on the other hand . . .

PROLOGUE

The sun was setting in a flood of scarlet and gold as a small white van cruised to a halt on the Caversham Road. Heraldic colour arced majestically over the Thames valley, glowing in the edging windscreens and blanking out the visors of the traffic cops. The van, *Anansi's Jamaica Kitchen*, was driven by a calm, amiable Rasta who seemed to have been training himself from birth for trials like this: the impatience of a tailback, the heavy hand of site security, the uncertainties of arrival.

'Rare pretty sunset,' he remarked, smiling like a gentle god at the motorcycle cop who had come snarling up beside them. 'You interested in politics, Fio?'

His passenger was a young white woman – a very young woman, no more than fifteen or sixteen, he guessed – dressed in green, with a stubborn face and a mass of dark red hair knotted back under her scarf. She wore a yellow ribbon tied round one sleeve, indicating that she was not up for sex, and a broken chain – it looked like a few silver links from an identity bracelet – pinned to her breast, saying that she approved of the Dissolution of the Act of Union. She'd slung her bedroll into the back with the kitchen and cooking supplies; she held an acoustic guitar in a battered case in her arms. She wasn't talkative. He'd learned very little about her, except for those two signs and the name, Fiorinda. He seemed to remember that name on the programme, but he wasn't going to ask her was she a performer. That's never a cool question. Maybe she was, maybe she was one of thousands, roadworn rags-and-feathers kind of white girl.

'Not in the least,' she said.

He smiled at her cut-glass vowels. 'Nor me. I'm here to cook my food and sell my food, meet my friends, avoid my enemies.' The van eased along another car-length and stopped again. There certainly were a shocking number of private transport hypocrites turning up for this

I

organic-holistic politically engaged Countercultural rock fest. White Van Man slid a glance at the young woman's breast. 'But you' wearin' the broken chain?'

'You can approve of something without being interested in it,' said Fiorinda. 'I do that all the time.' She lifted her chin, roused from the forbidding abstraction into which she'd retreated almost as soon as she climbed into the cab.

'You may as well drop me off now.'

It had dawned on her that it was ridiculous to stay in the traffic line.

'Sure thing.'

White Van Man reached across and opened the door, which was old and cranky and answered only its master's touch. The van was moving slower than walking pace, no need to apply the brakes. Fiorinda tumbled out and he tipped the bedroll after her. 'Thanks for the lift.' She joined the moving crowd on the pavement and walked away quickly.

The main gates to the site appeared: the taste-free Leisure Centre buildings, a green bank covered with hawkers and their litter; smiling but determined stewards in dayglo bibs. Fiorinda slowed and came to a stand, the crowd parting around her as she gazed over their heads, stony-eyed, at the vast beauty of the sky.

She eased the bedroll on her back and swerved away.

A short time later she was sitting under a poplar tree beside the river Thames, her back to the water, face towards the fence that separated normal life from the Festival campground. The soundtrack of that other world drifted out to her: a thumping dance beat, the wail of an electric guitar, a didgeridoo, a crying child, a dog barking, a growling engine, all multiplied and sampled down into anonymous aural mulch. She took off her boots and retrieved the backstage pass that had been hidden in the toe of the left one. In her other boot she had money. Her sleeping bag was wrapped in a heavy polythene sheet that served as roof and floor, house and shelter and defensible territory. She had everything she needed . . . except, it seemed, the mere will to cross the boundary and join that *fair field full of folk*. She stowed the pass away again and sat with her chin on her knees, rubbing at her toes.

Her feet were sore. The silver-sequinned filigree of her outer skirts needed mending and her longest underskirt was sticky with mud. The weather was clear now, but it had been filthy earlier and further north. She wanted a real bed, a proper bathroom with a flush toilet and a room with walls: none of which she was going to find down by this riverside.

The light of that extravagant sunset flowed over her, so low and strong that it confused every outline. But shortly she became aware that there were three people right in front of her, crouching in the trees and bushes that blocked her view. She heard the snap of a struck match.

'Watch out, sisters,' said a woman's harsh voice. 'Think Iran, in the days when the Shah fell. You'll submit to his charm, slave for his cause, die on his barricades. Then after the revolution you'll end up chained to the stove in peekaboo panties, all over again.'

'Barefoot and not even pregnant,' added someone else. 'He's into population control, I heard.' There was a general chuckle.

'Is he setting this up himself, or is someone pushing him?' asked a third.

'He's acting innocent,' said the first voice. 'You know what a low profile he's been playing. But it's all scripted, every bite and shite. Think Julius Caesar. *Offer me the crown a few times. I'll refuse, I'll deny every rumour, then I'll reluctantly accept* . . . She grunted, and went on, 'Of course he's been targeted. Headhunted by the secret rulers. He has backers, groomers, bankrollers, all of that. But it wouldn't happen if he didn't want it.'

Fiorinda crept closer, listening intently, trying to see the speakers without being seen. There were three women, sitting in a row, passing a blackened old pipe between them. One of them had a shock of silver-white hair tied up on top of her head, another had a broad back and was dressed in dark red. More than that she couldn't tell. A rich, faecal smell arose. She drew back from the impromptu latrine and walked quickly to the path that gave campers access to the riverside. When the three had finished their pipe and their business, she was waiting for them.

At the end of this year, three hundred years of history would be undone. The Act of Union would be dissolved. Ulster had already joined Federal Ireland; now the three nations of Mainland Britain would become, finally, officially, separate states. In London the law and order crisis was going to keep Parliament from its summer recess; that, and the struggle to make the process of dissolution look organised. Meanwhile, the Counterculturals had gathered in Hyde Park, at Glastonbury, at all the traditional sites around the country, and, notably, here at Reading. It was supposed to be a peaceful two-week rock festival. The media people were hoping for trouble, and doing their best to whip it up. Maybe their efforts were unnecessary. The Countercultural Movement was out for some real part in the new government of England, and they already knew that violence didn't diminish their popular appeal. The grass roots activists (militant travellers, eco-terrorists, animal rights extremists, road-wreckers, green-aggression hippies) would surely be eager to use this showcase. But Fiorinda didn't care about any of that. She had come to Reading following a rumour, on a mission half of longing, half of vengeance. The conversation she'd overheard had convinced her she was on a fresh trail. He was here. She would find him, she would face him. She wasn't interested in anything else.

ONE

The Salt Box

The Christmas that she was nine years old, Fiorinda's gran gave her a strange Christmas present. It was a box, of plain, polished birch. It had a snug-fitting lid, which opened to show a space inside about as big as a Turkish coffee cup, lined in darker applewood and full of sparkling white grains. Gran handed this over, unwrapped, when Fiorinda brought her breakfast tray down to the basement on Christmas morning. Gran was not bedridden, but she liked to spend much of her time under the covers, tucked up like a nesting animal.

'Is it drugs?' asked the little girl.

'No! It's salt. Taste, go on, try some. And look here.' Gran turned the box over and twisted off the base to reveal another cavity, containing a soft mass like yellowish cotton wool, and things that looked to the child vaguely like the dismantled workings of a mousetrap. 'That's so you can strike a light without matches.'

'Is it magic?'

The old lady chuckled evasively. 'Why would I waste magic on *you*, you little heathen?'

Gran was a witch, a Wiccan. Her damp rooms in the basement of Fiorinda's mother's house were hung with magical things: glitter balls, crystals, plastic dolls, sequinned scarves, bunches of herbs. People came to her for spells or to have their fortunes told – discreetly using the garden door so they didn't have to meet Fiorinda's mum. The child viewed her grandmother's profession with indifference. Already Fiorinda didn't believe in anything.

'Is it old?'

'No, it's new. I had someone make it for you, one of my associates. It's for your future. You must take it with you when you set out to seek your fortune.' She closed the child's hands over the box, covering them with her own. 'You are the salt of the earth, that's what you are. I've seen it.

And the world will love you as meat loves salt. Now put it away, Frances dear, and don't let your mother know.'

The child was used to being told, by her gran, that she mustn't let her mother know. Most of Gran's secrets were pointless: either things Mum knew about already (like gin and sherry taken from Mum's sideboard, like probably-stolen goods accepted in barter for magical services) or things she wouldn't care about, like spells that didn't work, or scraps of highly flavoured gossip. The salt box seemed different. She hid it carefully. In time she would come to see it as a double symbol, a threat and a promise. The promise was that she would escape: that winds of change would blow away the chill, hateful tedium of her childhood. The threat was that she would never free herself from an embarrassing set of old-fashioned values. She would be in the new age, but not of it.

When she was eleven her periods began, and she decided to call herself Fiorinda. This was the year in which her mother was operated on for breast cancer. It was while Mum was in hospital that Fiorinda's Aunt Carly turned up. Fiorinda had a stepfather, her mother's ex-husband. She had two grown-up half-sisters and a half-brother, and there was Gran, of course. But she'd never known that her mother had a sister until Carly appeared on the doorstep, with a taxi driver carrying her suitcases. She looked young, incredibly much younger than Mum, and she was dressed in the height of fashion. She moved in and switched on the central heating, although it was only November. She brought with her a régime of hot showers, scented foam, music videos and channel-hopping, takeaway food and glossy magazines. Gran stayed in the basement. She didn't seem to like her younger daughter much. Probably she was thinking of how angry Mum would be when she saw the bills for all this. But Fiorinda, who lived for the moment, was thrilled.

Carly explained that there had been a big family quarrel, years ago, and that was why she hadn't been in touch. She said she'd last visited this house for Fiorinda's third birthday party. 'You don't remember, but I was here. You were a very bossy, precocious little girl, do you remember that? I gave you a pink wooden horse.'

Fiorinda wished she could remember, or that any sign of the pink horse remained.

The cancer was defeated, at least temporarily. Mum came home from hospital. Once she came into the kitchen (actually warm, under Carly's régime) and found Fiorinda resplendent in her aunt's expensive cosmetics. She stared for a moment, and Fio braced herself for the storm, but all Mum said was, 'I'm going to turn the heating down.' She left the room without a glance at her sister: head lowered, arms wrapped around her changed and vulnerable body.

Carly was blushing, Fiorinda was surprised to see. 'She thinks I'm a child stealer.'

'Is that why she hates you?'

'No . . . It's because of things that happened long, long ago. Why don't you have lodgers, Fio? She can't maintain this place on her salary.'

Fio's mum was a university lecturer. 'We did have lodgers. But they either didn't pay the rent; or they were junkies and trashed their rooms; or they had dogs that shitted everywhere; or they had babies that screamed. I don't think it would work, whoever they were. My mother hates people, any people.'

'Poor Sue.'

'What was she like? I mean, years ago?'

'She was a journalist. She was chic and sexy, she was demanding, she had tons of style—'

'I can't imagine it. What kind of journalist?'

'Mainly music . . . rock music. Didn't you know? What does she teach now?'

'Contemporary culture,' said Fio, with a grimace: contemporary meant something for old people. 'But what happened? Why did she give it all up?'

'She didn't give it up, it gave her up. She fell from grace; it happens. Sue took it hard.'

'I can imagine *that*. Oh. I suppose that's why she hates me to play—'

'What—?'

Fiorinda was forced to play the piano. In secret she had taught herself to play acoustic guitar and to sing, a little (the secondhand guitar came from Gran, and the basement black market). She wasn't ready to tell Carly about this. 'Oh, you know: she hates any kind of music but Beethoven, that sort of thing.' Until Carly came, Fiorinda's only access to non-classical music had been through her ancient radio alarm, on which she listened to chart shows, secretly, late at night.

Carly started putting the make-up away. The house had become cheerfully untidy under her rule, but she was careful about her own possessions: she left no hostages. 'You can play Beethoven, wow. What a talented niece I have. But I'd have to introduce you as just a friend if you came to see me, because you look so grown-up. You'd put ten years on my age.' She surveyed her handiwork. 'You're prettier than Sue. You

7

don't have ginger eyebrows. 'She *made* herself beautiful. You won't have to try.'

Life in the cold house became doubly miserable through that long winter. Mum refused to accept Fiorinda's new name, which led to pointless friction. Every evening she sat marking papers at one end of the dining table that stood in the back of their chill living room, her profile sour in the lamplight. The idea of Fio having a telly of her own that she could use in another room was vetoed, no reason given. So she listened to books on tape, at the most muted volume, because Mum hated headphone-leak. She never read *printed* books in Mum's presence because it would have pleased her. Every time her mother called her 'Frances' it was another flick on the raw. In the night she devoured her mother's library, relishing the privacy of the old relationship; and wrote songs, both words and music, which she hid inside the split in her mattress.

When Carly invited Fio to visit her, Mum tried to stop that too. Fio heard them arguing on the phone. (There was one, fixed phone in the cold house. It lived in the front hall, at the foot of the stairs, by the living room door, for maximum inconvenience and minimum privacy.) 'She's a *child*, Caz. She's *a little girl*. Leave her alone—' But Fio pleaded and Carly persisted and in the end Mum gave way. Fiorinda travelled on the Underground by herself (she had to do this anyway, to get to secondary school) into the centre of London. She ate in a restaurant for the first time in her life, she stayed the night at Carly's tiny flat in Kensington Church Street. Carly took her shopping, gave her clothes, make-up and a mobile phone. (The phone didn't work after the first day, but it looked great.) True to her word, she introduced Fio to the people she met in Kensington as 'the daughter of a friend of mine'.

In the summer, Carly invited Fiorinda to stay for a whole week. This brought renewed resistance, but Carly wouldn't take no for an answer. 'And when you're tired of this game,' said Mum, 'you'll dump the poor kid and I'll be left to pick up the pieces. That's what pisses me off.' Fio, eavesdropping from the landing, heard the defeat in her mother's voice and exulted.

Mum would have been furious if she'd known that Carly let Fio smoke dope. But nothing else remotely shocking happened: no stronger drugs, no vice. People came around and chatted, Fio was mostly ignored. She spent much of her time on her visits to the first-floor Kensington flat alone in the cubbyhole Carly called her study, drinking Diet Coke and playing computer games. She didn't mind. It was paradise compared to life at home. But this time Carly had been invited to a country house party, and she was going to take Fiorinda with her. They were going to stay with Rufus O'Niall, the rock star. Of course, this had to be kept secret from Fio's mother.

Rufus O'Niall had been a megastar before Fiorinda was born. He was practically retired now, even from special guest stadium sort of occasions. She'd have been more excited if she'd been going to meet Glasswire, or Aoxomoxoa and the Heads.

'I wasn't invited,' she said, uneasily. 'Won't that be weird?'

'Rufus is a billionaire or something, darling. He doesn't count the spoons. And he's a very private person, but he never goes anywhere without this huge entourage—' Carly laughed. 'Don't worry, you'll be lost in the crowd. But you'll meet people. You want to be a singer, don't you?' Fio had by now confessed her secret ambition. 'You'll need contacts. You can't start too soon.'

The journey and the arrival passed in a blur. Carly had been right, there was a crowd of people, the kind of people she had met in Kensington, only more so. Fio was shown to a room by a servant. The house must be five hundred years old – half-timbered, spartan, smelling of beeswax and lavender and dried oranges. The portraits on the walls were not of Rufus O'Niall's forebears, obviously not, since his skin was chestnut brown and the pictured faces were as white as Fiorinda's. But the sense of dynasty was right. Rufus was old money in the world of rock and roll. He and his band The Geese had reached that rare plateau of truly unassailable fame and solid wealth. Fiorinda began to feel thrilled. Later, when he took some of his guests on a tour of the manor grounds, she tagged along and tried to get next to the master. What was most incredible was that Carly's friendship with genuine celebrities seemed to prove that *Fio's mum* had once been on intimate terms with the famous. But she'd been warned not to mention her mother. Whatever it was Mum had done, apparently it still rankled in the music world.

She was trying to be cool, but feeling very uncomfortable. Used to the modest habits of her North London, mainly Hindu, neighbourhood, she felt terribly exposed in the clothes she was wearing. She was glad Carly had warned her how to dress, but she kept wanting to put her hands over her bum, to fold her arms over the outline of her breasts. And the men were no better. She supposed that if you were rich, walking about in your own private grounds was the same as being out at a fancy club.

As they climbed a flight of steps from the fishponds to a rose terrace, Rufus turned and glanced at Fio, who had managed to reach the centre of the group. He at once resumed his conversation with the fat, florid woman beside him (a movie producer). But a few moments later he turned again, and handed her a sprig of rose leaves. 'Put that in your pocket, sweet-briar,' he said, with a tender smile. 'Keep it for a souvenir.'

She hadn't known you could have rosebushes with scented leaves. She didn't have a pocket. She held the sprig in her hand, awkwardly, all the way back to the house. She was deeply flattered and excited. She started trying to think of the names of some of The Geese's hit singles, so that she'd have something to say if he noticed her again.

In the evening, after dinner, some guests disappeared. The rest sat around with Rufus in the great hall. People had been drinking quite a lot, and sniffing coke, but they were quiet about it. Fio had half expected them to be naked except for jewels and make-up, after the way they dressed in daytime, but they were wearing the same as in the afternoon. Carly was there, but she seemed to have decided to leave Fiorinda to her own devices, which was fine. Fio did not want to be shown off, or looked after like a baby. She had changed into her best scarlet teeshirt and a shiny long pink skirt. The teeshirt was printed over with little naked male figures, labelled jokily things like "French Polish" and "Turkish Delight", though you couldn't see much difference between the faces; or the sets of wedding-tackle. She had tried it on in the exclusive shop where Carly bought it for her, baring her tiny budding breasts without shame: they could stand up for themselves. 'Well,' the attentive assistant had said, impressed, 'I thought that colour wouldn't suit you, dear, but it certainly does.'

Scarlet gave Fiorinda's creamy skin the pure glow of a candle flame, it made her strongly marked brows and lashes look made-up, which they were not . . . for some reason, Carly had forbidden her to wear make-up on this visit. There was talk, and silence; someone strummed a guitar. It was oddly like an evening in the cold house, except that the setting was ancient instead of merely old-fashioned, and there were more people. Fio felt ignored. She went over to the hearth, where there was a fire of cherry logs, because the June night was chill. She gazed into the flames and then sat down, as if by chance, with her back against the couch where he was sitting, the rock-lord in state surrounded by his courtiers. She hoped that she would think of something intelligent to say: somehow contribute to the conversation and get noticed. Instead, Rufus began to stroke her hair. She felt his fingertips on the nape of her neck, and then circling her ear.

She was half stunned at the liberty he was taking. How did he know that he *could do this*? How could he just *stroke* her, as if she were a cat or a dog? But of course he could do what he liked. For Rufus O'Niall, everything was allowed.

'Can you do magic?' he murmured, so that only she could hear. 'You look as if you could.'

'My gran's a witch. Not me. I think it's a recessive gene. You need two copies.'

Rufus laughed very quietly, like a rumble of soft thunder.

'What about your parents?'

'Oh, they're dead. My gran looks after me.' Dead parents were simpler.

Someone challenged him to a game of chess, and he left the couch.

Fiorinda's room was next to Carly's. When Rufus came to find her in the night she was sitting by the bed, still wearing her scarlet teeshirt and her pink skirt. She hadn't wanted to take them off. She'd have felt stupid waiting in her pyjamas, especially since she was half convinced that she was imagining the whole thing. But here he was. Rufus said, 'I thought you'd be tucked up under the covers by now, sweet-briar.' He took her in his arms and carried her off to his own room, which was sumptuous, but she didn't get a chance to take much in.

In the morning she woke in her own bed with no clear idea of how she'd got there. Carly was shaking her gently. 'I've got to go back to London,' she announced. 'Right now. I'm sorry, sweetheart. Something desperately important's come up, it means lots of money.'

Fio was hazy about how her aunt made a living, but she nodded.

'You'll be all right, won't you, darling? I'd hate to drag you away. You know Joel, and Mittie.' These were Carly's neighbours, a gay couple who lived in the flat upstairs. 'They'll look after you and bring you home tomorrow, or Monday.'

Fiorinda had been told by her school friends that she would never get a husband, because her Mum was a depressive and had had breast cancer. In the comfortable bourgeois community that surrounded her mother's house, it was taken for granted that people with bad genes would not reproduce themselves. (It was easier for the community to accept this idea, since it was equally taken for granted that bad genes were almost unknown in people of Indian ancestry.) The well-to-do Hindu girls weren't being cruel. They meant that she should prepare herself for another kind of life, and they were concerned that she showed no sign of doing so. Fiorinda didn't mind. She liked the feeling of being one of a kind. She liked the feeling that she had nothing to lose. She'd been very surprised at what had happened, but she'd had no qualms about losing her virginity. It might be a big break, and anyway it was worth a shot. In the entertainment business, most people have to start out working for free.

She went back to London with Carly's friends, but she knew it wasn't over. Sure enough, about two weeks after half-term, Rufus came to find her. He was waiting in a taxi one afternoon, discreetly parked down the road from the school gates. He took her to a flat, a luxurious but poky little place which he used 'sometimes' he explained vaguely. She knew he'd used it with the other girls; she didn't mind. It was the start of a regular affair. Sometimes he was waiting in the morning, waylaid her and carried her off, and she never reached her classes; sometimes he only 'borrowed her', as he put it, for an hour or so. He gave her presents, which had to stay in the flat as she couldn't take them home, but there was never any suggestion that he would offer her money. She felt that was a good sign. The rewards she'd get for this would be of a different order. Weeks passed. In August, Mum thought Fiorinda was going into school to the holiday-homework club, but she was meeting Rufus. She found that he would talk to her, and plagued him with her insatiable, devouring curiosity. He said she asked more questions than a three-year-old. The sexual part of the experience wasn't very sexy for Fio, but she didn't mind that. The strange and important thing was that she was actually getting to know him, getting to *know* this big, flamboyantly handsome grown-up man as a person. Rufus was lagging behind her, but that would change. He would come to recognise Fio as a person, instead of a forbidden pleasure. He would like her, instead of feeling addicted and guilty, the way he felt now. She began to think with impatience of the years – at least three years, to be reasonable – that must pass before they could be seen in public together.

In September, without warning, he vanished.

She didn't know the address of their flat. When he stopped coming to pick her up she took the Tube to the approximate location and walked around trying to find it, but she couldn't. She realised, then, why she'd paid no attention to details like street names. She must have known, though her daydreams had seemed so real, that this was how it would end. He would simply be gone.

Since the country house party she had hardly heard from her Aunt Carly. She guessed that Carly had found out about her going with Rufus, and naturally didn't want to get involved. But she had nowhere else to turn, so she went to Kensington Church Street. She still had her entry card for the front door, but when she got upstairs there was nobody in.

12

When she'd been knocking and ringing at her aunt's door for a while Joel came down from the floor above.

'Hi, Fio. Long time no see. Carly's gone away for a few days. Can I help?'

'It's private.' But though she knew she *could not* chase Rufus, she was too weak to resist this opportunity. 'I don't suppose you know how I can contact Rufus O'Niall?'

Joel had a key to Carly's front door. He opened it and hustled her inside, into Carly's tiny, smartly furnished living room. 'Rufus has left town,' he said, folding his arms and glaring at her. 'He suddenly rushed back to the Seychelles, which is where he more or less lives these days. With his lovely wife and kids. You don't want to contact him. How old are you?'

She bristled. 'D'you think I'm too young to have sex?'

'With someone your own age, maybe that would be different. Rufus O'Niall is a low-down dirty dog. He's old enough to be your grandad, and *you* are well young enough to get him arrested, except that it won't happen. Maybe he actually took pity on you, kid: he can't have fled the country for fear of discovery. His sad taste for underage totty is something everyone knows and nobody tells . . . Do you hear what I'm saying? You have nothing on him. Go home, don't come here again. You do have a home?'

'Yes.'

'Thank God for that. How did you get involved with Carly Slater, anyway?'

'She's actually my aunt,' quavered Fiorinda, frightened by his anger.

Joel frowned. 'Your *aunt*?'

'Yes!' Fiorinda had been forbidden to mention this, but she was stung by the term 'underage totty'. 'She's my aunt. Her mother is my gran and lives in our basement.'

He stared for a moment, in silence. 'Remind me, what's your name? Your real name.'

She was so intimidated she confessed the hated truth: 'Frances. It's Frances Day. But that's my mother's ex-husband's name: she uses it, but he's not my father. My real name is Frances Slater. Carly is my mother's sister.'

'So, that makes you . . . your mother must be . . . Sue Slater? The journalist?'

'Yes.'

'Oh, my God.' Joel came up close and looked into Fio's face intently.

He backed away again, looking stunned. 'Wow. Your aunt is really something.'

Fiorinda wondered what was going on. Probably he'd guessed why she was here. But though she knew she'd been stupid, her problem wasn't *that* weird.

'Why did you want to see her? Did you think she'd give you Rufus's private number? Because you can forget that—'

'No! I don't want him involved! Not really, not at all. But I need help. I think I'm pregnant.'

'My God,' said Joel. 'What a mess.'

The sisters had a confrontation, in the kitchen where Carly had one day painted Fio's face, and remarked, 'I'd have to introduce you as just a friend.' Naturally, Carly denied everything. She insisted she'd been trying to help, trying to give poor Fiorinda a life. She was as appalled as anyone at the way Rufus had behaved, she'd had no idea he would do that, she was devastated, it was awful, a really horrible coincidence, she felt terribly responsible . . . But before the denials started, Fiorinda, who was present at this meeting, had seen the gleam of triumph in her aunt's eyes. She wondered what her mum had done to Carly, in the long ago, to lay the fuse for such a savage, cold-blooded, long-planned revenge. But she wasn't curious about the details. She decided, then and there, never to see her half-siblings again, never to have anything more to do with them.

If this was family life, the hell with it.

She refused to have an abortion. Having an abortion would make it all too real. Her gran provided cantrips and potions that didn't work, her mother seemed too sunk in her own despair to take much notice. She stopped going to school in the fifth month and completed the pregnancy in deep denial, trying to stay thin and hoping to the last minute that it was all a bad dream. The baby was born surprisingly strong and healthy. When it was three months old it caught pneumonia and died, after which Fiorinda left the cold house forever.

She followed the weird sisters into a low-rise tented township. New arrivals were wandering, laden: seeking friends, eyeing-up pitches. Families were cooking, tribes erecting totem poles and lofting big gaudy marker-balloons. Dogs ambled, bare-arsed toddlers tottered, smoke wreathes eddied. A band of dancers, pogoing in a trance that might keep going for days, had blocked one of the vehicle access lanes. Fio's three witches briefly joined the dance and passed on: the old one with the silver topknot, the one whose broad back was robed in blood red; the third in yellow and blue, with a bald head, a scalplock and an eagle's feather.

Fiorinda had moved from the cold house to a central London hostel, answered an advertisement in a music paper and started singing with a band called DARK. She'd been with them ever since. They'd brought out an album, but there were beginning to be rending and tearing noises. She had started doing some gigs alone. She was moving on, with the band or without them, on a trajectory that, in her mind, led only to one end. Rumours had been rife for about a year and a half that Rufus O'Niall, semi-retired superstar, was moving into Countercultural politics: that he was coming back to the soon-to-be-history UK; that he was going to take a major role of some kind. Nothing had happened, yet. He hadn't been mentioned in the media coverage for this summer of Dissolution Rock. But that was like Rufus, Fiorinda knew. Backers, bankrollers, groomers? The old witch was wrong. He had no need for any of that. He would arrive without fanfare here at Reading, which everyone knew was the *real* Dissolution Festival. He would be elusive, he would be relaxed, secretly drawing people around him—

Even now she could feel Carly's soft fingertips, the first blissful silky touch of expensive cosmetics on her skin. She could see her own face in the mirror, strange and lovely. *I'll have to introduce you as a friend* . . . She had understood, afterwards, that her aunt was what they used to call a procuress. Fiorinda had been procured, prepared and delivered to her own father, the client. Most probably (she'd denied this too, but it was obvious) Carly had also been the one who made sure Rufus found out. She had told him, or had someone tell him, that the latest box-fresh girl child he'd been enjoying was his own daughter.

But he must have had some idea, he must have suspected. I don't look like Carly but I do look like my mum, I know I do. If he didn't know about me and Mum and Gran, why did he ask me like that, *can you do magic?*

Lanterns began to be lit. She crossed a swathe of petrol-stink, and the gut-thumping judder of an electric generator bit her bones. The masses were exchanging tickets for wristbands and filing through the cattlegates. The witches ducked through an unofficial doorway cut in heavy plastic-coated mesh: she followed them. Now she was in the arena. Some band or other was playing on main stage, far away, but the witches had joined a small crowd outside one of the other venues, a big conical marquee called the Blue Lagoon. In the middle of this crowd, there was a man. They'd found their Thane of Cawdor. He was wearing a hat and a long brown leather coat. He had his back to Fio, but he was tall, he carried himself with a casual presence of power, and he was obviously the centre of attention. It was Rufus. She couldn't be absolutely sure until he turned his head, but—

What was she going to say to him? After four years . . . But the first year she didn't count, she tried to cut that year out of her memory. After three years of making something of herself, shaping her talent and using it. Don't say anything, don't let him see you, not at first.

No. You will never be ready. Take your chance as it comes—

In the distance there was a ring of hawkers' vans, bright as a funfair. Beer vendors with coolboxes were swinging big greeny yellow trunch-eons of chemical light. She wet her lips.

You knew I was someone's daughter before you touched me. If you cared . . . If it made a difference when you knew I was your *daughter, then how could you—?*

How could you leave me to face them all alone—?

> And now stop crying
> Slide the knife between
> Razor into there
> Always be there,
> however small it goes,
> between the bleeding
> space between screaming
> where it doesn't matter
> Live within the pain,
> Live in the pain,
> Live . . . for . . . this moment . . .

'Oh, hi, Fio!'

Coming towards her – just emerged from the backstage entrance of a smaller, emerald coloured tent across the way – was a vision of perfection, wearing a slim black dress and a long grey padded jacket with gauze sleeves. Her skin was misty gold; black curls caught up in a knot behind her head, brow and eyes obscured by a glittery effect like insect wings. Her name was Allie Marlowe, she was a sort of friend of Fio's. 'Shit,' muttered Fiorinda.

She remembered White Van Man's plan to meet his friends and avoid his enemies. Allie was a music-biz socialite, one of those people you might dismiss as a groupie or hanger-on until you realised (before she noticed your dismissal, if you were lucky) what an important role she played. Right now Fio didn't want to meet *anyone* she knew, but she absolutely definitely desperately did not want Allie Marlowe to witness her first meeting with Rufus O'Niall.

'Hi, Allie.' It was too late to flee.

'Fancy meeting you here!'

'Fancy meeting you,' said Fiorinda. 'I've just arrived. How's it going? How's the *boîte*?'

Their friendship had been founded when Fiorinda did a gig with DARK at a big club in Brussels that Allie was managing. Fio had ended up going home with Allie, and they'd talked all night. Since then, Allie had displayed flattering interest and look-through-you indifference roughly alternately whenever their paths crossed. She was an excellent barometer, if you were in any doubt about how you were doing. This time she seemed actually *embarrassed*, which Fio thought was a very bad sign, until she realised that Allie – eyes flicking from side to side under her dainty futuristic veil – was *personally* embarrassed, nothing to do with Fio, at being caught wandering around by herself. Socialites, like rock-lords, should never be seen without an entourage.

'Oh, I've moved *on*,' she exclaimed, warmly. With Allie it was always 'Oh!', a round-mouthed big-eyed home-alone pause before any possible statement, to give her time for second thoughts. 'I'm not running the club anymore. Oh, Fio, I must give you one of these—'

Fio accepted the handout, which Allie had taken from a businesslike grey attaché case: a surprising item for a style-monster, but Allie never made mistakes, so it must be right. She peered at it in the half-dark and discovered a list of events called 'seminars' and 'workshops', with titles like *The Death Of State Education* and *Human Rights – Who Needs Them?*

'What on earth's this? Is politics really the new rock and roll, then?'

'*Paul Javert* is going to be speaking.'

'Who he?'

Allie rolled her eyes. 'The Home Secretary, Fio. Where have you been?'

'Touring. That means he runs the police, doesn't it.'

'Look, don't you realise this is *serious*? If you don't know who Paul is and what he stands for, I think you'd better come along and find out. Trust me, Fio. Westminster is the place, nothing's going to happen out here in the sticks. So . . .' She glanced at Fiorinda's bedroll, her boots, her ragged fancy skirts, and winced, visibly. Allie didn't like Fiorinda's grunge-waif style, and had tried to persuade her to smarten up, to no avail.

'Are you looking for someone, or—'

'Looking for Aoxomoxoa,' Fio improvised. 'I was supposed to meet him and the lads—'

'Oh! The Braindead Ones. Yeah, they're here. Unless they've been chucked off the site. Apparently Sage arrived completely smashed and got into a fist-fight with the security people within minutes. Look, I'm in a real rush. See you tomorrow, and remember, *be there.*'

She flitted away into the dusk, leaving Fiorinda airkissed, flustered, humiliated, puzzled, and with a vague, wild idea that Allie Marlowe must be having an affair with the Home Secretary. What other explanation could there possibly be for her enthusiasm? Or the attaché case. The crowd outside the Blue Lagoon had vanished. The canvas doors to the marquee were roped shut; nothing was scheduled in there tonight. She went and stood listening to the dark and silence inside for a few moments, tasting her anticipation. He is here.

She wandered on, looking out for skulls, wondering if this crowd really was different, revolutionary, dangerous. Digital facemasks, bodymasks. Carnival plumes and banners, the painted and the naked and the students and the straights, all jostling together. Just the normal rock-fest scene, as far as Fiorinda could see. It would be good if she *could* find the Heads. She didn't believe the chucking-out story, that was just Allie's way of saying she hated Aoxomoxoa.

Sage and his band had been wearing digital skulls for heads, for years – a mark of deference to their late, great gurus, the Grateful Dead (an oblique influence on the Heads' actual music, which tended to vile noises and weird multimedia tricks). It was no longer so easy to pick them out in a crowd, now that masks were commonplace, but they were sure to be out here among the masses somewhere. They liked to see life.

She spread her sleeping bag that night in an ancient army-surplus mess-tent, next to Sage's preposterous great van, and woke to the sound of birdsong, leaf shadows dappling the canvas roof. She'd cleared the detritus and arranged the overspill of Heads' belongings neatly on her polythene (the van's annexe had no groundsheet), when the chief Head himself appeared at the entrance. He came into the tent – immensely tall, skull mask already in place – and perched himself in one of his giant pixie poses on a stack of hardware.

'I don't remember asking you to do that.'

Sage liked chaos. Fiorinda the grunge-waif was secretly, innately neat.

'Yes you did, Sage. You said, "Please, dear Fio, tidy up this jumble sale, as I know you hate mess, and then I will be able to find things, and I will be eternally grateful."'

'Fuck. I did not.'

Aoxomoxoa's name in private life was a relic of the band's history. They'd originally called themselves Purple Sage, but people had kept thinking it was Purple *Haze*: which had pissed them off, so they'd been forced to change it. Fiorinda had met him when the Heads had come backstage after a DARK gig, in Amsterdam. They'd been best friends ever since.

'You wouldn't know any different if you did, you were drunk as a whole stink of skunks. Sage, you didn't actually hit anyone over where to put the van, did you?'

The Heads' version of Allie's chucking-out story was that Sage had decided he didn't have to park his rig in the scummy hospitality area if he didn't feel like it. Site security had demurred. There'd been 'a pointless argument'; and the van was here in Travellers' Meadow — otherwise reserved for well-connected hippie clans with live-in wheels. 'Nah. I never hit the bib people no more, 'tisn't sporting. I *reasoned* with 'em. Honest . . . Where've you been, brat? Why'n't you turn up with DARK? People have been worried. I was too wrecked to think of asking you last night.'

'I had a fight with Charm,' said Fiorinda gloomily, picking up her sleeping bag and shaking it. 'Worse than ever. Horrible. I said I'd meet them here . . . but I think we're finished after this. We'll hack it through the gig and then I will be fired, or I will quit.'

Charm Dudley was DARK's frontwoman.

'What kind of a fight? Didja hit her?'

Fiorinda ducked her head and retired behind a curtain of red curls. 'I may have done.'

'Hahaha. So, I think you can fuck off telling me how to behave . . .' The blank spaces that hid his eyes lit on a white covered bucket standing in a corner. 'What's *that*?'

Sage's van was a monster; there was always something wrong with it. Last night she had learned to her despair that the composting unit was not functional. The Heads didn't care, indeed, she suspected they'd have hated the van if it ever managed the separation from squalor it so falsely promised. Fiorinda had taken the law into her own hands.

'It is a bucket with a lid. I went out and bought it from White Van Man. He's doing them as a sideline. I knew because he gave me a lift in yesterday.'

'Off of White Van Man, Fio. Not "from" . . . Watch yourself.' He went over for a closer inspection. 'I hope it's not a *chemical toilet*. I won't stand for that. We will fix the composting thing, how could you doubt us?'

'No you won't. It has never worked properly, and the nearest Portaloos are ten hundred miles from here, and if the weather warms up they will get *maggots*. I *cannot* cope with maggots squiggling around inches under my bottom. It's only a bucket. It can be cleaned by organically sound methods. But I insist on the lid. I can't help it, I'm addicted to civilisation. What are you doing up so early, anyway? Diarrhoea? I'll go for a little stroll then, if you don't mind—'

'Nah, we're off out,' said Sage, unhooking his one-shouldered dungarees and lifting the infamous lid. 'Going to town, to the LSE. Some kinda green nazi party political conference. You ought to come, Fio. It's your kind of gig. Lotta long words. I see you're still wearing the yellow ribbon. You're a wise girl. But don't you ever think you might be missing something?'

'True intimacy is not to do with sex,' said Fiorinda, laughing.

Fio, Sage, Cack and George breakfasted on corn patties and coffee with a heavy shot of Cognac, from the White Van, and drove off to London, leaving Bill and Luke to mind the shop (a sixth Head had quit after a severe health scare. You needed a superb constitution to survive the Aoxomoxoa lifestyle). The roads were Sunday morning quiet. Hyde Park, where they left the van, was heaving. So was the LSE. Fiorinda was amazed to see such a crowd, on a Sunday lunchtime, in a place that didn't even have a bar. There was no one on the door at the main venue. They walked in and stood in the front hall, people-watching: Sage and the lads waxing astonished to find themselves inside an actual seat of learning, admiring the marble mugshots of whosits, wondering if you had to pass some kind of *exam* to get into the gigs? Fiorinda let them wax, though she considered this performance too stupid to be funny. Tv crews, some of them from proper mainstream channels, were pointing cameras and snatching soundbites. Immense numbers of people, not all of them young, not all of them funky, were peering at hand-lettered notices, clutching printed handouts, shouting at each other and into phones: purposeful, inspired, throbbing with incomprehensible excitement. I mean, thought Fiorinda, suppose they actually took over the government? Would that be *fun*? Sending out Income Tax forms, cooking the unemployment figures . . . Is that *thrilling*?

'How important is this conference?' she asked Sage, casually. 'Do you think any seriously political rockstars will be here?'

'Oh yeah.' His mask, which was something different from the simple fx the other Heads wore, writhed into a boneyard sneer. 'I'm sure rock and roll's own great Pretender to the Countercultural throne is around somewhere. Didn't know you were a fan.'

'I'm not. Not at all. Just . . . intrigued. Slightly.'

She didn't know what he was talking about. He wouldn't describe Rufus O'Niall in those terms, would he? Not to Fiorinda. The Heads never mentioned her father to Fio. They must know the whole story, but they drew a veil; they were a tactful bunch of drunken laddish idiots. She couldn't bear to ask him to be more precise. But it was another sign. That made two messages from fate, counting Allie last night. She'd missed him last night, she would find him *here*. But why had she yet to hear his name or see his picture anywhere?

The lads wanted to hear one of the big name speakers, because you might as well. She ended up sitting with them in a large, heavily raked lecture theatre listening to the President of China talking about The Environment. The Heads were disgusted to find that they were watching a video, even if the video took the form of a free-standing image. 'Might as well be watching Michael Jackson jive,' growled Sage. 'If yer frontman's not going to be physically there, it's *okay*. But you hafta say so on the tickets,' complained Cack, shocked by the duplicity of the politicals. Also, there was something wrong with the ST ear-buttons. Whoever, or whatever, was doing the ST, was comfortable with words like *if* and *but* and *and*, not too happy about anything more strenuous.

The Heads left. Presumably the rest of the audience could understand Mandarin because they stayed. So did Fiorinda, folding the President's meaningless speech around her like a cloak; composing herself within its shelter – almost like being wrapped in Sage's music, or whatever you called that stuff of his. Funny that the second most powerful person in the world should have the same appeal as an Aoxomoxoa and The Heads gig. At Question Time, when heavy numbers started filing out, she joined them and went hunting for a VIP lounge, a backstage, a track for insiders. Quite by chance she ran into a human gridlock at the foot of a nineteenth-century staircase and saw in the crush ahead of her a silver topknot, a bald knob with an eagle feather scalplock and those broad shoulders in dark blood red. She reached a desk. Smiling but determined door police, supported by security muscle, wanted her name, wanted to scan her. She had to sign something. The smiling but determined ones were turning a lot of people away. Fiorinda got through. She didn't see what happened to the witches. Reading her handout as she slowly climbed the stairs, she found that she'd signed up for something called *New Faces For The Upper Chamber? Enrolment Only*: and Paul Javert would be speaking. Explained the security. But what did the man who runs the police have to do with the former House of Lords?

'Complete bastard waste of time,' said one passing delegate to another.

'Some kinda fuckin' fake-green peerage for fuck's sake,' agreed the second. 'Total sham.'

'All they want is our names and numbers, for later attention.'

I'm sure you're right, thought Fiorinda, with a qualm of unease. Could she have just done something dangerous? She didn't care. She was backstage of this thing and she'd seen the witches again. That meant he would be *here*.

If anywhere.

The workshop (or was this one a seminar?) was in an antique, buttoned-leather armchairs sort of library. There were vistas of London rooftops through the windows, there were hungry-looking tv and webcast folk, and there were a lot of vociferous people. As Fiorinda arrived a small posse of men in suits made their entrance, accompanied by a security escort (not literally in suits, but you could tell what they were as easily as if they were policemen). Allie Marlowe, wearing an even smarter long black dress but the same grey jacket, was with this party. She saw Fiorinda and gave her a complicated smile: the smile someone gives you when you have guessed a puzzle that they thought you would not crack.

'Hey, Fio!'

Sage and Cack and George had come up beside her, grinning (they couldn't help it). 'We saw you'd signed up,' explained Cack happily. 'So we did too. What's this one?'

'I have no idea,' said Fiorinda. 'It was an accident.'

'Better ask our beloved leader,' offered Sage. 'There he is, Fio, if you want him.'

A lot of people had surged forward after the suits. Over by the windows on the right of the room, another lot of people were pressing around a man in a long leather coat. Fio immediately went over there, blood thundering in her ears—

It was the person she had glimpsed outside the Blue Lagoon marquee. But it wasn't Rufus. At such close range and without the hat she knew this instantly, but she couldn't believe it. She circled around, trying to get a good straight look, irrational conviction fighting with the evidence of her eyes. It had to be the Three Witches' Thane of Cawdor, but it wasn't

Rufus. This man was much younger, much less heavily built than he had seemed in the dusk, and he wasn't white, but his skin was lightish, more milky-tea than chestnut. She stared, unable to believe she could have made such a mistake. She had been so *certain*. It was the coat that had fooled her. A long brown leather coat such as Rufus had worn in the days when he used to come and fetch her from school. The big, sleek, soft and expensive animal skin coat had seemed uniquely glamorous; it had become inextricably linked in her childish mind with Rufus O'Niall—

The not-Rufus caught her eye, raised an eyebrow and smiled wryly. She recognised him, though they'd never met. He was Ax Preston, lead guitar and frontman of the Chosen Few, or more usually the Chosen – a band from the West Country, not very commercial, but adored by the critics. It wasn't Fio's kind of music, but he was supposed to be an ace guitarist, bit old-fashioned, bit left wing. Did he really have pretensions in Counter-cultural politics? Not that Fiorinda cared.

She turned away, glad she wasn't prone to blushing.

She saw it all now. Rufus O'Niall wasn't even in the country. The whole rumour of his entry into post-UK politics was baseless, the idea that he was bound to turn up at Reading a figment of Fiorinda's imagination. How could she have built so much on so little? She'd have walked straight out, but that would have been difficult, given the crush, and anyway, the Heads were here. She might as well stay, hide herself again in a shelter of meaningless noise.

Everyone milled around: immensely too many to be seated at the table where the suits had arranged themselves. Organisers imposed some kind of order and the suits' leader started to make a standard sort of speech, as far as he could be heard above the hecklers.

'We're going to make England great again,' he shouted (against a loud, determined anti-car chant from back in the stacks). 'But we need *your* help, *your* ideas, *your* input.'

'You mean you need to cut a deal with the Counterculture!'

Whoever said that had a voice like a foghorn. All eyes, even Fiorinda's, turned to the speaker, a colourful character with a shaggy bleached crest and – going by what you could see – a full complement of heavy piercings and tattoos. There was a murmur of non-political interest, because it was Pigsty Liver, of Pig Liver and the Organs – a big name, in idiot-commercial terms. The Organs were headlining at the Hyde Park festival. Rockstars all over the shop, thought Fiorinda. But not the only one who counted. The anti-car chanters were being removed. An ardent fan who had climbed the Economics stacks to get a better look at the Home Secretary lost her footing and fell with a crash. The suit who must be Paul Javert leaned forward over his clasped hands, oblivious of all the row, and grinned.

'And are you in a position to offer us a "deal", Mr Pigsty?'

General laughter. Even in this context, the Big Pig was a crowd-pleaser. He claimed he had undergone a personality change after having a pig's liver transplant: a brazen fabrication, but the basis for videos where the Organs rolled in mud, pretended to eat live piglets from a trough, appeared to fuck a large white sow, and so on. Sort of thing the punters loved. Pig groped the heavy steel loop he wore through the septum of his fleshy nose, picked a lump of bogey and ate it. His fingers were thick with rings, his teeth small, white and even.

'Yeah. I'll tell you about it later. First off I want an office at Westminster, with my name on the door. And a place on the Cabinet and a sexy secretary.'

More laughter.

Fiorinda prepared to slip into no-time: into the place she had found, had been forced to find or invent, in the terrible year. Between the seconds, between the *microseconds*, she could take aeons to deal with the fact that *it wasn't Rufus*, and return refreshed, and no one would know she had been gone. But because she had co-operated with the organiser types she was in the front row, elbows on the long table. Trapped by those old-fashioned reflexes again, she found it annoyingly hard to get her attention away from what was going on. The chief suit had turned Pigsty's cheeky response into a brainstorming exercise. Everyone in his immediate line of sight was being asked what *they* wanted from the new England. What a stupid question.

No need to let them have it all their own way, however.

'I'm sorry,' she said, when it was her turn, 'I don't see the point in giving you a wish-list. Government in this country happens in committee rooms, off-line and off the record: not in public meetings. It's been that way forever. I don't expect anything real's going to change because the flag gets easier to draw.'

'I see! Well, that puts me in my place!'

'I don't know what possible use you could have for our wish-lists. Unless you're hoping we'll give you some free copy for your party's next advertising campaign.'

He frowned. Fiorinda noticed that Allie, sitting two places to his left with a laptop perched on her knee, was gazing at him soulfully. She wondered if that confirmed she was bandying words with the actual Home Secretary, or was Allie just practising.

'I think the old should die more,' said Ax Preston, though it was far from his turn (he was in the front row on purpose, presumably, to further his vaulting ambition). 'If you're old, you ought to die. It's common sense. And end state education. There's no reason why kids today should have to learn to read and write and figure. We got computers to do that.'

'I think shit's going to be important,' said Sage, not to be outdone. The three Heads, chancing to have been drawn there because they were with Fio, were in the front row too. 'I think it's important that we have a policy for shit.'

'Shit, ah, I see. You mean, the chaos of random events? As in "shit happens"?'

'Nah. As in the brown stuff that comes out of my bottom. It's gonna be fuckin' crucial.'

'Could we,' said Allie, her familiar voice rising suddenly and sharply out from among the suits, 'could we please try to take this *seriously*. Something momentous is happening—'

'Oh, Allie, no it is not,' said Fio. 'The Dissolution is a rubber stamp. The legislatures have been moving apart for years, nothing new is going to happen at the end of December, it's a question of changing the signs on the office doors.'

Ax Preston grinned at her.

The Home Secretary didn't seem to recognise the Chosen's celebrated guitarist, or even skull-masked Aoxomoxoa, never mind Fiorinda – but he leaned behind his neighbour to whisper to Allie, who whispered back. The guy between them nodded and made a note . . . Then one of the genuine green-nazis pitched in (a famous one, by the way the camera people leapt to attention) to haul the meeting back on topic. How is the government planning to *implement* this idea of handing the Second Chamber over the Counter Culture? What *powers* would such a body have?

And so on. People shouted, people were shouted down. Pigsty kept asking for his office space and his sexy babe, and raised a laugh every time. Eventually the Home Secretary decided to show a video. The lesser suits shifted their chairs around, looking eager and interested: perhaps, in their minds, this was the whole object of the exercise. Organiser types unfurled a plastic screen. It began to display a painfully colour-distorted sequence of Merrie England images, lacking a sound track: Morris Dancers, Umbrellas, Fish And Chips, Steak And Kidney Puddings, Cricket Teams, Cottages With Roses . . .

25

'Great,' said someone. 'For the relaunch. Should sell a million copies. But are their faces meant to be that colour?'

'It's yer blue emitters,' said Sage helpfully. 'Triggering the emission of photons at blue wavelengths, yer need a nice clean current, for consistent high energy electron transitions in yer semi-conductors. I think you'll find central London's havin' one of them power dips.'

The mask Sage usually wore was a living skull, freshly stripped: the bone rose-tinged, eye spaces blood-blank; tooth enamel preternaturally bright. Today, for a change, it was the charnel version. Fiorinda noticed a suit noticing, apparently for the first time, Sage's *hands*, as skeletal as the mask, but much more disturbing: dry brown bones with black shadows between them, clinging rags of withered flesh—

The video struggled on. People shouted their scorn and derision, and left. Others stayed to catcall and slow handclap, but that was as far as it went. No violence. By the time the screen was rolled up again, the crowd had thinned out and quieted down and the suits prepared to leave with some dignity. The note-taker came sidling up to Fiorinda.

'Allie tells me you're a rising popstar, Fiorinda.'

'That's nice of her.'

He was youngish, plump, Asian, thick black wavy hair, taste-free weekend-casuals.

'I wonder if you'd mind telling me, what exactly does *muso* mean? Would that mean, a popstar who is a trained musician, in the er, the traditional sense?'

'Not necessarily. I suppose it means someone who cares about the art and craft of it, rather than doing anything that will make money. Being an artist, not a commodity.' She looked at the table, where he'd placed his laptop while he leaned there strategically, corralling her in place. On the open screen there was a list of names, including her own. Next to Ax Preston, it said *has ideas*. Next to Fiorinda it said *light voice*. Huh. I do not! Time to start smoking the heavy tars again.

'And that's good?' He gazed at her intently, as if not sure he could have heard her right.

'Well, obviously.'

Behind Mr Weekend she saw Ax Preston grinning again. He had nice eyes. She wondered was he laughing at her, or at the suit. The Home Secretary's party swept out in a wave of camera flashes. Fiorinda walked around looking at the books and then went to join the Heads in the knot of music-biz people around Ax Preston: fellow tourists in this strange land.

'Are you sure about standing for Parliament?' Sage was asking, affecting friendly concern. 'I c'n understand you quitting the band. But why don't you just get a job——?'

'I have not left the band,' snapped the guitarist. 'If you've started believing all the bollocks you read in the music press, Sage, it's time you booked yourself into rehab again——'

'You know, most people think the Chosen broke up about five years ago, so it's gonna be a big thrill, seeing you at Reading. I'm really planning to try and catch that.'

The Heads and the Chosen Few represented opposing traditions. They couldn't have been more different in their material, but their star performers had a kind of parallel standing in the Indie world: Sage the brilliantly commercial techno-wizard, Ax Preston the pure musician with the critical and political cred. There tended to be a natural hostility when their paths crossed. Put it another way, Sage liked to wind Ax Preston up.

The group around them was possessed of certain facts, which they now expected to be aired. Such as, a short while ago Milly Kettle, the Chosen's drummer and Ax Preston's long-time girlfriend, had suddenly become vocalist and rhythm guitar Jordan Preston's girlfriend instead. Such as, Sage had recently lost the final round in his messy and pricey attempts to recover the rights to the Heads' first album, the legendary *Morpho* . . . Promising material for invective, or, with luck, a more physical exchange of views——

'Oh! Could I talk to you guys?'

Allie Marlowe had left with the suits, but she'd come back. She stood hugging her attaché case, looking nervous and self-important. 'Oh, Paul would like to, um, put a proposal to some of you. I have a list of names here.'

She read out her list and dispensed slips of fresh-pressed plastic. 'You'll need those for ID. I'll be in touch. I think I know how to' reach you all. Must rush. Got to talk to Pigsty.'

The music-biz folk looked at each other in bemusement. 'Holy Fuck,' said a style-victim black youth with a crimson brush cut and the face of a depraved cherub, 'I think we're through the first audition. But what did we audition for? Does anyone know?'

His companion tossed back shining brown Cavalier ringlets. 'Oh, Oh, Oh, pass the plutonium, Darius. We've been sampled for destruction.'

Silly boys, thought Fiorinda.

'I know *I* had my particulars taken down,' said an older, booming voice—

That gave her a jolt. She remembered being scanned, at the enrolment table. Bravado aside, it was the first time to her knowledge that she'd been handled by the law: and *she didn't like it*. But happily, Sage seemed to have lost interest in plaguing the guitar-man, so they could leave, and she didn't have to come back.

After the LSE gig, Ax returned to the big house on the Lambeth Road that belonged to his good friend Rob Nelson, of the PoMo band Snake Eyes; who shared it with his three fabulous girlfriends (aka the Eyes) and various other members of the Snake Eyes tribe. He was staying there while the Chosen camped at Reading, because he needed to be at the heart of this thing, and he didn't want to be in the Park. Some time after midnight he left the house, stone-cold sober, and walked through the poorly lit, humid night, up the long, straight road to the river. He liked walking. It helped him think. When you walked you saw things, felt things, smelled things that occupied the outer layers of the mind, freeing-up the machinery. A stack of binbags big as a house, who did that, and was it art? A scuttling rat with an immensely long tail; a pair of barefoot, horrible-looking little children crouched asleep in a doorway.

The city was not sleeping. It was crawling with light and movement, but on Vauxhall Bridge there was nobody about. A full moon glided between broken clouds. Ax had talked to the band – his brothers Shane and Jordan, and Milly the drummer – made sure they were okay, warned them he was going to be away a couple more days, doled out praise and customised attention for each of them. Attention keeps people sweet, one of those little mechanical tricks he'd picked up. Obviously no substitute for real feeling, but you don't always have time for real feeling, and you always need to keep people sweet. He walked up and down, pondering the imponderables of life: like why was his dad such a shite, and what about that little red-haired girl?

A few years before, when the Chosen had had a rush of money, he'd done the traditional thing and bought his mum and dad a nice house outside Taunton, his home town. His parents were still living there, along with Ax's youngest brother and sister, but his dad – without telling Ax – had raised two mortgages on the property, spent the money and fallen behind on the payments. The situation had just gone critical, and so Ax had heard about it for the first time. It was amazing, the amount of fucking stupid behaviour his dad could pack into a life that should be problem-free. Get out of bed, go down the pub. What else had ever been asked of the bastard? And he couldn't even stick to that.

He wished he could *sort* that problem, once and for all. Since he knew he could not, he put it aside and contemplated instead the things that had gone down today: itemising faces, names, quirks of behaviour, facts and inferences; storing them for future reference.

The little red-headed girl was wearing the yellow ribbon, which meant the long stare she'd given him couldn't have the straightforward meaning. Ax liked dealing with yellow ribbon people. It was a good institution, he often wore it himself. It meant you could cut a lot of crap. If someone didn't want the warning to be respected, if they were just trying to make themselves more desirable, too bad. But why *did* she look at him like that? Fiorinda. He knew the name. Rufus O'Niall's daughter, but the less said about that story the better. Very young, very angsty: and obviously, now he'd met her, not your average babystar. Pity about the accent.

Rob was excited about this development with Paul Javert. And yeah, there was something in it. Pigsty the government stooge, recruited beforehand, the rest of them picked up as filler. For what? Didn't matter really. Whatever was supposed to be going on, it could be useful to be involved. Ax was wondering if he could keep a low enough profile in a small working party, especially with that mouthy fucker Sage around. He wasn't ready to make his move, not for a long time yet. But in that regard, Pigsty would be useful. A good attention-attractor, nice and loud and ugly. The suits were in the mood to abase themselves before *ugly*, and you could understand why.

The Pig was right. The government *had to* make some kind of deal with the Counterculture. A group of GM-related crop disasters in the last three years, a couple of home-wrecker floods in the crowded south-east, hadn't improved a situation that was getting rapidly out of hand. Those kind of disasters didn't kill people, much (compare multi-drug-resistant TB and viral pneumonia deaths in the same period!); but they had a weird effect on public morale. Did a daft dislocation of risk-perception express some deep, molecular knowledge, a sleepwalker's sense of the cliff's edge? The hardline Counterculturals would tell you so. Whatever the truth of that, there were now outlaw bands of eco-warriors roaming unchecked, 'releasing' farm animals, trashing science parks, sabotaging capitalism any way they could – and gaining more support, not less, from Middle England, as their violence increased . . . And at the back of it all, the economic meltdown, inescapable anywhere in Europe.

Classic situation. Frightening situation.

Got to admire Paul Javert's nerve. He must have known he'd get slaughtered if he came along to the LSE gig. But it was pitiful. These fast-track government types thought they were razor-sharp operators, keen political minds. It went right by them that they'd been breathing the same corrupt atmosphere, feeding on the same poisons as their voters. That's how they ended up coming to the only people who might handle the CCM for them, scouting for *advertising copy*.

He paused in his pacing. What if he could actually do it, one day? Take control, turn the situation around? Then he could look forward to becoming as deluded and full-of-shit as one of those suits this afternoon; and then later on there'd be the fun of watching everything he'd achieved trashed to fuck by the next new wave. Unless he saved them the trouble by ruining it all himself.

Still be worth it, he decided. I understand the deal, and I accept.

Footsteps, that had previously failed to penetrate his reverie, suddenly sounded close and loud. A solitary armoured policeman was coming towards him.

'Evening, Sir.'

'Evening, Officer.'

'Or morning, I should say. It's past two o'clock. Would you mind telling me what you're doing down here, Sir?'

'Thinking.'

The upper part of the man's face was concealed: a chinguard reached almost to his nose. The mask of armour studied Ax impassibly.

'It's not very safe at this hour. Any ID on you, Sir?'

Ax felt something like a white light dawning in his brain: the *certainty* of destiny. He produced the plastic card that identified him as one of the Home Secretary's chosen. The policeman examined it thoroughly, running the biometrics and God knows what other information through the datalink in his visor.

'Right you are, Sir. I suppose you know what you're doing.'

'I hope I do.'

They started to walk together, falling into step. 'Flag of St George,' said the policeman, with a nod down the river to Westminster. 'It'll be funny to see it on its own. Like a football match. But it's about time, in my opinion. About time we got back to basics.'

'To the reality of the situation,' agreed the Ax. 'That's what we need. Some reality.'

TWO

Innocence and Experience

Pigsty didn't get his sexy secretary, not yet, but when Paul Javert explained his proposal, two days later, it was in some kind of committee room in Whitehall. The Home Secretary wanted to set up a Countercultural Think Tank (he was relying on them to suggest a catchier title), enlisting popular culture icons sympathetic to both sides of the debate, to advise the government and reassure the public over the Countercultural problem. He'd decided that pop music was the key – universally accessible as no other art form, non-elitist, fun, and yet long-time associated by the punters with principled, non-violent protest against the establishment . . .

There were six suits. Paul Javert, Mr Weekend the notetaker (whose name was Benny Preminder), another man; and three women who hadn't been at the LSE gig. Paul Javert was in slinky black, like a fantasy thriller hero. The others were in hopelessly suitish leisurewear; it must be giving Allie serious pain to sit beside them. It was very clear this time that they had a special relationship with Pigsty, who sat flanked by equally well-hard Organs, putting his feet up, scratching, farting and looking insufferably smug. Fiorinda wondered if the suits genuinely believed that Pigsty Liver was a leading social satirist. Maybe they did. The Pig, with his aging raver ironmongery, was regarded as a talent-free idiot by anyone Fio knew, but he was a household name, and might look convincing to the unwary, sitting there bravely outlawed from suit-wearing, as one who has nailed his colours to the mast.

Mr Javert's other recruits (most of whom had been at the LSE; a few who hadn't) were something else again. Besides Aoxomoxoa and the Heads, and Ax Preston (the rest of the Chosen weren't here), he had Rob Nelson of Snake Eyes, Ken Batty from Direct Action, Martina Rage from Krool, the heavy metal feminists; DK the DJ (Dilip Krishnachandran), the Perfect Master of IMMix; Roxane Smith, the veteran critic, and that new techno boy-duo (reckoned very interesting by the Heads, though Fiorinda didn't get it) who called themselves the Adjuvants. Plus a devout Islamic ghazal singer from Leicester, who was supposed to be the Next Big Thing. All in all, a well-filled shopping trolley. Realism prevented her from including herself (she'd probably been thrown in to improve the girl quotient), but if you'd given someone with impeccable if eclectic taste free rein to collect the tastiest people on the English Indie scene, this was what you might get. Everyone clocked everyone else, covertly. Nobody explained to Mr Javert that he hadn't enlisted any *pop* musicians, unless you counted Pigsty and the Organs.

Fiorinda had come back against her better judgement because the Heads were coming. She amused herself pondering the fate of dead metaphors, while the others played the wish-list game. What colours? 'Mast' could be a word for penis, and 'nail' means a piercing, but what are these colours Pig's nailed to his willy? Something to do with nail varnish? Pigsty has stuck his ampallang thingy to his willy with puce nail varnish, which shows he is incredibly brave and determined. But what is this grist that the suits say we must give to their mill?, and if we're talking about eco-warriors lying to the media, what has that to do with pots calling kettles black? When do cows come home, and what have roosting chickens to do with bad guys getting their come-uppance? What does 'roost' mean, anyhow . . . ?

We need a caring hospice for figures of speech, she decided. We should treasure our clichés and use them tenderly because *soon nobody will know*. Dead metaphors, dead words, words that are themselves layers of played-out metaphor: the shells of dead sea creatures, sinking down and losing their shapes, getting embedded, turning into rock . . . Maybe cultural deracination is when no one remembers *deracination* means pulling something up by the roots. Or that if you do that, the thing will die—

Whenever Fiorinda spoke – which she did, occasionally, to break the monotony – everybody stared. It was annoying. Martina the feminist never shut up with her Riot Grrrl stuff, and nobody stared at her. When Ax spoke everyone laughed, including the suits, although they looked a trifle shifty as they chuckled – presumably because his 'provocative suggestions' (the poor should eat shit, the unemployed should be sold as slaves) bore some passing resemblance to current government policy. If you took a really jaded view. It lasted a couple of hours. Fereshteh the ghazal singer sat in her burqa, like a running joke in an ironic tv cartoon, and never said a word. After the show they were bussed (nice bus, no expense spared) to a tv studio near the river, where they had a big joint interview for a current affairs programme. Sage's loud insistence that Cornish Brythonic should be made the official language of the new English Parliament earned him cheers from the studio audience; and a good time was had by all. At the end, Allie handed out plastic *per diems* and told them when to come back.

The Heads were taking Ken to Whipsnade, where the animal rights people were running a feasibility study (read: another green riot) on the mass freeing of wolves and other climate-hardened predators. Fiorinda didn't approve. Wouldn't wolves either decimate or starve out indigenous predators and prey? Like minks did? 'Nah,' said Sage. 'Ax is gonna organise a supply of small children, in depots round the country: it'll help reduce the surplus population.'

'In little red cloaks,' said Fio. 'And pigs in straw houses. Releasing zoo animals is as stupid as your jokes, Sage.'

'The spiralling helix of time has brought one significant change,' announced Verlaine, the Adjuvant with the Cavalier ringlets; striking a pose. 'If this was Paris 1789, we'd all be either lawyers or journalists.'

Chip Desmond clutched his red crest and made retching noises—

'You're out of your brains,' Fiorinda told them. 'If anything, it's more like Paris 1968. A street-party, a few burned-out cars, and back to business as usual.'

'That's what I like about you, Fiorinda,' said Ax. 'You're not easily impressed.'

'What's there to be impressed about? This dumb PR stunt? Please.'

The van took off north. Fiorinda went down the pub with most of the others. Eventually Rob Nelson's three girlfriends, Dora and Felice and Cherry, came to pick him up in their battered pink Cadillac, and she went back in the car with them and Ax Preston to the Snake Eyes house. It was easier than deciding how to get back to Reading; and there was nowhere else that she wanted to be. Rob's place was full of Dissolution Rocksters. The only bed he could offer her was in a coffin-like closet on the top floor, with a mattress laid down the middle. It was called the Mugs Room. Actual mugs filled the rest of the space, ranked on shelves, hanging from the walls, dangling from the ceiling, stacked on the floor, obscuring the window – mugs in all colours, mugs adorned with witty comments; PR mugs; merchandising mugs, novelty mugs, pretty mugs, arty mugs, obscene mugs.

'No one ever wants to throw one out,' explained Rob, 'unless it breaks. They're a hassle of modern life. Trouble is, I said that on the tv, on a rugrats' programme? Tryin' to think of something non-horny to say about my home life? So, you can guess. They mount up.'

The closet had obviously had a long career as the doss of last resort. It looked clean, but it smelled of stale vomit. Fio decided she couldn't stand it, which turned out to mean she was sharing the big living room in the basement with Ax Preston. She was surprised to find that this was where he was sleeping. She'd have thought he'd be in the penthouse suite.

'It's not so bad,' said Ax, putting aside the guitar on which he'd been doodling quietly, in the pauses, all through the political discussion. (Like Jane Austen, Fiorinda had thought: scribbling a novel on the edge of the drawing room table.) 'You can't sleep until everyone else has gone, but I don't mind. I never sleep much, anyway.'

'Where do you usually live?'

'In Taunton, with the band.'

'Is that nice, living in the country?'

'Taunton isn't the country,' he said, frowning at the end of the spliff he was lighting. 'It's much worse than that. But it's where we were born. That's important. I want us to stay there.'

The way everybody laughed at Ax and everybody stared at Fiorinda had created an alliance. In the Whitehall meeting and at the tv studio they'd kept catching each other's eye, and smiling ironically.

'What d'you think they want from us?' she asked. 'The suits, I mean.'

'I don't much care. I'm wondering what use *I* can make of this.'

Ah well, she thought. There he goes. Everybody's crazy about something.

'Ax . . . do you watch a lot of television?'

He looked blank. 'Never have time for it.'

'Do a lot of stuff on the internet?'

'Shane looks after all that. I can't be bothered.'

'Okay, do you like to eat in fancy restaurants?'

'Fuck, no.'

'Well, the normal people in this country do nothing else but watch tv and click around in cyberspace; whereas the ruling classes spend their whole time grovelling and scheming to get a table at this week's top restaurant. Face it, you've got *nothing in common* with them. There's no way you are going to get them to . . . to vote for you, or whatever it is you want.'

'Maybe I know what's good for them better than they do themselves.'

'That wouldn't be hard. But.' She was lost for words. Unlike the silly boys who spouted radical ideas with one eye in the mirror, there was something un-self-regarding in the Ax that made his obsession more embarrassing than funny. She wanted to save him from himself.

He looked at her, narrow-eyed: off on his own angle. 'What d'you make of Pigsty?'

'I think he's genuine,' said Fiorinda, immediately. 'He's not putting it on for the punters, which is what I assumed before I met him. I think he's just what he makes himself out to be. The kind of crass, stupid, self-satisfied libertarian bastard who would bugger a five-year-old in the name of free love.'

'Nothing wrong with buggering a five-year-old,' said Ax, in his *eat the unemployed* voice. 'As long as the kid's having a good time, whose business is it.'

'*Exactly*. Yeah, you got it. That's *exactly* Pigsty.'

They laughed. 'But we'll keep our opinion to ourselves.'

The suits adored the Big Pig: so the rest of them were already drawn into this complicity. Fiorinda nodded, wondering why *she* had to keep quiet. Why was she getting involved in this thing? Maybe it was a good career move. Maybe it filled a horrible blank.

She had been lent a manky sleeping bag. There was a proper bed made up for Ax on the couch, with a duvet and sheets. He gallantly offered it. Fiorinda counter-offered that they could share.

'Yeah, okay,' said Ax. 'Thanks.'

She glanced at the yellow ribbon, which he was also wearing today – and made a pragmatic decision, based on the irritating alternative of lying there wondering if he was going to make a move. The ribbon worked fairly well, but it was asking a lot to expect it to function when you were sharing a bed with someone you hardly knew. 'If you like, we can do sex.'

'You sure that would be okay?'

'No problem. Ribbon just means you're not *looking* for it. I don't mind, honest.'

'Right. I'll see if I've got a condom.'

'If you want. I don't care. I'm clean, and I'm not going to get pregnant on you. They gave me the injection in hospital when—' She stopped, but had already gone too far. 'When I had the baby,' she finished, casually.

'You had a kid, oh, right.'

'Not any more. It . . . he died.'

'Well,' said Ax, after a moment, 'that's a bad break.' He reached out, touching her for the first time, and stroked back a lock of the red curls that tumbled round her face. 'You've had hard times, I know. I very much admire the way you have come through them.'

She stared at him, like: *what weird language is this?*

'Do you want that fuck?'

'I'll see about the condom,' said Ax, hoping he wasn't making a horrible mistake. But what he was doing felt right. He would go with it.

For Fiorinda it was okay, except that he turned out to be the considerate type, whereas she was not going to get aroused by him unless he broke into her when she was dry, the way her father used to do it. She couldn't tell him this, and didn't feel like faking. 'I'm going to have to masturbate myself. Do you mind?' 'Why would I mind?' said Ax (sounding taken aback at finding himself in bed with a girl who said *masturbate* when she meant wank), 'you do what feels good.' Then the sex was fine. They did it four more times during the night – something neither of them had expected.

The Dissolution Festival at Reading unfolded its all-embracing programme. Rock bands rocked, circus troupes trouped, folksingers sang, poets declaimed. Anything Celtic was violently heckled. Aoxomoxoa and the Heads headlined to the usual huge, adoring, laddish crowd. The plan of bussing of artists around the country to other sites did not happen, owing to crisis conditions and economic meltdown. A secret gang of personal transport wreckers haunted the parking fields, leaving every morning a fresh swathe of terminally immobilised vehicles that were a real hassle to deal with.

Fiorinda and DARK did a miserable set on Red Stage, which was mainstage, in the rain at lunchtime. Everything went wrong, and such few people as happened to be hanging around in the arena pretty well ignored them. The next night they were indoors at the Green Room. Things were tense. They were all severely drunk, and very shaken by their Red Stage failure. Fil Slattery and Gauri Mostel were sullen, Cafren Free silently miserable. Charm was in a savage bad temper, and Tom Okopie the bassist was too smashed to be his usual steadying influence. Added to this catalogue it turned out they had a real crowd, not just hardcore DARK fans, but actual punters who had heard the buzz, and maybe even bought the album. DARK were famous (relatively speaking) for fucking-up royally whenever people looked like liking them. It could have been a disaster. Instead they flipped into a state of high energy and played like demons, Fiorinda's pure, ferocious vocals and wild guitar taking everything by storm. She was *radiating*. So much so that, with the set two-thirds done, she looked around, caught everybody's eye, and launched them, unilaterally, into 'Stonecold' – her own teenage-vagrant anthem, and a *killer* tune, which Charm had axed from the set in a fit of last-minute frontwoman autocracy. She just couldn't stop herself.

'Stonecold' was huge, the crowd loved it. Charm went along with the coup with a face like thunder, until the end of the song. Then she came over, glaring like a demented stoat, not quite steady on the feet, and said something audible and sarcastic to her vocalist, to the effect, Fiorinda's shitful megastar dad would be proud of her dirty tactics—

Charm never mentioned the fact that the megastar dad had allegedly got his twelve-year-old daughter pregnant. Otherwise it was no holds barred. Ever since she'd found out who Fiorinda's father was, the taunts had been endless.

Aoxomoxoa and the Heads were in the mosh, breaking the celebs/ punters barrier with their usual aplomb. They had a grandstand view of what happened next: the incandescent teenager in her sparkly blue party dress, squaring up to the queen of northern radical-dyke rock. Charm looks mean and nasty, no surprise. But though Fiorinda might dress like the ballerina on the musical box, and might look fragile, she stands an easy five foot five in her army boots, which gives her a couple of inches over Charm; and she's not afraid to make herself useful. Doesn't let the height disparity worry her: hauls off and lands the demented stoat a clip that sends Charm flying, guitar howling, into a stack of amps—

'Wooeee!' yelled Sage, punching the air. 'That's my girl!'

They removed themselves from the scene, however, during the stage-invasion that swiftly followed. Shame to leave a good ruckus, but as George said, they'd be doing the kid no favours, giving their seal of approval to that sort of unladylike behaviour.

DARK had an impromptu debriefing when they'd been hustled off. They hardly bothered with the latest incident, but cut straight to the chase, the real problem, the power struggle—

'This is my fucking band,' yelled Charm. 'I say what goes on the set list and that's—'

'Look,' said Fiorinda, biting back tears of rage and despair. 'Don't be such a brainless shit. Okay, I wrote it, I'm sorry. But *it isn't relevant who wrote it.* "Stonecold" *works* for us.'

'*Fuck that!*' screamed Charm, eyes popping. 'Who's "us" *princess*? You want the same crap megabucks stadium success as your dad, and DARK is not going that way!'

'I want us to get somewhere,' shouted Fiorinda defiantly. 'Don't you?'

'FUCK YOU, Daddy's girl—'

'You're just scared, Charm. You just can't stand the heat.'

'I can't stand any more of this,' muttered Cafren Free, pale blonde head in her hands.

Tom Okopie stayed with Fiorinda when everyone else went off to the bus. Plump, black, cuddly Tom had always been nice to Fio, far as rock and roll feudalism allowed. Don't let Charm get to you, he told her earnestly: it's right-on, constant fuck-ups, constan' revolution, freedom to flail, that's what DARK's about, proves the band's integriry . . . But Tom was totally pissed and he was Cafren's boyfriend. He couldn't really be Fiorinda's ally. Tom belonged to Cafren, DARK belonged to Charm Dudley, and Fiorinda had no place to lay her head.

She returned to the van where she found Sage alone and *incredibly* unsympathetic. He'd seen the whole thing and hadn't even come backstage to back her up. What d'you expect, he said. You were fantastic, but it's not going to get you nowhere at this fucking rate. You're too big for Charm to handle, an' she's not going to hand you her band on a plate. Give her some space, stupid brat. He told her she ought to pack in the public violence or take up mud-wrestling, *which was an absolute fucking cheek*, coming from him. Advised her she was going to have a shit of a hangover, and left on some sexual prowl or other. She crawled into the annexe and lay there spinning, hating everyone, too proud to cry herself to sleep.

Notoriety sometimes pays. Fiorinda snagged an invitation to do a solo gig at the Best of the Fest club, a smoky late night cabaret, where she went down a treat. She stayed away from DARK, but went to a couple more meetings in Whitehall, and spent a couple more nights at the Snake Eyes house. One chilly August morning, when the two weeks of the Festival were nearly over, she met Ax in the arena. They were both queuing to buy breakfast from a van. He was wearing that leather coat, and had a guitar case slung over his shoulder, which made her smile. See Ax Preston, see guitar.

'Oh, hello,' said Fio. 'What are you doing here? I thought you were staying in London.'

'I am, but the Chosen played the Blue Lagoon last night.'

'How was it?'

'Not bad.'

He had refused to play the 'Jerusalem' solo for them. And the crowd went crazy, but he still refused to play it . . . the howling cascades of notes singing in his head, in his fingers, in his balls, in the muscles of his forearms: but he knew it was right not to be persuaded. Better withhold, deny yourself the quick hit, however much you wanted it. He'd been thinking *well, they're not watching the telly now* (though millions *were* watching, the punters who didn't see themselves as Festival mud-slinger types, but who were still riding this wave): which had annoyed him. He didn't want to fall into the trap of trying to impress this girl. It would be doubly stupid in her case, because Fio did not want to be impressed. It wouldn't be like a bunch of roses if he did break through her guard, it would just piss her off. He wondered where she'd been last night. He was not going to ask. Better keep things cool and friendly.

'You next?' said the Korean noodle man, with a smile of contempt. As usual at these things, all the catering people by now hated all their customers indiscriminately.

'I'll have the flat kind, dunno what you call 'em.' He perused the list of fillings. 'With the veg, ginger pickle and seaweed.' Fio bought a bowl of miso soup. They walked off together.

Ax was looking at his food in deep dismay.

'What's the matter?'

'Fuck. I thought when it said seaweed it meant that nice dry shredded cabbage.'

His noodles had been buried under a mound of steaming kelp, actual *kelp*, yards of slick, disgusting marine leather. 'The bastard, he knew I didn't know what he was talking about—'

'So chuck it.'

'I can't do that. There's no bin. I can't chuck it on the ground. What d'you think this place would look like if people just chucked stuff on the ground?'

Like it does, thought Fiorinda. 'Don't panic. I'll have it.'

They did the transfer. Fiorinda burrowed in her underskirts and brought out the saltbox, balancing her biodegradable soupbowl deftly on her wrist while she opened it. 'Want some?'

He frowned at the twinkling white powder. 'Bit early for me, thanks.'

'It's salt.'

'You're going to put *salt* on seaweed and miso?'

'I like salt. Anyway, seaweed doesn't taste salty, it tastes of iodine.'

He'd been hoping for a chance to talk to her in a neutral context. He'd talked to everybody else, except that fucker Sage: basically just making himself known at this stage. But the times he'd been private with Fio he'd been sidetracked by the sexual opportunity. She wasn't physically his type, and she was fucked-up as hell, poor kid, but somehow he kept wanting more.

Maybe it was the challenge to his manhood. Getting Fiorinda to come wasn't the problem, oh no. Getting Fiorinda to respond emotionally to sex: that was a project.

'What about this Think Tank? I notice you're still up for it.'

Fiorinda was hungry. The Festival of Dissolution had given up providing food for its artists, and those government *per diems* were useless. She was trying not to waste her cash reserves on stupid bodyfuel. She chewed kelp doggedly before she answered.

'I think it's obscurely addictive. Like watching a dull arthouse movie that is somehow quirky enough to hold your attention. I suppose the media exposure has to be good.'

There had been a steady flow of attention. Pigsty was most in demand. Ax and Sage and Fiorinda were also popular, but media people were wary of Sage. He had no respect for them whatever, and could be murder to interview.

'They like you because of your accent.'

'Mmm. I know. It cracks people up. They like you because you give good one-liners.'

'And the dresses. The media-persons like your dresses. So do I. That's a good look.'

'Thanks. It's my one idea. I buy evening gowns from charity shops and wear them on top of each other. It's not original, but it's flash, and cheap, as long as you're fairly little and thin.'

'The website's crap, though.'

Fiorinda hadn't seen it. She shrugged, indifferently.

They ate and walked, catching the occasional nudge and glance from the sparse morning crowd. 'A dull black and white movie. It's a point of view. What're your plans after the end of the Festival? You going back north with DARK?'

'No,' said Fiorinda, sorry he'd raised the subject. She'd been enjoying talking to someone who didn't know anything about her fucked-up plight. It made a nice change.

'You could move in at Snake Eyes. Should be more space there soon.'

'Thanks, but I think I'll stay here. The campground isn't going to break up. A lot of people are planning on staying until Dissolution Day, that's the idea. HurdyGurdy are letting it happen, and the Thames Valley police aren't going to interfere. They reckon we'll disperse of our own accord when the weather turns nasty. I expect they're right.'

HurdyGurdy was the hippie consortium that had bought the Festival site from its previous owner, with the avowed intention of preserving it, 'for the Countercultural nation'.

'Hmm.' Ax came to a stand, annoyed that he hadn't heard this news himself. They'd reached a rubbish point, a hive of open-mouthed black bin bags in a wash of faultily aimed garbage. He took Fiorinda's bowl and chucked them both, making sure he did not miss. 'I hope you keep coming to watch the movie, anyway. I've got plans for this Think Tank, Fiorinda. I believe we could make a good team. You and me, and Sage – I'd value Sage's input, though he might be surprised to hear it – and the others. We could make a difference to this country's future.'

'I think you're out of your mind,' said Fio. 'You're a rock star, not a politician.'

'I don't want to be a politician. The time for politics is past. I'm going to be a leader.'

'Oh. Well, I go this way.'

Ax was heading for the Roving Presence Pavilion, which was in the opposite direction. 'I'm meeting some people in China. Can I persuade you to join me?'

'No thanks. See you later, then.'

'Yeah, later.'

Fiorinda didn't have anything special to do, she'd simply felt that the conversation was getting awkward. There was also the problem of having slept with someone a couple of times and not being sure if it would happen again. The moment she'd left him standing there looking a little forlorn, she wanted to turn back. She resisted the impulse, and decided to investigate the Zen Self tent. According to Luke and Cack, it had excellent rides: good as the Zorbsperience, which was the best thing in Violet Alley, the arena's official playground.

The tent was bigger than it had seemed from the outside. She looked into the booths around the inner walls and was disappointed to find that most of the things you could try involved getting hooked up to computers. Fiorinda liked playing games, but on the whole, information technology had passed her by. Her childhood in the cold house – where her mother used the computer and printed books had been Fio's refuge – had left her convinced that she could never catch up.

A few people were examining a coffin-sized cigar-shaped cylinder on a giant swivel arrangement.

'What's this?' she asked the Zen Selfer who seemed to be in charge.

'It's a centrifuge,' said the young man briskly. 'You get in there. We subject your body to stresses equivalent to several gravities. You lose consciousness.'

'Is that fun?'

'Well, it's interesting, because on the way out you will have a near-death experience. Anyone can have a near-death experience. There doesn't have to be a pathological reason. As the blood leaves your brain, and stays out, you get the tunnel vision, you see the bright light, you feel you're floating, you seem to be outside your body . . . You reach a beautiful place, you may feel you are being judged, you'll meet the people you love most, you won't want to come back. The whole thing. It's simply what G-LOC does to the cephalic nervous system. Want to have a go?'

'Um.'

'We give you a medical check first.'

'What's it about, though?'

'It's about consciousness. That's what all our stuff's about. You can get your brain imaged in action, you can get hooked up and see your own 40hertz oscillations. You can see a real-time simulation of the information-loading in the hydrophobic protein sacs of the neuronic cytoskeleton; or you can try the blindsight experiment. Over there, you can get the two halves of your brain virtually dissociated and experience being two people: try to contact your right-brain self. Or you could do the collapsed wave-function experiment—'

'Thanks for explaining everything. I think I'll just—'

'Most people,' said the young man, 'do the reductionist things first. Then they listen to Olwen. That's also somewhere to start. There's a workshop beginning now.'

In the centre of the tent there was a low, circular wooden staging. A woman in a yellow sari and a crimson blouse was walking about on this stage in front of a projection screen, fussing with her laser pointer and checking over her props: an amaryllis lily in a tall glass vase, a cage of white rats on a table, graduated plastic models of animal brains; a detailed plastic human brain that came apart. That must be Olwen Devi, the Zen Self guru. People were moving inwards. Fiorinda moved with them, as ready to listen to a lecture on the science of consciousness as she was to do anything. She sat on the grass, which here around the stage was uncovered, and remarkably green.

Olwen Devi led the group, which had grown to about fifty people, through some relaxation exercises, designed to be performed without too much disruption by a close-ranked audience. She talked about the extraordinary range of things we do, in which intentionality does not play the part we imagine: courtship, friendship, decision making, learning, ambition; and then about the animals that do things we would call human – ant farmers, bird artists, altruistic vampire bats, duplicitous monkeys. 'It seems we must either award self-awareness to the ants,' said Olwen Devi, 'or accept that hominids may have practised agriculture, and buried their dead with ceremony, before they reached the threshold that we have crossed – the state of *being conscious of being conscious*. Think of this: when you decide to perform an action (reach out your hand) the neuro-muscular preparation for that movement has already begun: around 350 milliseconds *before* the onset of volition. We act first, then we decide to act. We "think" first, then we know we are thinking. This can be shown by experiment. Perhaps our self awareness is merely an observer, after the fact.'

Someone raised a hand. 'But couldn't that reversal mean, guruji, that self-consciousness is a quantum effect, and not controlled by the time's arrow illusion?'

'It could be.'

Many of the students, or punters, had adopted the lotus posture. Fiorinda knelt, sitting back on her heels, her thoughts reverting to the hard lesson that *Rufus wasn't here*, that he wasn't going to turn up and she might as well leave. Part of her still didn't believe it. She was irrationally convinced that staying on would somehow make him appear.

'It could be that consciousness, the experience of being conscious, puts us in touch with a *plenum*, a sum of all states, where the arrow's direction is lost. Erwin Schrodinger once said, if we cannot find ourselves in our world picture – meaning that image of the world which is the work we do in our brains – it is because the sentient self *is itself* the world picture.'

What's all this to me? wondered Fio. As for near-death experiences, she'd had one, without any help from a centrifuge. It had happened when the baby was born. And slipping into no-time, leaving her body to take care of itself, was something she had learned to do at will. She could easily slip away while she was kneeling here. Perhaps that was what you were supposed to do, let the words wash over and meditate. Just look at that green, glossy blade of grass . . . Olwen Devi was right. She'd never thought of it before, but going into no-time did feel like two planes aligning together, two slides from a kaleidoscope lining up. The world that Fio perceived moved into phase with *this thing, Fio*, that was doing the perceiving, so you couldn't tell the two of them apart. She could well and happily believe that the effect was caused by something chemical going on in her neurons, but it still felt numinous and . . . an impossible perspective, like an Escher sort of thing. Now she was looking through the tent wall, and looking back to that moment in time where Ax stood, slightly lost in his shabby leather coat, nothing like Rufus O'Niall's. Ax became a focus point, a point on a disc, and from this point sprang lines of sight, which reached to another disc, another section through the helix of time and here was Ax again, in a different place, in that same old coat, around him a huge crowd. She had the impression he was selling tickets for something, or handing out flyers. They were going like hotcakes (where are these cakes, why are they hot?): and here he was again, an even bigger crowd, a flag with a red cross, people cheering, a knowledge of terrible events (an intense, violent feeling that she didn't want to look any closer at *that* information . . .) behind the sheer, resolute triumph on his familiar face—

Good heavens!

Fiorinda's eyes flew open. The Zen Self lecture was still going on. The lotus-kneed people around her were quiet. For a moment a smooth, brown, oval, middle-aged face seemed to fill her view, like a close-up on a tv screen. It was as if Olwen were looking straight at her, and knew what had happened to her. Then distance reasserted itself. Olwen Devi was far away on her little stage. Fiorinda got up and hurriedly left the tent.

Back at the van, Sage was standing half-naked beside the corpse of a sheep, which was hanging by its heels from a framework of raw timber. His slick black dungarees were twisted around his hips, blood drizzled over them and his lean, white, muscle-raked torso as if he'd been spattered by a fountain; the whole scene gleaming in sunlight. His natural hands, surprisingly clumsy, were absolutely covered in blood; he was flensing the animal with a long thin knife. The young sheep's head, adorned with a cute pair of sprouting horns, stood on the grass, gazing at Fiorinda with smothered, yellow eyes.

'Good grief. Where did you get that?'

'Farmer's market, up the road. We've been pursuing the feasibility study: bought this as a sign of good faith. It costs nothing, meat on the hoof. Got some potatoes too.'

'Did you kill it just now?'

'Yeah.' He stretched his blood-streaked arms to heaven. 'Yeah!'

'You are as a god,' said Fio. She sat on the grass to watch. 'I met Ax. Sage, you know him, sort of. Do you have any idea why he is the way he is?'

'You mean, why does the miserable sod think he has to rule the world?'

The sheep's hide slithered free and fell in a heap beside the shit bucket, which had been co-opted to hold its innards. 'Well, I did ask him that question, more or less, one weird occasion when we were chatting quite civilly. Far as I recall, the explanation is . . .' Changing to a different knife, he cut some generous collops of bluish-red flesh and laid them on the inner face of the fresh skin. Still life. 'Mmm, his dad's a bit of a shite, and he loves his mum, but the tv she likes to watch makes him puke. So, he needs to rule the world because he has a normal family background. Make of it what you will—'

'It's probably genetic.'

Sage grinned at her, went to the back of the van and emptied several buckets of water over himself from their rain butt. When he came back, masked and wearing a shirt of homespun grey under the dungarees, he had a yellow ribbon tied around one sleeve.

'Why are you suddenly wearing that?'

The skull smiled enigmatically. Neat trick. 'Felt like it.'

Fiorinda suspected some oblique, sarcastic reference to the Ax Preston development. She was sleeping with the enemy and she was sure Sage was pissed-off, though he hadn't said a word. But the skull looked innocent, and the meat, raw and bloody as it was, worked on her salivary glands. She attempted, for pride's sake, an assault on Head Ideology. 'Let me cook? C'mon, you bought it, you butchered it. If I don't at least cook it, how can I eat?'

'No.'

'Please, please, I won't do anything frilly, I swear.'

'Nah,' said George, coming out of the van bearing an iceberg lettuce wrapped in clingfilm and a blackened cooking pot, a litre of tequila from the Heads' vast store of alcohol tucked under his arm. 'You won't do it right, Fio. You know you won't. Look, we got you a lettuce. You could have ten sheep for the price of this.'

The barbecue was laden with charcoal, the charcoal soused with paraffin and lighter fuel. Cack commenced the cooking by hurling a lighted match and leaping backwards, and the chops were thrown onto the flames. George dealt with the potatoes; Fiorinda was ordered to sit down quiet and stop fussin' around.

'No, no, don't let her sit down! We're not ready! Shit, we gotta get *genteel* with this babe. We gotta get *suburban*, she's not just any rock-brat trash no more—'

Sage and Bill rushed up. Bill spread a clean sheet of newspaper with a flourish and arranged a square of cardboard beside it. Sage dropped to his

knees and presented a pastel-patterned serviette, rolled up in a *napkin ring*.
'Lunch is served, Mrs Preston, ma'am.'

'You bastards.'

'Hahaha.'

'You are *so full of shit*, Sage. Lay off!'

But she felt forgiven.

Soon everyone was sitting around the barbecue, gnawing meat and passing the lettuce from hand to hand. Fio brought out her saltbox, which all the Heads except Sage shared with an air of guilty indulgence, and it was surprising how good the meal tasted, although Luke did complain that the lettuce was chewy. However this was found to be the result of his taking bites out of the side still wrapped in clingfilm. Bill put the kettle on for tea while the potatoes bubbled sulkily. Potatoes always take too long. Fiorinda lay in the grass under the oak tree that she thought of as their own (dapple leaves on the annexe roof), and smiled to notice the blackened kettle sitting among the greasy flames, beside the blackened cooking pot. That strange experience in the Zen tent kept repeating on her, loaded with a dread so large and vague she couldn't get a handle on it . . . something about, my whole life, gone? What, *gone?* She willed it away. *This* was life, good as it gets: *déjeuner sur l'herbe*, mutton fat, tequila, paraffin and bruised grass—

'We could have a sheep every day,' mused George. 'Except they shit a lot in the van.'

'Except we don't need it,' Cack pointed out. 'You should only kill for what you need. And we don't fucking need to eat meat. It's cruel. There's plenty of calories in alcohol.'

'What are you going to do with the rest, Sage? It won't fit in your fridge.'

'Sell it, trade it, give it away.' They finished the tequila. Sage, who had eaten enough to build up his energy, but not to repletion, started rifling in a Japanese incense box with the letters NDogs burned into the lid, standing for *endogenous psychotropics*. 'I feel like bein' overwhelmed by emotion. I'm gonna do some oxytocin, go down the arena and pair-bond with something.'

'But Sage, you're wearing the yellow ribbon. You can't pair-bond without sex. That's silly.'

'You're true, Fio. Fuck, I'll take something else. What's the rest of you having?'

'I hate modern drugs,' said Fio. 'I want to do some whizz, get pissed and go dancing.'

Ax was making lists:

> Weapons
> Police
> Armed Forces
> Airports
> Roads
> Freight Distribution
> Communications?
> The World

There was something wrong with the item *Communications*. He felt that this was not a target. You would not gain anything by rushing to control the airwaves, charging into Broadcasting House and letting fly with automatic rifles. Other ways, the priorities were the same as ever in history. Put a cap on the enemy's powers of retaliation, secure your borders, get control of supplies. But not communications. Nah, let them talk. It will keep them happy. *The World* was why he was here, looking out of the eyes of a daft little robot, which was sitting-in on a meeting of utopian revolutionaries from Pan Asia, convened by the Chinese. The robot sat on a chair at a table in a room with dun-coloured walls, its little hind-legs sticking out in front of it. When standing it was about a metre and a half tall, and built something like an upright vacuum cleaner. RPs were small, so as not to look threatening. But if you clothed them in either skin or fur, it made people's inerad-icable tendency to treat the remote-logger like a toy much worse. So here was Ax, dressed as a consumer durable, taking part in a dissidents' talking shop thousands of miles away from his physical location. The windows were too high for him to get a look out, but he believed he was somewhere in Shanghai.

The PanAsians could not get their heads – or digital remote logging equivalent – around revolutionary rock and roll as a concept. They were computer nerds; they didn't have the context. Everyone who *could* understand tried to explain, but it was no use, the leap was too great. An assortment of cartoon domestic appliances, humming *Imagine* together, wasn't going to convince anyone of anything.

When they reached the religion item on the agenda, it was the European and the US delegates' turn to recoil. US and French-tradition radicals, trained from birth to foam at the mouth when they heard the God word, muttered and fell silent. The Chinese didn't like the topic either. Ax felt differently. Be practical: understand that for a significant part of the population of England, this is *mighty real*. So he paid a lot of attention and asked questions, while the South Asians and others bandied lines from the Koran and the Lotus sutra. At last they came to Ax's item, which, however it got mangled by the simultaneous translation, was meant to be about . . . Well, apparently he had proposed that the revolution had magic on its side. Yeah, explained Ax, going with it. For sure we all have to make our peace with God: but you can't *use* God, you can only hope that what you want to achieve is in accordance with His will. But we can use the magic, it's on our side.

Huh? What did he mean by magic?

'I mean *this*.' He raised the RP's skinny metal arm. 'Magic technology. We've got the big advantage that we're comfortable with things like RP, virtual realities, putting alien things in our bodies; doing strange things to our brains. I think we're in danger of losing sight of that, with all the emphasis on being ecological and green and getting back to nature. Not that I'm against getting back to nature, but—'

A West African Marxist – physically present, must be teaching or working here – leapt in joyfully, exclaiming, with reference to the model of the nineteenth century in Western Europe, that the creation of a proletariat leads to revolutionary man, and revolutionary individualism leads to the creation of anti-capitalist machines . . . ! A babble of voices joined him, straining the ST software with their enthusiasm. The machines, the magic futuristic machines, are actually Gaia in disguise, the Demiurge is with us, our mother earth and her secret informational armies, conspiring with us, we have the mandate of heaven . . . Ax had struck a nerve, a rich vein, and it's good when you do that. But he wished he could get them to stick to the practical. No use: they were stuck into the mysticism riff, obviously really getting off on it. Well, better add that to the list. Maybe it should be another list.

God
Magic

God he felt he could deal with. Ax could do business with God. He'd have to get onto Fiorinda about the other. Magic being a feminine thing, she was bound to know.

DARK and Fiorinda agreed on a trial separation. The parting was fairly amicable, possibly because Fiorinda had been taking Sage's advice. DARK returned to their native Teesside. Fiorinda stayed at Reading, going up to London for the Think Tank meetings with Martina of Krool when the Heads couldn't be arsed. If you believed the media reportage, every Festival ground, populated by campers who refused to go home, had become a pocket state of violent anarchy. But at Reading all was peaceful, though things were getting basic. Hippies washed clothes in the river and traded insults with the private security guards who patrolled those nice-looking houses, all boarded up, on the other side. Yellow leaves and lye suds drifted down to the watermill built by Sun Temple, patriarch of a tribe who were neighbours of the Heads in the Travellers' Meadow. It was constructed to a cunning design from the Whole Earth Catalog website, to derive maximum energy from the slow-flowing Thames, but sadly it had no corn to grind. A couple of kilos of wheat berries from the Organic Grocery van had simply vanished between the stones. Without grist, the mill turned on: a post-industrial aeolian harp, creaking and rattling in futility.

In the Whitehall meetings they discussed names-for-the-band. Counter Cultural Think Tank was hopeless. Some favoured The Dissolution Alchemists, which appealed to Paul Javert. Fio was holding out for The Dead Metaphors. Hours were spent designing a bus for the road show Paul was planning, and arguing about what they should wear on stage. The Heads started a small book on the incidence of the sexual-scatalogical swear words the suits employed to liven up their script. The word shit had special rating, and was greeted with a cheer. Two *shits* in successive utterances and they would jump up and start hugging and rolling around like footballers. Poor unfortunate suits had no idea how to defend themselves, just sat there smiling uneasily. Pigsty caused an impasse by refusing to let the cameras in for some tv coverage, but of course was forgiven. Could be he didn't want to get shown up. He wasn't impressive in the sessions. He couldn't produce anything resembling Ax's Lennonist one-liners, or Fiorinda's crushing put-downs. Couldn't even organise a childish wind-up.

It was the middle of October when the Heads decided to eat shit. It came about because HurdyGurdy's site managers, who were still running things, had banned them from the Blue Lagoon, because of the stage act involving human excrement. This was a tactical error, for the former Festival had become a bit of a heaving mass, and if you couldn't give the mob bread you had to give them circuses. The Dissolution Loaf – so firm, so brown – was served up in the Best of Fest tent, which had been ceremonially prepared, a trestle table laid on the stage with a white cloth and real knives and forks. Cack did the business, modestly at stool behind a red velvet curtain. His production was carried to the board on a silver platter, and carved by George to wild applause. It seemed like a sign that *everything's allowed*.

But then the rain began in earnest. Fires could no longer be lit, and anyway, there was no more wood to be had, unless you ripped it from the trees, and then the hardline hippies would kill you. The *hoi polloi* were best off, with their sleeping bags tucked into binliners in the fug of their little tents. In the vast open spaces of Sage's van Fiorinda and the Heads huddled, miserable and sour. The solar and compost powered heating had given up entirely.

'What' we stayin' on for, anyhow?' asked Cack, the puzzle apparently fresh and new to him. 'It was supposed to be two weeks, wasn't it? Why's everyone still here?'

'Because of the *Dissolution*, Cack. We're occupying the Festival site until the end of the year, until Dissolution Day. You lost the plot again, you arsehole.'

'And what's gonna happen then?'

'*Then* we all go home . . . I suppose.'

Cack was right. There was no sense or reason in hanging around in this wet field, living like refugees. 'I want to book in to the Holiday Inn,' whined Fiorinda. 'I want to sleep in a room with walls, and be clean, and have a flush toilet and a washing machine: look at my *hands*, they look like skinned toads. I want to be warm and dry, I want to have a hot dinner. We could try lighting a fire in the annexe. Is there *any* wood left?'

'Nah, we burned the last of old Sun Temple's mill; and the charcoal sack got left outside—'

'It *got left*, did it? Why is nothing ever anyone's *fault* around here?'

'Because that's the way we like it, Fio,' snapped Sage. 'You want laws, you want crime and punishment: go somewhere else.'

Sage and Fiorinda glared at each other. The Heads, dismayed, cast about for some way to distract their leader and their adopted princess—

Bill, the quiet Head – cadaverously thin, his skull mask always looking too big for his narrow chest and wire-coathanger shoulders – said, 'The Blue Lagoon has a wooden floor.'

Energised, they fired themselves up with appropriate drugs and ran round the campground, demanding support and illicit accelerants, neither of which were lacking. Without anyone except the Heads and their near neighbours knowing how it had started, the anarchist tribe of Festival staybehinds poured into the arena in the wet dark, many of them bearing paraffin torches. Sound engineers were dragged to Orange Stage and forced to ply their trade. The Heads put on a tremendous set, followed by various artists, and somewhere in the middle of this the Blue Lagoon was indeed set on fire. Nobody claimed responsibility, maybe many separate arsonists were involved. Fiorinda took over Orange Stage, with Krool and some unknown volunteers from the camper masses, and became alcohol-related furious about the way the staybehinds were waving their arms and singing along, these round beaming firelit mouths and ecstatic eyes, as if Fio was some kind of *children's entertainer*—

She dived, screaming. The slithery, resilient matrix of human flesh engulfed her. They passed her from hand to hand as if she was a sacred idol, as if she was the ceremonial turd: they were chanting joyfully, idiotically, *Live in the Pain!* She struggled free and ran, and found a place in the circle round the great bonfire. By this time not at all sure what was going on, still believing herself on stage and surrounded by howling music, she screeched that she was not doing this for pay, you bastards, this is not entertainment, this is me, this is what's inside me. So often she felt like a dammed stream, such a head of power, but she couldn't release it: desperately now, now, but it didn't happen. It was like sex, like the huge reservoir of arousal and lust in her that ought to flow like Niagara, but it was blocked, barred, she always had to *work* to get there, and that's not right. Only the baddest music understood her, only the most violent, pounding beat and wail came close—

'I'm so *fucking* miserable,' she said to Cack when Thames Valley Police had (reluctantly and ineffectively) come and gone, when the fire was dying down under hissing rain and the bodies of the fallen were being carried away. He had joined her, hunched under a fold of tarp, back of Orange Stage, bringing with him a sixpack of strong lager he'd picked up somewhere. 'D'you realise what's happening to this stupid country? Do you *realise*? Look, you see that bonfire? That's my life, that is. It's all going to go. By the time I'm grown up, everything I wanted out of life, a whole civilisation I *needed*, will have *gone up in smoke*.'

'Oh well,' said Cack. 'At least yore among friends. Have another beer.'

'It had a rotten acoustic, anyway. I'm glad I never played in there.'

The fate of the Blue Lagoon, well-covered in the media, brought new crowds to Hyde Park, to Worthy Farm and all the other venues, just as the weather was becoming impossible. Shane and Jordan Preston and Milly Kettle returned from Taunton. DARK called Fiorinda to tell her they'd joined a campground in the North East, and intended to live outdoors all winter. At Reading staybehinds who literally hadn't left the site since July shivered in their summer clothes, but they would not give up. Fiorinda wore her party frocks in extra layers, topped by a shapeless Dutch army surplus rain jacket, and divided her nights between Sage's annexe, Krool's women-only bender in the hospitality-area; and Ax's basement in the Snake Eyes house. She liked being of no fixed abode. The Heads were recording a new album, which meant they spent a lot of time at their Battersea studio, but the van stayed in the Meadow, and Sage at least went on turning up for the Think Tank. So did Fiorinda. She told herself that as long as Allie was involved there must be something in it: because Ax was obsessed and Sage could be pathologically whimsical, but Allie never made mistakes.

It was like the whole Dissolution Year phenomenon. You kept thinking you should walk away, but you found yourself hanging on, just to see what happened next. And she wasn't wasting time. She was putting a lot of thought (she didn't *seriously* believe the world was going to end) into planning her solo career.

In November something strange happened. Sage had a call from Alain Jupette, mastermind of the radical-political Eurotrash outfit Movie Sucré. Movie had been on the programme in July. They'd decided to come back to check out the action, and Alain wanted a meeting with Ax and Sage and Fiorinda.

Ax met the other two in the arena, which was looking more than ever like the centre of a refugee camp or a bedraggled mediaeval township. It was noon, but white mist still limned the eau de nil geodesic of the Zen Self tent and shrouded the blackened circle where the Blue Lagoon used to be. A thing like a tortoise on stilts loomed up: a hippie with a huge tray, the contents covered by a steaming cloth. 'Get your breakfasts here!' he bellowed. Ax bought three dumplings and handed them out. They weren't much to eat, a tincture of red bean paste in a mass of greasy dough, but they were wonderful to hold. Ah, thought Fiorinda, her fingers cuddling the heat. Hot cakes!

'You two know what this is about?'

'No idea,' said Sage. 'Power breakfast with Le Grand Grenouille, what a thrill.'

'Where we'll try not to say anything offensive,' suggested Ax, with a frown.

Fiorinda did not think Ax had recruited Sage to his cadre. They got on okay at the Think Tank, united in putting down Paul Javert, but there was too much previous between these two. Things like Sage describing the Chosen's music as 'complacent nostalgia' in front of a tv audience of millions. People remember words of that kind when the obscenities fade. And you wouldn't think *cynical manipulative crowd pleaser* would have hurt Sage's feelings, but it had. It was a difficulty in her life, because she really wished they could be friends.

Movie Sucré's long white bus had arrived overnight. Inside, Alain was waiting for them with Tamagotchi, obligatory Eurotrash kooky-girl. No sign of the rest of the band. Alain was wearing a scarlet quilted jumpsuit with a Ferrari badge on the breast pocket. Tama, in pink flannelette pyjamas and a fisherman's Guernsey, was making coffee that smelled divine.

'Where's the others?' asked Sage at once, as if he suspected an ambush.

'Oh, they are in here.' Alain patted a black box. 'Figuratively. We will perform, but too much is going on at home, we could not all leave civilisation in person.'

'I fucking hope you said so on the tickets.'

Alain laughed. 'Tickets! What tickets? Tickets for the Blue Lagoon? There are no *tickets* anymore, that world is over.'

'So, why did you want to see us?' said Ax.

'Well, it is the question of the British Squaddie. We want you, Ax, and your people, to know that we in Europe intend to deal with him strongly, and instantly, when the day comes.'

'Um, you're in Europe now.'

'Europe before,' said Tama, bringing the coffee. 'Europe afterwards, *maybe*. In between, every country for himself. Hello, Ax, we were in Shanghai with you. Alain was the brave little toaster, I was the cranky anglepoise.' She put down her coffee tray, tipped her naked skull into Ax's lap and bared her muscular, tattooed forearms.

'See my RP shunt scars, and now you want to see my new backflip?'

'She's such a clown,' said Alain indulgently.

'I am a fucking clown!' sang Tama. 'Don't ever put me down!'

The English took their coffee, exchanging puzzled glances.

'Afterwards? After what?'

'We prefer not to deal with Pigsty.'

'Pigsty?'

'Oue. I prefer to talk to you. Direct, offhand, like this, it's the best way. But we don't reveal any details and we understand it's the same with you. Only, when the violence starts there will be no time to discuss tactics through diplomatic channels, so you should know and accept it will be "open season" as you say, on those fucking mindless animals of yours, from the Baltic to the Sahara.'

'Wait a minute,' said Ax, 'What violence? I am not into violence.'

Tamagotchi sighed impatiently. 'That's fine,' she muttered in French, rolling her eyes. 'Fine.'

'Well—' said Alain. He looked into Ax's face, head on one side. 'Well, this is very curious. Ax, I think you will have to change your mind. This is not going to be a velvet revolution. Believe me, the scrap will come. Maybe sooner than you think.'

There was a pause. 'Hey, Fiorinda,' said Tama, eyes sparkling. 'Did *you* eat the shit?'

'I was there,' said Fiorinda. 'I certainly inhaled. But I did not put anything in my mouth.'

Then they were out of the bus, dismissed so abruptly they were still clutching their coffee beakers. 'What was *that* about?' wondered Fiorinda.

'Organised trouble,' said Ax, 'I do believe. Brewing, in London. Alain wanted to find out what I know. Which is nothing, so now he's happy. What you said, Fio: a few burned-out cars, back to business as usual. That's not for me. I'm in this for the long haul.'

They walked away. Shortly, Fiorinda headed off somewhere – leaving them, she hoped, to a rapprochement. 'Fucking frog-eaters,' said Ax. 'I hate the way they always talk English.'

'Yeah, and always with those *chi-chi* accents. They could easily pronounce it properly.'

'If they felt like it.'

The two young men stood together, self-conscious. It was hard to know what to say when there was no one else about. The skull's demeanour was forbidding.

'Sage,' said the Ax, nothing daunted. 'About Fio—'

'Shoot.'

'If she wants to fuck you as well, at some point, I thought I should tell you that would be fine. There's nothing exclusive going on: I'm happy if she's happy.'

'No.' Sage did something which didn't involve his hands, whatever it was, and the skull vanished. His natural features: wide nose, full lips, wide-spaced blue eyes, a close-cropped fleece of yellow curls, made a rare public appearance. 'No,' he repeated, face to face. 'I'll stick with playing the big brother. I think it's more what she needs. If I'd wanted to have her, I shoulda ignored the ribbon, shouldn't I. Only I know why the kid wears it, see.'

'So do I.'

'Well, you're a heartless bastard then.'

'I don't think so. I think it's okay, me going with her. It seems to work.' He glanced down at Sage's unmasked hands, one with mere stubs for the two outside fingers, the other lacking the two first fingers and half the thumb. 'So that's what they look like. Tough. Was it the infant meningitis? I read you had that.'

'Yeah.'

'Good job you're into mixing, Sage. You'da been in problems if you'd wanted to play a guitar.'

The skull reappeared. Curiously, its expression was now almost affectionate.

'Right, Ax. Well spotted.'

In the first week of December the Countercultural Think Tank was up for a full-scale political reception. It was to be held in a prefab venue, installed specially for the purpose on the edge of Hyde Park. Here the great and the good of the CCM would gather to meet the Home Secretary's radical rockstars. The Prime Minister was going to turn up. Paul was inexpressibly proud and excited. Most of what was supposed to be ready for D Day was not going to happen. There was *no way* the English were going to have national identity cards in time, if ever. Border disputes and the division of capital assets would grumble on for decades. But Paul's initiative on the Countercultural problem was reckoned to be a great success. It had captured the public imagination.

Pigsty was also thrilled about the reception. He took an obsessive interest in the details: the carpet, the curtains, the floral decorations, the buffet, the dimensions of the stage. Nobody else was enthusiastic. Only Pigsty Liver and the Organs were to play. The rest of them would have to stand around making small talk with an assortment of high-ranking suits and the green nazi aristocracy. Didn't sound like fun. But pity the poor VIPs, invited to meet some of the best radical talent in English Indie music and subjected to nothing but a brainless, derivative Organs set.

The event started at dusk, on a cold day of heavy cloud and still air. Around the prefab, big sleek dark cars cruised onto the grass and disgorged those guests who felt they could get away with personal transport hypocrisy. Further off, beyond the metal barriers put up to cordon the site, clusters of campground folk stood and stared, some of them waving banners and placards.

At the door, security men checked everyone for recording devices or weapons, and temporarily divested them of their mobiles and pagers, so they wouldn't disrupt the Organs' performance. Fiorinda, who had come up from Reading with Krool, endured the search, surrendered her phone and went off alone. The grrls were ardent networkers, they'd be making a big thing of circulating; Fiorinda didn't want to play. For a while she stood and listened to Paul Javert, who was behind her, talking to another suit about the wonderful team he had created. But we've done *nothing*, she thought. Absolutely nothing, except rehearse the usual stupid arguments about whether you can have terrorism in a good cause, fill in some slack moments on the tv, and talk drivel to interviewers. We haven't even agreed on a decent name.

The Chosen arrived in a body. Paul zoomed over to intercept Ax: brought him back to introduce him to the PM.

'Axl Preston, lead guitarist from the Chosen Few. Axl, because your parents were big Stone Roses fans, isn't that right, Ax.'

'Guns 'n' Roses,' said Ax sadly.

'Ax is our Lennonist,' said Paul. 'He comes up with some killing lines, so witty—'

The two men, with identical wide, fixed, shallow smiles, stared at Ax expectantly, like dogs begging for biscuits.

Fiorinda moved away, grinning to herself. Poor Ax. He had not been looking forward to this event. Arguably there were people here who were actually doing what Ax talked about, and that must be so frustrating. Especially since they were *doing it all wrong*. She wandered, spotting the Heads in their skulls, Rob Nelson and the Eyes looking very flash; but she didn't want to join anyone. How strange that something like the Countercultural Think Tank could get itself an existence, a website, a place in politics, articles in the papers, headed notepaper, stacks of tiring documents, when the content of the package was *nothing*. Most of the Lords and Ladies of Misrule were in very correct evening dress. Probably, thought Fiorinda, especially the ones who are secretly behind the most ruthless humans-must-commit-mass-suicide (or if not we'll help them along) eco-terrorism. But here they are, looked dead pleased to have been invited. How insane.

Torn between longing to be introduced to the Prime Minister and feeling completely, defiantly out of place, she drifted over to the potted palms by the buffet table, where she bumped into Cecile Hunt, the Think Tank suit who had endeared herself to many because she so obviously detested Pigsty.

'I should introduce you to someone,' offered Cecile.

'No thanks. I mean, yes, I suppose—'

'I *hate* these things.'

'So do I. What's the point of a party if you can't get drunk?'

'You can get drunk. Go ahead, be a rebel. What else were you hired for? Look at Ken. He's going to be legless in about ten minutes.'

But she didn't want to be drunk, not here. In any case, the milling about was over. It was time for the musical entertainment. Pigsty and the Organs moved on up. Security men stood in front of the double doors, only exit or entrance (isn't that a fire hazard? wondered Fio) from this crowded room. Pigsty was wearing vr goggles, leather jodhpurs, jackboots: a new, shaggy Afghan waistcoat open over his sixpack belly; the chains between his nipple rings swinging and glinting. He strode to the front of the stage, the image of a cleaned-up but still scary Countercultural monster.

'And now,' he roared, 'all you RAVERS. It's time to GET DOWN!'

The lights went out. There was a thunderous drum roll, and a fusillade of wild bangs, wild yells, crackles like machine-gun fire: an incredible, shapeless racket. Typical Organs, thought Fiorinda, a bored sigh rising in her throat. *Get down!* wailed someone: grabbed her and dragged her to the floor.

Some lights came on again. Her knees were warm and wet. She was crouching in a pool of blood. Cecile lay beside her, face upturned and eyes wide open, the side of her head and her lower jaw blown away.

Where had the gunmen come from? Through the roof? The prefab was full of choking smoke, coloured smoke from the stage act, grey smoke that smelled of cordite: no, they must have come through the doors, but how? How did they get past the security? How many of them were there? Three? Four, five? People were running, pushing and fighting each other, to the other end of the prefab: but there was no exit that way, no way out . . . The gunmen were going into the crowd, like shepherds among blundering sheep, still firing. There was Ken Batty, the Think Tank's earnest politico, lying on the floor screaming, a horrible mess of blood and some grey, puddingy stuff falling out of a rip in his belly. There was a man in a dinner jacket, trying to crawl and falling on his face, oh, God where's Ax . . . ?

. . . and then, right by her, she saw someone dragged out from under the buffet table. It was Martina, blood in her dreads and all over her *Red Sonja* jerkin, but who was that holding her? It was *Pigsty*. He held Martina and snogged her, very deliberately, mouth all over her face, hand inside the laces of her jerkin, squeezing one of her tits as if he was trying to wrench it off, then he hauled off and shot her in the jaw. Fiorinda backed away, staring, electrified, her mouth open . . . and someone grabbed her again. Not Cecile, Cecile was dead. It was Fereshteh the ghazal singer, dark eyes gleaming through the eyepiece of her veil, drawing Fio with an iron grip into the shelter of the palms. There they stayed, clinging to each other—

Somewhere off in the distance, sirens began to wail—

They were found, and hauled out. The room was full of the sounds of people crying and screaming, full of a confusion of moving bodies; the air smelled foul. The men who hauled them out looked like hippies from the campground. They were not rough, only insistent: they hustled the two young women out of the prefab. Firorinda thought they were being rescued, she kept saying *I'm all right*, because she thought the hippies should go back and rescue someone worse off. But then they were bundled into the back of a small van. No one else in there with them, no windows. Sirens all around, but they could see nothing.

They didn't speak to each other.

The van didn't go far. They were delivered into a big tent, one of the Hyde Park indoor venues. It was brightly lit, the slick heavy-duty membrane of the empty floor shining like the surface of a black pool under the lights. Pigsty was on the stage. He was holding a big hand-gun. With him were the Organs and a few other hippie goons of the same hard-nut type, armed with automatic rifles. Allie Marlowe was up there too, looking very frightened. Down on the floor near the stage, surrounded by more hippie goons, stood a small group of people Fiorinda recognised: there's Rob Nelson, in his electric blue suit, all bloodstained. There's DK the DJ; there's those silly boys, Chip the black cherub, Verlaine with his ringlets; there's Roxane Smith—

There's Sage and there's Ax. They're alive . . .

Sirens were yelling wildly out in the Park. There must be a whole fleet of police cars and ambulances, whoever had called them, converging on the scene of the shooting, rushing to sort out the survivors from the dead. Pigsty didn't take any notice of these noises, nor of his Think Tank colleagues. He was watching the back of the tent, waiting for something. Another vehicle pulled up. Two more hippie goons appeared, holding a man in evening dress between them. It was Paul Javert. They brought him up to the stage. There was blood on his face; couldn't tell if he'd been shot or just beaten up.

'What went wrong?' he gasped, shook his head and spat out some blood. 'I thought we were mates. I thought we understood each other.'

'Nothing went wrong,' said the Pig. 'The plan changed.'

Blam! There goes Paul.

Paul's body was dragged away. A hippie goon came up with a foam fire extinguisher and smothered the bloodstains, came back with a bucket of water and splashed it casually around. It was Paul's plot, thought Fiorinda. Paul had a plot, and maybe Allie was in on that, she knew something anyway, but she wasn't expecting what happened tonight. It was Paul's plot but the Pig has double-crossed him and taken over. And *this* is what the Think Tank was all about, *this, not nothing* . . . But she couldn't hold it together, couldn't think. Fear and shock took over, please God, I never provoked him, never challenged him, I didn't laugh at him, I kept my head down, didn't I? *I knew he was dangerous—*

What is he going to do with us?

Pigsty watched Paul being hauled off. He bowed his head, took a deep, fierce breath. 'Now I want the Ax and Sage. You first, Sage.'

Tall Sage walks out from the guarded corral. The skull is looking unperturbed. Neat trick.

'Take off the mask,' orders Pigsty.

The skull vanishes, the crippled hands are bare.

'Will you kneel to me?'

Sage kneels, like he's been doing it all his life. Doesn't look up, doesn't look down, no theatrics.

'Will you obey me, Sage? Will you accept me as your boss?'

'I will obey you,' he says. 'I will accept you as my boss.'

'That's good, that's enough for now. You can go.'

Sage gets up and doesn't know where to go. Decides to return to the corralled group. This seems to be okay.

'Now I want the Ax.'

Pigsty is going to kill Ax. There's no question. Looking back now you know you've seen *the desire to kill Ax* smouldering in his eyes, every time Ax came out with one of those smart one-liners, every time Ax made it clear that he is very clever and Pig is dumb as pigshit—

'Well, Ax. Will you kneel?'

Ax kneels. Everyone waits, knowing this can't possibly be enough. Pigsty pulls down his zip, heaves out his prick, which looks enormous, weighted by the thick steel thong through the glans. He starts to piss. Ax kneels there, piss on his hair and running down his face.

'Will you say, "thank you, Boss"?'

'Thank you, Boss.'

'There,' says Pigsty, zipping up. He waves for Ax to go away, Ax retreats, wiping his face on his sleeve.

Pigsty takes another of those deep, deep breaths. He stands tall, the coarse nobility of his features suddenly apparent under the bright lights. The men holding Fiorinda and Fereshteh release them and they join the others, the hippie guards stepping back.

'Now you're my team. Not Paul's. Mine. Okay, let's go. We got a lot to do.'

He took them back to the building where the Think Tank sessions had been held. It was brightly lit, and people were rushing about. News of the incident in the Park had clearly already arrived. The Organs and the hippie goons left their rifles in the vans, but they were probably still armed. No one dared to make a break for it. Maybe no one even thought of trying. The Pig led them with a swagger, talking to someone all the while on a heavy-duty radiophone, used his keycard to pass through security doors, up to the familiar room. How strange the place looked now: the stately, indifferent pictures on the walls in their gilt frames, the polished table, the coffee trolley in the corner.

'Sit down.'

One of the Organs brought in a small tv and put it on the trolley, where everyone could see it. They saw the scene in the Park. Benny Preminder (whose absence from the reception nobody had noticed) was on the screen, standing against a background of flashing lights, darkness, bloodstained people wrapped in blankets, sobbing people being comforted, covered stretchers being carried out of the prefab. The reporter with him was explaining to camera for probably the fiftieth time that armed ultra-greens had burst in on the Home Secretary's reception and opened fire on the guests, killing at least thirty people, and that Pigsty Liver and the Organs had retaliated.

'Mr Preminder, what *happened* here? Can you explain why the security was so inadequate, at an event of this kind, that gunmen could get through it? And how did Pigsty and the band come to be armed?'

'These are not normal times,' said Benny Prem. 'In extreme cases, normal rules do not apply. If it hadn't been for Pigsty's ability to fight back, there would have been a lot more casualties before the police arrived. As it is, many innocent lives have been spared. Surely a horrific incident like this proves that those on the positive side of the Counter-cultural movement have to be free to fight fire with fire.'

This is what it was about, thought Fiorinda. *This*, not nothing. Feeling like a guilty child. They had all of them stayed out playing by the riverside too long, refusing to go home (but Fiorinda never, never wanted to go home): and this is what happens. The monsters get you.

'Prem can be on the tv,' said Pigsty, dismissively. 'He can do the talking. That's his shit. Now I'll tell you something Prem doesn't know. We're setting off the green Blitzkrieg, as of tomorrow. It's a done deal, gonna happen all over, there's a shitload of us, finally going for it, no more pissing around. We're mad as hell and we're not going to take it anymore. Gonna save our mother earth, in England's green and pleasant land, and I want to do a proper job of it. The only question is, are you brainy types going to help me?' He reached down, pulled up the big hand-gun out of the waistband of his jodhpurs, cocked it and rested it on the table. He grinned at them. 'Or not?'

A moment of stunned readjustment, then Ax says, 'Yeah, I'll help you. Get me some maps.'

The others sat, bloodstained, immobile and hardly breathing, while the maps were fetched: listened to Pig explain how he'd been approached by Prem and agreed to take over Paul's plot; but *then*, Pig had decided he was going to take command for himself. Listened to Ax calmly discussing the whole thing; able to realise that Ax was saving their lives. But Rob began to get restless, began to twitch like a limb to which circulation is painfully returning, having been cut off. He started to mutter: *he killed . . . gotta . . . he killed . . . gotta do, can't let . . .*

'Get him out of here,' said Ax, casually. 'He's bothering me.'

Fiorinda and DK – who happened to be sitting on either side – took Rob by the elbows and moved him out. Pigsty's goons didn't stop them, but followed closely. 'Get me a phone,' said Fio, imitating Ax's manner; and this worked. A phone was produced. But then she couldn't handle it: she didn't dare to make that call—

So DK called the Eyes. They were safe. They were still at the Park, but they could leave. They would come at once. 'What's going on there—?' DK demanded.

'I don't fucking know,' answered Felice. 'We're coming and get our man, okay?'

On the steps of the building Rob wept and struggled, beside himself. The hippie goons stood by while Fio and DK held him, until the pink Cadillac rolled up out of the streetlight dark. 'He killed a sister. He killed a sister, man, the fucking bastard, I can't stand for that—'

'It's all right,' Fio pleaded. 'The Eyes weren't hit, they're okay, they're here now—'

'He means Cecile, I think. Rob, hey, that was an *accident*. Friendly fire.

63

The Pig is cool. Be calm, okay, the Pig is cool, you don't mean what you're saying.'

Fiorinda did not believe there had been any accidents in the events of this night. The Pig had known exactly who he wanted to murder. But Rob's losing it was also in some way a performance. He wasn't struggling *too* hard. They piled him into the car: the three Eyes looking grim on the front seat, Rob into the back, like tipping a wild animal out of a net into safe captivity.

'You're driving home again?' asked DK. 'Are you sure it's safe?'

'We can look after our sweet selves,' said Felice, 'Why'you think there's three of us?'

'That's how many it takes,' said Cherry. Her face was streaked with tears. 'What the fuck *happened* to you guys? What's going on? We thought you were all *dead*—'

'Any sister waits in hope for a black man to look out for *her*, is a fool,' said Dora, her voice shaking in the bitter fury of relief. 'C'mon, fellow-babes. I don't *care* what's going on.'

The Cadillac rolled away. DK and Fiorinda, released from their terrifying burden, stumbled into a hug, clinging tight, white-knuckled, bone on bone.

'My God,' he muttered, '*My God*—'

'We're still alive,' she whispered. 'We're alive, hang onto that.'

They were taken back. Then, in the familiar room, there followed an extraordinary session in which Ax handed over detailed knowledge of how Pig's 'green Blitzkrieg' should be run. Where the arms factories were, and the places where they made instruments of torture for that profitable global market. The most effective way of closing an airport or tearing up a major highway. The most poisonous chemical plants and how to decommission them without disaster; *leave the nuclear power stations alone*. The channels of communication that must be kept open and frequently fed, calming the people and the world out there beyond . . . Often in the Think Tank, Ax had teased Paul Javert – letting slip hints of how much politically and socially useful information he kept stored alongside his Lennonisms. Now it all came out. There was no one taking notes, and if the Pig's wishes had been obeyed there were no recording devices in this room, but that didn't seem to matter. All that mattered was that Ax could keep talking, holding the Pig fascinated, so Ax went on doing that, while the hand-gun stayed on view, sometimes pointed idly in one person's direction or another; the hippie goons stood around, and of course, Pig was joking. He couldn't shoot anybody, not in here, he just liked to see them scared.

Fiorinda remembered Martina's terrified face. He could do anything he liked.

Pigsty's tremendous physical strength and resilience became evident. While Ax turned grey and sank into his chair, while his hands began to tremble, Pig stayed bright as a button: not stressed at all by the events of his busy evening, showing not a sign of fatigue. Twice he sent the guards out, once for cigarettes and once for curry. (Ax vetoed alcohol, the Pig took this like a lamb.) And still the facts poured out. Verlaine and Chip, Fiorinda and Sage started to give each other wondering looks.

Finally it was over. The last phase blurred, the Pig abruptly satisfied. They were taken to another part of this big old building, where two connecting rooms and a bathroom had been prepared, evidently prepared in advance for this night of planned emergency; with camp beds and blankets. Ax went straight into the bathroom and threw up, ran a lot of water, came out with his head and face dripping, wiping his mouth, and collapsed on one of the cots.

The others grouped round him.

'Ax,' said Sage, softly, 'you've got a warehouse, haven't you?'

'An implant,' whispered Verlaine. 'You *must* have.'

'Yeah,' said the Ax. 'You're true. Don't tell Pigsty . . . I think he'd tear my head off.'

In the morning, Ax was separated from the others and sent away on a tour of the provinces, on what seemed like a rampage of mob violence but was actually pretty structured; Ax should know because he'd structured it. Within a few days he knew that the decision he had made was in some sense justified. Pigsty really did have an army, an army of wild young men and hardened green-violence veterans. It was growing all the time, and the Pig really was in command of this army, so far as anyone could be. There were no other leaders left, at least none prepared to claim responsibility after massacre night. The wild rumpus couldn't have been stopped, not without a major escalation of violence and death, but what was more shocking, more disorienting, was that nobody seemed to *want* to stop it. The police, the government, they were going to stand by and let the thing burn itself out. So that's what Ax was doing, or directing: the burning out of this energy. Guiding the destruction as best he could along less than utterly destructive channels, he felt like a lone paramedic at a massive traffic accident. But this paramedic was the same person who had allowed the drunk driver to take the wheel. He'd been so determined not to peak too soon – and to be honest, hoping the violent part could be avoided entirely. But there you go, Ax had got it wrong and Pigsty was the boss: well on his way to declaring himself King, Emperor, Idi Amin, Milosevic.

At least there were remarkably few human fatalities. Considering. Yet.

It was horrible, but it was quite an experience leading Pigsty's barmy army. There came, maybe inevitably, a moment when it started to feel right. It was in a vast supermarket, outside Wolverhampton – a staged event, this one, with a local tv crew in attendance and Ax himself leading the action – as the mob (still overwhelmingly composed of young men and older men, hardly any women or girls) let rip with blowtorches and chainsaws. *This had to happen*, thought Ax. Two hideous little children sleeping in a shop doorway, their names are Want and Ignorance . . . cannot make terms with those children, they've grown to monster size, they can only be driven out by force. He had just made a stupid speech about the crimes of profiteering fat cats and the real, terrifying price of cheap food, but though stupid, it was also true. Smash! Destroy! He had never wanted it to be this way, but maybe there was no other way, the crashing chords, the violence of sound and meaning fused (they would put his 'Jerusalem' solo on the soundtrack for the tv item, he'd made sure of that . . .). Jerusalem.

Later: the Disney version. It was March, and the postponed Dissolution Day had come to pass. The retired Prime Minister who'd been ceremonial head of state since the royal family quit, had quietly resigned. President Saul Burnet (aka Pigsty) would take office now: a figurehead post, but a substantial and fitting compliment to the leader of the CCM. Fiorinda and the Ax – best candidates for romantic Countercultural prince and princess – featured in the parade, rolling up Piccadilly and down the Mall behind Pigsty's biker escort, in a coach left behind by the royals. It was balmy weather, the sky was clear and china blue, the buds on the plane trees swelling and unfolding in sheeny golden-green. The cheering crowds included many conventionally dressed Londoners, but few tourists.

They hadn't seen each other since December. Ax had been delivered to the luxury hotel where Pig had his London HQ just in time for the start of this show. He didn't know what had been going on for her. He had not been allowed to communicate with his friends while he was on tour. He only knew they were still alive, all those who had stayed alive that night in December, alive and more or less okay. He wanted to talk to her about the *rightness*, the immense power of certain moments, was that magic? She ought to know.

'I've been thinking,' he said. 'What happened was terrible, but I can use this—'

Today the formalities would be concluded at last: Northern Ireland already someone else's problem, Wales and Scotland now to go their separate ways. Then it would be time to explore the new relationship between the English government and the CCM, how would that power-sharing go? Interesting to see how things went in the continental EU also, where versions of the Tour scenario were playing at several national venues, to some degree or other. Alain had been right about that non-velvet revolution. Now that he was free again, Ax would be able to find out more. Fiorinda was looking so good. At first he'd thought it was a new dress, then he'd known it was one of the old ensembles – green silk under spiderweb lace and sequins – cleaned up and mended. There was jewelled netting threaded through her beautiful hair.

'We're still together, you and me and the others. We can still make a good team.'

Fiorinda had been staring out at the crowd. She turned her head. Trust Fio, she was not impressed by his pitch. She would never be impressed, by anything he did.

'Ax, you are beyond belief.' She shook her head and added, with such loss and finality she could have been speaking from an open grave, 'I'm never going to write another song.'

And the crowd went crazy, a background of senseless rejoicing behind his familiar face.

THREE

Cigarettes and Alcohol

Ax was in the Zen Self tent. He hadn't been interested in the place before, because Olwen Devi was Welsh and, by definition, none of Ax's business (be practical: set your limits). But Dissolution was past and the Zen Self circus was still here, so he'd decided to come and check it – see what Fiorinda and the Heads were on about. He had meant to accost one of the Selfers, get the spiel. Instead he moved through the little crowds around the installations, stopping and staring and then passing on, brooding on the grief he was having with Fiorinda.

He hadn't known how much he'd been looking forward to seeing that girl, until they were suddenly together in the royal coach and she froze him out. Things had been no better since. He was back where he'd started, with the stone cold eyes, the clipped chill voice, the *so, do you want that fuck?* In times like these, a lover isn't for sex. A lover is someone to reach for in the night, someone whose existence in the world you can cling to when you're hard pressed. He'd been imagining that was what they were for each other . . . but no way. She'd been living in Pig's hotel under some kind of house arrest, which couldn't have been fun. He'd thought she'd relax when he took her back to the Snake Eyes' place: it hadn't worked.

She said the world where they could have been right together no longer existed.

Ax said he thought they needed each other more than ever, now everything was fucked.

She said, 'I'm not going to be any rockstar political gang's comfort girl, *allowed to tag along* in return for sexual favours.'

So then Ax had to face the difficult question of what Pig might have been up to (although at least she was *alive*, and in okay physical shape, more than some people could say). She brushed that off, hurtfully as possible. 'Oh no. Pigsty won't touch me. He'll *protect* me. I'm the Ax's main squeeze. I'm safe, as long as you and he don't fall out.'

'Look, Fio,' said Ax, 'this is *not fair*. We're all equal under the Pig. You, me, anyone. You think Pigsty or his goons would hesitate at anal rape? You're kidding. Believe me, I've seen them in action. You're not being "allowed to tag along". You're vitally important, you have been from the start, if that's what's fucking you up. You're the one with the verbals, the one the suits respect, and so do we all.'

Still the curled lip, the hostile eyes, the relentless tongue. 'He'll probably knock me on the head, however, when he finds out I'm sterile.'

'You are not *sterile*. You had the injection: it's reversible—'

'Not the one they give to single mother thirteen-year-olds who have just given birth and have no one to read them their rights.'

It was impossible, he couldn't reach her, and he hated and despised himself for taking the sex anyway. Well, it was his own stupid fault for building up a crappy fantasy. He'd come to like and respect Fio very much, but he hadn't thought of himself as romantically involved, before massacre night. He'd regarded her as a project, a friend in need. What a fucking stupid way to behave. Not knowing what is happening, not thinking it out, just *falling*—

It had been a relief to go down to Taunton, where repossession was looming again. That'd been a bizarre experience. Contrary to the look of the thing, Ax didn't have any money, certainly none to spare to pour into his Dad's black hole; not this time. He'd been pleading with the finance company, thinking, fucking hell, don't you guys realise a word from me to the Pig and your heads might get blown off?, and at the same time could have kissed their feet for *not realising*, for still managing to live in a world where nothing had changed.

His Dad didn't realise anything. Ax's dad would keep repeating on him like a bad curry, until the hideously distant day when the bastard could be stuck in a nursing home.

And throw away the key.

Old people ought to die more. When he'd said that, what he *meant* was that old people in this country might as well be dead, considering the kind of life most of them had to endure—

Taunton had been only lightly bruised by the violence of the Deconstruction Tour: some broken plate glass, a couple of burnt-out buildings, nothing to mention. But there were no young men. Apparently a bunch of hippies, led by one of the Organs, had been through all this area on an aggressive recruiting drive. It made for a strange atmosphere, especially at night. Ax had walked about the quiet, dark streets, and understood that Pig had done this deliberately. The idea of Ax raising an army in Somerset was laughable, but it was a chilling insight into the way the Pig's mind worked (we never thought he *had* a mind. What fools we all were) and a view of the situation that had to be nipped in the bud.

The fingernail and thumbnail coming together, nicking out the disastrous growth before it has time to get started: he could feel it. And there was Fio again, one of those Think Tank Fio-riffs about words that *make sense*, language we can understand with our senses . . . raising a cruel, ridiculous nostalgia for the good old days of jamming with Paul Javert.

His brothers and Milly had been here on Reading campground since the coup: good thinking on their part, safety in numbers: safety in being seen to be part of the Countercultural nation. He'd insisted that he needed to talk to them – wanting to know how much freedom he had. His barmy army escort had agreed to drop him off, no problem. He'd told the band he hoped they could go home to Taunton soon. But Ax would have to get back to London. Probably have to stay there now, in the Snake Eyes house; or find somewhere of his own. What about Fio? Would she move in with him?

He kept wanting to call her and talk to her, see if anything had improved. Like, right now. It would be no use. Fiorinda and telecoms didn't mix. Her cut-glass accent, her mulish little white face on a postcard screen, communicated nothing.

Fuck. Relationship-grief was a distraction he badly did not need.

Was it the sterilisation? Women will do that, a defence mechanism, tell you anything but the real problem. If she wanted to have a baby . . . okay. As long as it was just one. Whatever the injection had done, they'd get it fixed: sure to be possible.

In front of the quantum-dissociation experiment he stood, distracted from his trouble by a technical puzzle. What were the Zen Selfers running all this stuff on? Power supply was fucked to hell all over the country in the aftermath of the Tour; so that the campgrounds, with their dodgy little generators, were relatively well off. But these slick big-science installations looked too hungry to be feeding off a little chugging petrol engine out the back of the tent. Ax was very interested in novelty energy sourcing. There would come a time when the problem of power was not transient, and it might not be far ahead.

It was on the list called *Solutions to Problems*:

Find a means of supply that can survive without the socio-industrial complex.

But Ax had envisaged being on the sidelines for years working on that list. Instead of which he would have to spot the future solutions that must be around in embryo, and save them *now*, if he could, while struggling with a raft of horrible present and pressing dilemmas—

'Good morning, Mr Preston.'

Ax looked round and found a woman in a sari standing at his elbow.

Ax had prided himself on being non-famous. Fans might get excited in context, but no one was ever going to pester *him* in the supermarket. The Tour had put an end to that happy state of affairs, at least for the moment. He sighed. 'You can call me Ax.' But he remembered this woman's photograph from the Festival programme, so he was able to return the compliment (if that's what it was). 'And you're Olwen Devi, nice to meet you.'

'Is there something you'd like to know?'

'Well, yes. How're you keeping all this stuff going? Off a petrol generator?'

Maybe they had a landline all the way from some busy Welsh wind farm. But that was not the answer. All those renewable resource things were the socio-industrial dependent National Grid concept, dressed in green. They didn't solve the problem Ax wanted to solve.

'We make our own power.'

'How d'you mean?'

'I mean, literally. We use ATP, adenine triphosphate, the energy currency of all living things, from our own cell metabolism.'

'You mean, like a . . . like a potato clock?'

'Something like a potato clock. Would you like me to explain?'

'Hmm.' The Fiorinda problem flew out of his mind. He took a better look at this woman. The morning was chill; spring had turned bitter since Dissolution Day. Olwen Devi wore a bright red and green plaid shawl, trimmed with black piping, around her shoulders – a colourway offensively drab-yet-garish to his English eyes. Her face was a smooth oval: half-circle eyebrows, high round cheeks, round brown eyes, businesslike smile. What is she like? She was like a calm, confident, Welsh Hindu primary school teacher. He could imagine her standing no nonsense.

'Okay. Explain it a little. No need to get too technical.'

She led him away from the drifting, idly interested campers to the decking in the centre of the tent. They stood among the collection of lecture props.

'Every cell of your body contains little powerhouses called mito-chondria.'

'Yeah.'

'Which . . . it's a fascinating process—' Olwen Devi's hand edged as if magnetically attracted towards her laser pointer, the controls of her display screen. Ax gave her a firm look.

'Translate fuel into work potential.'

'Right.'

'We've developed a means to draw on this power, through the skin, and amplify it.'

'Oh yeah? And then what can you make it do?'

'Well, light and moderate heat are the easiest applications. Those can be seamless. Otherwise, unless your machines have been designed bottom-up for the ATP, there's an interfacing problem. We're envisaging a set-top technology, in the medium term.'

'But you're already running this whole show like that? How long—?'

'We've been running the Zen Self tent on human metabolism power since last July. In times of high demand it can be exhausting, like running uphill. But everything here is highly energy-conserved and we are many: it's never too much to handle. Of course it would be another huge step to move on from experimental conditions.'

'Guruji, how would you like to work for me?'

'Please don't call me that. A guru is a chubby fellow with a penchant for half-nakedness, glistening like a raw egg as he rakes in money from the gullible. Also, it is a title for a man. I tolerate it from the punters: I don't like it.'

'Then, er Dr . . . Devi?'

'Just call me Olwen.'

A bunch of Zen Selfers, most of them wearing some garment in that tacky Welsh red and green, had come to see what was going on between their boss and the Ax. They didn't look surprised, no more than Olwen herself. It was as if they'd been waiting for him to turn up.

'Okay, Olwen. What about it? Not now, but if I'm in a position to hire you, one day?'

The Zen Selfers looked at each other, grinning. Olwen Devi shook her head at them a little.

'Mr Preston, Ax, we believe we're already working for you.'

'Huh?'

'We've been hoping you would come and see us. We would have sought you out, but we were afraid that might be tactless. Everyone knows that you have defended the country's science base wherever you could, but still . . . you are *dux bellorum* of the CCM.'

73

Ax didn't known what a *dux bellorum* was. But he thought of the Tour, and what these people were, and their position here. It was something he hadn't considered at all.

'Yes,' said Olwen, calmly. 'And yet we've chosen to stay on. You see, Scotland is an established European state. Ireland is a thrusting economic miracle. Wales is small, confused and vulnerable. We have our skill resources, our software, and pockets of highly developed sustainable technology, but the way things are going, very little of what we have will stay in Welsh hands. It's a gold rush over there since Dissolution. We saw what was coming and decided to leave. Our parent company stayed behind. But we believe that the work we want to do is safer *here*, in the heart of the Countercultural movement and its anti-science fury: because of you. Because we are under your protection.'

'My protection.' Fucking ironic, indeed.

'As for paying us, we consider ourselves well rewarded for the moment, and we plan to make our own fortunes. But if you could extend your protection and look out for Wales, when you come into your kingdom, Ax . . . that would be a bonus.'

Ax had never before had anyone speak to him as if they shared his sense of destiny. He was amazed, and a little frightened. 'What about your, um, parent company?'

She shook her head. 'Oh, they won't be cherry picked. They are not vulnerable.'

He felt that this subject was closed. Okay, forget the parent company. 'Could you do . . . stage lighting?'

'Fuck shit,' muttered one of the Zen Selfers. 'Sudden death.'

'I can't see that, at present,' said Olwen sedately.

'What about, say, really heavy computing power? Where's your mainframe?'

She raised her right hand. On the middle finger she was wearing a ring with a large, golden-white stone, brilliantly cut but slightly cloudy within. Not a diamond, maybe a white topaz? He'd noticed it already. 'Here she is.'

'I see. Does the ring come off?'

The Zen Selfers grinned some more. 'Not easily,' said Olwen. 'Serendip and I are very close.' She eased the gold band aside. Sunlight falling through the dome was caught, glittering, in a barely visible filigree, like spiderweb, between the jewel and her skin.

Ax had shivers running down his spine. He thought of the meeting in Shanghai. High tech is magic that works.

74

'What about the actual Zen Self shit? Does *that* have some alt-tech rationale?'

'The ATP development is an aspect of the Zen Self project. We are looking at all the ways in which Self and the world are connected, and how those connections can be reconfigured towards our final goal. If you mean, could you use the science of consciousness for your revolution, I'm not sure. But there is surely a synchronicity. When technology – applied science – becomes magical, what does science become?' The Zen Selfers had dispersed, at some signal Ax hadn't noticed. Olwen stepped down from the round deck and began to walk towards the tent entrance. He followed. She was right, they'd said all that could be said for the moment. 'Did you know the Upanishads were first translated in Europe during the French revolution?' She turned to him, absurdly symmetrical dark brows raised in mild enquiry.

'I never knew that.'

'Well, mysticism is not for you. But we understand each other?'

He had no way of knowing whether this ATP technology was worth anything. The Welsh can be plausible buggers, adept at making fuck-all sound momentarily impressive, they have to be, don't they. He'd need to try and find out more about it, from another source . . . But he was sure Olwen Devi was going to be a valuable acquisition, some way or other. Without knowing it, he'd been looking for someone like this, exactly like this.

'Done deal. You work here, I look out for you. And for Wales . . . if that's ever an issue.'

They shook hands, like market traders. The ring on her middle finger felt warm as flesh.

The Pig's hotel was a blank white tower on Park Lane. It had been empty, with a skeleton staff, due to lack of trade, when Pigsty decided he wanted to move in. The foreign owners had made no problem over leasing their place as a Presidential Palace, as long as someone would someday pay the bill. As soon as Ax was back in town, Pigsty called a meeting of the Countercultural Think Tank in one of the conference rooms. This turned out to be a grotesque replication of the old conditions. No eighteenth-century pictures on the drab corporate walls, no ornate white plaster ceiling high overhead. But here was Pigsty, flanked by his drinking buddies, at the head of the table. Here was Benny Preminder taking notes, and here were the radical rockstars, wondering why they'd ever signed up for this charade.

Some significant gaps in the ranks, otherwise no change.

The President hadn't done this before, he said, because he didn't want to take Ax away from the Tour. From now on they would meet often. 'You're my Cabinet,' he told them affectionately. 'The government can do the government shit. *You* work for me. Ax is Prime Minister, 'course; an' I hereby appoint Sage my Minister for Gigs. The people want that roadshow Paul was promising them. I want you onto it, Sage. We're gonna lose all artistic credibility if we don't get touring soon. The rest of you can have titles when I think of 'em.'

It lasted a couple of hours. They were still alive at the end.

Downstairs, three Eyes and four Heads and three Chosen were anxiously waiting. They'd been required to turn up, but President Saul aka Pig had decided at the last minute that they were not allowed into the meeting. The hotel lobby was noisy and chaotic, full of Pigsty entourage and hangers-on: stray campers from the Park, hippie goons from the barmy army, fresh-faced teenagers who'd run away from home to join the circus of the hour, and, having reached it, sat giggling or ready to weep on the stained and ripely hungover luxury-hotel upholstery – might as well have signs hung around their necks reading Please Kill Me And Eat Me. If the foreign owners could have seen the state of their public rooms (where the cleaners seemed to have abandoned a losing battle) they might have had qualms about that lease. But they couldn't check it out easily, owing to Pigsty having made a clean sweep of webcam eyes.

The Pig's Cabinet – Ax and Sage and Fiorinda, Rob and DK, Chip and Verlaine and Roxane, Fereshteh in her enveloping veil – sat down with the others. It was the first time they'd all been together since massacre night. No one spoke for a long time.

The body count after that night had ended up lower than first estimates, only twenty-three actually dead. The English nation, including the government, seemed to feel that was a reasonable price to pay for the taming of the CCM, especially since most of the fatalities had been out-and-proud green nazis: advocates if not perpetrators of the most murderous eco-terrorism. The funky new President was fine. Even the Tour had been fine, now it was over.

The day after the Dissolution ceremonies Ax had had a phone call, an invitation to lunch at a gentlemen's club in the West End. He'd gone along, and found himself sitting opposite . . . Was it someone from Special Branch? The Home Office? MI6? Didn't seem to matter. No labels, just someone who wanted to talk to Ax. Middle-aged Asian guy, very well-dressed, thick silver grey hair brushed straight back, giving him to understand that the facts were known and the situation, Paul Javert murdered and Pigsty for President, was something the country could live with. He'd talked about youth and age. How young people, if they are of any worth, are convinced that what they *do* is important. Older people come to understand that . . . there are no new moves, everything that we do has been done before time and time again, it's what you *are* that matters, the personality brought to bear on these inevitable actions. Ax had listened, having difficulty just chewing and swallowing, thinking about ethnic origins, and how he didn't really have one, himself. *I'm not from anywhere.*

But what had shaken him was the way this well-rooted, well-finished someone had *waited*, when he'd described the situation everyone could live with, watching Ax's face with a deeply disturbing kind of respect. The unsaid words had hung between them: that if Ax planned to change the situation, then that would be okay too, because he, Ax, was too dangerous to be messed with.

So he had what he'd wanted. Already, right now. Reach out and take it.

He hadn't known that it would feel like this.

He twisted his Dissolution Fest wristband around: clear plastic, with a shimmering rainbow border. Everyone was still wearing them, probably end up like the Masons, shoot your cuff and obstacles disappear, *oh, I see you're wearing a Reading DY wristie, and with all the colours, access all areas, oh well that's different* . . . His head was full of cottonwool. How long since he'd managed to cop any REM sleep? About a year, it felt like. His hands were cold as ice. He put his coat back on and stuck them in the pockets, felt marginally better inside the trusty leather armour . . . 'Is there some-where we can go and talk?'

'What about the Garden Room?' said Fereshteh.

So they all trooped through the lobby to the hotel's breakfast buffet and coffee shop, where there was a garden courtyard, formerly glassed over, now open to the cold sky after some hippie prank. It was sad and empty, big hothouse plants quietly dying in their pots and troughs. The broken glass had been cleared away, but there was a scum of litter over the marble pavement, empty cans and bottles in the water feature.

Ax sat on the steps by the pool, where a clogged fountain struggled to rise, and looked around at the rest of them. Three brave, beautiful Eyes in bright woollen coats, red and green and blue, fun-feather plumes at the wrists and throat; and their stocky plum-dark beau. DK the party-animal with his receding hair tied back in a ponytail, big sunken circles under his pretty eyes, far strayed from the *dao* of fun. Roxane Smith, flamboyant ex-man, veteran of God knows how many waves of rock idealism, looking like shit, the damage only emphasised by a Chinese-opera-scale slap-job. Rox's young boyfriend Verlaine (aka Kevin Hanlon); and Verlaine's *other* significant other, Chip Desmond.

Shane and Jordan and Milly, Fereshteh the ghazal singer, five skull-masked Heads; and Fiorinda in one of her party dresses under a drab, matted sweater, looking even more like shit than Rox. Walking wounded, all of them. Only Fereshteh, alert and composed in her burqa, seemed relatively okay – and the kids, Chip and Verlaine, who were just too fucking *childish* to stay shattered for more than five minutes at a time.

'Well,' said Ax, at last. 'Let's start at the beginning. Most of you were at the LSE that day, and I don't believe any of you were there by accident, or out of idle curiosity.'

'What d'you mean by that?' said Sage.

That amazing mask had maintained a merry and even-tempered grin through the Cabinet meeting. It was now a bleak closed door, and what the fuck made the difference Ax couldn't begin to tell, only it was there. Sage and the Heads had spent three months with the rural divisions of the barmy army, killing surplus farm animals and stuff like that, and had behaved so well they'd earned the privilege of visiting their families. Sage had been to Wales, to see his ex-girlfriend and his kid. Ax wanted to know how that had been, now Wales was a foreign country, and especially in the light of his talk with Olwen Devi: but it would wait. Anything to do with Sage's kid was territory where the guy's worst enemy might fear to tread, at the best of times.

'I mean, some of us might not like to admit it, but we all have the agenda.'

'Yeah,' said Rob, leaning forward, elbows on his knees, coal black fake-astrakhan lining of his coat a rich frame to the lemon-yellow of his suit. 'We wanted to make a difference, got snared into that shit-for-brains Think Tank because we hoped it would *come to* something. But what the fuck do we do now?'

'This thing has turned truly hateful,' murmured Felice. 'As bad as it gets. I'm scared. I'm like, I'd leave the country, but it's *my country*.'

'I think we're all scared,' said Ax, 'but I'm afraid this isn't as bad as it gets. Unless we're very lucky, we'll lose a lot more ground before we come to the bottom of this slide.'

'Just a harmless little market adjustment,' remarked Verlaine cheerfully. 'Or the end of the world as we know it. Whichever label sells best will win out.'

'Yeah. That's about it. Well, you know the story. According to the hardline CCM we've reached the limit of what this planet will stand. We all ought to commit suicide, but we're doomed anyway. The truth is, things could get a whole lot worse for the lesser spotted flycatchers and so on, without several billion humans having to worry much at all. But there's such a thing as a self-fulfilling prophecy, and being in the middle of the crash at the end of the longest economic boom in modern history doesn't help. We're in real trouble, and we're not alone, either. One reason why the English government is happy to settle for Pigsty is that they see what's happening in Italy, and France, and Germany and the Benelux. They know we're better off than we might have been.'

'Aside from a few dead bodies,' murmured Fiorinda.

Ax sighed. 'Aside from a few dead bodies, yeah. I haven't forgotten them. I'm saying that since what happened, happened, we haven't come out of it too badly so far. But because this is so widespread, and because we *are* pushing the limits, in terms of numbers versus resources, in the short term, things are likely to get worse now the shit has hit the fan, in ways we can't avoid. If you need convincing, I could give you detail—'

This offer brought back, with vividness, the grey hours of *that night*. Everyone recoiled.

'That's okay,' said Sage hurriedly.

'We believe you.'

'Not necessary, Ax.'

'You're the man with the plan.'

'Just tell us what you want us to *do*—'

He had not understood that they would be waiting for him. He had hardly thought about them while he was on the Tour, except for praying to God he would see Fiorinda again; and except that their faces would come to him sometimes, vividly, on the edge of the sleep that eluded him. Faces around a table, willing him to carry on, keep going, *we're with you, Ax*. But here they were, still with him: and he hated what he had to tell them.

'We have to concentrate on doing what we *can*. First off, that means tackling the CCM masses. That problem is *not* solved. No way. Getting rid of the leaders doesn't matter, and appeasement won't work, because the real problem is not the proverbial minority of troublemakers, or committed revolutionaries, depending on your point of view. The real problem is millions of angry, confused citizens who have spent the last few years seeing their savings wiped out, their prospects vanish and their self-esteem destroyed. And unlike Scotland, Ireland and Wales, the people of England don't have the lovely feeling that the world is young and early struggles will bring success . . . Misery. Normal, gut-wrenching human unhappiness. That's what fuels the drop-out hordes, that's what will keep on feeding the CCM, and keep it dangerous. Fact is, I think one of our major concerns as a culture, *if we get through the rough patch*, is going to be finding new ways to make terms with normal unhappiness . . . because the ways that used to work, such as wage slavery, will be gone forever. But right now, we're talking about crisis control.'

It was strange how these successful rocksters – all of them at the sweet end of a monstrously unfair system, if only the Heads were in the superleague – had started listening, really *listening*, when he mentioned gut-wrenching unhappiness. How Fiorinda and Sage especially lifted their heads, like they had heard some distant, magical, inevitable summons. Shame he had to bring them back to earth.

'We have to manage the Countercultural nation, keep them from breaking the place up, stop the green revolution from turning into a reign of terror. How can we achieve this?'

'Shoot more people,' suggested Fiorinda. At least this time she cracked a tiny smile.

'Thanks, Fio. I'll hold that one in reserve . . . No, I think the best thing we can do, for the moment, is carry on with the job Paul Javert hired us for. Accept President Pig. Work with him, work around him, get on the road. Free concerts, big ones.'

Silence. They stared at him blankly.

'You mean we hang on,' suggested Verlaine, hopefully, 'in deep cover. Limit the damage as best we can, and wait for our chance to take over the government?'

'Er . . . no. I am not planning to take over the government. Wouldn't do me any good. I agree with Pigsty, let the suits run the bureaucracy. It's the function of the government to be disliked, and people have to like us, or we won't be able to do what I want us to do.'

Ax picked up a stem of dry bamboo, debris from one of the neglected plant troughs, and began to poke at the base of the fountain, to give them something to look at while they thought it over. To work for the Pig. To endure him and his hippie goons, and look as if they liked it. It was a tough offer.

'Is anyone going to pay us?' asked Rob. 'Just out of interest.'

Ax grinned ruefully. 'I doubt it. No one was offering to pay us for the Think Tank stuff. Financially, the whole thing is a bust, I admit. But the media exposure should be good.'

'Hey,' said Chip. 'No probs. We have Aoxomoxoa to bankroll us! If I run short, I shall come straight to you, Sage.'

The skull gave him a dour look (which crushed Chip utterly, for a minute or two). 'I'd have to decide if it was a worthy cause.'

'Listen,' said Ax, 'I didn't expect the Pig's coup. I didn't see it coming, my fault entirely, and, for the record, I feel like shit about that. But now we're on the other side. We have to start from where we are and work with what we have and *I don't want any more violence.* Pigsty is convinced that he needs us, and convinced that we are his best mates, weird as his reasoning on that may seem. And he's the President. That gives us some kind of leverage, some power for good in a bad situation. I want to use it. Will you help me?'

'Okay,' said Sage, 'if that's what you want, we'll do it.'

The others all nodded.

'I think I see it,' said DK. 'Catharis, joy: the power of the everlasting beat. Yes, for sure, the best of drugs, a drug that truly heals. But no one can rave twenty-four hours a day, Ax. Not without dedication, and the dedicated are not your problem. The barmy army recruits will flock to your gigs, and *then* they'll go out and break the place up.'

'I was coming to that. We're gonna sell them community service. They'll accept rockstars as charity work promoters: it looks familiar. We'll get them cleaning hospital toilets, replanting hedgerows, picking up litter, chatting to old ladies in geriatric wards. God knows there's enough that needs doing. And they'll love it. We know they will, because we've all been there. Being nice to people is a drug with a very pleasant kick, even when it's cut to shit. It's the way we're wired, we get good juice from caring for each other. So, we'll give the patients rock and roll for heavy medication, voluntary work as routine antidepressants. If we pitch it with enough conviction, they'll buy it. As we all know only too well, human beings will do *any fucking thing*, no limit, if it is seen to be normal and taken for granted, and the role-models say it's okay. The Counterculturals are no exception.'

'Circuses,' said Roxane, 'and occupational therapy . . . Yes. You left out the bread, Ax. The drop-out hordes will need to eat. They'll need the necessities of life.'

'I do have some plans for that aspect, but for the moment it shouldn't be our problem. There are rich hippies. We'll scrounge off them, if the government won't pick up the tab.'

No one else had any comments.

'It's like . . . shuttering,' said Ax. 'We've had the industrial revolution, we've done that. The walls will stand on their own, we can knock away the supports. We can go back to *being ourselves* – except that we don't ever go back. We go on, further along Verlaine's helix of time. If we can *just get through this part*, this difficult passage, we'll be there. Over-population, from which every other problem stems, will be a pulse that we've passed through. The truly liberating tech – for which over-population was in many ways the price we had to pay – will be up and running. There could be, for the first time in history, a genuine human civilisation. For everyone, not the élite few who have always had a sweet life, any time this last however-many thousand years. I intend to try and keep things from going to shit, here in England, through this particular shake-down, because I want to give the future that *could* happen a chance. That's my project, that's always been my project. To make this turning point the beginning of civilisation, instead of a fall into the dark ages. But the only kind of good state that's going to endure is one where nobody has to make an effort to do the right thing. Utopian revolutions that demand discipline and self-denial turn rotten in about six weeks, because default human nature reasserts itself. That's why I want to give to the Counterculture . . . shit, to the whole country, if I had the chance, a model of life where we only take time off from having fun, from making art, from *being ourselves*, to concentrate on each other, like the social animals we are meant to be. The lesser spotted flycatchers may even be reasonably satisfied, if my idea comes about. And yeah, before anyone says it, I know it won't work. If I succeed beyond my wildest dreams, it'll be partial, fucked-up and temporary. Partial, fucked-up and temporary will be fine. If we can get that going, for just a few years, just here in England, we'll have made our mark. Something will survive.'

So he'd given them the manifesto. He hadn't meant to do that, and he wished he'd kept his mouth shut, because he could see that not one of them believed a word of it. Oh well. They would still do what he told them, because (like Saul the Pig himself) they badly needed to be told what to do. At least the fountain had responded to his persistence and was rising more strongly: nice touch.

'But on the way to Ax's rock and roll café society,' said Sage, after a polite pause, 'there is this roadshow—'

'Yeah. You'll need help, Mr Minister. You better get on to Allie, she's the one . . . Where *is* Allie, by the way?'

'She's upstairs,' said Fereshteh. 'She couldn't face everyone. I think maybe because she knew, and she didn't warn us. I mean, she didn't know there was going to be a massacre, but she knew something.'

They were uncomfortably silent.

'Well, tell her we need her,' said Ax. 'Soon's she can hack it.'

'She's been spending time with Anne-Marie and Lola and their kids. It seems to help.'

Anne-Marie was old lady to Smelly Hugh, the Organs' second in command. Lola was President Pig's wedded wife. She usually kept (or was kept) out of the public eye: a side of the Pig's life that didn't fit well with the outrageous-outlaw image.

Roxane and Verlaine glanced at each other. 'What about Benny Prem?' said Verlaine.

Ax was looking at Fiorinda. God, she looked terrible, sitting there oozing anger and misery, hair tied up in a scarf that looked like a dishcloth. The party frock, full-skirted blue taffeta, sprinkled as if with splinters of emerald, made her look like a *mental patient*. Oh, Fiorinda, why are you like this? He couldn't help comparing her to Fereshteh, who had come through the same ordeal, so serene and strong. He noticed, a change that had passed him by until this moment, that she was no longer wearing the yellow ribbon.

That ribbon, originally a clubbing signal, had been born out of social exasperation: *there has to be a way to strike up a conversation, dance, flirt even, without the other person getting narked if you don't suggest a fuck after thirty seconds . . .* Inevitably it had come to mean other things, inevitably people often wore it when they *were* on the pull, and taking it off signalled some kind of plighting troth with a new partner. Ax suddenly remembered that Sage, sitting beside Fiorinda now, had been wearing the ribbon, on some bizarre whim, before massacre night. Not anymore. He clocked this information, and Sage not touching her but very close, with bitter, blinding insight—

'Prem? He's a government suit. If they're happy to keep him on, after what happened, that's their business. If we can live with Pigsty, we can live with him. He doesn't matter.'

The meeting degrouped, and he knew it had gone well enough because everybody (except Fiorinda and Sage) found some reason to come up to him and say a word, touch his sleeve. Even Shane, poor kid: with his heartfelt, justified sadness about the band. Ax followed the Heads into the Sunlight Bar, a spacious grope-dark locale where the *de facto* senior officers of the barmy army liked to gather. He detached Sage and took him off to the terrace.

'How was Wales?'

'Didn't look any different.'

'Did you take a passport?'

'Forgot. They don't want passports, anyway. They spit on EU

passports. They want national identity cards, and I aren't got one of those. The border was nothing. But I'm in deep shit at Cwm Gared over this business. Marlon had been seeing his dad on tv, offing the poor sick moo-cows, dumping them in mass graves . . . Did his head in. Fucking media people—'

Ax was staring out at the righteous Countercultural squalor in the hotel gardens: the teepees, the bare-arsed toddlers, the dogs, the woodsmoke, the heaps of refuse. *Silent Spring* he thought. Magpies, herring gulls, rats. Nothing takes them down.

'Well,' he said, 'I suppose I better regard you as some kind of blood brother, since you've decided to take me up on my earlier offer.'

'Huh?'

'I'm talking about Fiorinda.'

The skull stared at him, doing a thing that might have raised its eyebrows if it had any. 'Oh, I get it. I've been in your bed while you was off on tour. Well, thanks. How do you think I managed that? Sneaked back here in my spare time and *climbed up a drainpipe?*'

'Don't care how. I said, it's okay. Just wanted the development out in the open.'

'Ax, *if* it's any of your business, I haven't touched her. What the fuck are you on about?'

Ax realised he was way out of order. He'd insulted Aoxomoxoa, stupidly, needlessly, and it was *the last thing he should be doing*. But he didn't see how to take it back.

'Nothing. Forget it. Fact is, I don't know what's wrong with that girl. You've seen what she's like. She's letting herself go. Won't eat, won't sleep, she looks like *fishbones* . . .'

'How strange. When everything is so hunkydory.' Sage concentrated on his cigarette for a few moments. 'Ax, d'you remember that tv show? When I was slagging off the Chosen Few?'

'I remember.'

'After which you sought me out, took me on the town, insisted on us talking all night while getting me legless drunk, and I couldn't work out why. You said then that you always tried to listen to the people who made difficulties.'

'What's your point?'

'Maybe you should listen to Fiorinda.'

Eventually, freighted with beer and white powder, Ax went back to the house on the Lambeth Road. He wasn't drunk; he was in the mood where nothing will make you high, just tired. Fiorinda was in bed, wearing a greyish and raggedy underslip, and reading by candlelight (the power supply was having a scheduled brown-out). Her lovely hair – her best feature, in Ax's opinion – was in such a mess it would soon be dead-cat whitey dreadlocks of no return, a style he hated. The slip hung dismally slack from her skinny collarbones.

He went and sat on the floor in front of his Les Paul and touched the strings vaguely, without raising a sound. His fingertips were tender from lack of use. The rest of the guitars were valued and respected pieces of equipment, but this Gibson was his lady, his favourite instrument, constant companion. In that gleaming, dark red, classic form lived the first big gig, lived the first time he'd seen a crowd go wild, lived everything he most passionately loved to play, everything he'd written (though not the 'Jerusalem' solo). The years of living with the band in that house, which had belonged to Milly's mother, until Milly's mum and her stepdad moved to Spain; with the overgrown garden where they never did any gardening, the double garage where they had first played together . . . Rehearsals, tours, recognition, critical acclaim. A whole life, a whole world. Gone.

'Maybe you should set fire to it,' suggested Fiorinda.

'Probably wouldn't be a bad idea.'

He stubbed out his last cigarette and crunched the empty packet. He'd been smoking tobacco all night; no wonder he felt disgusting. He turned around, on his knees.

'Fio . . . I love you. You're right, I know you're right. We are fucked, it's horrible. I'm *just trying to be positive*, stupid as that may sound. Please be nice to me.'

'Ax,' said Fiorinda, dryly, 'I begin to suspect you love a lot of people.' But she sounded mollified. 'Oh, come on. Come to bed. Come and rest your weary head, idiot.'

He'd known that the word, which he'd never used on her before, would have an effect (although it was a word she would perhaps never use herself). That, and telling her she was in the right. People are so easy to handle, as long as you pay attention to the details: problem is that you forget to *handle* the people who matter most.

The Minister for Gigs proved to have a talent for delegation. The organisation of the post-Deconstruction Tour was directed by Allie Marlowe, with help from Ax and Fiorinda and DK. The Heads turned up *just about* for their spots in a punishing schedule which dragged everyone, sometimes in the same venue, sometimes scattered, all over the country. Otherwise they kept company with the barmy army. They cooked up batches of home-made napalm on Reading campground, and went crop-spraying the swathes of 'green concrete' monoculture that the government had purchased for destruction as part of their CCM appeasement: a stupid crowd-pleasing stunt that Ax hated. Sage had never flown an aircraft before, but he picked it up. No more problem than driving the van.

There was no murderous violence in the Cabinet meetings, only the ever-present threat of it, but there was ugly stuff to swallow. In May, President Pig intervened personally to insist on the summary execution of all fifteen prisoners currently sentenced under the restored death penalty. Fired with enthusiasm by the experience, he summoned Ax to the heavily guarded family suite on the hotel's first floor (a very disturbing place) to discuss the formation of a Countercultural justice system, with public hangings, flogging and branding for crimes against Gaia; what did Ax think? He was anxious for Ax's approval for what he'd done about the death row cases. 'We gotta get tough,' he insisted, alcohol-stunned eyes wandering around the room, unable to fix on Ax's face. 'Child molestors, that kind of shit, we gotta be hardline there as well as on the green agenda.'

The suite reminded Ax of another thing Fiorinda used to say in the Think Tank. It's all costume. There's no distance between the Counter-culture and right-wing family values.

On massacre night Ax had saved his friends' lives and his own, and he could tell himself he'd saved many more lives by taking control of the Blitzkrieg. Now he was trapped. The Pig was popular, the government satisfied. There was nothing Ax could do, except walk away (if Pigsty would let him go); and he couldn't bring himself to do that.

A few days after this interview he was on the south coast, doing lunch with some ancient ladies hauled out of that other, vastly more numerous death row, for the pilot of the CCM Volunteer Initiative. 'I'm glad my mother had me,' said the spry wheelchaired ninety-eight-year-old next to him. 'If she hadn't, I wouldn't be here with you now, would I?' The way she said it, you'd have thought the decade she'd spent lying, dying of boredom between threadbare sheets, sometimes in her own shit, had been wiped clean off the slate by this particular salty-aired sunny day as she sat gumming her fish and chips for the cameras.

After the publicity lunch he talked to the matron of one of the long-stay hospitals in the south coast conurbation, and asked her what she needed. Everything, she said. Economic meltdown had not been easy on the low-income poor-health sector of the geriatric bulge. Donations in kind would be best, as credit was difficult. She'd love some volunteers, nice mature ladies for preference. 'What about young men?' said Ax. There were more nice, mature ladies than you'd think among the drop-out hordes, but they tended not to be at a loss for occupation. Matron (not her title, but it seemed the natural term) looked down her nose, but she was desperate. 'I would *consider* young men. As long as they were clean and tidy.'

'I'm gonna make you eat that tone of voice,' said Ax.

The media called them Ax Preston's Chosen, but that was already the name of his other band, so they quickly became The Few. They moved into a huge building near the Park that had been standing empty like the Pig's hotel and set up their headquarters: a press office, a club venue; studios, a works' canteen, hostel beds for teenage runaways. They called it The Insanitude. After the post-Deconstruction Tour Ax tried to get his friends out of the hostage situation, arguing plausibly that they should go back to their home towns, spread the message in the regions. The Chosen returned to Taunton; the Heads retired to Reading. But the Pig started to get restive about it, so the others stayed: Chip and Verlaine at Rox's flat in Notting Hill, Allie and Fereshteh and DK at the Insanitude, directing the refitting. Fiorinda and Ax went on living at the Snake Eyes house.

Fiorinda helped DK to run one of the Insanitude opening-nights, keeping him company in his eyrie above the ballroom while he played merry hell with state-of-the-art immersions. She wore the new filter glasses, the latest clubbing accessory, to shut out the assault on her visual-cortex: looked down through blood-brown lenses at the huge crowd of dancers swirling around in an ornate but dolefully derelict Victorian hall. Maybe they need never bother to redecorate; virtual scenery would be enough.

'What did it used to be?' wondered the mixmaster, mopping streams of sweat and chewing gum at a terrible rate. Forty-something, motormouth Dilip could lose or gain fifteen years in a moment, depending on his mood or the light. He was young tonight, he was flying. 'This hideous heap, this pile of architectural dung . . . was it a factory? A power station, a *mental hospital* ?'

'Do you really not know? You were living in the Park all last summer.'

'Was I? Oh well, I only saw it from afar, a big lumpen empty building.'

'You're having me on.'

'Mmm hmmtitum . . . I've never been interested in sightseeing. What a beautiful gown you are wearing.' He did something that made the dancers shriek, ejected his gum, stuck it on the underside of the desk, searched in vain for a fresh stick. 'What do you think of the Pig, Fiorinda?'

'I think he's a braindead, brutal creep,' said Fio, far enough from sober to relish the feeling of speaking dangerous treason.

'So do I. I also believe Ax did what had to be done, he had no other choice, and he is still doing what has to be done, and all power to him.'

'Exercising the art of the possible,' agreed Fiorinda. 'Same old, same old. But don't get me wrong, I know Ax is doing his best.'

'And here are we, torn between Jupiter and Apollo, or something equivalent appropriately Hindu that I can't think of, but let's be shamelessly multicultural: you want to come over to the north wing after this, back to my pad?'

'Sure.'

'That is, um, that is—'

'As long as it would be okay with Ax,' supplied Fio, resignedly. 'S'okay. He won't mind.'

'Ah, Fiorinda.' He swung around from the desk and wrapped her in arms like friendly, roving snakes. 'Sea-green, oceanic, spellbinding, Fiorinda.' His breath was sweet and hot. She reached over his shoulder, took off her glasses and was plunged into deep water, filled with mysterious shapes that thrummed at her like another kind of sound: then flipped to the roaring surface, stretched over the peaks and troughs of a series of gigantic mid-ocean waves. Dilip was lovely and warm, in the middle of this huge cold sea. 'Actually,' he confessed, nuzzling her throat and at the same time leaning back to do something new to the illusion. 'I *was* having you on. I know where we are. We're in Buckingham Palace, for a changing of the guard, what could be more fitting, ah, green-eyed Fiorinda—'

Her eyes were grey, or in some lights hazel, or maybe even brown. But it would have been a shame to correct him when he was on a roll.

Ax arranged for Fereshteh to get him up to speed on British Islam, or English Islam, as they should now call it. She and Allie were occupying a suite of Insanitude rooms together: a makeshift arrangement, like Ax and Fiorinda living at Snake Eyes, that seemed likely to persist because it was impossible to make plans. No sign of the roommate, when he turned up. Allie was keeping a low profile: functioning okay, but nothing like her old self. He was startled and intrigued to find that Fereshteh was still wearing the burqa.

'You're not a male relative, and I feel more comfortable this way.'

It was certainly interesting to watch her hands and her eyes and guess at the shape of that smile in her voice. How old was Fereshteh? Her hands said young, but her rich singing voice had all its growth, which he knew in a woman normally meant late twenties. Was she fat or thin? A little fleshy, he judged, but graceful. They talked about Islamic background, and how Ax would have to learn Arabic if he wanted to get very far: both of them skirting round the obvious, which was *how can a woman put up with this?*

'I don't get it,' he said, at last. 'Okay, I heard about how women get a better deal in the Koran than in the Bible, and Muhammad was an early feminist, and wearing the veil is actually liberating, but give me a break. You and I both know that what *happens*, among the faithful, is heavy inequality.

'Qur'an.'

'K'ran.'

'Better. Whenever you say the name of the Prophet, you must say Peace and Blessings of Allah Be Upon Him.'

'Muhammad, Peace and Blessings of Allah Be Upon Him. But how can you *agree* to something that says you're less than a man, and you have to go around with a bag over your head because you're responsible for sexual attraction and he isn't, all that?'

'I don't have to agree, Ax. I only have to accept, to stop fighting with the way things are. Accept the will of God, and be at peace. That's what Islam means. But not only Islam thinks like this: *In la sua volonte e nostra pace*—'

'That's not Arabic.'

'No, it's Italian. It's a line from Dante's Paradiso. *In His will is our peace.*'

For himself, he could feel the attraction: some kind of bedrock. *Accept* was a riff that kept playing in his head just now. For a woman, a courageous, competent, talented human being like Fereshteh, it was incomprehensible. He shook his head. 'Nah, I still don't get it.'

She reached out to straighten the sleek dark braid, tinged with rust-colour, that lay on his shoulder. 'Oh, Ax. You're like a little boy. Your information chip let you down, huh?'

'It doesn't help with understanding things, it's only a stack of facts and some ordering software. So, are you ever going to take that off while I'm around?'

'Not until we put out the light.'

*

89

In July Fiorinda moved back to Reading. Too many hurtful things had been said and done since that horrible ride down the Mall. Being with Ax had become a commitment with no joy in it: an unhappy marriage. They were better apart. She found a vacant hut, sturdily made out of car body panels, in one of the furthest-flung camping fields, arranged her possessions and sat looking around, seeking things that dated from before the Ax. Her guitar, a few dresses. My life is over, she thought. This isn't my life now, it's something else, a useless aftermath. That was the way she'd felt since Massacre Night. It wasn't Ax's fault, but maybe it was the reason they'd broken up. She picked up the saltbox and held it in her palm. She felt no nostalgia for the cold house; those years were dreadful to recall, but this double-edged talisman was still precious. A present for a little girl who is going to live beyond the end of the world.

She began to work for Olwen Devi, on a scheme training human gut bacteria to chew up and neutralise shit, wherever it was laid (but not before!). As Sage had predicted, it was getting direly necessary to have a policy for the brown stuff. She didn't like being a pharm animal, but she knew she had to *be there*. That was what the Few were about. She wasn't going to let Ax down, just because they had personal differences. There were exercises you did, physical exercises rather like T'ai Chi, which *perhaps* expedited the pharming, due to quantum entanglement or something. She was doing them one morning, while her breakfast tea kettle sizzled, when Sage arrived. When she'd finished he was sitting at her open door.

The skull was chipper enough, but it was lying through its teeth. The rest of him looked bone weary. The Heads had been ill with some bug or other, and then Luke had gone down with a viral pneumonia. There was nothing a hospital could do for him, and Head Ideology scorned such places anyway. They'd been nursing him as best they could in the van for the last fortnight. Fiorinda was not allowed to help. They said she was too young, and what the fuck would Ax say if she got sick?

'How is he?'

She didn't invite him in. He looked as if he needed the sun and air.

'Okay, sort of, for the moment. George is with him.'

'Is he going to get better?'

The skull contemplated. 'No,' said Sage at last, stonily. 'I don't think so.'

She said nothing. Her fire burned with a strong, young, yellow flame; the effect of the exercises made her feel distant and sleepy. So this is what we will do, she thought, as she crouched waiting for the water's note to change. We will die . . . well, that's not so bad. Without premeditation she reached out, and a flame crept into her hand. It curled there confidingly, the little wild creature, full of life: such a consoling thing, a fire. Sage moved in the doorway, a boot heel striking—

She looked around. He quickly looked away.

'There's a letter for you. I brought it over.'

The campground post office was busy, these days. Cellphone networks had collapsed as the hippies chopped down masts all over the place – leaving abjectly mobile-dependent music-biz folk lost and bewildered.

The short letter was from Carly.

> Dear Fiorinda, excuse me writing, but I couldn't get a number for you, you famous person you. I don't know if you want to know this but I thought you ought to be told—

'My mother's sick again,' she said, when she'd read to the end. 'Sounds as if she's dying.'

Summer turned to Autumn. Throughout Europe the Countercultural revolution flared and smouldered, fuelled by economic crisis and social problems. In England appeasement of the CCM seemed to be working, but conflict between Yorkshire's Islamic separatists and the police had reached the proportions of a small war. In the cold house Fiorinda endured the hated company of the dying woman, not knowing if it made any sense to stay, sure she could not leave. At least she didn't have to deal with Carly, who made no further contact. She thought of Saul the Pig in his hotel suite with his bodyguards, Ax the manager organising every-one, the Few obediently doing what he said was good for them, and all the barmy army lads, all the campgrounds, all those thousands upon thousands of people who had never gone home. From a distance she could see it happening: Ax's future, the rock and roll lifestyle written over everything, the nomadic idleness, the emotional intensity, the excess, the tantrums . . . She saw no hope in the development. A certain model of human life becomes accepted: once we were manufacturing workers, then we were venture capitalists, now we're rockstars. The world stays the same.

Sometimes she thought about the magic. But Sage had been right to look the other way, because there was nothing to discuss. Magic, when you hold it in your hand, turns out not to mean anything useful. It's like life, it's like death: it's not *for* anything. It just is.

*

The trouble in Yorkshire, which had been rumbling since before Dissolution, was getting very bad. Girls of Pakistani or Bangladeshi extraction were found dead if they had so much as left the house unveiled or without the escort of a male relative. Schools were closed, 'Anglo-Saxon' companies attacked, mixed-race families harassed. Terrorist bombings and racial gang fights were daily occurrences. People who had direct access to satellite tv started seeing the map of England on CNN (shorn of Scotland and Wales: you didn't even recognise the 'headless chicken' shape, first few times you saw it), with Yorkshire outlined in jagged red. People who didn't were fed a milder version of events.

President Pigsty had decided there was a Countercultural issue. He was outraged over the honour-killings, dress codes, all that oppressive stuff. He ordered the toughest nuts of the barmy army up there, to liaise with the police and sort the bastards. When the Cabinet demurred he told them they better mind their own business, they were a bunch of fucking popstars and he was the President. But there was no change in Yorkshire, and the Pig's pride was touched. One day in September he announced at a Cabinet meeting that he was tired of hearing his Prime Minister tell him he didn't know what he was doing. He'd fixed up for Ax and Sage to go north. Let them solve the problem. If they were so fucking clever. They were leaving tomorrow, no argument.

When the meeting broke up, the others gave the two of them space. No one knew what to say. Suddenly they understood they were still hostages, still at the Pig's mercy.

Ax and Sage went back together to the Snake Eyes house and up to Ax's room, the one he'd shared with Fiorinda. It was twilight and there was a brown-out. Ax fussed with candles. To Sage this was nostalgic. At Reading they had ATP lighting now: a limited system, but beyond futuristic – a glimpse of a world that challenged Head Ideology in ways he didn't know if he could tolerate.

He sat down. 'Well? I suppose we have to go?'

'Yeah,' said Ax. 'I think we do.'

They hadn't been seeing much of each other. Without withdrawing his support, or causing trouble with the Pig, Sage had been quietly going out of his way to annoy Ax – with the Heads' perfunctory attitude to their tour engagements, the napalming, and general non-cooperation. Ax had accepted the situation. He knew it was his own fault, for impugning the guy's honour (to get suitably mediaeval about it) that time, over Fiorinda. He shouldn't have done it, and he'd wished often he could apologise, but some things are better left unsaid. He was surprised and relieved at Sage's attitude now.

'And we can take it that the secret rulers are happy for the barmy army to be involved?'

Ax was sitting next to him on the bed; the room didn't have much furniture. He leaned back, head against the wall, thinking about Benny Preminder, sitting there so demurely, making his notes. Bastard. 'Oh yeah. The government's using the barmy army, whether or not Pig knows it. It's better than sending in the regulars. Which is the next step.'

'So what are you planning to do when you get there?'

'I've no idea.'

'No brilliant solution to the Islamic Question on that chip of yours?'

'I keep telling people, it's a datastack, not a wishing well. I'm only fucking sure that street fighting is not the solution. This is a problem of emotional identity, it feeds on that stuff.'

'Fine. Let them be the Islamic Republic of whatever.'

'Right. Then would you evacuate the non-Islamic population? Or let them stay, and watch the ethnic cleansing start up? Where exactly would you set the borders of that republic? Use yer head, Sage. No, there has to be some way to convince the Islamics they want to be part of the new England. Maybe we have to find it . . . and without offending the Pig. Last thing I want is to challenge that fucker's authority.'

They sat in silence, both of them absently watching the candlelight, and the shadows that played on the red Gibson; on some sheet music lying on a table; a saucer of dry catfood with which Ax had been trying to lure one of the Eyes' cat's pretty kittens into his life; a scarf that Fiorinda had left behind.

'Pig's goons aren't going to be very impressed,' Ax remarked gloomily. 'I've never touched a firearm. I managed to avoid them on the Tour. What about you?'

'I can use a shotgun.' Sage took off the masks and flexed his crippled hands. The right was worse off: that was the one with only half a thumb, the surviving fourth and fifth fingers lumpy and crooked from long ago efforts to build up their strength. 'My left hand's more or less functional.'

'I thought you was right-handed.'

'Yeah, I was. Converted to ambidextrous by years of vicious bullying. Ah, it won't be hard. Things like that never are.'

'Easy enough for you to say. You're the guy who juggles chainsaws.'

'First time I've heard you admit you've seen our stage act.'

'Must've read about it somewhere.'

'Hahaha. So we go up there, you and me, and what, we *shoot people*? My God.'

'I hope it doesn't come to that.'

'But it might.'

They contemplated the future, the real future of what had happened to them on massacre night, not the daydream. The sheer monstrous impossibility of Ax's project.

'Well, now we know,' said Sage at last, 'why Fio was getting so fucked-up.'

Ax flinched. 'Please, could we not talk about Fiorinda.'

He hadn't been too concerned when she moved back to Reading. It was just a spat, he'd known they would be together again. But now . . . She was living in that house, mother still dying: refusing to be visited, refusing all help. The last time they'd spoken on the phone, she had looked so bleakly unhappy and withdrawn. He was terrified. The only comfort he could offer himself, in those grey early hours when Ax never slept, was that hopefully she was too down to get it together to slit her wrists or swallow enough paracetamol.

'Sorry.' Sage restored the masks and got to his feet, unfolding, as always, to unexpected heights. The skull's stark grimace was irrationally cheering. 'Okay, we're off to the wars. Now let's find some company and get stinking drunk.'

FOUR

The Straight Path

Ax did not get drunk. Talking with Sage had made him realise that being treated like that by the President didn't matter. The Islamic problem was something he had to tackle. He had a hill to climb. Looking at it concentrated him so he forgot to drink, or if he remembered, the drug had no effect. Maybe the calories from the alcohol went straight into bitminding, who knows. In the morning Sage was found in the mugs room, curled up peacefully beside a savoury pool of vomit and urine. They woke him up and hosed him down, then Ax and Sage went off to talk to media people about their expedition until it was time to set off. Ax went on thinking about this hill on the train up to Doncaster, while Sage slept, folded into an impossible-looking pose on the opposite seat in their ancient first-class compartment. Sage could sleep anywhere.

In Doncaster they were taken to the disused office block on Chequer Road that the barmy army was using as a base. They were received there on an upper floor by someone called Gervase, who sat behind a desk, in a big open-plan office that still bore traces of its previous occupants, and explained that the barmy army in Yorkshire had no use for their presence.

'I'd like to see you two dudes do your free concert or whatever it is, and get on the next train back to London. We're running a war here, not a pissant rock gig.'

Gervase wore his new piercings and his custom-tattered camouflage with an air of self-satisfied irony. His accent was more offensive than Fiorinda's, though not so perfect. You had to feel a certain sympathy with the pleasure he took in being rude to the famous: but he was frightening. Ax had met others of this chilling type: the kind of guy whose response to massacre night had been to realise that joining the hardline CCM was a smart career move.

'A war?'

The Pig wannabe stared at him. 'What else would you call it? Now, if you rockstars will bear with me, we'll take care of your gear and I'll get someone to drive you to your hotel.'

He picked up a sheaf of papers and pretended to read. The hippie goons at the doors of the office stared ahead of them. Either ex-regulars, or they'd soon got the idea. Ax stood up and went to the windows above the street. He thought about the rivers, the Don and the Trent, and the line of the Great North Road: the old Roman road to London. Strip out the confusion of modern civilisation and you could easily see, on a map, why this place had once been a guarded gateway to the south. And here we are again. How long does it take to complete the fall? Not long. Not when the stumble and slide is being helped along by so many venal *idiots*.

It was late evening and there was a police curfew, but there was a crowd on the pavement for Ax and Aoxomoxoa. Gervase's soldiers were shoving them back. Sage had got up too. He was prowling the deserted desks, turning over the spoor of the accounting firm that had died here, very suddenly, some months ago. But the skull's eye sockets appeared to be watching Ax with lively interest, to see how he would jump.

It was one of those moments when you have to take one fork or another. Am I going to backtrack and be a visiting celebrity, or am I going to be something else? Maybe, ignobly, it was a pure rockstar reflex that swung it: that's *my* crowd, you smug bastard. 'Sage, let's go meet the public. Take care of the gear, Gervase. We'll call you later.'

The lifts were non-functional. They went leaping down the stairs, passing the occasional startled hippie. 'Hey,' said Sage, 'what happened to not challenging the Pig's authority?'

'It'll be okay, I can fix him.'

The guards at the reception area on the ground floor seemed to have other orders, but Ax made it clear that he was going through. Faced with the hero of the Tour and your actual Aoxomoxoa, paragon and nonpareil of glorious English louthood, what could they do but give way? A few minutes later Ax and Sage were working the front row, and accepting eager, thrilled invitations to come along to the barmy army's favourite club: marching away, the lads forming up behind them, roaring out the Deconstruction Tour song:

> Oats and beans and barley grow
> Oats and beans and barley grow
> Do you or I or anyone know
> How oats and beans and barley grow?

At least they were clearing the street; police should like that.

The club was a dank basement arena, given over to drinking and male bonding, the sound of yakking voices louder than the generic dancetrack. The moment they walked in they were surrounded all over again. Ax knew he'd made a risky move, but he didn't think it was too dangerous. He could handle the Pig, at least this far. He put the problem out of his head and got back into Tour mode. It wasn't hard. The lads were okay, nothing like as bad as the merciless hordes at the post-Deconstruction Tour concerts. They just wanted to get near, grinning all over their faces, laughing stupidly, bursting with pride.

Sage went off with some local connections of his napalming pals. Ax stayed with the first bunch: managed to get them past the gobsmacked stage, get them talking. One particular kid was intensely up on the Chosen, eager to discuss what had been going on in the making of *Dirigiste* (which album he kept calling *Dirigible*, but never mind); picking up the references to past greats with heart-warming accuracy. It was a shame he couldn't have the attention he deserved. Maybe another time.

'You know what it was like for me?' said another of them – a young black man in a Deconstruction Tour teeshirt, shaken voice and shining eyes of someone who has *seen the light* – 'It was like, the world was in shades of grey, fuckin' shades of grey. Suddenly it went into colour. Everything was green and bright and alive, and I was doing *something good* for the first time in my life. Fuckin' magic, Ax!'

'Not *only* green,' said Ax. 'That would be monotonous. If you're going to have only green, you might as well have only grey. Extremists are all alike, we want variety.' If he'd learned one thing on the Tour, it was how to talk pleasantly to drunken louts who had got idealism. How to understand that what for him was the aftermath of a hideous train-wreck was the major event of their lives, their righteous time, the moment when they had become real.

'But what about this Islamic situation? What do you guys think of it?'

The barmies and their mates from Doncaster town looked at each other.

'They say we're protecting the pimps,' burst out the *Dirigiste* boy; 'it's not fuckin' true, Ax.'

'There's plenty of Islamics that run working girls,' protested one of the civilians, a white youth with premature medallion man tendencies. 'Fuck's sake . . . It's *them*, fuckin' minicab drivers with big guns, they won't fucking give up—'

'That's why we gotta get military: go for the nests, burn them out.'

'The way it is now, it's horrible. Most of what happens never gets on

97

the news, I bet *you* don't even know some of it, Ax. Nail bombs, car bombs, shootings, and all these dead girls.'

'We knew this Paki, we knew he'd killed this girl, his cousin or something, only for walking down the street. So we took one of his girls and we cut her, not that badly, you know, but enough so he'd understand, and we sent her—'

'But it's no good, they won't learn. There's only one way, got to finish them off.'

Assisted by their medallion man pals, the barmy army lads were happy to explain what Gervase was planning. The police were useless. All they wanted to do was play with their fuckin' helicopters. No, the barmy army was going to *get military*. They were going to go into the Islamic towns, in strength, and . . . It was bloodcurdling, and all too possible. To these young men, the idea of turning Leeds-Bradford into Stalingrad or Sarajevo was not monstrous. Many of them had done time in the regular army, had seen active service; they were used to that culture. Or they were from the south, or from the other side of the Pennines, which made more difference than you'd think. Ax kept a straight face, listened, asked questions, and set about turning their feeling on the scorched earth plan around. It would need more then one conversation in a bar, but nothing like making a start. Eager to offer him the best they had, they brought out a little very pure smack to be smoked. It was Islamic smack, but they didn't think Ax would mind. In a way it was like, *proof* that he was right. They could still get on with the Islamists, still do business with them.

Someone offered to go and fetch Aoxomoxoa.

'Nah,' said Ax. 'Leave him alone, he's fine where he is.'

'Oh yeah, he was a junkie, wasn't he. He hates the stuff, I read that.'

Ax leaned back on the dank red banquette. Thinking, with great clarity, *this is what you do*. You get a buzz going, enough so that they buy the album. They buy the next two out of punter-inertia. By the time they realise your music is not what they thought, it's too late, you've *changed their minds*. Ripping up motorways makes them feel so good about themselves, with luck they'll take the next thing you ask them to do on trust . . . So there was heroin in Yorkshire. There was very fucking little of it in the rest of England. Since legalisation and government analysis started, the exotics had been disappearing from the street, and Dissolution hadn't helped. Someone had synthesised a good cocaine substitute (you really wouldn't know the difference); but there was no satisfactory replacement for the classic hard stuff. Suddenly it struck him, with more force than the mellow hammer blow of the drug itself, *that there was a problem here.* A problem for the future. The third biggest economy in the world, or was it now the second? Are they going to let us, in Europe, get away with this legalising everything, uncoupling the drugs from the crime? They are not. *Most certainly not* if it goes with what looks vaguely like a left-wing revolution. What then? Opium Wars. Now there's a bad problem, but never mind, got to be a solution, it'll come to me.

Sage, being reasonably sober, tired of the defoliation enthusiasts and came back to check on Ax. When he spotted what was going on he went off alone to prop up the bar. There isn't a single woman in the place, he noticed. Strange, I thought we were the feminists.

Someone new came up beside him and gave a huge fake start of astonishment.

'Oh my God. Has this place just gone costume or are you *really* Aoxomoxoa?'

'I'm Aoxomoxoa.'

'My God! Could you *stand there*, while I run home and fetch my copy of *Arbeit Macht Frei*? . . . and you could sign it or, oh no you don't do that, well just *touch* it or something. My God, if I'd known—'

'I'm staying for a while. You can find me again.' Sage did not get off on being a gay icon, and he was not at this moment in the best of tempers; however, the skull grinned benignly, the skeletal hands accepted a cigarette from the guy – who seemed to be genuinely *trembling* with delight. 'So, how do you feel about having the green liberation army in town?'

The gay guy – thirty-something and fresh-faced, limp brown hair cut in a bowl fringe – looked up: looked around, leaned close. 'It sucks. Having the barmy army in town *sucks*. Listen, let me tell you—'

Somewhat later Ax was alone. His soldiers had left him to get back on duty and the civilians had gone off with them. He was thinking over the facts and inferences he'd picked up, ordering and sorting, reviewing possibilities, when Sage appeared and sat beside him, looking big and wired.

'Hi, rockstar. Where've you been?'

'Hi, other rockstar. Around. Being worshipped. I haven't felt so famous for quite a while. I came back before, but you were busy so I went away again.' Empty sockets, black in this low light, surveyed the remains of the club crowd. 'Ax, I don't think I like our side.'

'Nor do I, the way they are. That's partly why we have to be here, straighten them out.'

'Oh yeah? You're going to straighten them out are you, *smackhead*?'

'It's none of your business, Sage.'

'Isn't it?' The skull flashed him an ugly glance.

This discussion might have continued, but it was interrupted by the sound of gunfire. They looked at each other. The steady firing broke off, then started up again appreciably closer. 'Hmm,' said Sage. 'Sounds interesting. Let's get outside and see what's going on.' They made for the exit, through a jostling crowd. 'Glad I didn't check my coat,' muttered Ax.

The street was in near to complete darkness, municipal lighting a casualty either of the Tour or the local situation . . . but a compact group of men could be made out coming towards them, rushing up the roadway between the High Street Generic stores. The men ran and dropped, alternate rows: fired and jumped up and came rushing on. Many of them seemed to have white scarves wrapped round their heads. This was the enemy. Three police helicopters rattled overhead, glittering blue and white and red, dipping like giant dragonflies above a pool. But it was the barmies who were returning fire, from alleys and roofs and upper floors of buildings. Those ordered volleys gave the scene a strange, choreographed quality: you looked for the film crew. A barmy army squaddie came running, laden. He seemed very relieved to have found them, thrust an assault rifle at each of them and gabbled a mouthful of instructions, orders, something . . . No use, they couldn't understand his accent. He was gone, the video kept on unfolding, but they had no part in it, and no ideas for improvisation. They stood staring, amazed; oblivious of danger.

'I think Pig sent you up here to be killed,' shouted Sage, through the racket, 'Gervase is supposed to arrange it. And me, on account of the Pig is convinced we are best mates.'

'I don't know how the fuck he got that impression. But you could be right.'

Ax looked at the weapon he'd been given. It was a British Army Issue SA80, box fresh. The feel of it, its weight and heft, brought a flood of olfactory illusion. Ax could smell blood, the warm metallic butcher-shop reek of massacre night.

'I suppose we better head for that office block.'

When they reached the block they found it livelier than they had left it, full of the bustling disorder familiar to Ax from the Tour. No sign of Gervase. Someone took them down to a big room in the basement where a burly young-middle-aged black man was drinking tea over a table full of maps, computer terminals and landline phones. He was wearing the combat uniform of a British Army Infantry major, with a discreet pink triangle replacing the bar of colours on his tunic. With him was an elderly gent in more casual dress.

Ax stared. 'Richard!'

'Ax! There you are. We were getting worried. Good to see you again—'

'Sage,' said Ax, grinning with relief, 'otherwise known as Aoxomoxoa, this is Richard Kent, friend of mine from the Deconstruction Tour. I'm glad to see you too, Richard.'

'Pleased to meet you,' said Richard Kent, holding out a hand, fascinated to discover that Aoxomoxoa really did wear that mask in private life, as it were.

The rockstar kept his hands to himself. 'I didn't know the regular army was involved.'

'Actually I resigned my commission last year, because I felt I could and should be part of Ax's new wave.' Richard shrugged. 'Now it seems I'm in the army again.'

'Where's Gervase?' asked Ax.

'Ah, unfortunate. Beauvel-Horton was killed, a few hours ago, a drive-by.'

'Shame,' said Sage. 'We hardly had a chance to get to know him.'

'I don't think you missed much. This is my lover, by the way, Cornelius Samson.' The elderly gent looked like he deeply disapproved of the skull mask, but he nodded. 'Another regular soldier, before he retired. But we have seen the light. Or jumped on the bandwagon, if you prefer.'

Ax had been wondering how to deal with the question of those British Army SA80s. Was he supposed to pretend he didn't know what was going on? It would have been hard to stick that if things were made so fucking obvious, and he'd had to deal with Gervase. But with Richard and Cornelius he was on familiar ground. On the Tour, there had always been a great deal that had to be left unsaid. Those who understood one another had formed a network and worked together, over and around the criminally insane.

There was a burst of renewed gunfire, somewhere up above. 'It'll be over soon,' said Richard. 'This is the pattern. Terrorist tactics by day, in-your-face shooting up the streets by night. We know the shootists come from towns just north of here, or Doncaster itself, but we can't stop them getting in, not without building some kind of Berlin Wall. A house-to-house search operation might do the trick, but we haven't the authority for that, nor do we want it. We have a problem, Ax. We're in this too deep, it's like nothing we've done before, and we're finding no solutions. Thank God the President sent you along. We've been begging him to do that, as you probably know.'

'Yeah,' said Ax. He sat down at the table. 'Okay, I have an objective, not a solution. I want to get the violence away from the population. What about those famous moors, wilderness space with a challenging micro-climate, good venue for war games—'

Richard Kent sat down too. 'Get them out of town? How are we going to do that? This is outright war, near as damn it, and this is how modern warfare works. Terrorism, street bombs, soft targets. Centres of population are what it's about.'

'Then we'll invent post-modern warfare. Time someone did; the present version stinks. We've got a situation where certain cities and towns are no-go areas, in effect an Islamic territory within Yorkshire. That's bad, but we can use it. We blockade those cities and towns. Everything that has to go in and out: water, sewage, power, we can get at those. We've mine workings that have been linked to the gas supply, to channel off the methane: we can use that. We can cut off their water, make their toilets back up, spread farm slurry on their market gardens. We fuck them up so they have to come out and get us, and do it selectively enough that we don't cause a humanitarian crisis, much—'

'No more blowing up trains, though.'

'Definitely not. I never meant to blow up any trains, it just happened. We might waylay some consumer-goods freight trucks though, that's always fun.'

Sage quietly took a chair. He watched, and listened, as the major and the elderly gent pored over their maps, on paper and on monitor screens; Ax relentlessly telling them the details (but they didn't seem to mind) and showing them what could be done. Just astonishing: massacre night again, but this time Ax among friends. To see him like this, this focused power, put a different perspective on things. Hippie orderlies came and handed out more tea. The police liaison officer, a sober, taciturn guy called Kieran Matthews, turned up, along with other barmy army *de facto* officers. They all listened, and made difficulties.

'It's a shame your green maniacs got away from you and trashed the Air Force bases up here, Ax,' complained one barmy commander. 'God knows no one wants this to escalate any further. But if the conventional forces have to move in, they'll want local air power.'

Richard and Cornelius looked at each other and laughed.

'Yeah, I was sorry about that,' said Ax evenly. 'Those planes are so pretty.'

He looked up, and around the table, including Sage in his glance. 'A lot of things got away from me on the Tour,' he said. 'But I trashed the Yorkshire fighter bases on purpose. I knew about this situation, obviously. I didn't want the Islamics to be able to use them. And, let's understand each other, I didn't want to make things easy for the Air Force either. I wanted it to be hard for any full blown violent-opposition-group conflict to get going. To me that was as important as the green agenda.'

The barmies nodded gravely, apparently unaware that they themselves were the other paramilitary force that Ax had been determined to forestall.

'You did a remarkable job,' said Richard, 'As we now discover.'

'Yeah, but Ax, we are still a nation state. Green is good, but we gotta be able to defend ourselves, you havta see that—'

'I see it. But first we have to *stay* a nation state, which begins to look doubtful.'

Silence around the conference table as everyone, for a moment, looked beyond this stirring game, and met the shock of reality: the grim possibilities dead ahead—

'Fabius Maximus,' said the elderly gent. 'Quintus Fabius Maximus Cunctator, dealing with Hannibal's invading army, in 216BC or there-abouts. Avoided the kind of battle they were trying to force on him, wore them down by cutting off their supplies. Much the same as what Ax has in mind, *mutatis mutandis*. Who, by delaying, saved the city and the people of Rome.'

'If you say so. Yeah, delay.' Ax looked deflated, the never-in-doubt focused power gone out of him. 'That's all I've got, so far. Move the fighting out, leave the police to police the streets, make life normal as possible again. Let's see how it works out.'

The police liaison officer got up and said he had to go. He shook Ax's hand.

'I'm glad to have met you, Sir. We'll be in close contact, but if there's anything I can do—'

'There's one thing,' said Richard, when Matthews had gone, 'that I have to point out. If we do this, Ax, if we become guerrillas, we'll be forcing *them* to become an army.'

'That's happened,' said Ax. 'I just saw it. That's the situation. Better engage with it.'

So they talked on, identifying targets, and ingenious ways to use the landscape. The crunch came in the morning, when, after a few hours' sleep, they had to start implementing Ax's plan. The barmy army was already organised into guerrilla-sized groups, each group a judicious mix of clueless amateurs, ex-army or TA types and green-violence veterans. When they moved out into the countryside, the rockstars went with them. Same as the Few and the gigs, the community service, Olwen's projects. They had to *be there*. There was no way they could stay back in Doncaster sticking pins in a map, and retain artistic credibility. So those SA80s were not video props. They were real. They must be used.

In October Sage turned up missing after a skirmish over a water pipeline. They went back for him, to a deserted moorland village. They'd have done it for anyone, but the idea of having to carry on without *Sage* upset everybody, not least the Ax. They had him located in the cellar of a house that had been blown up by a homemade mortar bomb. The only approach allowed by the steep and narrow street – ancient cobbles under frayed tarmac – was covered by a sniper ensconced in the church tower. Shots came out of the body of the church as they moved through the churchyard. Ax walked, in the strange emptiness surrounding the sparse pattern of fire, around the building; found a door and blew out the lock with a short burst that was lost in the other noise. None of the Islamists in the nave saw him as he crept up the stairs to the tower. There he found the young man, alone with his high-powered rifle in a dusty space broken up by big diagonal rafters. Sixteen or seventeen years old, the same age as Fiorinda: blooming with new muscle and height. He'd dropped the rifle. Maybe he'd run out of ammunition; it didn't look like a weapon that would take kindly to the kitchen sink variety that was coming on the market now. He had no way out, unless he jumped through one of the tower's windows. No one had thought about his exit, fucking poor planning on their part, he's a marksman, he's valuable. He was clutching a grenade, about to pull the pin, yeah.

'Allah Akbar!' he yelled, this angry young man with fine dark eyes alight; serene.

God is great.

I don't want to live at this price, thought Ax. *I don't want to.* But the assault rifle – this was a first, never before used it where he could and must know just what happened on the other end – came up of its own accord: a terrific racket, Ax splattered in blood and tissue and fragments of bone. Snatched up the grenade, tossed it out into the grey graveyard, stayed alive.

Meanwhile Sage had rescued himself, and the kid Chris who had been trapped with him. Whatever he'd had to do to achieve that, the skull stayed blank as a Hallowe'en toy for a couple of hours after he rejoined them: a disconcerting thing to see. But he was fine later.

In November they once camped in a ruined monastery. The Islamists had had no part in this destruction; most of the buildings had been bumps in the grass for hundreds of years. No picnickers now, no virtual reality show in the restored tithe barn: a thin sweeping of snow, a black night, frost and stars. They were looking for the herb garden, which Ax knew should be around here somewhere, and talking about food – oblivious to the small heap of human corpses that lay in the shell of the church. The Islamists had a habit of dumping bodies in churches, in the (largely mistaken) belief that this would shock or distress the enemy. The barmies had shovelled some earth over the remains when they moved in, but the ground was hard and they hadn't got very far.

Something moved in the darkness, in the enclosed space in front of them.

'What's that?' whispered Ax.

It looked like a human figure, greyish and fuzzy in outline. It appeared to be climbing *out* of the stone box of a table tomb. They were both armed. It was easy to get attached to having a weapon, that comforting weight, slung over your shoulder. But they didn't have the reflexes, not at this moment anyhow. They stood and watched. It seemed to be alone; nothing else stirred. It started coming towards them. A waft of foul air preceded it, and as it came close enough they saw that, though moving and limber, it seemed to have been a long time dead. The teeth had no lips to cover them. Only the eyes, sunken and wet, had survived. It stood looking at them, then it moved away, heading towards the east end, where the bodies were lying. Ax started forward – to accost the phantom? To prove it was someone in a mask, to ask it what interest it had in the poorly buried flesh?

'No,' said Sage, stopping him.

They backed off. Found the herb garden, but didn't fancy harvesting anything from the dry, wintering bushes. They decided not to tell the lads, just posted a double watch and sat up all night themselves. Nothing else happened.

*

And between these and other adventures, back to the nearest non-Islamist town: clean up, shave, delouse (the crusty-tendency in their group was incorrigibly verminous, everyone had to live with the fallout). Become rockstars again, get drunk, find some friendly girls to fuck among the barmy army's camp following. Of course, don't touch the locals – a veto that was becoming sinisterly easy to observe. Local girls – Hindu, Christian, Muslim or nothing – didn't come out to play. Women were disappearing from the streets, from daily life. Catch up on the Islamist incursions into Lancashire and Teesside, join the latest government and police failure to negotiate. Do the goodwill ambassador, think of plausible reasons why Muslims still living in *this* town shouldn't move out. Try to stem the polarisation: get nowhere. The only battle they were winning was a private objective Ax had spoken of to no one but Sage – a vindictive determination to get the number of casualties higher for combatants than for non-combatants. Of whichever persuasion. They'd done that. The anti-civilian terrorist actions were way down. For what that was worth.

dreams of the young sniper's head coming apart. Soldiers are also human.

In December they were holed up in a conifer plantation, towards Wharfedale. The weather was vile. They'd used larchpoles from a stack of thinnings they'd found as flooring for the benders, but the mud got in everywhere. There was nothing to eat in this forest, even the hippies admitted that, and supplies were low. They had sent their two most respectable-looking individuals – disguised in more or less clean clothes – off to find a corner shop that would take cash money (much of the Islamic territory that surrounded them was running on complex barter systems), and now they whiled away an afternoon, sitting out in the cold under a stretched tarp, as if around the campfire they didn't have because of the smoke. As usual, the barmies were talking politics. Brock – their battle-reenactment weapons nut, broad as a bear, grey hair in a bushy ponytail – was trying to persuade the hero of the Deconstruction that selfish human interests should be as naught, compared to the fate of one red squirrel. Or tropical cloud forest tree frog.

'You got to do it by force, Ax. Torch the car depots, raze the fast food joints. Like we did, and you didn't try too hard to stop us, did you. Turn back the tide by force, there's no other way to save the planet for the species that *deserve* to live.'

'I've thought about it,' said Ax. 'I care more for human beings, myself.

But if you don't, I think you still have to put them first if you want a lasting solution to the problem. I think it works out. If you create a culture that is good for people, genuinely good for their peace of mind, health and happiness, then you get a situation which is okay for the planet. Not ideal in your terms, Brock, but okay. Maybe there won't be much wilderness, maybe we end up living in a garden, that we have to manage fairly thoroughly—'

'Ah, fuck that, Ax. If it's wild it's nature, if it ent wild it's *gone, dead*—' Brock lifted the sword that he was working on (he loved sharpening his swords) and glowered down the blade. 'There's no compromise on this issue—'

'But it's true,' said another of the hippies. 'England is a fucking back garden already. Wherever you park yer bender, you get some fucker claiming ye're in his face—'

Sage did not contribute to these discussions. He just listened, as he was listening now, lying on his back staring up at the cracked, muddy grey-green plastic of the tarp, taking in the Ax manifesto at a remove and thinking: *how fucking strange*. What if he can actually make it stick . . . ? It was a pity the two most pass-for-normal barmies had to be the two youngest – fifteen-year-old Chris, and a seventeen-year-old third generation hippie kid called Zip, who was rebelling against his background stylewise. It was a six-mile hike to the nearest settlement, but they'd been gone too long. Shoulda vetoed the foraging. But rank was not like that in the barmy army. You got groups of weirdly straightened-out hippies, polishing their boots, putting hospital corners on the bender tarps and howling Sah! at each other, but the infection was mainly all the other way. You don't tell 'em what to do unless they clearly want to be told. Under fire. They find it reassuring to be yelled at under fire.

And here at last were the two boys, humping their rucksacks, exhilarated by success. They'd found a friendly corner shop. They'd bought potatoes, onions, carrots, tinned fruit, fresh milk and pitta bread: and news. The Hindu shop owners had warned them to go home and stay indoors, because the army was in town. The Islamist army, that is: on their way to do some fighting. Yorkshire Hindus, though of two minds on the subject of proper marriage for their daughters, could be relied on to be neutral or wary towards the Islamics.

'That means us,' said one of the ex-regular soldiers, happily. 'We're on. Fancy doing some drugs, Ax, mate? May as well celebrate now, might not be here tomorrow.'

'Brock,' said Sage, sitting up. 'How about if we go and practise the sword fighting again?'

When he returned to the bender it was dusk. A pan of dahl and vegetables stood on the chemical stove. 'Why does it fuck you up?' said Ax pre-emptively. 'Because you got caught, that's why. If you had never been addicted, you wouldn't panic about the occasional.'

'It fucks me up, because I don't think you are doing that for fun. I think you're doing it because you need it, and in the position we are in, with the authority you have, I don't like to think that that's your frame of mind. Also, my experience is that if you need heroin, using it does not make you need it less.'

'I'm writing to Fiorinda. Want to add something?'

'Ah, I'm wasting my time. Go to hell then: what the fuck do I care? Okay, pass it over.'

'It's not a very good letter, but it'll have to do. You missed the conference.'

This landscape had never been conducive to the cellphone revolution, but the barmy Signals core handled it fine. They managed a nightly postcard-screen 'video conference' by landline and mobile transmitters; including the police and sometimes (if he spared the time), the President. It was secure as hippie nethead talent could make it, which was pretty good. They'd yet to spot the enemy profiting from what went down.

'What happened?'

'The kids were right. We're going to meet the Islamists tomorrow morning.'

They took the pan of stew out along a Forestry track, far enough to escape from the camp's dim stench into the scents of moss and water, stone and fresh-cut timber. A blackbird was singing in the twilight. The night was going to be cold, but there would be no frost: the sky was thick with cloud.

'Why do they never harass you about your green credentials? It's always me.'

'That's because I'm the one who napalmed half Suffolk. My cred is impeccable.'

'Fucking perverse. I hated that stunt.'

'I know, I know. It was fun, though. And it got me well in with your barmy army, which—'

'Probably was no bad thing, in the light of this business. Ah, okay.' Ax leaned back against a larch bole, pulling up the collar of the battered leather coat. 'At least if we get killed tomorrow it means no more body lice.'

'No more a shitload of unpleasant things . . . yeah. Hardly any loss at all, really.'

The skull and Ax grinned at each other.

I have never felt more alive, thought Ax. Never more alive, and never nearer to the unforgivable, the unthinkable. Despair, giving up.

'Where I was born,' said Sage, 'in Padstow, no one I knew thought about any future beyond the next chance of getting whammed. My drop-out parents didn't give that attitude much of an argument. I started gigging with the mixing boards to finance the drugs, basically. Went well to the bad, way too far with the smack. Got hauled out of that and agreed to go to university to prove I was clean. I was so *fucking* bored it was intolerable, packed it in after six weeks and went back to gigging. I'm sure I made the right decision, financially and every other way. But it does occur to me, tonight . . . if anyone had trained me to have some *ordinary, normal* ambition, long ago, I might be safe in some far away silicon valley now, pondering my golf handicap.'

'I'm sorry I got you into this.'

'If it hadn't been for you I'd have been dead last December. Technically, it was Fiorinda who got me into this. She'd put her name down for the fatal seminar, so we did too.'

'I wonder why she did it.'

'No idea. We'll have to ask her sometime.'

'I spent a miserable adolescence,' said Ax, 'because I knew I didn't want to do anything but play guitar, but I thought everything worth doing in that line had been done . . . I would lie awake agonising for hours about the problem.'

Sage laughed. 'I can imagine that.'

'Yeah, well, I know your opinion. I worked out a solution that satisfied me: I decided being original or fashionable or mass market trend didn't matter, so I should stop worrying. But I still needed an audience. I started thinking about where would this audience come from, and looking at the future prospects for rock and roll as an art and craft, rather than a machine for making unreal money for World Entertainment. Didn't look good. I knew I'd have to do something about it. Went on from there, really.'

'And this is why we're here? So that you could be a fucking latter-day B.B. King?'

'You could look at it like that.'

The blackbird stopped singing. High overhead there was a sound like tearing silk. They both looked up, with intense anxiety: nothing crossed the darkened aisle of sky.

'That's definitely a fighter plane.'

'Shit.'

'Air power is the point of no return,' said Ax. 'I'll pretend it isn't, when I find out where the planes are coming from. But it's the end. No pulling out of this. Fucked.'

At night the slightest wind roared through the timber, sounding like a hurricane. Ax lay awake, listening to the weather, which he knew was due to get worse again before morning. He could hear Sage's quiet breathing, didn't think he was going to sleep at all himself. No problem, they still had NDogs in the first aid. He could dose himself with energy when he needed it.

Tomorrow they would go out on the moor, and if barmy army intelligence was correct (which it often was, surprisingly enough), they would meet a matching unofficial army of about fifteen hundred Islamists who had been lured out to hunt down the guerrillas. There would be, when this group and other remaining outliers joined the main strength, about two thousand of the barmy army. Soldiers, survivalists, hippies and clueless volunteers, equipped with assault rifles, shotguns, pistols, cross-bows, machetes, samurai swords, maces, police riot shields, helmets from World War II, re-enactment armour, any fucking thing . . . How this strange life closed the world down. It had been a big relief, be quite honest, after those months of unremitting tension after massacre night, to fall into the pattern. Never looking beyond the next tactical move, the next target, the next meal. No time to think . . . except in black hours like this, when thinking was cruelly unprofitable, and he couldn't stop himself. The sniper, other faces, all of them human, no longer human now: dead meat. Lucky Sage, he didn't feel the same gut-sick horror. They hadn't talked about it, but Ax knew. Head Ideology, it seemed, could accept *kill or be killed* without much trauma.

Accept.

But the Islamists were not going to break. They were not interested in making peace, and they had no incentive to make terms. Meanwhile the Pig, instead of resenting Ax's popularity up here, had simply lost interest. Ax could handle the gut-reaction (not shared, far as he could make out, by other non-white barmies: to their credit? Yes, to their credit) that he was on the wrong side. He was getting less and less able to deal with the organised murder, *that was achieving nothing.* He should get back to London, before his influence with the President evaporated. The barmy army should quit, stop pouring petrol on the fire.

Pretend what happens next is not your business: except that it soon will be, because the military solution is no solution, and the trouble won't stay in Yorkshire. The Islamics are inextricably part of this country. Give them up for lost, give up the whole thing—

Sage rolled over. 'You still awake?'

'Yeah. What time is it?'

Ax's watch was a piece of retro handicraft: you couldn't read it in the dark.

'Middle of the night time. What does it matter?' But he stretched out his arm, resignedly, so Ax could touch his wrist. It was just after three thirty, by the clock function figures that glowed through the skin, about an inch above where the skeletal-hand masks would stop.

'That's a clever thing.'

'Nmmm. I think I don't like it. I'm gonna get Olwen to take her spell off again. It's giving me future shock.'

'That's a daft remark, coming from you. I suppose the masks aren't *useful* for anything.'

'Except intimidating people.'

'And hiding behind. But they don't interfere with your closet-hippie belief that we should all go back to getting up at four a.m. to milk the moo cows, the hardy few of us that survive—'

'You're not going to inveigle me into one of your insomnia conversations. Go to sleep. Or not, I don't care.'

When they got up, before dawn, it was raining hard. One of the trucks was so badly grounded they couldn't shift it; the other refused to start. They covered everything and set out on foot. After an hour they came out of the plantation, above a shallow upland valley: clad in straw-grey winter grasses, crisscrossed by fresh tyre tracks, alive with barmy army guerrillas, sitting round their camouflaged trucks, wandering to and fro, readying their unorthodox weaponry; in the thick, small rain strangely hard to spot until they moved. It was called Yap Moss, this place: about halfway, on a north-east, south-west diagonal, between Ilkley Moor and the Brontës' Haworth. The great Muslim-controlled conurbation of Leeds, Bradford, Halifax lay to the south. Another December the ground would have been sodden and impassable, but this (in spite of what the guerrillas felt about the weather) had been a very dry year. The barmy commanders consulted with their young Alexander. The groups came together, split again into larger companies and moved into their positions: and shortly the Islamists came over the hill, in about half their reported strength.

Ax and Sage's company was in the centre, at the lowest point in the valley. It was intended that the enemy should believe they'd found all their quarry when they saw this mass of barmies: that they would commit themselves to the low ground and get caught. Down they came. Fewer in number, better armed, looking much more like a model army, they dropped and fired and jumped up and came on, like that night-patrol in Doncaster magnified.

'Transmission mast,' said Ax to Sage.

'See you there—'

Don't go to meet them, let them come on. Those organised volleys are not as dangerous as they look, here are no serried ranks to be mown down. Fire when it is stupid-time, when there's really no chance that you won't hit *someone*. Soon, in the racket and the blur of smoke and rain, the fighting will be hand to hand, then the Islamists will lose their advantage. Now it's happening, a mêlée like a dancefloor. There's Sage, using the Roman legionary's stabbing sword Brock gave him, easier for him to grip: the skull glimpsed, grinning, perhaps their eyes meet, but it's difficult to say. What hard work it is, how cold the rain, how sickening the thrust into flesh and the grappling, the warm blood, warm as the sweat that bathes your body. The slamdancing crowd heaves, something has happened. It should be step two: the Islamists have committed themselves and our reserved forces, that have been taking advantage of every dip and hump on Yap Moss, have risen out of the landscape. A barmy Signals voice in Ax's ear confirms, yes that's where we're at. Now we push them up the hill again, yes it can be done.

The strangest thing is that if you look up, if you ever dare, you can see all round you quiet, empty stretches of the straw-grey Moss. It would be possible to elbow your way free (well, cut your way) and get out. I'm tired, I don't want to dance no more, let's go get a drink. There's a hippie in a gasmask. What, *seriously*? The Deconstruction Tour did its best to rip the heart out of this country's capacity for organised violence, but there are still some chemical plants around . . . No, it's not a gasmask, it's some weird gaming accessory. Islamists must think we're mad, avatar masks and fancy dress—

Transmission mast. There it is. So we're up the hill. This may mean we've won, at least it means we have the advantage, what happened to the rest of the Islamists? For a moment, with that spidery tetrapod looming out of the rain – which had become a fine, stinging hail – Ax had the wonderful illusion that the battle was over and it hadn't been too bad. But here they come, another rush. The voice in his ear told him what was happening: about five or eight hundred Islamists had been waiting on the ridge, and it's all to do again. Pull the company, such as has remained in reach, together. Slamdance over to the open base of the mast, not much shelter, but a focus, and now we can use the rifles again, firing into the wall of this renewed advance. Sometimes you can think in this. As if walking in the night . . . Do the mechanical things, concentrate your mind on something else entirely. He realised that Sage was beside him. So they had made it. They dropped together behind a heap of stones, an old cairn that stood by the mast. Breather.

Ax stared ahead of him, listening for the voice from Signals, hearing only static—

'What're you thinking . . . ? Christ, don't start *posing*, get *down*, you stupid fucker—'

'Space programme.'

Sage tipped back his head and cackled, skull's jaws parting on open-throated darkness.

'Yeah, very funny, but think of what is happening to us: no GPS on this battlefield. Cellnets wrecked in the name of landscape preservation, global mobiles fucked, satellite owners changing the locks because we can't pay the rent. I don't see us going back to a terrestrial based system. We may have to put up our own hardware.'

'Oh really? Launched from where and with what?'

'That's what I'm thinking about.'

'You, beyond belief. Better get back on. Are we winning?'

'Yeah.'

The fighting was becoming scattered, spreading out. Their position between the great metal limbs would soon be out of the loop; the Islamists were giving ground fast. It's over: nothing left to do but fire from comparative safety into what begins to be a full retreat.

'God, I *hate* this,' muttered Ax, coming down. 'I fucking *hate* the whole thing—'

'Could be worse. We haven't had to torture anyone yet.'

'Oh, right. We're having a *clean* war. But we know what's going on: and some of the most evil stuff is being done by our side.' Suddenly he turned on Sage. 'What d'you mean *had to*? Under what fucking circumstances would you feel you *had to*—?'

'Figure of speech, Ax. Calm down.'

'Fuck. Let's get after them. No point in staying here 'til we run out of ammo.'

Ax went charging out across the ridge; the others followed. Some of the Islamists had formed a block and were departing in order, others spilling out in all directions. The weather was worsening again, the hail driven by a bitter wind: and suddenly, right overhead, that sound like tearing silk. Three silhouettes zoomed out of the cloud: three unmarked fighter planes, shearing down, raking the field with machine-gun fire. Everywhere bodies dropped, either hit or diving for cover. The block of retreating Islamists kept going, some of them falling: it was not at all clear whose side the planes were on. Ax stood staring up, trying to identify them. Where the fuck are they coming from . . . ? The voice in his ear was reporting victory but *not anymore*. This is not a victory.

Someone grabbed him. It was Brock, the big mouthy ultra-green. 'Ax! Fucking hell, come on. Yer not going to bring down any fighter planes with that popgun, let's *get off the hill*—'

They ran: Sage and Brock in the forefront with Ax, Chris and Zip; and some of the rest of their group – including Jackie Dando, Romany ex-squaddie, the man with the smack, someone Sage would not have regretted much if he'd been left on the Moss. Soon Ax came back from his blank-out, stopped short, changed direction.

'This way. Ground gets more broken, better cover—'

Of course he was right, he was always right. Through swerving gusts of hail they could see the upland folding into valleys, a furze of bare tree branches almost underfoot: and then they were dropping into a narrow gorge. There Sage, jumping down from the rocks above, almost landed on top of a lone Islamist.

He'd been hiding among some boulders, using a phone. Sage got the phone. Brock and Jackie got the unknown, hauled him to his feet, relieved him of a rifle, held him by the upper arms. He was a slight young man, in battledress that looked weirdly clean and tidy, like his mum had pressed it for him, a neat bandana around his brow. 'Who were you calling?' said Jackie, amiably. 'You won't get a taxi to come and pick you up out here, Ahmed.'

The prisoner stood, mouth tight, eyes bright, staring at Sage, who was checking the phone and finding out something disturbing. He handed it to Ax, – the skull looking *oh, shit* – and came up very close to the prisoner, invasively close and malevolent.

'You're French,' he said. 'What are you doing here, mademoiselle?'

A second's stunned panic. Then she burst into life, threw off the startled barmies, pulled a small automatic from inside her flak jacket: almost blew a hole through the mask before they disarmed her. The tableau resumed, Sage well in her face, that skull looking uncannily *natural*, peering out from a sage-green British Army Issue balaclava—

'Yes, French, and a woman,' she spat at him, glaring defiance. 'So what, English?'

'Well, I'd rather be a woman than a frog-eater,' said Sage, grinning, wiping saliva from the skull's chin with the back of a skeleton hand. 'Just *about*, rather.'

'Suit yourself, exhibitionist asshole.'

'I bet you know something about those planes,' said Brock.

The rest of the group had caught up. They scrambled into the gorge and stood there staring at the prisoner. About twenty men – some gaps in the ranks, some walking wounded, some strays from other parties. All of them dirty, unshaven, dishevelled, many of them pierced and scarified like savages.

Ax repeated Sage's question, more gently. 'What are you doing here?'

'I am fighting for the cause of religious freedom,' she answered, visibly struggling now to assemble her English. Her eyes flickered, taking in the size of them, their numbers, the threat of their sex. She looked sick. 'That's all you will get out of me.'

'Right,' said Ax. He walked away, sat down on a rock and stared at the ground. At last he took out his own phone. 'You may as well relax, everyone. I've got to talk to some people. Sage, could you come over.'

Sage went over and sat next to Ax. The hail flew into their eyes and faces, bounced glittering from the ground, rattled on stone. Beside their rock, a very dead sheep lay festering on the brink of the noisy little stream. What was that in the water? Iron stain? Ah, no: too dark, and crimson, rather than rust. It was blood, from some dead or dying human body fallen in, back towards Yap Moss . . . There'd been reports of foreign nationals spotted fighting with the Islamists. This was the first solid confirmation.

'I bet she does know something about the planes,' said Sage.

'Yeah. Fuck. Looks like we've got international intervention. Non-government, I suppose, like us. Not that the French have much government at the moment. But it makes no difference. I was afraid that was the explanation. This is very bad.'

'What are we going to do with her?'

'I'll get a police helicopter, we'll take her to Easton Friars. It's not important . . . Sage, I'm finished. I'm not going to pretend this can be fixed. I'm not going to carry on.'

'Okay.' Sage looked up into the darting white hail and the grey sky. 'Sounds reasonable to me. If the Islamists have outside support, we are fucked to shit. Might as well admit it now, instead of pissing around for about ten years first. But if you quit, the barmies will quit. Does that mean we give up and let the real military move in?'

Silence.

'Ax?'

'I've got an idea. No, it's more than an idea. I *know* what to do. I think I've known since we came up from London. I just couldn't face it.'

'You gonna to tell me what the idea is?'

'Not right this moment. Sorry.'

'Oh, no problem.' No problem, except Ax looking as if he was about to jump off a very high building. See if he could fly. 'Just remember, before you make any strange moves: the President is holding my band hostage, as well as your girlfriend, your brothers, your drummer, and the rest of the Few.'

'Don't worry. I can handle the Pig, and this will work.'

They walked a few miles, to a headland where the helicopter (a very special concession: the police treasured those machines) could pick them up. The lads went on, out to the road: to rejoin their own groups, get medical treatment, or find their way back to the camp in the forest. Ax and Sage and the prisoner were taken to Easton Friars, outside Harrogate, present quarters of the barmy High Command. When they arrived Richard Kent was waiting in the great desolate front hall.

'Congratulations. Come upstairs, to the habitable regions, we've made arrangements for mademoiselle up there. You two'll want to clean up.'

'Suppose we will. Congratulations?'

'I hear you won a famous victory.'

'Old news.'

The house had been standing derelict before the barmies arrived. It was ruined still: damp seeping through the bare walls, shards of plaster fallen from the ceilings, dust-sheeted furniture that no one had bothered to remove rotting in situ. While Ax spent the next day with the commanders Sage explored, opening doors: surprising fieldmice, spiders, ghosts. He found the prisoner alone with her chaperone, in a vast empty room on the first floor. She seemed pleased to see him. The mask didn't scare her anymore now she realised it was merely a rockstar's affectation. Shame.

'So your friend is Ax Preston.'

She'd been treated nicely and politely questioned, and in the end had made no difficulty about telling them who she was with. Her outfit called itself the Force Expéditionnaire Internationale. They were French and German and Netherlanders, mostly. She didn't know all the nationalities. Maybe some Russians. They were all Muslim, and it was their right and duty to join the *jihad*. She'd come over by sea. The planes were 'borrowed' from the French Air Force. She didn't know about the pilots, or what weaponry they had, or where they were flying from.

'He's a superb guitarist, I know this. But how is he your Prime Minister? It's curious.'

Sage chose one of the rotting chairs and sat in it, cautiously. Outside tall windows, Easton Friars deerpark stretched gloomily to the horizon. Bit of a doer-upper; plenty of room to sling a frisbee, though. The chaperone smiled, and pretended to go on reading her book.

'Countercultural Prime Minister. It's a hybrid system. No idea. Because he wants to be.'

'*Quoi?* What kind of reason is that?'

He shrugged, took out a packet of cigarettes and offered them. She shook her head.

My friend, he thought, had the bizarre foresight – before the crash – to get a data wafer planted in his head, that holds a phenomenal amount of information about this country. He knows where the sewers are laid, how the contour lines run, where the bodies are buried. I'm not going to tell *you* that. The fewer people know about it or realise it the better. Richard knows, I'm sure: but he's okay. But it's not the reason. Fucked if I know what makes him do what he does. He's just the Ax.

In the operations room, the same group of people as Ax had met that night in Doncaster talked over the girl's revelations and Ax's idea; and how to negotiate the necessary arrangements. Richard Kent was concerned and puzzled that Sage had been left out of the loop, actually barred from this meeting by Ax himself.

'It's for the best,' said Ax. 'Trust me.'

'But won't he—?'

'Oh, I will get some kind of shit, but it will be okay. Head Ideology will see me through.'

'I suppose you know what you're talking about.'

The same helicopter carried them to Bradford, some days later: Ax and Sage and the girl. They were to deliver her personally, unharmed, to the leader of Muslim Yorkshire – and by his own reckoning, the paramount leader of all English Islam – Sayyid Muhammad Zayid al-Barelewi. The Muslim leader and Ax had never met. He didn't negotiate, he didn't do tv: he had steadfastly refused to have anything to do with the Infidel. Yet he'd agreed to this proposal, understanding that it would be an opportunity for a private meeting. The barmy army chiefs had been incredulous. Ax had known it would be okay.

The machine landed them at a motorway junction north of town. From here they were taken, in a cavalcade of huge black off-roaders, into the city centre. Then they walked, surrounded by a hollow square of smartly turned-out Yorkshire Muslim soldiers, in battledress and white turbans. The streets were calm. There were women around, with and without the veil; even children; everyone behaving naturally. In this community armed men did not have the profile of a revolutionary aberration, or a nightmare intrusion. They were in keeping, they belonged to the order of things. Ax's heart sank. This calm was terrible, a reason for Fiorinda's mourning, the end of a world, an unbearable loss: but he had to bear it. Accept.

'Ever been here before?'

'Nah. Leeds, Durham, Middlesborough, Newcastle, Halifax . . . Beverley. Weird place, Beverley. Never played Bradford, that I recall. You?'

'Don't remember. Take off the mask.'

The skull looked dubious. 'Ax, I don't think so.'

'Take it off. Please. No rockstar fancy-dress here.'

They reached a street where the substantial Victorian houses on one side had been razed, replaced by a mosque and another building inside a walled courtyard: the Sayyid's home. At an Arabian Nights gateway, candy-pink with gilt cartouches of Arabic lettering, Ax and Sage surrendered their weapons. The escort dropped back. There was a crowd of hawk-faced young guardsmen inside the gateway. They started muttering to each other. When Ax tried to move on there was suddenly a wall of bodies in his way, rifles levelled.

'What's going on?'

'No Anglo-Saxons!' they shouted.

'Let me pass. It was agreed, you have to let me pass.' He was so keyed-up he hardly realised he was facing a row of trigger-happy assassins. Some of the escort that had brought them from town hurried forward, in a panic. They hustled Ax and Sage and the girl back, and got between. There was a heated exchange, unintelligible to the strangers: something had gone terribly wrong.

'It's not you, Ax,' called someone, suddenly, in pure Estuary English. '*You're* okay. It's him. No one said you were going to bring fucking Hereward the Wake along with you.'

'Told you,' murmured Sage. 'I'm not Anglo-Saxon,' he yelled, 'I'm Cornish.'

The mask reappeared. That or the fellow-subject-races appeal swung it. They were in. Within the gates there was a courtyard of combed, rose-pink gravel. A guy in white with a green sash and a turban came out to greet them: with him a platoon of sprucely uniformed women soldiers, green scarves low over their brows. The women took possession of the French girl. They marched her away: looking back over her shoulder, looking frightened. Poor kid, too bad. Hope they just send you home.

He would do what he had come to do, that was certain. But was there any way to do this without making it a betrayal of Fiorinda? From the start and forever, make it something she would understand? Walking along these corridors, everything beautifully clean and serene compared to life with the barmy army: yes, it's peaceful on the other side. At the entrance to the Sayyid's diwan he almost couldn't take another step. Sage caught his arm.

'You okay, Ax?'

'I'm fine.' He pressed his hands to his temples, briefly. 'Future shock.'

The diwan was a large, long room: plenty of space, plenty of people – that is, men – either in white or in suits. So this was the private meeting. Well, naturally. The Sayyid was in the position of strength. He could treat this as a coup, the English Countercultural Prime Minister, forced to come unarmed into his den. They were led through the company to the far end of the room, where there was a raised dais. They were introduced by Sayyid Muhammad's son-in-law, who was their guide, to Sayyid Muhammad's brothers, brothers-in-law, and finally to Sayyid Muhammad Zayid himself.

The leader of English Islam was a suit: a strongly built, thick-shouldered businessman, very conventionally dressed, with a domed forehead and a badger-striped beard. He looked like his photographs. He was briefly polite, and then asked Ax to wait: he had something very important to discuss with somebody else just now. Okay, a standard move. Ax didn't mind. While the Islamic leader pretended to do this very important stuff with his brothers, he took time to *look*, because he must know this man. What is he? He chooses to wear English formal clothes, not the robes. He doesn't wear a turban. What is in his eyes? Sayyid Muhammad noticed this attention and returned it, and eventually beckoned Ax to his side.

Sage stayed back, among the onlookers. Ax and Sayyid Muhammad Zayid sat together on a dark blue couch, trimmed with gold cord, strange hybrid of the caliph's palace and some nice, solid, Yorkshire living-room suite, and they talked.

Of course they had to go over the ground of the failed negotiations. The inferiority and corruption of Anglo-Saxon culture, the outrageous irregularity of the barmy army police action. Of course, the Islamist had to get pre-emptively stroppy about the disgusting way Infidels treat their poor degraded womenfolk. Ax took it all, without pretending to be very impressed. It was verbiage. He knew he could do business with Sayyid Muhammad, if only he had the right key. In a sense they had already reached an understanding, a distant but real engagement, dating from the time Ax had come to Yorkshire and initiated the blockades. Someone had chosen to put a brake on the anti-civilian terror tactics. Someone had accepted Ax's alternative to urban mayhem. It was this man. This man, who was surely no happier than Ax – no matter what he said to his own public – about the arrival of the internationals.

Time to lay the cards down. 'I suppose you will send that girl soldier home,' said Ax. 'But what are we going to do about the rest of them: the foreigners on our soil, muscling in on our quarrel? It's a problem, Sayyid Muhammad. I'm hoping you and I can find some answers.'

Sayyid Muhammad Zayid looked at his bold visitor in silence, for a few moments. 'It is very interesting to meet you, Mr Preston. No, more than interesting. It is an *honour* to meet the hero of the Deconstruction.'

And there you have it. The Tour. The more Ax himself found out, or realised, about things he'd done and instigated on the Deconstruction Tour, the more he was just *appalled*. Musta been on drugs. Or temporarily completely out of his mind, after massacre night. Yet everywhere he went he found that the Tour had made him friends. He had struck a nerve. Somehow all that reckless burning of the boats (no going back) had been what people needed: a moral turning point. And now this descendant of the Prophet, revered Qur'anic scholar, him too, seduced by green violence.

Fucking bizarre.

'It's an honour to meet you too. And a crying shame if we can't work together. I know that the Muslim community has a lot to offer in this new England. What about that saying of the Prophet, *Salla-llahu alayhi wa salam*, "All the earth is a mosque"? In the Hadith, in the Chapter of the Prophet's tradition, 3172 if I remember right. Muslims have always known that they should regard the living world as sacred.'

'Ah, and a scholar too.'

'Not me. But I've been trying to learn, from Muslim friends. There's the sixty-seventh surah, also. *Live on what He provides, but always remember that you will all one day be answerable to Allah*—'

Sayyid Muhammad smiled. And shook his head.

'Mr Preston, I appreciate your courtesy. I would like to help you. But there is nothing to be done. You and I both know it. There is nothing I can do, and nothing you can offer, except territorial recognition. Discussion is pointless.'

'I don't think discussion of the Holy Qur'an can ever be pointless,' said Ax.

Sayyid Muhammad Zayid frowned. He gave Ax a long, measuring look, which Ax returned. Then he straightened, and his manner changed. He became something else than the guy in the position of strength giving Ax a nice, kind brush-off, and they started to discuss the Holy Qur'an. Ax must have acquitted himself okay (though he felt like an eight-year-old playing chess with the person who invented chess), because after a while the Islamist said, 'We should continue this in private.' He stood, Ax stood. He beckoned to one of his brothers.

They went to a room on the first floor of the house. Sayyid Muhammad's brothers and son-in-law came in with them. It was furnished as a study, with a mihrab set in the eastern wall, and windows overlooking a court-yard where a fountain played. The Sayyid sat at his desk, gesturing to the chair on the other side. He was stern now, on his dignity. The brothers, brothers-in-law, son-in-law, settled in the background.

'Now we are private. Let's speak frankly. What do you want from me, Mr Preston?'

'Ax. I want you to end this so-called war. I believe you can do it. I believe you want to do it. I think it's substantially by your choice that Muslims in the rest of England have not, at least not yet, been drawn into the conflict. I think that means you understand the danger, and you don't want to see this country torn apart, anymore than I do.'

'Maybe you're right, maybe not. Maybe I have different priorities. But I asked what do *you* want. You personally, Mr Preston. I have the impression that you are telling me something that wasn't one of my expectations for this meeting.'

Ax nodded. 'Ax, is fine. Yeah. I want to become a Muslim.'

'Hmm.' Sayyid Muhammad Zayid considered this young man. Obviously of mixed race, no telling exactly what went into the mix: North African? South Asian? Saxon of course; some Chinese? Allah only knows. Taller than average, no more than average build. Almond-shaped brown eyes. Dark hair drawn back from regular, clean-shaven features—

'You think if you do this, I will be able to give the English government peace, because of the effect of your conversion on my people? Is that your reasoning?'

'I'm hoping for something on those lines.'

'You're very sure of yourself. You think you are so important?'

'I'm not sure what effect this will have on the negotiations. I'm sure I want to do it.'

'Why?'

'I need some kind of bedrock. I think Islam can give me that.'

'I see. And you don't anticipate any difficulties? With your President, with your "barmy army", with the dissolute way of life you've led up until now?'

'No problems with the President or the army. Plenty of difficulties with my way of life. I don't know whether they can be reconciled. Things would have to move on both sides.'

'You're a very arrogant young man!'

'I'm trying to tell you the truth.'

Sayyid Muhammad leaned forward, intently. A warlord, a forthright Yorkshire businessman, a spiritual leader. Maybe it was his turn to want to *know* who he was dealing with. Ax could see that the businessman and community leader was tempted by the prize of a celebrity conversion. The warlord needed a big inducement, or he wouldn't even try to call off the fight. Was Ax in person enough for those two? But there was another Sayyid, the one who had allowed himself to respond to a fellow human being . . . It would take more than one conversation in the diwan to get to know *that* man. Another time.

'If I thought this was some cynical ploy—'

'If this is cynical, it is cynical to know how many beans make five. I think it's what has to be done, and I know it can't be undone later without making things worse than ever. I also meant it, as far as I understand myself.'

'Well, go on then, lad. If you've made up your mind. We have witnesses.'

Shahadah. The declaration. It has to be done. Accept. Sort the details later.

'I testify that there is no god except *Allah* and that Muhammad is the messenger of *Allah.*'

They went back to the diwan, and from there to a hall where a banquet had been spread for the honoured guests. Still no women. The men from the diwan, and more, came pouring in, excited by the obvious success of the meeting: everyone wondering what was going on. Didn't have to wonder long. Sayyid Muhammad Zayid quickly made things official, with an announcement in English and in Arabic to the whole company. You couldn't blame him, and Ax had agreed to this. It would do no harm. Pig already knew, the barmy army already knew what he had been planning. If it turned out to feel right, and depending on how he was received . . . Ax Preston has declared his Islam. How strange that sounded, very strange.

Only person here of any significance who hadn't known, was coming up now to join him, mask inscrutable. Please, Sage, don't give me a hard time . . .

At least the news seemed favourably received, on the whole.

And now, Sage's physical presence at his side, what a relief, a babble of conversation rising in waves. Sayyid Muhammad, having seated Ax at his right hand, tactfully, blessedly left him alone, and got stuck into some neutral but important topic to keep his brothers and the son-in-law occupied. Ax stared at the handsome platters of food, wondering if he'd ever want to eat again. What the fuck have I done?

'Well, you're going to be interesting to live with come next August.'

'Huh?'

'Ramadan. Good idea not telling me,' added Sage – dealing stoically with the double irritation of conventional eating irons and having to eat with his right hand. 'I might have felt obliged to do something weird and drastic myself.'

'Sorry.'

'I fucking hope it works, that's all.'

'It'll work.'

Ax decided to blow out the actual settlement talks after the first day. Maybe it was his imagination, but he found the way Sayyid Muhammad talked to the government people – his air of condescending to the bureaucrats, already having dealt with their *shaykh* – alarming. He and Sage spent a month travelling around meeting imams and other Yorkshire community leaders, while the Expeditionary Force was dismissed, and the barmy army guerillas were collected up, moved back to Doncaster, and (more or less) disarmed. A few Islamist weapons were handed in to amnesty points: no one tried to push that just at present. The English government made concessions. Muslim and Hindu leaders agreed to an equal rights for women agenda; and to cooperate with the police over recalcitrant offenders in their communities. Ax wasn't much interested in that part. No paper agreement was going to roll back the neo-conservatives, only time would tell. But he was glad it went through.

In that month of public relations, one of the deputations they received was different from the rest. The soldiers wanted Sage and Ax to do a gig. Just the two of them. It was great that the Few were coming to tour the north, with a brilliant line up of guests, but it wouldn't be the same. Peace Tour later, now the Ax and Aoxomoxoa. One night, something rare, for both the armies. Sayyid Muhammad would like it. He'd never been to a rock concert before.

'You don't know what you're asking,' Sage told them.

Well, it was a challenge. They worked something out that seemed as if it would work. But right until the actual night, they didn't know what it was going to be like. It didn't sound promising: Ax Preston on guitar, Aoxomoxoa on scary visuals, horrible noises and violent athleticism. They had no idea, until they were in the middle of it, that they had produced something stunning: and what a feeling then, eyes meeting across the stage in amazement, the huge civic centre hall packed, glittering sea of enraptured faces swirling out there in the void . . . Ax grinned at the skull and looked away from this zing of glances to segue into 'Dark Star', a surprise for him, something they hadn't planned. Now that is true love, Sage. I *hate* the fucking Grateful Dead, and I'm going to start hating them again the moment I get off this stage, but just for tonight, here you are, here's a nightfall of diamonds for you to play with, yes I thought you'd know what to do—

In the second set there was more stuff that had not been planned. Ax kept up, not really surprised at the mayhem; Sage was known for it. Amused to find himself playing the man's part in this extended *pas de deux*: his role to *be there*, rock steady under the pyrotechnics, anticipating, taking the weight, so that Sage could not lose the beat, could not falter, could not fall. He was effacing himself, but he didn't mind. The

'Jerusalem' solo would have been a touch tactless. But more than that: he'd had Sage supporting him, through these gruelling months. Taking the weight, always there. Time Ax gave something back.

They had agreed that they would do no encores. Sage wanted to finish with 'Who Knocks', a track from the Heads' latest album, *Bleeding Heart*.

Ax had not been sure that they should do this. 'Who Knocks' was a little too appropriate, and the immersion (even diluted to mere visuals for a concert hall) was fearsome. But he'd let himself be persuaded, and here it was, the final number. The faces, the whole hall drenched in red and slippery intestinal silver: distorted, excoriated images, that teased the eye with the promise of shuddering horrors, never giving you a straight answer . . . sound that goes with them compounds the fascination, stirs up reactions that you can't control, and at last here's Sage, menacing and graceful, just *standing* right at the front of the stage, singing:

Who knocks?

singing about the beauty of women, and their terrifying subtleties, and the things of which we know we are capable, any one of us . . . Yeah, tactless as hell, but a different tactless from 'Jerusalem', this was something that should be said. He is a brilliant performer, thought Ax, watching from the shadows. I don't know why anyone would want to buy this stuff and take it home. (Fucking bizarre lives they must lead, Heads fans.) But in performance he is superb. Great voice too, the bastard. Crying shame he hardly ever uses it. God, what are they making of this? This hall full of men—

Sage walked off, the stage went dark. There was an accolade of stunned silence, and then the roar.

In the dressing room, Sage drenched in sweat, ebullient. Ax yelled at him, because of the second set, Sage completely unrepentant, says, I knew you were okay. I can't never keep those stupid lists in my head, too bad . . . Back in the hall the house lights must be up, so far only producing a stubborn, thunderous clapping and stomping resistance. In time they'd realise no one was coming back. A knock on the door. Both of them used to being surrounded by a protective blur of people in this situation, they forgot to be on their guard, they let the person in. It turned out to be a starry-eyed Aoxomoxoa fan, who wanted to tell them he had got the whole thing, the whole Aoxomoxoa and Ax command performance for the soldiers at the end of the Islamic war. He would love to send them a copy.

Well, fuck. It had not occurred to either of them that this whacking great new civic hall might not be proofed, so it hadn't occurred to them to advertise that recording devices would not be welcome. Sage was up against his own ideology anyway, owing to the attitude of his departed gurus. At a normal Aoxomoxoa and the Heads gig the rule was sure, go ahead, try.

Both the performers display staggering self-control, thank him nicely, send him on his way.

'Fuck,' said Sage. 'I didn't want that recorded. Did you want that recorded?'

'No, I did not.'

He'd realised halfway through that this brilliant thing would be gone forever when it was done, nothing left but disparate fragments, the working records in Sage's boxes, nothing you could put together again. The feeling that this was *once, once only* had added considerably—

'Ah, the fans.' The skull grimaced in resigned contempt. 'Who can figure 'em? No taste, no refinement of feeling. Let's get out of here, before anything worse turns up.'

They went back to the hotel suite, both of them still dazed, ears ringing, thoroughly spaced. They'd been on stage for three hours, one short break. They opened a bottle of vodka, some stupid generic brand, and barely chilled, but never mind. Sat collapsed opposite each other, across a glass-topped coffee table, impressively ugly thing. Big windows full of gleaming, impenetrable dark (suite was on the top floor). How strange and disorienting still, to be indoors, to be unarmed, to have no lads around.

'That was really good,' said Sage mildly, at last.

'Yeah.'

'And the war's over. You did it, Ax. Not too painful, being a Muslim, is it?'

Ax's conversion had yet to make serious inroads on his dissolute way of life. He'd declared his Islam, genuinely. He didn't know, and wouldn't speculate, on how much traditional practice he would come to follow. He would need time. This was the way he'd decided to play it, fuck of a sight better than getting caught out later. It satisfied everyone so far. The Islamists understood that they'd *got Ax,* and knew that this was a major acquisition. They weren't going to make difficulties. They were going to say (they did say), well, being a Muslim is a practical spirituality. Ritual is important, but deeds and intentions matter more.

With luck, they wouldn't notice for a generation what they'd done to the ringfence.

'I'll keep them happy. I can do it.' He swallowed vodka and stared at the top of the coffee table. 'But I'll tell you one thing I won't do. I won't do this again.' He looked up, passionately earnest. 'Never. Anyone ever asks me again to play a game of soldiers, *forget it*.'

'Right. I'll drink to that.'

'I will die first.'

'Hey—' Sage reached out and grasped Ax's hand (from Sage, a gesture of most unusual intimacy). 'It's okay, Ax. It's *over*. You stopped it. You don't have to do that no more.'

He got up, quickly, and loped across the room. 'I'm starving, what d'you think's the chances of getting anything to eat?'

It was after midnight. 'Zero. I think there's a chocolate bar in the fridge, or some peanuts.'

'Ecch. I hate chocolate and the peanuts will be salted. I'll have a cigarette.'

Ax's phone was lying on a hotel dresser, quivering patiently. Sage picked it up, checked the fridge (nothing); tossed the phone to Ax. 'Call for you.'

'Who is it?'

Sage had walked into his own room. 'Dunno. Didn't look.' It would be Fiorinda. He flopped on the bed. Will I kneel to you, he wondered. Will I call you boss? Yeah, why not. As long as you can provide this level of entertainment . . . And if you ever give me the chance, I will *try* to protect you from the horrible things you feel compelled to do to yourself. Lit a cigarette, couldn't hear the conversation if he wanted to, Ax was speaking so low. His body flooded with sweet exhaustion. Is it really over, can we go home?

'Sage—'

So he got up again. Ax was standing by the coffee table, strange expression on his face. 'That was Fio. We have to go back to London. At once. Pigsty's killed a little girl.' ·

'What?' said Sage, stupidly, 'an accident?'

'No. Sounds like . . . not an accident.'

They looked at each other, caught: not surprised, not shocked enough. A confession of something like fugitive, guilty knowledge, for the first time shared.

FIVE

Who Knocks?

Fiorinda was on the platform at St Pancras, alone; coming into focus out of the crowd, in a winter coat they didn't know, her face pale and bright, hair glowing like a beacon fire as it tumbled out from under a dark knitted tam-o'-shanter. It was mid-morning, the station was busy. She kissed them both: reaching up on tiptoe to touch her lips to the grim reaper's grin. They went into a café in the Eurostar terminal and found a table.

'Are you really okay? No hideous injuries you've been keeping from me?'

'Not a scratch.'

'I dislocated my shoulder once,' boasted Sage.

'He fell out of a tree—'

'How thin you both are.' She wrapped her hands around her coffee cup, real *English* coffee again, after so long in the wilderness of that scary aromatic stuff – as some ungrateful journalist had pointed out. Tasting of nothing, but at least it was hot.

'Nah, we are blooming. You should have seen us after Yap Moss.'

'There's nothing fit to eat up there,' complained Sage. 'Only evil northern ethnic muck. Fried Mars bars, chip butties, black puddings, dog pie, all disgusting, they can keep it.'

'It is *amazing* the amount of perfectly normal foodstuffs he either cannot or will not eat—'

'Ah, come on. I ate the worm omelette—'

'Only because our hippies had you convinced they'd found some unusual, but of course not threatened in numbers, species of earthworm packed with weird alkaloids—'

'I don't believe in the worm omelette,' said Fiorinda, laughing. 'If you had an omelette to put the worms in, you could have eaten the eggs.'

'What ignorance. You don't make a worm omelette with *eggs*, Fio. You skin the worms, beat them into a kind of patty, and fry it like a burger—'

'Takes fucking hours.'

'Piss-poor energy audit—'

The traditional blank wall, she thought: this cute, evasive double act is probably all I'm ever going to hear. Will they babble about dugouts in their sleep?

'Well,' she sighed. 'The good news is, no nuclear power stations blew up.'

'And the bad news?' said Ax. 'Where is Pigsty now?'

The people in the crowded café must have noticed it really was Fiorinda, Aoxomoxoa and the Ax sitting there, but no one was letting on. At Ax's question there was a guilty quickening of attention at nearby tables: not a head turned. They knew Ax didn't like being stared at, they were respecting his privacy. This is fame indeed, thought Fiorinda. Stone Age fame. When she'd told the media people to stay away from the station today, their response (relayed back to her, through the San's press office) had been like, hurt astonishment: *what do you take us for?* Of course we'll play it exactly the way Ax wants. How could you doubt our tact in this sensitive situation? Where will it end? she wondered. For my Ax, for us all. If it has any further to go, that is. If it isn't finished.

It was a week since the night she had called Ax in Bradford. It hadn't been possible for them to leave straight away: had to handle the story then and there, before the Islamic negotiators heard about it some other way. Tact and sensitivity for the nation's hero hadn't stopped the media from leaping on a devastating Countercultural scandal. The way they felt about Ax was something different. The fact that the funky green President was helping the police with their enquiries was all over the shop.

'He's at the hotel. The police want to move him, but I don't think they should, not yet. In a strange environment, where he can't believe there are no spying cameras in the room, he might stop talking to me—'

Ax frowned. 'To you?'

'Well, yes. It's okay. I've been doing it for days. There's an unused bedroom in the suite, I talk to him in there: police right outside the door, and I have a panic button.'

The two young men were staring at her, appalled.

'What, *alone*—?' said Sage. 'You've been alone with him?'

'Fiorinda, that's got to stop—'

'Ah, bother. I didn't think. I should have broken it to you gently. It's the way things turned out, and I'm fine about it, true. Look, let's start again. From the beginning.'

*

After her mother died, Fiorinda moved back into the Pig's hotel, voluntarily returning to what had been a prison for her. Why did she do this? Ax and Sage were gone. She wanted to rejoin the Few, but she didn't want to live in the Snake Eyes house, in the room she'd shared with Ax. There was a slight antagonism between Fiorinda and Rob Nelson. Nothing serious, but something she didn't want to have to deal with every day. Also there was the issue of sexual independence. She didn't want Dilip, or any other guy she might go to bed with once or twice, to get the feeling that he knew where he could easily lay his hand on her. No thanks.

Anyway, she moved back. Allie and Fereshteh had already done the same, on the excuse that refitting was making the Insanitude uninhabitable. They resumed the old arrangement: a room each, on the floor above the Family Suite.

So there they were. The women in President Pig's *zenana*, of their own choice, everyone keeping up Ax's crisis management plan: the community service shifts, the tv discussions, the hassling of rich Countercuturals for money: the gigs, the personal appearances (but never away from London for more than a night). An infrastructure was forming: volunteers who had become recruits to Allie's administration, other bands and artists joining the gigs and the social work; no one new that Fiorinda yet distinguished from the crowd.

The Chosen stayed in the West Country. The Heads took the opportunity to spend more time with their families. George Merrick had a wife who was a potter, in St Ives (however that worked, the odd few weekends together over the years; but it seemed it did). Bill Trevor had a dress designer girlfriend in Bristol. Whatever Peter (Cack) Stannen did when he wasn't being a Head he went off and did that. But they were never away long. They had to keep making sure Fiorinda was okay. Because if you're not, said George, we better move to another planet before the boss gets back.

It turned out that she did most of the talking with the Pig. The suits tended to address things – memos, e-mail, personal approaches – to Fiorinda, either because of the accent, or because she was Ax's squeeze; and none of the others wanted the job, not even Rob. She began to lose the *horrible, constant,* sexual fear of him, which she'd taken out in bitter anger against Ax when he came back from the Tour. She was still very scared. It was an ordeal to walk into the room where the Countercultural Cabinet meetings were held, an immense effort to stay calm and endure the Pig's constant groping and scratching of himself, always convinced that big hand-gun was about to reappear.

He didn't have many official duties. The new England was still shaking down, no one really knew what the funky green President ought to be doing. It was just as well. Without Ax, the Pig as Ceremonial Head of State was way, way out of his depth. He was happiest on the tv, wearing a flak jacket and talking about 'the war'. Then he became another person, the crude-but-honest noble savage Paul Javert had invented. But the war palled, and she could see panic growing in him, more dangerous than the most brutal confidence. Benny Prem kept wanting her to get him to sign things and agree to things that he wouldn't like. Now that the excitement had died down, Prem was tired of being bossed around by a lump of wood. Do it yourself, she said. I'm not going to get my head blown off for your sake.

She hated the little inadequate-male grin. Those sickening white baby-teeth, like Peter Pan.

She was buried in the problems of the Countercultural Volunteer Initiative, Ax's new deal. She kept thinking, *this is insane. I'm not a bureaucrat! I won't quit while you're away because that would be mean, but just you wait 'til I get you home, Ax Preston* . . . But they were all working ridiculously hard. They would meet, the Few and friends, when they could, at that pub by Vauxhall Bridge where they used to gather when they were the Think Tank: drink like fish, laugh like hyenas, watch the news from Yorkshire.

Then at last it was Yap Moss, and soon after that Ax had made peace.

They were wondering what would happen when Ax and Sage arrived back. Pigsty didn't seem bothered; he was proud of the peace and smug that he'd got his feminist agenda into the settlement. But everyone knew Ax would have to be really, really careful.

Late one night Fiorinda was in her room, sitting on her bed softly playing guitar, crouching over to lay down notes, in black ink on manuscript paper. It was the way she had always written her music and probably always would: by hand, late at night and secretly.

Ax had been right about the effect of so much exposure. *No Reason*, the album she'd recorded with DARK, had been selling madly since it was reissued. Her solo debut *Friction*, which she'd recorded last year, between post-Deconstruction tour gigs, amidst all that stress and confusion, was, bizarrely, getting hailed as something special. Fiorinda had money, for the first time in her life. At least she no longer had to wonder exactly who was going to pay her hotel bills. And she would go on making music, it seemed, although the world was over.

Felt guilty about having told Ax that she would never write again, truth was, she'd only said that to make him feel bad—

Someone knocked on the door. Instant dread and panic: *why did I move back here? If the Pig wants to he'll come in, the door is nothing, he can blow the lock out—* The knock came again, this time in the pattern that meant Allie. She hid the music under her pillow and went to open up. Allie came in and sat on the bed, biting her lip, that round-eyed home-alone stare imploring.

'What's the matter?'

'Oh, Fiorinda, we need to talk to you.'

'Who's we? All right.'

Allie went off, and came back with Pigsty's old lady, and Fereshteh, and Anne-Marie Wing and her partner Smelly Hugh, the second in command of the Organs. They all looked very grim. They sat down on the hotel furniture and stared at her so desperately she was plunged again into terror. '*What is it?*' she gasped.

'It's okay,' said Allie quickly. 'It's not about Ax.'

'Lola wants to talk to you,' said Smelly Hugh.

The President's wife was like her photographs, only a little older: a bottle blonde Mrs Leisurewear whose bright make-up and aerobic-toned body said sadly, I know I'm not really pretty. I know I have no style. She was dressed for outdoors in a mink-lined trench coat, and clutching a big Harvey Nichols straw-look tote bag.

'I don't want to talk,' she said. 'I want you to come with me, somewhere.'

'What, now?' It was about one a.m.

'*Yes*, now.'

'Why?'

'I'm not answering any questions. You have to see for yourselves.'

'Are we all going?'

'No,' said Smelly Hugh. He appeared to be sober, for once in his life. It didn't suit him. He was looking absolutely haggard. 'I'm staying here. My kids are downstairs.'

'I'm staying too,' said Annie-Marie, giving her old man a look of deep contempt.

Fereshteh was wearing a long, long-sleeved and high-necked embroidered shift, and the hejab – serious piece of headscarf, close around her cheeks, low over her eyes, showing not a millimetre of hair – but no burqa. Maybe she counted Smelly Hugh as a relative. Feresh, like Rob, could be a little hostile towards Fiorinda. Something like, *you abuse your position as Ax's squeeze, white girl.* Only never spoken. But there was no sign of that now.

'I think we should go with her, do what she says.'

133

'Oh, I think so too,' said Allie. 'Really.'

Fiorinda could not handle the Family Suite. Fereshteh and Allie were in and out of there all the time, doing women-and-children stuff: Fio couldn't take it. She'd barely spoken to Mrs Leisurewear, ever. That must be why she didn't have the slightest clue what was going on, what kind of emergency this was.

'The Pig's gone out drinking,' said Anne-Marie. 'We've got all the kids in our suite. If he comes back, I'll tell him they're asleep and he'll go away. I've done that before.'

'Okay,' said Fiorinda, 'but if this is so serious I want to call Rob, and Dilip if he's reachable, get them to come along. Does that make sense?'

The others looked at Lola. She nodded, yes.

So the four women set off, the hippie nightwatchmen downstairs encouraging them with the usual tired comments (*you on the pull again, Fiorinda? what's it worth not to tell your boyfriend? etc*). They took a black cab, into the cold early-hours drizzle. It was a long ride, out of the centre, through Stepney and Stratford to Manor Park. Lola had the cab stop by Woodgrange Station and they walked through grid-straight dark streets: a town-planners' dream from before words like *organic* or *natural*.

The house was number 113, Ruskin Road. It was divided into two flats. Lola let them in to the hall, and through the front door of the ground floor flat. It was as cold inside as outside. The rooms were furnished and they smelt occupied, but in some perfunctory way: an occasional retreat, an investment property between lets. In the front room there was a soft, bulbous three piece suite, upholstered in terracotta to match the floor-length curtains at the windows. Lola gave the housekeys to Fiorinda and sat on the sofa.

'Go on,' she said. 'Have a look round.'

'For *what?*' demanded Fiorinda.

Lola stare at her, with an expression of blank horror. 'Take a good look in the cellar.' She turned her face away from the young women's gaze.

Feresh took off the burqa with the air of someone stripping for grim action and they looked around. Furnished rooms, an empty bathroom, an empty kitchen. An unplugged fridge containing a half-empty Corona bottle. A carton that had held cans of bitter. Two mugs by the sink, a stained sheet of newspaper with a date six months old. The silence was eerie.

'Thank God it's not a brown-out night,' said Allie. 'I'd hate to be doing this by candlelight.'

'Has anyone got a torch?' asked Fio. 'In case—?'

They hadn't. Shit. Not very well organised.

'Do you two know what we're supposed to be looking for?'

'Something terrible,' whispered Fereshteh.

The upstairs flat showed fugitive signs of habitation: a tube of toothpaste in the bathroom, a centrefold model from some men's magazine stuck to the living room wall; a jelly sandal belonging to a child. On a student desk in one of the bedrooms stood the remains of a roll of parcel tape, well-used. They tried the lower flat again, and this time found the door to the cellar. One of the house keys opened it. They went down the stairs. It was a bigger room than you'd expect under a house this size. It held a big black chest with deep drawers, a video recorder of ancient make, a bentwood chair, a camera tripod and lights. A painted Satan face in *trompe l'oeil* detail covered one wall. There was nothing else unusual; the normal debris: cardboard boxes full of rusting paint cans, old cans of car body filler. A row of dusty, empty glass demijohns. Paint-brushes stiff and rotting in a jamjar on a cobwebbed shelf.

'What's that smell?' said Allie. 'It's like formaldehyde—'

'Do we have the keys to that chest?' wondered Fereshteh.

They did. They opened the drawers, one by one. In the top drawer, a power drill, ancient make. In the second, a pair of scissors and a ball of twine. In the third a crumpled and grubby bundle of children's clothes. They looked at these clothes without touching them: and then at each other. They shut that drawer again.

The deepest, bottom drawer was empty, but as Feresh pulled it open they heard something shift. Kneeling on the floor, they hauled the drawer right out. Fiorinda reached inside and rapped. 'It's a false back, this is hollow. I can move it.'

The chest was against the back wall of the cellar. Behind the panel there was a hole hacked through the brickwork and into damp earth beyond. Fiorinda and Allie together dragged out a large wooden box: a roughly made box of black-stained composite. They used a blade of the scissors to pry off the lid, which had been nailed down. A strong smell of formaldehyde rose, mixed now with decay. In the box, wrapped in a blue bath towel, they found the body of a little girl. She was on her side, naked, hands behind her back, knees bent and legs folded under her. Withered parcel tape was strapped across her mouth, and around her waist, binding together wrists and ankles. Her sunken eyes had been wide open when she died. Someone seemed to have soaked the body in preservative, before packing it away.

Fereshteh gave a choking gasp, barely managed to push herself back from the box before she threw up . . . Allie just turned away, hands over her face.

Fiorinda knelt looking down, feeling neither shock nor horror, but a dizziness that cleared almost to a sense of relief.

Ah, so here it is, so this is it . . .

Things came into her mind that she had hardly thought before, for such a long time. How naïve and ignorant she had been the day she arrived at Reading, convinced that Rufus O'Niall, ageing Irish megastar, was about to emerge as the leader of English Countercultural politics. What an incredibly stupid idea. Barbecue fuel, bruised grass, the aural mulch of Festival noise, the mind of an angry, stupid, arrogant little girl . . . How strange it was to revisit her grand obsession, how hard to believe that she had so desperately wanted to see her father again. Here in this cellar, the worthless, cobwebbed relics, the things you thought were of value, which you hardly recognise when you come across them again—

Back to the present, and a rush of useless pity: put that aside. She had to think about the man who had saved her life. What would this murdered child mean to Ax?

She sat back on her heels. 'You okay, Feresh?'

'Yeah. I'm okay.'

'When we were vetting the Pig,' said Allie – forgetting to say Oh! – 'back when I was working for Paul, we found out that he likes kiddie porn. No one was too shocked. It isn't uncommon, is it. I think Paul was actually pleased. It meant we had a hold on the guy. But someone – it wasn't me, I swear – found a big hint of something worse, and I don't know what but I know . . . we buried it. Because we'd gone too far, because we'd invested in Pig; and Paul liked taking risks. He liked being right when everybody thought he was wrong, that was his self-image. I didn't know a thing about gunmen at the reception. Not one thing. But all the time, I knew something like *this* might be what was buried. I couldn't tell anyone, I just couldn't. It's not something you can easily say, is it?'

'We all knew,' said Fiorinda. 'The three of us. We knew there was something. Why else did we got back, except to wait for this to surface?'

'No,' said Fereshteh. 'Not me. He was in power, so I needed to be near him. That's all.'

'Oh, I know about that,' said Allie, wiping her eyes. 'I have done that.'

'Me too,' said Fiorinda. 'Me too.'

They knelt together around the dead little girl, in the stunned silence that tragedy exacts. Then Fiorinda stood up. 'I suspect she's not alone, but I don't think we should search any further. Let's go back upstairs, wait for Dilip and Rob.'

They went back upstairs. When they came into the front room Lola gave them one look and burst into tears. She curled up in a foetal ball, face hidden in a cushion, still hugging her tote bag. They waited in silence: long enough for Fiorinda to wish fervently that she still smoked cigarettes, and for Allie and Feresh to stub their way through most of a pack. Then the men turned up.

'Sorry,' said Rob, 'bomb at the Insanitude.'

'God.' Fiorinda had opened the door. 'Aren't we supposed to be at peace? Scare or real?'

'Real. Not the mainstream Islamics, they're outraged. Some other bastard fools.'

'Many hurt?'

'Not many, none seriously,' said Dilip, shrugging. Bomb boredom. 'What's going on?'

'The Pig's old lady decided to tell us something. Brace yourselves. It is not good.'

All five of them went down to the cellar again. Rob and Dilip looked at the dead girl, touched nothing, said nothing much. Then they all came back upstairs and stared at Lola.

Fiorinda went and sat on the end of the sofa.

'Lola, sit up and talk.'

She sat up. Her expensive make-up had survived the tears. Frightened, desperate eyes looked out pathetically (if you accepted the pathos) from a geisha mask.

'Tell us what you know.'

'I don't know anything. He used to come here. He used to bring kids here, to take pictures, make videos, nothing else: that's all I knew.'

'I don't believe you. You didn't bring us here just to show us his hideaway studio.'

'*I didn't know, I didn't know!*'

'You knew she was there. Were you here when she died? Did you watch?'

'*Fio—!*' breathed Dilip, horrified.

'Shut up. Were you here, Lola?'

Mrs Pig shook her head violently.

'But you believe your husband killed her. Why? Can you prove it?'

Lola thrust the tote bag at her. It fell open, spilling a heap of multipurpose recording discs and big, old, plastic video tape cassettes.

'Oh, okay. I see. But why now? That kid has been dead for weeks, and I'm afraid she may have company, under the floors, behind the walls. What made you decide to call a halt, suddenly, after letting it happen for so long?'

The Pig's wife grabbed the bag back, glaring in dumb misery at her tormentor. She dug in the bottom of it and pushed something into Fiorinda's hands. A pair of pants for a girl about three or four years old. They were pink lace, with bows; and bloodstained inside.

'Right,' said Fiorinda, stone hard. 'Yeah, I suppose that would do it.'

'I found them today,' sobbed Lola. 'They were just under her bed. I asked my baby, and she told me . . . she says, Dada says it's okay, and she won't make her pants dirty again, she'll be more careful. I never believed he would do that. Not his own flesh and blood—' She collapsed again into her foetal ball, stopped sobbing and just lay there.

Fiorinda left the sofa. The five of them moved to the other side of the room, where terracotta-curtained windows shut out the winter night, the street, the great city.

'My God,' said Rob. 'What are we going to do?'

'Fiorinda—' Dilip tried to put his arm around her.

'Don't touch me. We're going to call the police.'

'*What?*' Rob's stunned expression broke into anger. 'No! You don't take that on yourself. We get hold of Ax, right now. We talk to Ax, we think very carefully before—'

'I can't deal with stupidity at the moment. Sorry, Rob. We do not contact Ax. We do not sit around thinking what kind of spin we can put on this. We call the police. Now.'

'She's right,' said Allie, tight-lipped, huge-eyed. 'I know it could be a disaster, but she's right. It's what Ax would say.'

So they called the police, and the police came to 113 Ruskin Road and took possession.

'That was ten days ago,' said Fiorinda, in the café on St Pancras. 'I got them to do nothing, just take Lola's statement and keep a discreet watch on the hotel, until after your Bradford gig. We tried to act normally, except that Lola took the kids and left, right that night before Pig got home. She's at her mother's now. The morning after I called you, armed police came to the hotel. We thought there'd be a gun battle, but it was easy. They told him they wanted to ask him a few questions about that house, and he said, I want my lawyer. Simple as that. The hotel is practically empty now, except for him and the Met team. The Organs and all the other people, Pig's entourage, moved out as soon as the police would let them.'

'Fio,' said Ax, 'I don't think you should be going anywhere near him.'

'The police asked me to come to the suite with them, to try and avoid violence, and I did. That's how I come to be talking with him. He won't talk to anyone else, including his lawyers, about anything but evil cameras, and how they are pointing at him everywhere. With me, he tells me the lot. It is speeding things up a great deal: knowing where to look for the bodies, things like that. So I'm going to go on doing it. Sorry.'

They were looking at her as if she was a piece of broken china.

She sighed. 'Okay. I know what you're thinking. I know you both know the whole story about me and my father. I'm grateful that you have never, either of you, brought it up before. Or not much.' So there it was, out in the open for once. The fact that Fiorinda had been seduced by her father when she was twelve years old, had borne his child when she was barely thirteen; and seen that child die. Everybody in the music biz knew it, and really it was bloody good of all her friends to let her pretend they didn't. The hum of the crowded café seemed to rise, rushing in to fill their helpless silence.

'You know the miserable story, and I'm sure you know the other rumour, which I am certain is completely untrue. But it isn't relevant.'

Like hell, said the glance that flashed between them.

'No it *isn't*, so lay off, both of you. I can do this. I want to do it. And me helping the police, for which they are dead grateful, will help you to manage this, Ax. Trust me.'

She smiled at them ruefully. 'My poor heroes. What a homecoming.'

There was a small commotion at the entrance to the café. Three idiots with skulls for heads were blocking it, grinning cheerfully (they couldn't help it) and waving their arms.

'Hey, my band!' Sage jumped up, slung his bag over his shoulder: kissed Fiorinda on the cheek, touched Ax's arm lightly. 'See you later—'

They watched the Heads depart. 'He told them to look out for me,' said Fio. 'And they did. When I was at my mother's house I used to come down and find them drinking with my gran in the basement. She thought they were great.'

'He never said anything about that to me.'

'Nor me, but I know he put them up to it. I don't know what they'd have done if anything had happened.' Fiorinda suspected that the Heads were armed. It would have been out of character for George Merrick not to get that sorted, after massacre night. She wasn't going to mention this to Ax. It would only upset him. 'Died in my defence, I expect. The Heads are weird about Sage. He's their sacred icon.'

'He's a very loveable guy.'

'For all his faults,' suggested Fiorinda, grinning.

'For all his evil faults. And winding me up something rotten, whenever he feels inclined. Okay, I changed my opinion. I can change my opinion, can't I?'

The Few, she thought, were going to be *amazed* at the new relationship, the new body language, the whole double act. She was amazed herself, although she'd been forewarned by the letters. She had loved getting those letters (handwritten, what a sweet gesture); but she'd been gobsmacked that they came with a cuneiform scrawl from Sage tacked on the end. Sadly, not even George had been able to decipher the full text (no use asking Sage: it would only piss him off). But what a formidable team they made, Ax and Sage united. And so natural, once you saw it, unlikely as it seemed until you did—

An elderly woman, very soberly dressed, went by their table, and stopped with the little double take people do when they have decided to give the beggar some spare change after all. Came back and patted Fio on the shoulder. 'I'm so sorry for your trouble, my dear.'

'Thank you,' said Fiorinda, reaching up to touch the hand, smiling. The old lady nodded shyly at Ax and hurried away.

Stone Age fame.

'Shall we go?'

They went back to Snake Eyes, found the house quiet and reached their room unmolested. Ax hung up his leather coat, took the Gibson out of her case and restored her to her place; sat down on the bed and started to roll a spliff. Fiorinda sat by him. 'What a considerate guy you are,' she said, knowing what the grass was for. 'Well . . . did you meet any nice sheep?'

He grinned at her: that flashing smile she remembered.

'No lasting attachments. And you?'

'No lasting attachments.'

'Thank God for that.'

He took her hand, kissed it, and held it while he looked at her. What a phenomenon she was, this Fiorinda. At that first meeting of the Countercultural Think Tank, how everybody had stared . . . How could they help it? She's a *sixteen-year-old girl*. How can she be talking to us like this? Where are the strings, who is making the kid's mouth move? Where did she get those cold, wise eyes, where did she find that tone of contemptuous authority? The skull-masked Heads sitting there grinning, like: *haha, we knew! We found her!* – especially that one mask more flexible and expressive than most naked human faces. Ax had known the kid's reputation (drinking buddies with Aoxomoxoa, for fuck's sake). He'd put it down to hype, and Sage being wilfully bizarre. He hadn't expected anything like this. He had thought then, *I will have her,* without any sexual meaning at all . . . and even now it was not lust he felt, or not pure lust, but something more painful: the shock of realising he had missed six months of her growing up. Was she actually taller? At Fiorinda's age, it could easily be. Still thin, but she no longer looked like fishbones. She looked well put together, clear eyed and strong, her hair crisp and bright as copper wire on the surface, deepening to wine in the soft depths. I must never leave her again. Never, never.

'Ax. I was so afraid you would be killed.'

'Me too.' He lit the spliff, and handed it to her. 'I would love to fuck you now, but I could understand if you're off the idea, with all this Pigsty stuff. If you don't want, it's okay.'

'You have a point. I warn you, you may be off sex yourself after you've seen the Pig's video diaries. But oh no. Soldier home from the wars gets to fuck girl. That is the rules, I wouldn't want to break the rules.'

'Hmm.' He wanted very much to have her, but was not sure about the terms.

'Even if he's turned into a Muslim.'

'Ah—'

Ax realised with horror that *he still had to deal with that.* He'd convinced himself it was better not to try to explain until he was back where he could touch her. Now the news about Pigsty stood between: and he had nothing scripted, he was helpless—

'Oh, don't look so terrified. It's okay. Ax, you believe in God, everyone knows you do. That's something people cannot help, it is just the way you are wired. If you had to sign up for something organised, you might as well be a Muslim as anything. They're all equally horrible.'

'Good.'

'Long as you don't grow a beard.'

'I will not grow a beard.'

'What about getting circumcised?'

'I plan to avoid that if possible. I have heard it is extreme pain.'

'So, do you want that fuck?' Smiling at him so tenderly, with her heart in her eyes—

They finished the spliff as they stripped. Slipped into bed: God what a *joy* to hold her. She reached down her sweet cold hand to his balls and he buried his face in her hair, laughing for sheer relief and thinking, if all the rest is about to go to hell, there is a good thing I have done.

About eight in the evening of that day, Ax and Sage and Allie and Fiorinda were in one of the smaller presentation rooms in the mezzanine at the Pig's hotel, with DCI Barbara Holland and some of her team. The room had been shut up for months before it became this impromptu video theatre. The air smelled of carpet glue and stale coffee, withered business stationery was arranged on every desk. The police techies muttered to each other, occasionally focusing in on a detail: replaying or trying another angle. An unspoken delicacy had separated the civilians, Allie and Fio together down at the front, the two young men further back and several rows away.

It was going to take weeks, or months, to analyse the material that Lola Burnet had handed over. This disc was one of the simpler records: no computer generated backdrops, props, animation to be stripped out. It involved Pigsty and other adults, and a child. The adult faces and hands were blurred, very professional job, all attempts to restore them had so far failed. Only Pigsty had been identified. The others were all men, and seemed to be four separate individuals – but not even these facts could be relied on. Once an image has been through a mixing desk, anything might have been changed. The desk that had been used, for all the discs, was a generic High Street model: could be the same machine as one that Pigsty had in his possession, but that had yet to be proved.

Fiorinda could not concentrate. There was no point in being moved or even sad, her pity would change nothing. Her mind kept straying to the implications of the scandal. Was this the end of the Countercultural Cabinet? What would happen now? Beside her, Allie wrote on faded hotel-corporate notepaper, *Dachau, Buchenwald, Auschwitz*. Fio nodded. Yes. Maybe it was because they were faceless, but they were like death camp guards, those men: no orgy, just drab, braindead working stiffs, plodding through their dehumanised routine.

The movie ended. 'Of course, nothing that has been digitally manipulated is evidence,' said DCI Holland. 'That's the law. None of this material can be used in court.'

'But you don't need to prove anything,' said Allie. 'He's confessed.'

'Not exactly,' said Fiorinda. 'He knows he's guilty as hell, and he wants to be punished. But he is not guilty of murder, as he never meant to kill them. He sticks to that.'

'We still need evidence, no matter how he pleads.' DCI Holland looked at Ax and Sage. 'Only a few of the amateur recordings involve other adults. We believe they were made some time ago, same vintage as the commercial kiddie-porn videotapes. But they've been copied and re-copied. Everything's heavily tampered. This next one is a little different.' She held up a plastic cassette, bagged and sealed. 'The picture and sound quality are poor, but for some reason he didn't enhance them; and there are other differences: it could be an original.'

They watched. It was the same routine, familiar by now to Allie and Fiorinda. The child who does not want to be there, who keeps asking, *can I go home now*, who tries charm and tries co-operation and tries pleading, and then just panics: but nothing works. The adults barely speaking. In this movie they were wearing hoods over their faces instead of having their features blurred out; and long white robes over their naked bodies. There was a fire, and candles. It looked as if they liked the idea of the Klu Klux Klan or some other secret society thing. The scene seemed to be happening in a cellar, and there was a Satan face on one wall.

'As you can see,' DCI Holland murmured, 'this isn't 113 Ruskin Road, but very like it—'

Shortly, Fiorinda said, 'I don't think it's original.'

'Why not?'

'Because the original would be more than thirty years old, the tape would have rotted away. Probably the difference in quality is because it's been copied on older machines. I think the cellar in Ruskin Road may be an imitation of this one . . . The little boy is Pigsty.'

They stopped the tape, plugged their cassette player into their Conjurmac, cut and pasted the child's face, rebuilt it, lined it up with photographs of the adult—

'She's right,' said one of the techies, 'I think she's right.'

'Oh, *what* a surprise,' said DCI Holland, with a bitter sigh.

'What goes around, comes around,' muttered another of the techies.

'Doesn't it. Always.'

The movie kept moving as planned. When it ended, the Chief Inspector turned to Ax. 'I think we'll stop there, Sir. Mr Preston—'

'Ax.'

'Ax. And Mr Ao-ah-um-er—' Poor woman was baffled as to how you address Aoxomoxoa; even umasked, and revealed as merely a very tall blond, with cornflower blue eyes and the body of a world-class gymnast. Fiorinda noticed again the way the police treated the two of them: with reserve, naturally, because we are all implicated in this, we are all under investigation; but with *serious respect*. It was most clear in DCI Holland. The techies were more just old-fashioned fascinated and pleased at being involved with celebrities.

'Sage.'

'Yes. Thank you both for coming in. I won't subject you to any more of this tonight, but we will have to ask you to view more of the material. And answer some questions.'

'Of course,' said Ax.

The techies were packing up. 'And thank *you*, Fiorinda,' said DCI Holland, warmly. 'As ever. You'll be seeing him tomorrow, usual time?'

'Yes.'

'Mr Preston, now that you're back, we'll need another meeting with your press office. I hope we can co-operate fully over handling the media. Could we—?'

'Yeah, sure. Let's fix it now. Allie?'

Allie and Ax went out into the corridor, fixed a time. The police took themselves off.

'How is she coping?' said Ax.

'Fio? Just amazing. She's held the whole thing together for you.'

'I know *that*. I have not been on another planet. I meant, with this shit.'

'I know what you mean,' said Allie. 'I think she's okay. The only sign of . . . well, the first night when we'd found the body, she was *vicious* to poor Lola Burnet. It was shocking. Suddenly she . . . she was like some people think Fiorinda always is—'

'Yeah. Talented little monster, you have to feel sorry for her, but she's not capable of normal emotions. Only we know different, don't we? God, I wish I could keep her out of this. But I can't.' Allie didn't know what to say. To feel *flattered* that Ax was confiding in her seemed a cruel response to the anxiety in his eyes. She wanted to touch him, but those video diaries poisoned all gestures of affection.

'I'm so glad you're back, Ax. We've missed you.'

'Yeah.'

In the meeting room Fiorinda and Sage were sitting where he had left them, in silence. He sat down again beside Sage. Somewhere overhead the grown-up version of that little boy, those soft little limbs, that sweet, open face, was watching tv with his burly police bodyguards, who never let him out of their sight (except when he was with Fiorinda), in case he should harm himself. Ax had been to visit Pigsty, before the video session. What could you call it? A courtesy call? Pigsty a little gone to seed. Wanted to get back to his tv. Spoke of what he'd done as a terribly bad habit, that he'd taken up again because he was under a lot of stress.

'I didn't kill them, Ax. The deaths was accidental. That's a fact.'

'When my mother was dying,' said Fiorinda, 'all that time, I went on hating her. I could not stop myself. I hate her now. It's not to do with my father, I know she wasn't to blame for that. It's to do with years of her being miserable and ignoring me . . . It is so easy to be brutal to someone who is helpless. It is instantly addictive, *instantly*, once you start. She was dying in pain and loneliness and I could not be gentle. Couldn't even fake it, most of the time. That is such a vile state to be in. I think it's hell. I've been thinking, that's where Saul Burnet lives, that's where he *lives*, the child, the person he might have been. That's the place where his emotions survived. It's very strange. When he talks about what he did to those other children, when he's saying really hideous things, *he becomes human*. And I pity him, and I feel that we are not so far apart. The rest of the time he's still a complete jerk, with his cunning little plans to get round the system. God, he's mortally afraid of being declared a head case . . .'

She wiped away the tears that were running down her face. 'I'm so sorry for him.'

Later, around midnight, the Countercultural Cabinet were gathered in the Sunlight Bar. The big, low-ceilinged drinking hole was empty, otherwise. No bar staff: they were serving themselves. They'd come to find Ax, hoping that Ax home from the wars would have some brilliant solution, but Ax wasn't doing them any good. He was in a booth by the terrace, Fiorinda in his arms and her head on his shoulder, neither of them taking much notice of anyone. Sage was in the window seat opposite, staring through the dark glass into the night. The others, grouped around these three, were getting drunk, but not at all merry, wreathed in cannabis smoke, but not at all mellow. Gallows humour impelled them to discuss *Bleeding Heart*, the Heads' new album, which was raking it in, usual Aoxomoxoa and the Heads style. And that gruesome hit single, too.

'What do you do with all your money Sage?'

'Don't think he spends it on clothes,' muttered Allie.

'It all goes on running that van,' said Chip. 'How many four-star gallons to the millimetre?'

'Van doesn't run on petrol, so there.'

'Doesn't run at all, mostly,' said George Merrick. 'Can't get greener than that.'

'So where does the fortune go?' insisted Verlaine cheekily. 'What's the secret vice?'

'I give it away.'

'What, all of it?'

'Nah, just most of it.'

What was 'Who Knocks' about? The lyrics weren't provided, you had to piece them together. There's this cannibal in a cellar (God, it would have to be a cellar, wouldn't it), sitting among bones and bits of flesh, that used to be beautiful girls (lot of spooky, delicate detail about the beauty of *parts*: hair, eyes, ears, etc). There's a staircase with a door at the top. He's watching this door, up there in the shadows. Someone's knocking, it's the woman he's just killed and eaten, she wants to come in, he's very scared, should he let her in?

Well, in the end, does he let her in or doesn't he? We need to know, and it is not clear.

'Can't remember.'

'You are so weird, Sage,' said Anne-Marie. Since *that night*, the second utterly terrible night in their history, Anne-Marie and Smelly Hugh had switched camps, and been accepted. Anne-Marie was okay, if she was a bit of a crystal-swinging folkie, and Smelly wasn't a bad guy. 'Why d'you have to do a song about a serial killer anyway?'

'Tisn't about a serial killer.'

'How d'you know it isn't? You just said you've forgotten what it's about.'

'Because I'm not a serial killer.'

Sage had taken off his mask for the video session. The skull was back in place, but there wasn't much sign of that glorious monster, Aoxomoxoa. The person there in the window, tired and still, absently fending off the banter, was much more like the Sage that Fiorinda and the Heads knew; and now Ax. But *the guy in 'Who Knocks' is meant to be me*, he said: and the implications blossomed like cancers. Aoxomoxoa's dangerous affinity for horrors, those hideous death-camp passages in *Arbeit Macht Frei*, jumbled bodies like strips of withered leather . . . How far from Sage's personal darkness to what Pigsty *did*? How far from those dead children to the heart of the Counterculture?

Everybody is thinking the same thing, thought Fiorinda. We went to that seminar, out of pique or curiosity or for some other reason that seemed important at the time, looking for the leader of the Countercultural Movement. And we found him. But the leader wasn't Ax, it was Pigsty. That's what we have to face now, delayed reaction, finally hitting us. Paul invented him, we accepted him. We went along.

'Why do you think he's protecting those other bastards?' said Dilip, eventually.

'I don't think he's protecting them,' said Ax. 'I think they may be dead.'

'You mean he's killed them, too?'

'Not exactly. Remember the death row thing? Five of those men were re-offending lifers, on paedophile charges. I think Pigsty's friends may have been among them.'

After the Deconstruction Tour, President Pig had intervened to make sure that the fifteen prisoners awaiting execution, under the restored death penalty, were swiftly killed.

'*God,*' said Sage: and then, frowning, 'Why didn't you tell DCI Holland that?'

'Because I only just thought of it.'

The emotional atmosphere deteriorated further, if that were possible.

Abruptly, Sage jumped down from the window seat. 'Ah, this is no good. C'mon, let's go somewhere, out. *Not* the San. Let's see if Allie can get us in somewhere cool and fashionable.' The skull wore its craziest grin. 'C'mon, come on. On your feet, out of here, all of you, let's hit the town.'

Late the next day they met at the Insanitude, in the room that the Few had refitted as their office: with the windows overlooking the Victoria Monument, the stacks of flyers and posters; the workstations in rows, littered counters around the walls. A ring of scuffed tables and chairs, secondhand classroom furniture bought very cheaply, had become the forum where they talked things out. Ax and Sage took places on either side of Fiorinda. The alert, don't-even-think-about-it physical presence they'd brought back from Yorkshire made them look like her body-guards.

Everyone pitched in to bring Ax up to date. How the government was keen to co-operate with his crisis plan, not so keen on funding. They had no money for their own concerns, never mind for the Counterculture. Luckily the dangerous element in the drop-out hordes (still growing, still roaming around desperate to be *part of something*) – which meant, roughly, the young males – seemed happy for the moment with free gigs, good works, beer money, the occasional dodgy vegetable curry. In some regions the Initiative was working very well, some not so good. The returning militarised barmies would present a new challenge . . . There was a danger that employers would use the volunteers as free labour and dump their unskilled staff, simply exacerbating the problem. 'But it doesn't happen much,' said Fiorinda. 'They know that's not the intention, so they work out how to give our drop-outs simple chores that do not cause much damage and displace no one.'

'Good, that's good. Better than I'd hoped.'

'They like the romantic packaging, but they know they're buying into a protection racket. Do just what the Countercultural movement wants, or else.'

Everyone laughed, happy to have Ax back, to have these three installed: Fiorinda and her bodyguards, a wall nothing was going to get through, an inevitable triumvirate.

'Right,' said Ax, grinning. 'Wouldn't want it otherwise. We need them scared.'

Pigsty was formally charged and taken into custody. Fiorinda persuaded him to co-operate with the psychiatric assessment. She went on visiting him, in the remand centre at Lloyd Park in Croydon, the Category A public sector prison that had replaced the disgraced Wormwood Scrubs. The story in the media grew in baroque detail, but the expected eruption of Countercultural violence did not happen, not even in Saul Burnet's native Northampton.

The Chosen came up to London and had a terrible conference with their frontman and with Kit Minnitt, the band's manager: Milly storming out, Shane and Ax in tears, tough guy Jordan not far off. But then, instead of quitting as he had threatened, Ax started gigging with them: driving down to the West after dark, meeting the others wherever they were playing. No advertising, people just arrived and found Ax on stage, and were thrilled: and the fingers still worked, though it seemed to Ax that they should not. They began to work on the album, their first since *Dirigiste*; that would become *Put Out The Fire* – the valedictory, the immensely personal goodbye from the Chosen to a lost world, that seemed to belong to everyone who'd been travelling with them through these two years. The title was not a reference to the end of the Islamic Campaign, but to a classic Who track. It meant, that song is over. There's no going back.

It was amazing how normal life went on seeming in this interlude – normal in terms of what they'd started to call normal. Work like workaholic bureaucrats for manager Ax. Do your volunteer shift on the hospital cleaning, the hedge planting, the classroom aiding; whatever's going. Late at night, if you get the chance, do some drugs and get on the town with Aoxomoxoa. Lean on the big strange guy's ferocious energy, like all those global punters, until he pounces on some willing unknown and disappears with her. As Dilip said, watching Sage on the pull was like flat racing: over too quick to be entertainment.

'Have you noticed,' said Verlaine to Chip, 'how he keeps away from *her* on the dancefloor? Because when he's smashed out of his brain he can't trust himself—'

'He keeps away from me too,' sighed Chip woefully, 'I tries not to take it personal. You are way off, Pippin. Haven't you *noticed?* It's classic, innit. The endless one night stands, the mask, the outrageous homophobic remarks—'

'Don't get your hopes up,' said Verlaine unkindly. 'I'm right.'

They'd been missing their telly, for which they had no time under Ax's régime. Triumvirate-watching was shaping up as an excellent soap-substitute.

Ax had meetings with government suits; and went to visit his old lady in Hastings, the one he'd met at the Volunteer Initiative launch. Her name was Laura Preston, nice coincidence. She was ninety-nine now, and still glad to be alive. She said she thought bringing back National Service was a good idea, but there ought to be something for the girls. His postcards from Yorkshire were up on her wall.

The shrinks said Pig was sane. He would stand trial, and it was time to talk the thing out.

Saul Burnet's parents were members of a magical cult: not mainstream Satanist or Pagan, something of the group's own invention. He was sexually and violently abused by both his parents, and others, when he was four and five and six years old. Then his parents split up, he went to live with his maternal grandparents and had no further contact with that lifestyle. In his early twenties he began to collect kiddie porn, and made contacts that drew him into sexual violence against children. He got scared when some of his confederates were arrested, and gave it all up. When he returned to the habit and started using the house on Ruskin Road, he avoided all former contacts. No one, not even his closest associates, knew anything. He would bring children there, have sex with them in the cellar that he'd set up to look like the room he remembered from his childhood, and record the action. He had to frighten them, hurt them and particularly immobilise them, or he didn't get a good ex-perience. But he knew it was wrong and he only did it when he really needed to do it. He'd been forced to do four children this way during the past five years, due to the stress of the Organs' success, and then Paul Javert's Countercultural Think Tank, and all that had followed. On each occasion, although he admitted he'd tortured them, the death had been an accident that he could explain. He had tried to preserve them, because that was what seemed right, like the ancient Egyptians. He believed that his wife must have been secretly filming him, and that was how she had found out about the house.

'Four bodies have been found,' Fiorinda went on. 'Three little girls and a boy, where he said they would be. No more, though the police have taken the place apart. In most respects Pigsty's version checks out, except his story of how he procured.' She gazed ahead of her for a moment. This word gave Fiorinda trouble. Her bodyguards, though they did not stir or look at her, seemed to the rest of the circle to have moved closer . . . 'procured the children. He says he "bought them off the internet", but the details aren't convincing. So that's it. Everything I've told you has yet to be fully investigated, proved, names named; stand up in court. But it will. Including the torture, to the point of death. Nobody, not the police or Pigsty's defence team, has any doubt of what's going to happen.'

'So that's why he hated cameras,' murmured Roxane. 'The fear of getting caught—'

Fiorinda gave Rox a puzzled look, surprised anyone could be so dense: 'No. It's because he hates to be *reminded*. Cameras make him feel sick.'

'The trial won't come up for months,' said Ax. 'It could be a year, or two. But as the law stands, and the way Pigsty has reacted, he's going to die. He's heading for the lethal injection, no question.'

'Maybe it's what he wants,' said Dilip quietly, while the rest stayed silent.

'I'm quite sure it is.' Fiorinda had started some careful crosshatching in the margin of her printed notes. She spoke without looking up.

'But what do *we* want,' said Ax. 'Should he die, or should he live? Well?'

The office was barred to its normal traffic, no one in here today but the remains of the Countercultural Think Tank. It was the beginning of February. Weak, clear, morning sunshine streamed through the naked windows: made a glowing aureole of Fiorinda's hair and bathed Ax's long-fingered, well-knit hands in silver; but left untouched the rosy dark- ness of the skull's blank eyes.

'Are you going to go on wearing the mask, Sage?' asked Roxane, suddenly.

Three other deathsheads turned on her as one, displeased at being separated from their chief. 'It's a fair question,' said Sage. 'We've thought about it. Yeah, we are. If we stop wearing the masks now, that says the next weird-looking person you meet is probably a murdering paedophile Satanist. We better reverse the drugs legislation, fold the green volunteer programme, let fast-food capitalism and gun-culture supermarkets and green concrete agribusiness back in. Clear the campgrounds, shoot down any resistance . . . I don't think that makes much sense.'

'A good answer.'

'Probably have to have some kind of global ban on the Heads' music too. Then I wouldn't be rich an' famous any more, and I wouldn't like that at all.'

'But I asked you something,' said Ax, with a faint smile. 'I mean it. Round the table.'

'Ah, God.' Rob looked disgusted. 'How can we answer that? It's not our business.'

'It might be.'

'Ax,' said Felice, 'I'm not in favour of a life for a life. But you just came back from a *shooting war* that started halfway up the M1. People die by violence all the time in this city, and all the cities of England. This is the times, we got the law for these times. Okay, you say *he's ours*. Dilip says, *he's ours*. I hear you. But I'm sorry, I don't see the death of one murdering bastard like Pigsty as a big issue.'

'Good point,' said Sage.

The other two power-babes made it known that they were with Felice.

'What about you, Sage,' asked Cherry, 'what's your choice?'

'I've spent the last couple of months playing paintball with live ammunition, in defence of the nation state. It was a lot of fun, but I don't know: somehow I still can't stick judicial murder. I vote for life.'

'I say he lives,' said Roxane grimly. 'I hate the death penalty. It stinks.'

'Lives,' said Chip, his round, cherub face almost looking grown-up.

'Life without parole,' said Verlaine, pushing back his ringlets. 'It's the only way.'

'He would be better off dead,' said Dilip. 'Back to the clay, remoulded in the hands of the Divine. But that's too bad. We cannot let him go, we must carry him round our necks like the albatross, we cannot pretend he didn't happen, we have to keep him by us over the years, assimilate, accept, who knows, maybe redeem our shame, our boss. Lives.'

'He should die,' said Fereshteh, in a low voice. She wasn't wearing the burqa, only the hejab scarf. She never wore the burqa again inside the Insanitude, but the change was hard on her. Her liquid dark eyes looked to Fiorinda for support, but found none: she quickly lowered her glance, trying to make a veil of just *not looking* at anyone.

'Fiorinda?' said Ax.

'I think it is cruel,' she answered, concentrating on her crosshatching, the clipped accent well to the fore. 'I think it is torture, because I don't think he can recover or repent. He's not capable of that, Dilip. But he has to live.'

. Ax kept talking it around. In the end they all said live. Even the power-babes and their man, even Smelly Hugh. Even Fereshteh: because that was the answer Ax wanted. It was a process of ruthless attrition. He didn't go after their hearts and minds, just their bare assent. They didn't have to mean it, he was satisfied to nag them into *saying* the right thing. That's Ax, thought Sage. Always the art of the possible, always willing to take partial, fucked-up and temporary, if that's what he can get. How strange that that's what makes him such a clever guy – the way he's prepared to settle for a fuck-up.

'Okay,' said Ax, at last. 'I said, it might be our business. Or my business. I went to see the Prime Minister again yesterday.' He looked around, gathering them all in. His expression was reserved, bleak: not a hint of triumph. 'He made.me an offer. Not unexpected, but . . . I suppose you could call it flattering. I made him a counter-offer. He said yeah, it'll happen, probably within the life of this Parliament. There's been a revulsion of feeling across the parties, and ironically, Pigsty helped it along, hustling for those fifteen lethal injections. Whole lot of support for the view that the death penalty experiment has failed. That was what I was expecting. I told him I wanted a commitment *now*, or I won't take him up. I asked him for a referendum, and he agreed. If I don't get the response I want, I'm going to quit, and they can pick themselves another funky green ceremonial head of state.'

The others sat and stared. They had known the Presidency was on the cards. For everyone except Sage and Fiorinda, the rest was a shock.

'This is important to me,' said Ax. 'The guys offering me this job are the same guys who knew the truth about massacre night. They knew Pigsty was a cold-blooded murderer when they made him President. They accepted him because it suited them; now they're glad of the chance to be rid of him. I want the Presidency, yeah, I admit. I think I can use that position. But I'm not quite hypocrite enough to take it over Pigsty's dead body.'

'A referendum takes forever to organise,' said Roxane. 'The CCM won't wait. They want a new Countercultural President *now*.'

'Day and a half to pass a bill,' said Fiorinda, doodling hard. 'If there's a will to do it, and cross-party support. A month or so to print slips and mobilise the polling stations. Electronic voting software is fucked-up by Dissolution problems, but the traditional method is still on the shelf, and in working order . . . It's like corporate music publishing. If they don't care, they'll sit on your stuff for years. If they're keen, it's hyped and out all over the world in a week.'

'So, they will be voting on whether or not to retain the death penalty?'

'They'll know what they're voting for,' said Sage. 'We can make sure of that.'

'Sage,' said Fiorinda, getting next to him and away from Ax, as the meeting broke up. 'Are you registered to vote anywhere?'

Skull looked a little shifty. 'Not sure. I might be, down in Cornwall.'

'Have you ever voted?'

'Ah . . . No.'

'Thought not. I better tell George. You will never handle an electoral roll all by yourself.'

The skull got on its dignity, gave her a mean glare. 'I will sort it, okay. What about you, brat? Where are you registered, huh? No fixed abode brat.'

'Actually I hate the idea,' said Fiorinda, suddenly bitter. 'I don't want to vote for anything, ever. *This is not my world.* But with luck I don't have to worry about it this time. The most likely date is March the twenty-ninth. I won't be eighteen.'

Not eighteen yet. My God.

Fiorinda was tired out. She went back to Lambeth Road with the Eyes and Rob. The others retired to the Insanitude canteen. Sage went looking for Ax, who had vanished. He found him alone in the Fire Room, over in the north wing, so called because it was one of the few rooms of the six hundred with a chimney that worked, and it was small enough to be heated by a fire in the grate. The room was lit by one meagre electric lamp, with a parchment, tasselled shade from the nineteen fifties, on a table by the hearth. Ax was sitting by the fire. He looked round and smiled wanly.

Sage pulled up a chair. 'You knew about Pigsty's kiddie porn habit, didn't you?'

'Yeah.'

'So did I.'

They watched the fire. Sage took out a pack of the government-licensed anandinate cigarettes he perversely favoured, offered them.

'No thanks. I don't know how you can stand those things.'

'So denounce me to the Campaign for Real Cannabis. I can't be fucked to roll my own, it takes me to long. Anyway, I like the advertising . . . Ax, arguably we made a shit choice on massacre night. We stayed alive. Arguably we made a shit choice when you came back from the Tour. We could have fled the country or something. But you are not responsible for what happened to those children.'

'I knew he was a bastard,' said Ax. 'I didn't know he was a psychopath.'

The skull looked at him in silence for a moment, then turned away and stared into the flames. 'Maybe the line between the two isn't so easily drawn as you think . . . You know about me and Mary Williams, don't you? Of course you do.'

'I remember some of what got into the papers,' said Ax, diplomatically.

'Yeah. Well, it was all true. All true. I used to beat her up. Me hitting her was basically our relationship, that and the smack. I hurt her badly enough to put her in hospital a few times, including once when she was pregnant.' Sage looked down at his masked hands and closed them into fists, the virtual ghosts that replaced the missing fingers moving with uncanny realism. 'Not so great for needlepoint; but they work fine as weapons.'

This Ax knew. He'd seen those weapons used, up in Yorkshire. Sage in a fist fight was a thoroughly alarming proposition.

'No wonder you hate heroin.'

'Oh no. No, no, no, never blame the drug. It was me. And I am perfectly sane. What I mean is . . . well, I'm not sure what I mean, except you're not to blame.'

'How tall were you when you were sixteen?'

'Same as I am now.'

'*God.*'

'Yeah. Fucking ridiculous.'

Ax thought about the sixteen-year-old giant junkie, prowling the little streets of Padstow, seeking for meat. 'If it was so bad, with Mary Williams, how d'you come to have a kid?'

'I didn't know Mary was going to decide to get pregnant. Never crossed my mind. Contraception was her business. It's girl stuff, right?' The skull grinned in self-contempt. 'Got the injection, soon as I found out. I'd've had it done permanent if I'd been old enough.'

'But you made her do a DNA test.'

'That was later, when she set the lawyers on me. I was being nasty, I never had any doubt he was mine. I used to have him with me a lot, first few years. But her lifestyle changed, she got bored of trying to show me up, I don't know . . . There's a court order, but that was also me being nasty. I don't pursue it. I'm not even sure if it runs any more, now Wales is a foreign country. I've seen him once since Dissolution. Don't know when I'll see him again. He's eleven this year. I have an eleven-year-old son, isn't that weird.'

'You love him?'

'I try not to think about it.'

'Sorry.'

'What can I do? She hates me. I hate her too. Nothing personal, just the whole fucking *idea*. Ah, horrible. She doesn't want me around, she doesn't want her kid to be with me, and I can't honestly blame her.'

'Have you hit any other women, since?'

'Haven't hit anybody since, not seriously.' Ax smiled. This would exclude some crowd-pleasing showmanship on the tv and other public occasions. And fair enough. 'Except a few Islamists. Oh, and George. I hit George occasionally. He doesn't mind.'

'Bizarre lives you Heads lead.'

'I suppose we do.' Sage finally lit the cigarette he'd been holding. 'Ax, I—'

The sentence stalled. They sat staring into the red caves between the coals.

Nothing's really changed, thought Ax. The administration is the same dodgy team that Paul Javert was playing for, same bunch of amoral chancers. The peace in Yorkshire may not hold up. We're still deep in shit. But Fiorinda calls the police, the hippie-goon régime collapses like a house of cards, and suddenly it feels as if we have a *chance*, first time since the coup, to pull ourselves out of that swamp where murder is law . . . Astonishing girl. He had asked DCI Holland *what the fuck* (expletive deleted) did she think she was doing, having a seventeen-year-old kid interview a murdering paedophile, alone in a room with him? She'd answered: ordinarily you would be right, but this is *Fiorinda*.

The girl who told me, the first time we were alone together, the first night I took her to my bed, *Pigsty is a childfucker*. In just about that many words. How did she know?

Maybe that was a stupid question.

He'd had a terrible struggle, since they came back from Yorkshire. But tonight he felt that he was back on track, his mind quiet in a way it hadn't been for a long time, the future out of his hands . . . Insh'allah. Whichever way things went, it would be okay. Shit. If I come out of the game with *nothing*, except Fiorinda and Aoxomoxoa, I'll still be well up on the deal.

He smiled, thinking of Yorkshire adventures. He just unfolds, this guy—

'Listen, Sage. Would you do some oxy with me?'

Sage looked up, startled out of deep abstraction. The skull went blank, and stayed blank long enough – measurable seconds – for Ax to get alarmed. It was something he'd been thinking about, doing the intimacy drug, but maybe this really wasn't the moment. No, it was okay: the mask came back to life and he was getting the *you, beyond belief* grin that he considered his personal property.

'Yeah,' said Sage. 'Yes, I would.'

'Not now, but if we are ever through this. Next time there's a good time.'

'Done.'

'Good. You were saying—?'

'Was I?' Sage shook his head. 'I've forgotten. I was probably going to say, that's enough about Mary and Marlon. I just wanted to tell you—'

'Yeah.'

'C'mon. I came up here to stop you from moping. Let's go find some company.'

Sage had been living, in so far as he needed a place to sleep, at the Heads' studio in Battersea. That weekend he took Fiorinda and Ax to his cottage in Cornwall, a retreat that even the bând rarely visited. It was on the north coast, in about twelve acres, halfway up a hill on an execrable washed-out track. The Atlantic was on the other side of the hill; a tumultuous small river ran through the land; there was a tiny village two miles away. He had done almost nothing to the cottage since he bought it, except to get decent crystal cable laid, set up the parlour as a studio (where he'd written most of the *Arbeit Macht Frei* and *Stonefish* immersions: place should be hideously haunted); and move a big, low bed into the living room. He slept down there, couldn't be fucked, drunk or sober, to negotiate the narrow, crooked, low-beamed staircase at night. The place was otherwise a miracle of inconvenience, especially for someone with Sage's hands. Most of the domestic appliances were left over from when it had been a decrepit holiday let.

The weather was terrible. Sage and Ax did old jigsaws, Ax having discovered a stack of them in a cupboard. Fiorinda read the children's classics she found in a bookcase upstairs. At twilight, when the rain eased off, they walked to the pub: down the track, the river rushing in spate over its granite boulders beside them, hazel catkins beginning to shake under the bare oak branches; primroses shining like milky stars in the high banks along the road.

On the night they *didn't* get astonishingly drunk at what was known (though who was locked out was unclear: it wasn't the local police) as a lock-in at The Powdermill, Fiorinda sat dreaming by the hearth. Ax and Sage had both fallen asleep, on the sofa and on the bed. There was no sound but the whisper of the flames.

Sage's property was called The Magic Place. The name was on a stone marker at the turn-off, in Cornish. He'd shown it to her when they arrived. Nothing to do with Sage, it had always been called that. It wasn't the cottage that was supposed to be magic, but a stone, he thought. Or a tree, or a pool in the river.

She had asked him, do you know which word is which?

Don't get smart with me, brat. Certainly I do. That one's magic, that one is place.

How do you say it?

I've forgotten. Have to ask George.

They'd been alone because Ax, who had driven them down in his precious classic Volvo coupé, had kicked up a big fuss when he saw the track. He was walking up the hill, fuming, to make sure it didn't get any worse. *Fucking perverse, why do I have to put up with this—?*

I'm glad you're here, Sage had said, the mask doing *enigmatic smile*. Always meant to bring you here.

I'm here, she thought, reaching out to the fire. My friend, my brother, I'm here. A handful of flame lay quivering in her palm, and she had that Escher feeling, the two planes sliding into one. She looked round and found Sage, unmasked by sleep, blue eyes wide open. 'So you can still do that,' he said.

'Please don't tell anyone,' said Fiorinda. 'Not *anyone*.'

'I won't.' He turned over and, as far as she knew, slept again at once.

Sayyid Muhammad Zayid had come to London and taken a suite at the Savoy (never backward with the panoply, Muhammad). He did not try to influence Ax on the question of Pigsty and the death penalty. Perhaps he even agreed that the perpetrator of such crimes, if found guilty, should live out his guilty life. But he'd come down because he was sure Ax would be the next President, and what was on his mind was *shari'ah*. They had discussions – the Islamic entourage in attendance, Ax alone – which were good and friendly, in which neither of them shifted their position in the slightest. One day Ax arrived at the suite and found to his horror that Fiorinda was there, alone with the Sayyid and his brothers-in-law. Fiorinda, straight-backed on the hotel sofa, hands in her lap like a princess in a fairytale, wearing a grey voile shift over glistening cream satin, her hair burning through a grey cobweb scarf. When Ax came in she smiled at him, made her excuses, took her coat and left.

'So that is your wife,' said Sayyid Muhammad.

'Ah—'

'She's a charming young woman, intelligent too. You did well there, lad.'

'Muhammad, could you do me a really big favour? Could you . . . not use that term, when Fiorinda is around.'

'She seems like your wife to me. I think I must call her your wife.'

'Big favour. Please.'

Sayyid Muhammad smiled at the young man's instant, visible anxiety. 'You *are* under that little lady's thumb: well, it's natural for a while. But you be careful. You know, the difference between Islam and Christian, on the matter of women – and it's a real difference, though I've never argued with you on the civil rights issue, I'm all for that kind of equality – comes down to the danger of idolatry. We recognise it, we guard against it, the Christians don't. We're so weak, where they are concerned, every man is the same. We would put them next to God, and that is not allowed.'

'How can you talk about the people of God,' said Ax, 'and say *we*, when you're leaving out half of them? What is Fiorinda then, a djinn?'

She is a fine lass, thought Sayyid Muhammad. She dresses extravagantly, but a sight more modestly than most Christian girls: and she has something very strange in the back of her eyes. 'There are such beings, in some sense. This is a matter of revelation.'

Ax had been going into djinn, and the whole ingenious project of making modern science line up with the magical and supernatural hierarchies of the Qur'anic cosmos. It was interesting stuff.

'Yeah, right. As long as we stick to *in some sense*, and it means an Islamicised term for autonomic software agents, or mysterious big number behaviour. I can go with that.'

'Well, mysticism is not for you. But government is, so let us return to that problem.'

Ax sometimes wished his prophet of choice had had the tact to get crucified and bow out of it, instead of sticking around to set up a religio-political state. He sat down, frowning.

'Muhammad, to me *Islam* means faith. It means accepting the will of God, and accepting that the task of the human community is *to become* the presence of God's mercy and compassion on earth. You'll never convince me it has anything to do with headscarves. Or how much you have to nick before you get your hand chopped off. I don't know if I'll ever be in a position to influence the lawgivers, but if I was I'd be no use to you. You may as well forget it.'

'As long as we're talking,' said Sayyid Muhammad, imperturbably, 'I'm in with a chance.'

Times and times he had crossed London, from Paddington to Battersea, coming up from the cottage – yes, using public transport. Always, why not? I like to see life – without hearing a single English voice, sometimes without hearing a word of English spoken. No chance of that this evening. The Eurostar invasion rolled back, tunnels not functioning at all at the moment. No tourists. No oddly garbed munchkin Japanese girls, no vast middle-aged North American couples. Posters and video clips everywhere about the referendum. He joined the patient crowd on the Underground platform, thinking about the last six or seven years. On tour and gigging, plugged in and working at the cottage, working with the Heads in Battersea, plenty drugs to paper over the gaps . . . could have gone on forever. On the Circle Line train, he obstinately stayed by the doors propping up the carriage roof (*you* can move down, sunshine, you fit better); and played the game of desert island Londoners – the ones he liked the look of, the ones he'd have to feed to the sharks. There's a clay-coloured soulful, sexless face from the Levant. I'll have hir. There's a face from West Africa, young but traditionalist, scarified cheeks like a ripe fruit bursting. She's okay. One from the Horn, *very* superior profile, but he looks sulky. Sharkmeat. A black haired, pale-eyed, white-skinned Irish girl, chatting hard with her sparky hejabed girlfriend whose looks are from the Gulf somewhere (keep those two). Red braces type, possibly Norman French – standing out still after a thousand years, that hard T-junction nose and eyebrows, slab cheeks, I will keep him on trial: and they are all English. Ginger Scot in a cashmere overcoat, a senior suit of the first order. Don't usually see those on the Tube, maybe he's a devout Countercultural suit. Now there is a stunner. What went into that? Thai-Vietnamese-Irish-Nigerian? Wonder if she'd like to fuck Aoxomoxoa . . . And they're all English. Presumably, pragmatically, since they're still here.

Wonder what they make of me.

Wonder are they feeling merciful.

Change at Baker Street, and here we wait and wait. Green Park, and out into the pale, warm powdery twilight. Sometime during massacre night, I decided I was going to stay with this. Not sticking around to get vengeance on the Pig. No, no, no. Perish the thought. Simply because it would be a crime against the Ideology to walk away from something *so fucking strange*. But when is it going to end? Trouble ahead, trouble behind. When will the state of affairs formerly known as normal resume? Never, he began to suspect. Things are going to get stranger, much stranger. This isn't nearly over, it has only just begun.

The gates are open. The hippie guards were sitting outside one of the sentry boxes, deeply involved in a crap game. 'Hi, Sage.'

'Hi, slackers. Maybe we should invest in a flock of trained geese. Ax here yet?'

'Dunno, haven't seen him. Try the Fire Room.'

Instead he found Fiorinda, playing the piano alone in a dusty drawing room.

'What's that? Scarlatti?'

'Yeah.' There was a bottle of wine on the grand piano. He topped up the glass beside it and took bottle and glass off to a row of assorted armchairs. Something Insanitude must have been going on here, but the room had an air of weary dereliction.

'Hey, don't take my wine . . . Bring it back here.'

So he came back and leant there watching as the serene music spilled out from her hands. 'You managed to find your way to the polling station?'

'I did. Very sweet and old-fashioned, the whole thing. I had no idea.'

'Sage, tell me this stupid referendum is going to work out.'

'This stupid referendum is going to work out.'

'Are you just saying that because I asked you to?'

'*Aargh.* Don't do that, Fee. It pisses me off. Have you been out much today? I've come across London, looking at people. I think they've voted for him.'

She shrugged. 'Then I'm glad. Oh well, why not. The hero of the hour, with a battle-hardened army at his back, having embraced the religion of the coming age . . . asks the people to elect him king. Sure, of course. Since we are heading for the dark ages anyway. It's not what I would call progress in a positive direction.'

'You been talking like that to Ax?'

'No. But I've been thinking it. This is not my world. No matter what the result is, my world ended on massacre night. Look what happens to me. You and Ax go off to war, I stay behind to look after Ax's baby project, and manage the household. Until you get back, and I'm required as a pet again.'

'Don't be so snivelling ridiculous.'

'Okay, what if I had wanted to come with you, join in that game?'

'Fuck, *no!*'

She smiled nastily. 'Right. Not that I remotely want to go off and kill people, but I know exactly how you think on that sort of question. You, and Ax, and all the caring menfolk of the Counterculture. I can see my future. I'm not built to play Red Sonja, so I have to be the lickle princess. There aren't any parts for me as a human being in this movie.'

'Better than being one of the lickle serving wenches. You *are* in a brilliant mood this evening.'

'Ax is worse. He's pretending he doesn't give a shit, but the pretending is painful to be near. He's not here, by the way. He's off somewhere playing with the band.'

'Okay, c'mon. Leave that. Let's go find Roxane. Nothing s/he likes better than a good rousing election night. S/he'll cheer you up.'

For six weeks Ax had been working the crowd. Roxane and Dilip had been his best allies, Chip and Verlaine surprisingly reliable filler. They'd been careful not to do too much, they hoped they'd done enough. The Counterculture was believed to be split between those who would vote for Ax and those (the majority) who would not vote at all. The rest of the country . . . well, no matter what they thought about judicial murder, after they'd heard the arguments, they'd vote for the hero of the Tour and of the Islamic Campaign; and for keeping the CCM in a safe pair of hands. Unless of course they didn't. Could go either way.

An overwrought party mood developed in the Insanitude. In the smaller venues there were drumming programmes and other semi-magical rituals going on. Tv, radio and webcast people wandered around, licensed but confused. Dance music started up early in the club venue in the state apartments. On the fly-eye wall screen in the Office, and on big and little tvs set up here and there, the coverage rolled into action. Political figures from the neighbour states offered their comments. Hardline Counterculturals of the campgrounds came on camera to explain that Ax was selling his soul to the squares with this referendum; and tv was just a shite-spreader for the evil empire, the socio-industrial complex; and hello Mum. As the evening progressed, channel-hopping converged on mTm (many-To-many, the nearest the world came to a global Countercultural telecoms company); and the trashy-intellectual English terrestrial channel 7 (popularly known as CultTV). CultTV had gone straight for the jugular. They were treating this as a general election night with all the trimmings: the talking heads, the coloured maps, the swingometer, the dancing pie charts, the video-booth clips and e-mail from *soi-disant* ordinary citizens; the big gig in Birmingham, where Snake Eyes were headlined.

'It'll be close,' said Rox, uneasily. 'There's been a massive turnout. That could be good: but it could be bad. They've never been asked to vote on this issue before. And they *will* vote on the issue, just because we don't expect them to. It's always the way.'

Ax finally came in around one a.m., looking calm and distant. The Chosen had been playing the campground at Taplow (former neolithic theme park), in Buckinghamshire. He sat with Rox, Fiorinda and Sage, and talked a little with a nice polite tv woman. Chip and Verlaine were insufferably chirpy. The fly-eye was set to default to Channel 7 and the results, whenever there wasn't anything more interesting to be found. Its cells began to switch to the map of England, until the whole wall was maps of England, filling with cute little guitars.

By two-thirty they knew it wasn't going to be close at all. Ax had a landslide.

'Looks like we're on,' he said to Fiorinda, wrecked by unacknowledged tension, but grinning with relief. He hugged her for the tv people, and everybody cheered.

Fiorinda and Dilip did another club night, in the immersion box together: Dilip pumping up the springtime, breeding lilacs, sending the sap shooting, breaking open the seedcase bodies of the dancers with a near-lethal dose of phototropism . . . 'Ah, Islam, Islam,' he sighed. 'The English are fools for it, always were, the disastrous spoor of this infatuation is all over the former Empire. Did I say disastrous? Shame on me. But why did they not prefer Hinduism? Because we poor Babus, with our taste for fussy office work and teatimes, we are are are too confused, too cheerful, too bumbling, too fuzzy, too like the English, in a word. So are you smashed enough to tell me truthful nonsense, what do you think of Ax now, Fiorinda?'

'You want to know what I think. What I really, really think?'

'Go on, go on, tell me tell me tell me—'

'I think he's the Lord's anointed. I think he has the mandate of heaven. I think he is rightwise king born over all England. But still—'

'But still you are the cat who walks by herself, green-eyed Fiorinda—'

'But still nothing's changed.'

Pigsty would stay in Lloyd Park Remand Centre until his trial came up. On one of her visits Fiorinda found out that Lola Burnet was coming down from her mother's in Norfolk for a conjugal weekend. For some reason this gave her a bad feeling. Well, she had her reasons: but this particular *for some reason* was the fact that Lola had given the Insanitude as her contact address. Who is she staying with? she wondered. Why didn't I know? Fereshteh and Allie were both living at the San again, while looking for a London flat together. Perhaps her friends thought loopy Fiorinda was not safe with Lola. Would grow fangs and try to tear the woman apart if they should meet. Not far wrong. But she had decided to keep silent about *what she knew* – without proof, without any evidence. Her part was over, leave it to the professionals. She could not explain her antipathy, so she said nothing to anyone.

One April dusk Sage, coming up to the Insanitude from Battersea, met Chip and Verlaine and Rox just leaving. They were going to the Easter Vigil at St Martin's in the Fields, and tried to convince him to join them. The new fire, the blessing of the water and the holy oils, the chanting and the candles, it was so great, so primitive, like the mysteries of Eleusis, insisted Chip. You have come to weep for Adonis, it's such a turn-on, the whole thing. When the priest goes, like, *lumen Christi*, or even in English: I just die!

'Sorry,' he says, the skull looking between bemused and distaste. 'Got to meet Ax and do some tv. Er, thanks.'

Fereshteh went to Lloyd Park with Lola that evening. The staff treated them respectfully. They searched Lola and her weekend case. They did not search the veiled Islamic woman, Ax's close associate, with any officious thoroughness. In the rooms where Lola would spend the night with her husband the two women embraced in tears, and parted in silence.

At the Lambeth Road house, some of the Few and friends had gathered to eat together; and stayed together to watch Ax and Sage being dead genial and relaxed on a late night rock programme, getting teased about cronyism as they both insisted, laughing their socks off, that Snake Eyes was their best thing, reaching new heights, best sound this year—

Well okay, says the show's presenter. Let's hear some of this fabulous PoMo sound—

Newsflash—

The Few and friends didn't like newsflashes. They all sat up. At least nothing horrible can have happened to Ax or Sage; or Rob or the power-babes. What does that leave? A wide field. It is Pigsty. He is dead. His wife has smuggled a plastic shooter into the conjugal flat, someone having disabled the surveillance in there for her; or previously taught her how. She shot him dead and then shot herself. Lola is still alive, but seriously injured. It's just happened, all this, but a group called the Daughters of Islam has claimed responsibility for Lola's act—

Fiorinda, electrified, turned on Allie Marlowe before the newswoman had finished her autocue. 'I'm going out there. Will you come with me?'

'What do you want to go there for? What can you do?'

'Sounds like Lola's dying. I want her to tell me something, if she can, before she goes—'

Lola Burnet was in the prison hospital operating theatre when they reached Lloyd Park; her situation had been too desperate for her to be moved anywhere else. Fiorinda and Allie had been there for an hour, waiting for news, when Fereshteh appeared. With her were two other women in fiercely modest paramilitary uniform: heavy scarves, long brown tunics over trousers, Sam Browne belts, epaulettes, all that. Fereshteh was dressed the same. She was looking shocked and distraught; but proud of herself too, her secret revealed at last, big eyes glowing, patches of bold scarlet in her honey cheeks—

Fiorinda jumped to her feet. 'How did she convince you to do this, Feresh?'

'She asked for help,' said Fereshteh simply. 'We helped her. I'm not ashamed of that, I'm just sorry, terribly sorry it went wrong. I didn't know she would turn the gun on herself!'

'What did you *think* would happen? You thought she'd live happily ever after?'

'He had to die!' cried Fereshteh. 'She had a right. We had a right. *Ax wanted this*. He couldn't say so, but *we know he did*. You're the one who should be ashamed, not me. The way you protected that monster—'

'Ax did not want this. You fool, you idiot. She should have been in here herself!'

'We know what she did, when she was helpless and terrified of him—'

The Daughters of Islam stood solemnly, looking on.

'My God,' said Fiorinda. 'I don't know what the police will do to you, but I will not forgive you for your part in this. Ever. You better stay out of my way—'

'You never liked me. To you any woman is just competition. You only like *men*, don't you, Fiorinda. Any kind of man, any dominant male with a big dick. Maybe Ax should ask himself how close you used to get to the President, while he was away all that time—'

Sage had arrived with Ax, who had been waylaid by the prison governor. He'd come into the hospital visitors' waiting room at the start of this verbal cat-fight, and stopped at the door. At this point he was forced to wade in, grab Fiorinda and move her out.

She didn't struggle, she knew she'd be a fool to struggle, there was absolutely nothing she could do. But he didn't think it was safe to let go until they'd run the gauntlet of the prison staff and were outdoors. 'If you want to hit someone, hit me.'

'No,' she said. She walked away from him and sat on the low wall that surrounded the car park and the bus stand. In the distance, partly blocked by buildings, the perimeter fence, with its brilliant lights and rolls of razor wire, stood up against the hollow, empty night.

'A child murderer taken out of the equation and rendered harmless,' she said, distinctly, 'is worth something, even in this fucked-up disaster movie. It means the damage that was done to Pigsty stops here. That thread is broken, at least, of all the thousands, the thousands. A child murderer murdered is worse than meaningless. It says the system just goes on.'

'Most people are not as rational as you, Fee. Most people will take the solution that looks like a solution, without thinking it through the generations first, see if it checks out.'

'Lola was getting hold of the children for him. It had to be her, who else? She was doing it to keep her precious family life intact, she thought it was a price worth paying. Oh well, what does it matter. I don't care . . . Ah, poor Feresh, she's right, I never reckoned her. I didn't look any further than the veil, I counted her out. My fault. I'm still never going to forgive her. What a joke, eh? Fereshteh and the Daughters of Islam. Paul Javert let a terrorist slip through his vetting, and we never spotted her either.'

'Looks like it. Made fools of us all.'

'You know, I start to wonder about Ax's buddy Muhammad, and this—'

He shook his head. Not meaning no, she understood: meaning *it's not worth it.* You can investigate, dig deep, uncover the shocking truth. Where does it get you? Some place like this prison car park tonight. Fucking nowhere.

Allie came out of the hospital wing, Ax behind her. They walked up and stood with Sage.

'Well, it's over now,' said Allie.

'What? Is she dead?'

'Yeah,' said Ax. 'Died about ten minutes ago.'

So here we are, thought Fiorinda. So this is where we are at. Doomed to play Stone Age royalty to forty million post-civilised people, while our world falls apart; and we have failed at the first test. Fereshteh and Mrs Leisurewear have wiped the floor with us. Oh, poor Ax. But they were looking at her with such pity and anxiety she couldn't stand it. As if *she* was the one with the problem.

'I am not a piece of broken china!' she yelled. Jumped up and stormed away madly. Ax came after her, caught her and held her. The two of them walked slowly back, his arm around her, her face very pale but tearless, and calm again. The resilience of this girl is amazing.

'What are we going to do now?' asked Fiorinda, after a long silence. 'Ax said Pigsty had to live, and he is dead.'

'Bury it,' said Allie. 'Do something to distract them. Look as if we don't care and hope the Daughters of Islam story dies of not being fun. It's all we can do.'

Yeah, bury it. Accept the defeat along with the victory. And go on.

SIX

Sweetbriar

It takes longer to organise a big splashy day-to-night rock concert than it does to pass an Act of Parliament; but not that much longer, if you have everything in place. Post-Deconstruction Tour and general crisis conditions had to be accommodated, but Allie's team was used to that. A flattering number of VIPs from the former nations of the UK managed to accept short-notice invitations. Public transport to the Rivermead site was organised like the WWII Blitz evacuation. Reading town agreed to accept a complete black-out, except for the hospitals and emergency services. The Heads had decided to take Sage's appointment as kapell-meister seriously, so they wrote the programme, mixing the bands with glee (and they *could have fucking waited* for a less fraught occasion to start developing this new game, but it worked out).

It was the fourth of May, hot and humid under low skies. The day-trippers started pouring in at dawn. Sanitation hell descended once more on the peaceful, post-futuristic grunge of the staybehinds. Hippies, actual hardline hippies, were heard talking about getting a Railtrack spur – or, hey, why not a superconducting levitation monorail? – to the site gates. There were twisters in Staffordshire, homewrecker floods in East Anglia, and the anti-nucleaires in the Rhône Valley might be bringing European Civilisation to a sudden close this afternoon; but that last wasn't a big topic of conversation, Green Apocalypse Boredom having set in many moons ago.

It was strange to be back for the opening of the third Dissolution Summer: to see the rebuilt Blue Lagoon, the Zen Self dome, the Mood Indigo tent where the shit-fest had been held, the dishevelled permanence that had overtaken all the ephemera of their history. The Chosen were on Red Stage early in the afternoon, which inconvenienced the tv schedule people, but too bad. The crowd seemed well pleased (though they howled and begged for 'Jerusalem', and didn't get it); and for once the frontman's girlfriend managed to be there. At five the Heads were on Yellow Stage, otherwise known as Scary Stage because of its accident record; however, nothing went wrong. Other stages, other acts, poets and fire-eaters, dance troupes, storytellers and tumblers, non-Few Name Bands: but these were the images of that sweltering May holiday. Aoxomoxoa on the big screens, stalking around with a hand-held mic, having given up his acrobatics and left the vision boards to Cack Stannen, singing or chanting the lyrics of 'Kythera', previously unintelligible to all but those trainspotters with the time and equipment to take a Heads track apart bit by bit.

> *Venus—*
> Lo in the western sky
> Can you see the green light
> That means go—

Fireballs, interstellar gases, balls of glowing plasma shooting through the crowd, Sage in black and white optical print trousers that took on pinwheels of whirling rainbow and shards of piercing gold from Cack's lasers, sweating so hard he appeared to be melting; the sun a small pale burning blob through the overcast, like the star of a different planet—

> Can you see
> the colours
> of the stars?

And Ax Preston, in subfusc brown jeans and a faded red Tour singlet (with the *It's the Ecology, Stupid,* message on the back) – holding this immense crowd of people, all of them longing to wave their arms and sing anthems, in silence, as he plays (fine-boned profile detached, intent; sleek dark hair braided and tied in narrow black ribbon) as if there's nobody out there but God.

At sunset Fiorinda was in Allie's new van in the backstage parking, hiding from the suitish, grown-up things that Ax was having to do. Allie had decided, now that Fereshteh was off the scene, that she didn't need a place in London: what she needed was to be mobile. No fixed abode Allie . . . The back of the van already felt like her Brighton flat, where Fiorinda had dossed a couple of times in the past: a rooted place, a lovely womanly bookworm's study; a little cloying. But the green-aircon worked. Anne-Marie Wing was there too, with four of her rugrats. AM and Allie were talking about the Volunteer Initiative, Anne-Marie interested to know the ropes. 'You park yourself on a crusties' lot? And move in with the message?'

'You don't often get as far as the message. The Countercyulturals who can handle volunteer work are the tip of the iceberg. Sometimes I've spent, oh, *hours*, explaining something like how to catch a bus. The world's become a very mysterious place to a lot of people out there—'

Ax's New Deal had been meant to keep the in-your-face eco-warriors from breaking the place up. Now they were running into the submerged mass of hopeless cases, and no one knew what to do. Where did their responsibilities end?

Is that a live metaphor or a dead one? wondered Fiorinda. Hull down in the killing cold water outside the citizen-ship, this mountain of rotten ice, the twisted and broken and bent-out-of-shape unculture. What a dangerous mess. She wished Anne-Marie would lay off. But that was what it was like today. Other bands, outsiders, guests, kept coming up all bright-eyed, worse than the media people, asking: *what's it all about?* What IS this thing, where are you heading?

We have no idea. Go ask the Ax, he's the one who knows everything.

Jet the baby was fastened on his mother's tit, Ruby the boy toddler watching the process with intent, professional interest. Eight-year-old Silver lifted out the books from Allie's cardboard boxes, with the air of a museum curator examining curious relics, and handed them to her little sister Pearl, who was using them as building blocks. Anne-Marie's oldest kid was thirteen, already fucking, already flown . . . Fiorinda watched the children, listening to backstage PA messages whispered in her ear. Allegedly there were half a million people packed into Reading arena. Maybe fifteen millions, hey, who's counting, why not let's say twenty! outdoors, countrywide, watching the show in front of big screens on all the sites with live transmission: the Countercyultural Very Large Array.

There can't be half a million people in Reading arena, she thought. That isn't *possible*.

'I'm going to open some wine,' said Allie. 'I'm sick of being sober. Sun's over the yard arm, I think I'm off duty. White or red, Fio?'

'Nothing for me. Not 'til after the show.'

'*God*,' said Allie, greatly impressed. 'Are you feeling all right?'

'Oh yeah, no problem.'

If the day belonged to Ax and Sage, it was Fiorinda's night. When she finally appeared, having been dead elusive for hours, she was dressed for the stage in a silver and white lace cowgirl dress and red boots, her hair a burnished storm. Sometimes Fiorinda was averagely pretty, sometimes beautiful, sometimes just a sulky, skinny white girl with a stubborn jaw. Tonight her fickle redhead's good looks had come out to play: she looked absolutely wonderful and she knew it. The New Blue Lagoon was packed, government suits and other VIPs taking up too much space in their raked seats, walls reefed high to allow the crowd to spill out across the arena; the mosh pit one deliquescent, amoebic mass, yelling in undamped delight when Fiorinda walked on, picked up her guitar from the piano stool and waited, grinning, for DARK to get themselves settled.

Charm Dudley, DARK's frontwoman, had decided she couldn't make it, which was, on the whole, a good thing. Friction between Charm and her space-time-devouring, spinning black hole of a vocalist had been a major problem when they were last together, in Dissolution year. And away they go, Fiorinda leaping into the attack, from that calm little grin to *instantly* amazing—

On the side of the stage, the Fiorinda Appreciation Society had gathered: crew and stars, by no means all of them male, all of them staring like rabbits caught in the headlights.

'How's that for Sugar Magnolia, Sage—?' murmured Dilip.

Sage, standing beside him, shrugs, 'All right I suppose. If you like that kind of thing—'

Skull gives Dilip a sidelong glance, a little crooked twinkle of acknowledgement, and they both resume concentrating on the rock and roll brat: who has calmed down a little and is singing that *Jesus doesn't want her for a sunbeam*. Doing it the Vaselines way, but louder.

DARK had not managed to get to Reading until the day of the concert. But that was okay, rehearsal had never been the band's forte. It only led to trouble. They arrived back at the Leisure Centre after their brilliant performance, sweating like pigs, grinning fit to split their faces, accepting with no false modesty congratulations from the non-Few famous. In the shared dressing room, which they now had to themselves, they decided they couldn't be fucked with showers. They jived around stripping off sweat-soaked clothing, sousing each other with cold water from the sink, gabbing happily about the terrible mistakes they'd made in various songs, the impressive company they were keeping, the thirst they had on them: sniffing up powder, pouring cooling draughts of alcohol down their throats. Fil Slattery raised the bottle on which she had been swigging.

'Absent friends—'

'Absent friends!' they yelled in chorus.

'Go on,' said Tom Okopie to Fiorinda, hopefully. 'Say it. You actually miss her.'

Cafren groaned, and cuffed her boyfriend gently around the head. 'Eee, Tom, trust you—'

'I miss Charm's guitar,' said Fiorinda, grinning hard. 'On stage. I fucking *do not* miss Charm. Absent is the way I like her. Sorry, folks.'

It was Charm Dudley who'd formed the band, with her friends Cafren Free and Tom Okopie; and enlisted Fil Slattery and Gauri Mostel on drums and keyboards. A year of thwarted-ambition hell, shit venues and flashes of genius later, they'd demoted Gauri from lead vocals and advertised. That was how Fiorinda had come to join them. Cue a different kind of hell, because Fiorinda and DARK were soulmates, utterly right for each other, but the mix was volatile. The kid was in a hurry, she was even more ambitious than Charm, and the effect of Charm Dudley and Fiorinda jockeying for control had quickly become awful.

Just awful.

The happy faces fell. They all looked at Fiorinda, and she looked back, the five of them reality-checked, deflated.

She had wanted DARK *so badly* in Dissolution Summer, when they had last played together: wanted DARK and been such a little horror she didn't see *why the fuck* she could not have . . . The sad thing was that she still wanted DARK, just as badly: and they wanted her too. But she was grown-up now, so she knew they weren't going to break with Charm. Charm and Fiorinda could not work together. Situation hopeless. Fiorinda sighed, and started hunting around for a towel to rub the sweat out of her hair. She suddenly didn't want to do the dressing room scene any more. It was like looking through a window at the life she'd lost (intense, painful, absorbing scenes of long ago); seeing it all going on without her.

'Hey, whose are the flowers?'

'Oh, they were for you,' said Cafren. 'Sorry, forgot—'

'Who the fuck sends me flowers,' muttered Fiorinda. She *did not like that sort of thing*, and it couldn't be Ax. He knew he'd git his head in his hands, yecch. She tore off the florist's paper, harbouring a vague wild idea that Charm might have Interflora'd her a bunch of pink roses, as an insult. There was no card or note. The roses had a sweet scent. No, not these roses, some other pink roses, long ago, and it was the leaves that were scented . . . Sweetbriar, what her father used to call her. Oh. Oh no.

something like a bright, silent explosion in her brain.

She had walked into one of those waking nightmares, the weird kind of migraine-without-the-headache she suffered occasionally, hadn't had one for ages, she'd forgotten how bad—

She put the flowers down, so clumsily they fell onto the floor. She felt very sick. Oh. This isn't a weird migraine, this is me feeling *very sick*. She felt so dreadful she thought she should yell out something like *oh shit, I've been poisoned*: but before she could get that together something started happening, an experience she couldn't stop, couldn't escape, couldn't deny—

Ah God, what is this? What is going on, does it show, I DARE NOT look in a mirror.

'Are you okay, Fio?' said Gauri, putting an arm around her.

'Yeah,' said Fiorinda, drawling, shrugging, hearing her own voice from a long way off, wondering how she'd got to be sitting in this chair; little snip in time. 'Oh, I'm *fine*.'

She managed to stay *fine* until they left, which wasn't long. Thank God for the awkwardness of the Charm issue, which made them probably glad to get away—

Tom thought Fiorinda was not okay. But there was previous between him and Fio that made it difficult for him to pay her special attention. And the red-headed kid had changed so much. Her beauty and authority daunted him, daunted all of them. If Fiorinda wanted you to go, she didn't need to say the word. You were gone.

After DARK the show was over. The day-trippers and VIPs were efficiently channelled off, and the bands came out and danced with the staybehinds. Cooling breezes flowed through the Blue Lagoon, where Olwen Devi stamped and whirled to highly evolved bangra, long ago classical training being put to use: thinking of Ax Preston and the future of all this (thinking about *the energy audit of stage lighting*, in fact). Zen Selfers, notable campers, faces and costumes named and namelessly familiar surrounded her – particularly the lean young giant in the skull mask, that sweet-natured boy, who seemed almost to be dancing *with* her. She started to feel a little confused about his motives. This would never do: she left the floor and made her way to the bar. But as she waited in the press of bodies, Sage was there again.

'Hi, Olwen. You got that boyfriend of yours staying tonight?'

'Ellis? Yes. He was tired, he's back at the trailer.'

'Shame.'

Olwen knew the Heads well. They were some of her best converts: genuinely, intelligently fascinated by the project. Their boss (as the band called him) was funny and crude and charming: an A student, a delight. But what was this? The skull's alert, inviting grin went on giving her the message, while she stared in disbelief.

'Get away with you, you joker. I am old enough to be your grandma.'

'If my gran could dance like what you can,' he said gallantly, grinning more sweetly than ever, 'I would want to fuck her too.'

The bar staff and the people by did not seem to be hearing this. She hoped not!

'Sage, I am afraid you are smashed out of your young brain.'

'I certainly am.' But there he stayed, waiting, exactly as if he had asked a reasonable question that deserved a civil answer.

'He's not my boyfriend,' said Olwen. 'He's my husband. He's a professor at Cardiff, he'll be going back tomorrow. We've been married nearly thirty years, but we have always spent a lot of time apart. It suits us.'

The mask came off. Sage beamed at her, pupils so dilated his eyes looked black instead of blue. He nodded, the skull snapped back: he turned and plunged into the crowd behind them, vanishing like a seal among the waves of his natural element.

'Hi rockstar.'

'Hi, other rockstar. You look very . . . *interested*. What have you been up to?'

'Not gonna tell you. Something I have had in mind for a while. Where's Fiorinda?'

'I don't know. I was wondering that myself. Let's go find her.'

No Fiorinda, anywhere. They found Tom Okopie and Cafren Free. Cafren thought Fiorinda might be in the Leisure Centre, where DARK had had a dressing room, and there had been a star-studded scene after the show. So they set off on this expedition, an adventure, many music-biz friends and enemies to avoid.

'Your parents gone?'

'Thank God. I really find my dad *fucking unendurable*, around things like this.'

'I like my parents,' said Sage, magnanimously, 'not both in the same room because that can turn ugly, but separately they are good. But I like going to visit them in their lives. I would very much appreciate if they would *stay out* of mine.'

'Yeah. If we're going this far, you could change those trousers. They are getting me down.'

The white singlet was fresh. The trousers were the eye-hurting Bridget Riley rip-offs that Sage had been wearing on stage.

'No. I like 'em.'

'Ah well.'

The Leisure Centre was empty. They strode along an endless-seeming corridor, feeling equal to anything: never got this whammed in Yorkshire but what if we had, we'd still have been useful . . . By some dimensional trick they missed (possibly he'd come out of a door; there were doors) Chip Desmond was heading towards them. They advanced on him with friendly intent. But the kid unaccountably veered away and scuttled off.

'What's wrong with him?'

'Looked as if he thought we were going to *eat* him. What's in that stuff you gave me?'

'Nothing special. Bit of MDMA, bit of acid, touch of toad venom. Coming up on you now, is it, Teflon-head?'

'Yeah. My God, if anyone had told me two years ago I would be taking unidentified candy from Aoxomoxoa . . . I must be outa my mind.'

The skull grinned at him beatifically. 'You soon will be.'

They came through the door of the dressing room together, laughing, expecting to find it empty; there was obviously nothing going on around here. But Fiorinda was there, wearing the cowgirl dress. She was standing in the middle of the floor, fists pressed to her mouth. She didn't move. She was staring right at them, but didn't seem to see them.

'Fio?' said Ax.

No response. He went up, put his hands on her shoulders—

'*Fiorinda?* What is it? Sweetheart, what's wrong?'

Sage had stayed at the door. As soon as he saw her move, as soon as she came out of that frozen rigidity, he turned to leave, sure he had no place here—

'*Sage,*' she wailed. '*No!* Please! Don't leave me! *Please!*'

He shut the door, came swiftly over. 'Okay, I'm here. I will not leave you.'

They sat her down. Her eyes were black, her pulse thready and racing, her skin as cold and clammy as if she was bleeding inside. Her hands were covered in small red scratches. They looked at each other, the Heads' patent cocktail dropping out of them like something fallen down a lift shaft, leaving them – for the moment – stone cold sober.

'Fio, what have you taken? Do you remember?'

'*Nothing.*' She was clinging to both of them, clutching Sage's ruined right hand, hanging onto Ax's shoulder. 'I didn't want to be smashed on

174

stage in case I fucked up in front of all those Prime Ministers and things, let you down. Not even a glass of wine.' Her breath was coming in gasps, small breasts heaving under the sweat-soaked lace. 'We came back here and there were some pink roses, for me: and *I didn't like that.* But I managed to . . . be okay. I was fine, really. Then the others went off and left me. They can't be too chummy. They think Charm would smell me on their breath and kill them. And then. What time is it? I don't know how long I've been here. Is it the same night?'

'What's wrong with pink roses?' asked Sage.

'*I hate pink, and I hate roses.*' She let go of Sage's hand, grabbed Ax harder, burying her face in his neck. 'I think my father sent them.'

Ax wrapped his arms around her, soothing her like a baby, *sssh, ssh, don't be frightened, I'm here.* Sage followed a trail of bruised petals to a sink. The remains of a bouquet lay there, torn to tatters. He turned over the fragments, flowers and leaves and stems: natural roses with real old fashioned thorns, dark thorns the colour of old blood, Fiorinda's scratches explained—

'Who delivered these?'

'I don't know. They were here, and Caf said they were for me. I have no idea.'

'Was there a card, a message?'

'No. No one told me they were from him. I KNOW BECAUSE I KNOW!'

'Leave it, Sage. The flowers don't matter. I think we have to get the paramedics. She's in shock, she's so cold, this isn't safe.'

'*No!*' Fiorinda jumped up, pushing him away. 'No! I'll be okay. No doctors no nurses no injections. *Please,* no whitecoats not even hippie whitecoats. I just want to get away from here. Please, please Ax. I don't want anyone to know, if people see me like this they'll think I'm no good, they'll think I'm a pathetic trashy hysterical babystar—'

'All right, all right.' He put his arms round her again. 'Ssh, little cat. You won't have to see anybody. I'll take you straight back to London.'

But she stared at him in new horror, in what seemed wild fear *for him:* like, how could he suggest anything so insanely dangerous? 'No, oh no! Not *London!*'

'What about my van?' said Sage, quickly. 'How d'you feel about the van?'

'*Yes.* Sage's van. Let's go there.'

She was shivering hard. Ax passed her over to Sage and sought for something to combat that icy chill. He found a thick dark jacket. They put it on her, and a sailor cap from the same heap of DARK's belongings, pulled down over her eyes. Thus disguised, they tried to walk her to the door, but Fiorinda's knees buckled. She couldn't do it.

'I'm gonna get the van,' decided Sage. 'I can bring it round here.'

'You sure?'

'Better than making her face the public, there are far too many people around. Fiorinda, I'm going to the Meadow, fetch the van and bring it here. You're gonna stay with Ax. I will be gone a little while, you'll look and you won't see me, but I'll be back.'

Fiorinda huddled on the chair, knees to her chin, wrapped in the dark jacket. Ax knelt beside her, holding her hand. She didn't speak, she was now completely *out* – teeth bared and locked in rictus, dilated eyes unfocused, the tendons in her neck and hands visible and taut as over-strung wire, breath coming fast and shallow. He talked to her softly, but he didn't think she could hear him. Maybe it had to happen. She had been so tough for so long. Maybe it wasn't serious. But he was terrified. Something appallingly precious, appallingly fragile, was breaking in his hands; he was trying to hold it together but *there was no way* he could succeed. It was a very long time before the door opened and there was Sage again.

'We're on. Short corridor, emergency exit, van right on the other side of it . . . Fee, big effort now. You have to pass for normal, for a short walk. Up. On your feet.'

She stood up, miraculously. 'I can manage. What do I look like? Do I look strange?'

'You look very cute and brave,' said Ax, tugging the sailor cap down to shade her face. 'You look like you're being rescued from the sinking of the *Titanic*.'

'I'm sorry about this, Ax. I'm sorry, Sage. I am *really* sorry.'

'Sssh.' Ax kissed her, hugged her briefly. 'Let's go.'

The corridor was empty. Fiorinda managed it well, between her bodyguards. Through the emergency exit into the leisure centre car park, running the gauntlet of the crowd, to where Sage's van was waiting. Sage jumped into the cab, Ax lifted Fiorinda, passed her up; climbed after. Sage took the wheel, Ax took the babe, on his knees, holding her tight; and they were out of there, no problem, except for a minor near-miss incident at the exit—

—involving the rear end of a taxi that was taking on passengers.

'Fuck!' howled the driver. 'Who the fuck does he think he is, the crazy fuck!'

'That was Sage,' Verlaine told him. 'Cheer up. You can tell your friends you nearly had Aoxomoxoa in the back of your cab.'

'Oh, well—' said the taxi driver, mollified, 'Aoxomoxoa. Well, he's a crazy fuck.'

'We're back to normal then' boomed Roxane, indulgently smiling as s/he arranged hir silk-lined cloak around hir in the passenger seat; the boys together in the back. 'For a little while there, I thought we had a grown-up Sage batting for us. Now that *would* have been bizarre.'

'I saw them, a few minutes ago,' whispered Chip to Verlaine. '*Boy,* they looked hot . . . Trust me, tonight poor old Fiorinda is nowhere. She is not even going to get her socks off.'

'You want me to drive you to *Notting Hill*? Jesus. Don't you know we got a fuel crisis on? Awright, who am I to argue? It's your money.'

The skull turned to Fiorinda. 'There. The night is ours. What d'you want to do? Wanna drive out to the motorway bridge and chuck cans at the slaves of the evil empire? Or shall we go into town, go people-watching among the common folk?'

'You c-can't take the van into town, Sage. *You know what happened last time.*'

'How about visiting the Ancient Britons, see if they died out yet—?'

'What Ancient Britons?' asked Ax, understanding that *last time* must refer to some incident two summers ago. Fiorinda had escaped, back into the days of innocence. 'Tell me about them. Eyes forward Sage, it is customary, although I realise it may not make much odds.'

'It's the Sun Temple people,' said Fiorinda, between chattering teeth. 'If you were a camper, you'd know. God, I'm so cold. They dug some ground, in a field out along the Oxford road. They t-try to grow pure native food things, fat hen, purslane, beechmast—'

'*Beechmast?*'

'Oh yeah,' said the driver. 'Old Sun is in this for the long haul.'

'But they're dying of starvation, or they *would* be if they played fair. None of it grows.'

'Or if it does the sacred holy slugs eat it.'

'Like sacred cows in India. Can't be touched. Sage keeps ent-t-treating them to hear the voice of the Mother, and top themselves. They get really pissed off.'

'I can imagine.'

'Well, they are *hardline*,' explained Sage. They were in the arena. The word sounds empty, no such luck, it's a shapeless mediaeval village having a carnival night. He swerved around a trail of people who had not been planning to give way. Maybe they couldn't believe the van was real. 'And here is Gaia giving them the clear message, *you are dead meat*, but they just go down the Organic Grocery van and stock up. Can't understand it—'

'Oh, Sage, I am in such a bad way. Oh, doctor, doctor, what do you prescribe—'

'Cannabis and red wine.'

'Chocolate.'

'No chocolate. Chocolate is for Aztecs.'

'You bastard, you are so full of shit. Sugar. I need sugar.'

'Think I got some dried fruit.'

'*Fuck* you. Oranges and bananas.'

'They don't grow here, babe.'

'Yes they do, *they do*. I've s-s-seen them—'

'Not for fucking long, then. How many times do I have to tell you, ignorant brat, global warming makes this country colder, not warmer—'

'God, that is *so unfair* . . . Hey, Sage, watch out!'

'Whoops. Hmm. You know, I really shouldn't be driving—'

'M-my least favourite Sage remark. Up there with *I did not tempt fate, fate tempted me*. You should *never* be driving you are a *menace*. Oh, Sage, don't kill anyone—'

'I'm not going to kill anyone. No, no, no. Look, they scatter.' But the van was going round in circles like a vast, lost dodgem car. 'Ax, have you spotted an exit?'

'How did you get in?' said Ax.

'Can't remember.'

'Head for Blue Gate.'

'That's what I'm *trying* to do, man. Only, I have to confess, I can't strictly see what is presumably out there, in the real world. Not in any sort of clear order.'

'Stop thinking about it,' advised Ax. 'Do it on physical, leave your mind out of it.'

'Good idea.'

'Tell me when we're at the van,' said Fiorinda suddenly, urgently.

'She okay, Ax?'

She was not okay. They should not have shifted their attention for a moment, her whole body had gone rigid in his arms. He could feel the cold that gripped her spreading, her lungs filling with icy water. But, thank God, Sage had managed to find his way onto an access lane. The van was rumbling through a different darkness, little elfin glimmers in the endless humped rows of tents: at last a thump and a crash as he pulled up.

'What did you hit? Oh, Sage, you hit something.'

'Water butt . . . We're home. I hope I didn't run over the annexe.'

'Where's the van?'

'Get a grip, Fiorinda. We are *in* the van.'

'Oh. I didn't know that.'

As she went ahead of them into the back Sage caught Ax's forearm and clocked the blood-specked weals on the inner side, as if measuring an index of her distress.

'You've seen her like this before,' said Ax.

'Couple of times. Not so bad.'

They followed Fiorinda. Sage touched the wall and a pearly radiance spread. Things had been flying about during Sage's navigation of the asteroid belt: a lot of unsecured stuff was on the floor. 'Don't worry,' he said. 'Anything breakable left loose in here, I broke it long ago.'

Fiorinda went and sat on a couch, knees up, arms locked around them, head bowed.

'Sage, can we handle this?'

'Oh yeah. Administer first aid, talk her down, she'll be fine.'

Stepping through debris, he started opening lockers, until he found a bottle of red wine. 'Fuck, an actual cork. Who bought this? I hate 'em.' He handed it to Ax. 'You do it. Ought to be a corkscrew in one of those drawers but I don't know. This van disappears things as if it was trained by the Colombian paramilitary.' He pulled a white box the size of a picnic hamper from another locker and advanced on the patient.

'Fiorinda, gimme a thumb.'

She looked up. 'I'm all right. I said, I took nothing.'

'But humour me.'

She gave him her hand, and hid her face again. Sage stood looking down at her. He tapped the implant on his wrist. 'George . . . Hi, George. Don't want anyone near the van tonight. Yeah. Thanks; later.'

'I have the corkscrew,' said Ax.

'Excellent omen. I have the NDogs. We are equipped.' He took a slim lacquer box from the first aid hamper, rummaged and selected a handful of poppers.

'You want some straighten-out mix?' He slapped a popper against his throat. 'Mmmph.'

'What's in it?'

'Adrenalin, mostly.'

179

'Gimme,' said Ax; and then, 'No, wait.' He was not a hardened NDogs abuser, and those things could be hellish treacherous. Because Aoxomoxoa does it all the time doesn't mean anyone else should try. 'Better not.'

'You sure?'

'Me, Teflon-head. I'll stick with what I have, you court cardiac arrest.'

'Okay, if that's the way you want to play it.'

'If you collapse, will your wrist let me get hold of George—?'

'Course it will. It'll probably work for hours even if I'm dead . . . Ah, no. Hey, Ax, I didn't say that. Come back. Don't panic, nobody's going to die.'

'I am not panicking.'

'Are you *sure* you don't want me to straighten you out?'

'I'm sure. What about Olwen? Could you get hold of Olwen quickly?'

The skull looked amazed. 'Why Olwen? What made you think of her?'

'She's a doctor of medicine, isn't she? She has emergency stuff. And I think Fio likes her.'

'She was a neurologist, don't know what you'd call her now. Yeah, she's on the campground. I scream for help, I think she'd come.'

'Okay,' said Ax. 'We're sorted, let's go. Operation serve the princess.'

So this was Sage's van, this battered, pearly-lit, gaffer-taped moon module, more of a Russian than a NASA ambience. The focus – for quite a while, at the beginning of all this – of Ax's covert and jealous curiosity. He'd been wrong, he knew that now. Whatever mystery bound Snow White to the giant space cadet and his crew, it was not fuck. The compartment they were in was already, surely, bigger and squarer than was possible inside a trailer; other spaces beyond; it probably went on forever back there. The windows were jet black, sheets of obsidian. There was a kitchen table, counters with lockers over and under them, couches bolted against the walls further down. He righted a chair, sat on it and began to roll first aid spliffs, watching Sage with Fiorinda. He'd taken off her red boots, but she didn't want to take off the jacket; and indeed, it was cool in here. They were muttering about Aztecs and fat hen, the brass buttons on the sailor jacket, are those things meant to be eagles or anchors? *keep talking to me*, she insists, every few seconds.

When he went to join them she sipped a little wine from the glass he put to her lips (her hands were shaking too much for her to hold it) and started to say that she was better – then suddenly dropped to the floor, fists to her mouth, stifling tearless, gasping sobs.

Ax on his knees beside her, holding her, 'Fiorinda *what is it*—?'

'I can't tell you there's nothing to tell please don't be angry with me, I can't help this—'

'Why would we be *angry*? No one's angry with you—'

But she was gone, incoherent, struggling like a panicked bird. He had to let go, he couldn't stand it. He could see the bones through the flesh of her arms and shoulders, so white and brittle, he was sure he would really *break* something. Sage took over, held her securely, reached left-handed for one of the poppers he'd laid out, checked the code and slapped it against the pulse in her throat.

'Don't do that to me!' she screamed, fighting him.

'Gimme another.' He took the second popper, did it again. Almost instantly she relaxed: her head drooped, her eyelids closed.

'What's that?'

'Pro. It's a prostoglandin cocktail: safer than melatonin, it starts a cascade that puts you under, very gentle, unfortunately it may not last.'

'She hates modern drugs.'

'I know. But I don't keep sleeping pills. Let's get her to bed.'

Sage picked her up and carried her, Ax following, through the van to a room at the end; laid her on a bed. They covered her up and left her.

Back in the Heads' kitchen, the air seemed filled with after-images of her terrified fluttering. Sage checked the screen in the white hamper.

'Did she take anything?'

'Nothing to mention. But you're always testing for things you know about already . . . I was wondering about those roses.'

'*What?*'

'Stranger things have happened.' He closed the box, frowning, and self-administered another dose of straighten-up; shook his head at the stinging hit. 'How Muslim are you feeling? Got some Chopin in the freezer.'

'I'll drink.'

They sat at the table, frosted Polish vodka and shot glasses between them.

'Is there any chance he could have been at the gig?'

'Who?'

'Rufus O'Niall.'

'I really don't think so. He definitely wasn't on *my* guest list.'

The megastar had returned to his native land after Dissolution. He'd been there ever since, living in a castle, playing the ageing celebrity states-man. Thankfully he'd never taken that rumoured leap into politics – not overtly, anyway. He was not someone they had to meet.

'He needn't have been with the VIP party. He could have slipped into the country privately and walked in here with the crowds.'

'He'd have been recognised; and anyway, why would he do that? Forget it, Sage. This is about a whole shitload of things that I shouldn't have let happen. This is not about one sad bastard called Rufus O'Niall.'

'No?'

'Come off it. She's been under incredible strain and she's *vulnerable*. A lot of people think Fiorinda is hard as nails, only too well able to look out for herself. They are wrong. She's not heartless, she's damaged. Sometimes she's like someone walking with broken bones—'

'Agreed. And how did she get to be like that?'

They stared at each other. 'Well, okay,' said Ax at last. 'I admit there are things I'd like to do to him. But it's no use thinking that way. Nothing is going to change the past. Fiorinda is who she is. She starts from now . . . *Sage*.' He didn't like the mask's expression. 'Lay off. As long as he leaves Fiorinda alone, we leave him alone.'

'Is that an order?'

'Oh, for fuck's sake. Listen, as far as the public record is concerned, *he didn't do anything*. Nobody sold the story to the tabloids. Okay, in our world no one is in any doubt of what happened. But that just makes O'Niall a rockstar who fucked a precocious twelve-year-old, and thoughtlessly got her pregnant. In our world, yours and mine, that's not a crime. It is shit behaviour, but it is not a crime. He didn't know his exgirlfriend's sister had set him up with his own daughter, to pay off some festering old score. If you want to go after someone, go after Carly Slater. If you can find her. Fiorinda won't thank you. She doesn't want that stuff dragged up, you know that's the last thing she wants.'

Sage downed his vodka, refilled the two glasses. 'What about the other version? The ugly rumour that says he knew she was his daughter, and that's why he was interested, for some fucking reason, and *he* was the one who screwed Carly Slater into setting her up?'

'People will say anything, once the dirt starts flying. As you should know.'

'Then who sent the roses? Someone expert at pushing buttons, evidently. Someone who knows things we don't know . . . What if he likes to remind her, occasionally, that he is in the picture? I don't think I can stand for that.'

'You've seen her like this before. Any pink roses or postcards from Ireland involved?'

'Not that I knew about, but—'

Ax slowly shook his head.

'You think I'm making it up?'

'I think Rufus O'Niall is not another Pigsty. He has a hateful taste for very young girls, but he is not crazy. He's not going to go obsessing over one of them, *his own daughter*, when it could make real trouble for him in his new respectable role. He's a rich, vain, Big Name bastard, with a reputation for bearing a grudge, and he is influential on the government of our most powerful neighbour. I don't need him for an enemy, I don't want Fiorinda caught in the crossfire . . . and if I *believed* your ugly rumour, I'd feel the same way.'

'But you've thought about it.'

'I'm stupid enough, vain enough. I'd like to avenge my lady's honour, yeah. I've thought about it, and decided to forget the idea. I advise you to do the same. Let it go.'

'What if I don't want to let it go?'

'I don't know why I'm listening to this. Sage, Fiorinda has had some very hard times, the scars will be with her for life, and I hate myself for letting her get into this state. But going after O'Niall stinks. It's not on the agenda and it never will be.'

'Okay,' said Sage, after a moment. 'We drop the subject.'

'I knew she was on a knife-edge, after Pigsty—'

'Yeah.'

They sat in silence. Ax watched the beautiful detail of the mask, and looked around the capsule, mildly curious as to why nothing was floating. Sage filled their glasses again.

'I could get Allie to run over the Irish party's hotel records, see if any of them ordered any flowers. If it would make you happy.'

'Nah, leave it. It would be very fucking stupid for us to be caught snooping.' The skull grimaced horribly. 'What a shit, eh. Not only divested of the last shreds of empire, but dependent on the powerful Irish tolerating our eccentric rockstar solution to the CCM. You think they enjoyed the show, your Celtic-nations VIPs?'

'I think they were keen to check us out. They find the size of the thing frightening. So do I.'

'Me too. I have visions of a runaway chain reaction. What if they *all* decide they want to leave home an' join your rock and roll band, Ax? All forty million.'

'It won't happen,' said Ax. 'Something worse and totally unexpected will happen instead.'

They laughed and shook their heads, and fell silent again. Future shock.

'You know,' said Ax, 'I used to wonder a lot why you hadn't jumped on her, back in Dissolution Summer; spite of the yellow ribbon. You obviously liked her, and you do jump on women, Sage. You are known for it.'

'Yeah, well. Sometimes even Aoxomoxoa can tell when he's not wanted.'

Soon as he spoke Ax knew he'd been tactless. He had a propensity for doing this to his friend, saying what should be left unsaid. But Sage didn't seem to have noticed. The skull's blank eyes were staring sombrely into the middle distance.

'Ah, you're right. Tonight doesn't have to have anything to do with O'Niall. To Fiorinda, what has happened to us looks bad enough: this trap she sees closing around her. Forced to live on beyond the end of the world, reduced to the status of a pet animal—'

'I hate it when she starts that one. That's *such nonsense*.'

'But it's the way she feels. It's the future she sees.'

They both looked up, sharply. She was crying.

In the room where they'd left her Sage touched the wall, raising a little light, and there she was: sobbing desolately, face buried, hair a cloud over the pillows, like a map spread out, a little country sinking into stormy seas. Ax felt himself grow in scale, he had to be big enough to hold her. He got beside her, stretching his arms across the immense distances: touched her and folded down the middle dimensions again, into human forms, Ax and Fiorinda, lifted the babe and hugged her, murmuring hey, ssh, I'm here.

Fiorinda stopped crying. She stared at him in horror, without a trace of recognition, scrambled to her knees and backed away.

'Sage!' she wailed. 'Where's Ax? Help, come quick, Ax is gone—!'

It was all Sage could do, stern and gentle, coaxing and cajoling, to talk her down this time. Ax was no help. A moment ago he'd been seeing himself and Fiorinda as the land and its defences, harmless brain-candy picture language, straight from his mood tonight. Now his control was gone. The Heads' cocktail, abetted by her terror, overwhelmed him, he *was* the monster, this demon his darling saw . . . He heard their voices, like the thin piping voices of strangers, victims, prey—

'hey, hey, none of that, it was just a bad dream—'

'Oh, I hate it when nightmares go on when you open your eyes—'

'Yeah, yeah, me too, the worst kind. But it's okay, you're in charge. Take over. You're not going to let a stupid dream push you around.'

'I take over?'

'Yeah. C'mon, you know you can do it. Now, this is Ax. Give me your hands.'

Ax's eyes were open, but his vision so disturbed he could hardly see. Cold fingers touched his face, tracing its outline. 'Yes,' she whispered. 'This is Ax. He feels right. This is my Ax.'

'Of course it is.'

'I'm sorry Ax.' Her face came into focus, blurred as if by rain. 'Did I frighten you?'

'Ssh,' said Ax, holding her. 'I'm sorry too. Sorry, Sage. Lost it there for a moment.'

They hugged each other, Ax and Fiorinda both of them shaking, recovering from a near-miss incident, things that had almost turned very bad. Another swoop in scale. The wide bed, surrounded by its walls of digital-studio hardware, seemed as if it was hiding the three of them, they were like little sparkly software people safe in the depths of the machine . . .

'Don't give me NDogs again,' said Fiorinda. 'I don't want to be asleep, being asleep is like being awake only worse. Ax, don't let him do that to me.'

'Ha. You think you're sorted now, don't you, brat? You can go whining to Ax, any time you think I'm pushing you around. Anytime he pisses you off you're going to come whining to me. It will probably work too . . . C'mon, if you don't like being asleep. Back to the kitchen. Drink some wine, smoke some spliff.'

'You won't send me to the whitecoats?'

'We will not send you to the whitecoats.'

'I'm so sorry, I know I'm being a horrible nuisance.'

'Leave that out, stupid brat. You are not a nuisance.'

'I'm all right.'

'I know you are. You have Ax, you have me, we're in the van. Everything real is good.'

They went back to the kitchen: and in some ways things were better after that. But she was not all right. She couldn't or wouldn't tell them what was going on in her mind. They had to give up asking; it upset her too much. She couldn't keep still. She had to pace up and down, bite her lips, dig her nails into her palms. She had to talk, incessantly, but could not complete a sentence. She needed to shit, they both had to go with her and hold her hands. Sage coaxed her into drinking a pint of dioralyte, because dehydration was obviously one of her problems: matched her gulp for gulp with the filthy-tasting stuff, assuring her he really didn't mind if she threw up all over him. That ended badly because she *did* throw up; and afterwards refused even plain water. Ax began to feel sure, deadly certainty, absolutely immutable, that this wasn't a temporary breakdown, a weird aberration. This was the truth. This thick, bloody spring of desperation was welling up from some haunted depth where the core of Fiorinda *had always lived*, and now she had fallen into herself, and she would never get out again—

They'd promised they would not to give her any more NDogs. But she was so distressed, so exhausted, they changed their minds and dosed her again, put her to bed again. Stayed with her this time, lying on either side of her, talking softly about neutral things.

'That was a very low key set you did.'

'It was meant to be.' Ax wanted a cigarette. He had to make do with one of Sage's Anandas, because she couldn't be left for a moment.

'An' you didn't play your "Jerusalem". You haven't made some kind of sacrificial vow about renouncing that solo, have you? Because of Pigsty and all that?'

'Nah,' said Ax. 'I wasn't in the mood. They would've sung along, and I really thought, this afternoon, if they started a singalong, with "Jerusalem" or with the fucking "Oats and Beans", I was going to have to *trash my gear.*'

'That I would have liked to see.'

Fiorinda stirred and murmured. Sage reached up and touched the wall. The dim light brightened; she was sleeping.

'What's that *feel* like? The ATP?'

'Tiring,' said Sage. 'Sometimes, if you're using it heavily. *Very* tiring, if you forget what you're doing. And hungry. But this—' he touched the wall again '—doesn't feel like anything. Feels like flipping a switch. The light-propagating gel is doing most of the work.'

'I've been talking to people about a pilot scheme in ordinary housing, in London. But I've never actually . . . How d'you turn it off?'

'Just vary the pressure.' Sage touched the wall again, darkness: another touch, light.

'And there's no power-source but your cell metabolism, and we can set this up anywhere? God. How bright can you get the light? Can you cook with ATP?'

'Bright as day: I'll show you when she's awake. You can slow cook, haybox things; or keep a well-insulated room warm. Piss-poor energy audit on grilling a steak, so far. But yeah, you can set up for ATP lighting anywhere. Move out the furniture, spray on the gel, move back in. The catch is, anyone who wants to use it has to take the treatment. A tricky concept to sell to the science-hating CCM.'

'Or to the only-natural-is-good general public. I'm thinking about it.'

She slept for twenty minutes, and woke crying, accusing them of breach of trust.

They returned to the kitchen and stayed there, fighting Fiorinda's demons. Sage had to do most of the talking, soothing, teasing, reassuring. For Ax, the nightmare was too real. But that was okay. He felt that they'd agreed on this division of labour. Ax would go down with her, into the dark: and Sage would keep watch, ride shotgun for them both.

Towards dawn they were together on one of the astronaut berths, Fiorinda wrapped in the sailor jacket, her head on Ax's shoulder, Sage beside them, bangra playing softly, the bass diffused to a filmy, miles-deep oceanic murmur. 'I hate the idea that evil is essential and com-plementary,' she said. 'That's what my gran believes, like a good pagan. Good and evil, both have to be worshipped. Oh, I despise that way of looking at things. I think suffering is the other side of reality, the stuff we have to respect. Evil is just what sad bastards do.'

'Not important at all,' agreed Sage.

'Important, but contemptible.'

'Okay.'

'But pain is valid. When you are inside it, you can live there. You can get to the place, level, state, don't know what to call it, where it's . . . breathable. *Usually* I can do that, but sometimes I daren't. Sometimes you can't get there, because you might be laying yourself open to horrible things that are lying in wait on the way. Do you want some more of this, Ax?'

'Thanks.' He took the spliff from her cold, shaking hand.

She stroked the sleeve of her jacket. 'Oh, I meant to tell you. It's not the *Titanic*, it's the Battleship *Potemkin*. This is Tom's stage coat. He likes to be a deserter from the *Potemkin* on stage, you know, from the Russian Revolution. In solidarity with the revolting masses of the fucked-up. We wouldn't let him, though, last night. He'd have steamed to death like a pudding. It's written on the hat. Look.'

'If you say so.'

He couldn't read the lettering. But an attack of dyslexia wasn't much to worry about, after the past few aeons (amazingly, according to his watch, less than four hours since they left the Leisure Centre), during which he had been utterly convinced that Fiorinda was never going to come out of this. That his darling was going to live the rest of her life in a state of unreachable terror: and it was *all his fault* . . . The Heads' cocktail was bottoming out, paranoia fading. He wondered what it would have been like, untainted by mood and circumstance, but he didn't think he'd ever fancy trying the same mix again.

Beyond the obsidian windows, the post-massacre-night world was a void, a hard vacuum. Open space inside the van was not so bad, but Sage seemed in real danger when he left them: which he did, occasionally, to fetch essential supplies or whack himself in the throat with another popper. But he always insisted he would be okay, and he always came back safe.

At ten in the morning Ax was sound asleep. Sage was lying awake on the opposite couch, unmasked, smoking a cigarette, staring at the ceiling.

Where are we?

It's somewhere in Northern Europe, early in Dissolution Year. An Arts Festival with a 'strange rock music' component, where DARK is on the same line-up as the Heads, and they are all in the same hotel. He is prowling the Northern Europe Breakfast Buffet, staring, through the protection of the mask, at the pickled herrings and the smoked peppers, the cucumber surprise and the chopped beetroot, the heaving platters of boiled eggs, baked meats, glistening cheeses, my God. At least it is colourful. George comes up beside him.

'Well, did you fuck her?'

'No.'

'Does she even know you want to?'

'Hope not. She's not supposed to know.'

The mask his brother Head is wearing doesn't do natural expressions, or it would be looking between bemused and exasperated. George has no idea what kind of night that was, and he isn't going to find out from Sage. He can't make out what is going on.

'Now lissen up, Sage. Some day soon she is going to take a fancy to one of those other blokes, the ones she *does* fuck because she is afraid to say no. And then where will you be?'

I will be here.

Didn't think it could happen. If some other guy takes her away, before she is ready to say yes, the way I want her to say yes, I will take her back. How could that be a problem? I'm Aoxomoxoa, and she belongs to me. How was I to know that the unscrupulous bastard who would take my baby down, knowing that he did not have her free consent, *and make her happy* . . . would be Ax?

'Hallo?'

She was standing in the doorway, barefoot, still wearing that grey rag of a cowgirl dress and the sailor jacket.

'Ah, Fiorinda.' He sat up, stubbed out the cigarette. 'C'me here.'

'I'm better.'

'I am glad to hear it.' He examined her face. She looked wretched, tallow-pale and huge shadows under her eyes: but herself again. 'That was a fun-packed few hours you gave us. What's the name of the Prime Minister?'

'Huh? What's he got to do with it? I'm *really* sorry, Sage.'

'Don't start that again.'

Ax had woken and was sitting up, combing back strands of fine dark hair with his fingers. Fiorinda tugged Sage to his feet and pulled him to the other couch, settled herself between them, smiled at them angelically. 'It's over and I don't want to talk about it, not right now, anyway. Except, thank you very much, both of you, and I think you ought to go and get yourselves some breakfast. You must be sick of the sight of me. I'm going to have a shower, if the van will let me. I want you to call Allie. Tell her I'm ill in bed, and she's to come and read me a storybook. She'll understand. We used to read to each other in Park Lane, when we were prisoners of the Pig.'

Sage didn't have Allie's direct line stored on his wrist, and none of them could remember the number. They had to hunt down a phone, the night ravelling up: parents, Prime Minister and his lovely wife, Fiorinda on stage . . . and then what? Where exactly did we *leave things?*

Sage tracked down Ax's phone in the cab, came back into the kitchen talking to Allie.

'What do you mean, *ill in bed,*' she demanded. 'She was all right last night.'

'I'm only saying what I was told to say. Girlcode, I assumed . . . Now the horrible woman thinks we've been beating you.'

'I heard that, Sage. I don't suppose you keep any books in that overgrown Tardis?'

'Oooh, shouldn't think so,' he said, looking straight at a clear-fronted locker stacked with ancient hardbacks and paperbacks.

'So there's no point in asking what you have. Shit. Those kids have been building suspension bridges with my entire library . . . oh, I'll find something.'

Fiorinda had switched the back of the door to the outside world to mirror and was staring at herself. 'What a disgusting object. Tell her I've

189

got Tom's jacket. And his hat.' She headed for the shower. 'And tell her to bring me some clothes.'

'Right. You get all that Allie? Bring the princess some clothes.'

Shortly Allie turned up, exquisitely dressed in a slim cocoa brown sleeveless shift over matching narrow silk trousers, bearing a smart overnight bag: Allie with her dislike of Aoxomoxoa well on display, prickly as a cat stepping into a dog's kennel; and not too pleased with Ax, either . . . very difficult. Fiorinda emerged from the shower, wrapped in a bathrobe that belonged to George Merrick, and rescued them: told them again to go, go.

'You'll want the mask, Sage,' said Ax, stopping him as they were about to walk out the door. 'You look terrible.'

'Oh yeah, forgot.' He peered at his reflection: deathly-pale, bloodless lips, suffused eyes, lines of fatigue deep as ditches. 'Adrenalin will do that. Thanks.'

Out into the heat and glare. It was shattering.

'Well,' said Ax. 'Another night to remember.'

They stared for a while at the crumpled water butt, then began to walk towards the arena. Green grass, blue sky, colourful campers, noise. It felt like an illusion, a paper world. Nothing meant anything, except the sense, already acutely nostalgic, of the immense peril (yet again) that they'd come through together.

'*What?*' said Sage. 'Why are you looking at me like that? What's wrong?'

'Nothing's wrong. I'm just very, very glad you were there. You were amazing.'

'Don't be nice to me, Ax. Anyone's nice to me this morning, I'm gonna burst into tears.'

'C'mon. Let's go down the Oz Bar. I'll buy you a steak.'

So they went down the Oz Bar. But Sage wasn't happy. He was edgy, fidgeting, he seemed to have had enough of Ax's company. They'd been sitting together for a few minutes, steak breakfast hardly touched, when George and Bill came into the tent, looking around. 'Oh, my band!' says Sage, jumps up and makes his escape.

Yeah, thought Ax, watching him go and understanding why. I cut you out, brother. Didn't even know I was doing it, though I did kind of doubt the brotherly affection story. But it was her choice, and you can't ask me to regret the way it went. I'll just have to hope you can forgive me, for knowing what I can't help knowing, after last night.

But nothing could be a problem, between Sage and Ax and Fiorinda.

The night they'd just spent together had been a voyage such as the legends of friendship are made of: and now it seemed to him that Fiorinda had been fighting demons for all of them, a rite of purification that had finally put to rest the horrors of massacre night, Pigsty's misery and death; all of that. The future rushed in on him (long gone the days when you could pin down the prospects in a couple of lists). He met the onslaught with a mind washed clean, exhausted but positive. Thirty thousand staybehinds on this site alone, insisting on living like Bangla-deshi slumdwellers, and more and more of them all over the country; where is this going to end?

I'll sort it somehow. The project is real now. It's happening. Better engage with that.

SEVEN

Big In Brazil

In mid-May it was Luke Moy's birthday, Luke being the Head who had died of pneumonia the summer after Dissolution. The Heads held a service in Reading campground's boneyard, a staybehinds' affair: no outsiders, unless you counted Chip and Verlaine. Fiorinda was there, some Zen Selfers; the Sun Temples (Sage's long-suffering neighbours were a forgiving bunch of hippie tribals); a congregation of assorted campers. This was when Sage was fucking Olwen Devi – a startling arrangement, two weeks and going strong, record-breaking stuff for Aoxomoxoa (must be the dead clever Sage, the one who wrote the immersions and built the avatar mask, who was getting it on with the guru). But Olwen wasn't at the service.

Luke would have been twenty-three. He was the only one of the Few and friends to lie here. Martina Wyatt and Ken Batty, who had died on massacre night, were represented by memorial plaques. The landscaping of the boneyard was still raw: a henge of car body panels, weird camper memorials. No plantings allowed but native flowers, lovely enough right now; no marble angels as yet. They laid the stone (a slice of polished serpentine, about eighteen inches square) and sat around it, talking. Smoked some grass, but took no other drugs: the Heads had decided it would not be seemly. Eventually they sang a few hymns. Luke had liked hymn tunes. The Zen Selfers were reticent about displaying their musical talent amidst the crap-at-it English, but if Aoxomoxoa was singing with them that was different. Which he was, because of all the utter balderdash Sage had laid upon the media folk over the years, the one about his grandad and the Methodist choir was perfectly true. The effect was beautiful, so seductive the whole crowd was trying to join in by the end.

Fiorinda held out. She didn't know the words or the tunes, and had no desire to learn.

The strains of the Last Days Of Disco song (*Dear lord and father of*

193

mankind . . .) sank to rest. Luke's cousins and his gran (Luke had no closer family) left to catch their train, declining an escort. The Heads and Fiorinda, a few Zen Selfers, Chip and Verlaine, waited a while in the afternoon sun to let the congregation thin out.

'It's getting to be like two complete worlds,' said Verlaine. 'Trying to occupy the same space.' He pointed, with a stalk of grass he'd been chewing, at the hedge that divided this raw garden from the bank of the Thames. 'Do they know we're real? *Are* we still real?'

'We were real enough when we put their lights out two weeks ago,' commented someone.

'I don't like it,' grumbled Bill Trevor. 'Gadgets, okay. But this beyond-futuristic stuff is getting personal. I don't want to end up transformed into some crackpot post-human elf.'

George and Cack laughed at him. 'You're sittin' there with a fuckin' skull for a head,' jeered Peter. 'Lissen to yourself.'

'Nah,' said their boss. 'We won't change. Doesn't matter what we do to ourselves, we'll be like Edwardians watching tv. It'll be the next generation, the kids who never knew any different, who cross the borderline.'

Fiorinda lay in the grass, in her tattered green silk over yellow underskirts, a donkey-eaten wheatstraw hat shading her face: a Counter-cultural Titania among her courtiers. Two weeks of sun had turned the skin of her arms and throat an amazing shade of deep fallow gold. 'What's it say on Luke's stone?'

'I rise from sleep,' George translated. 'And leave my dreams behind.'

'Is that what death is? Oh, I don't like that. I don't want to leave my dreams behind. Not even the bad ones.'

Sage laughed, hugging her shoulders as they stood up together. 'Hear that? Fiorinda wants to live forever. Get onto it, someone.'

They began to walk back towards the arena, Sage falling into step beside Fiorinda with his slow, deliberate stride: *deliberate*, she thought, because he takes it for granted he's going to be walking down, so to speak, to anyone he's with. Hands in his pockets. Even masked they must be hidden if possible: tucked in pockets, into belt-loops, curled into fists.

'I don't want to live forever,' she said. 'I meant, I'll be pissed off if it turns out, after all the hassle, that *this* was only a rehearsal, a daydream. Do you believe in life after death?'

'Not sure.'

'I never did, until my mother died. I wasn't there. She wasn't supposed to die that night, I'd gone off to lie down. The nurse fetched me, but it was too late. I knew then that . . . she had not stopped being. It was obvious, can't explain why. I still don't exactly believe in another life after this one. Doesn't make sense. But there's something. Something about time not being what we imagine it is, maybe? That means death is not what we think, either.'

'Maybe it's a topic I'd rather not dwell on. I have killed people, Fiorinda.'

'I know. Let's go down to the river?'

They'd dropped behind the others. They crossed a stile in the hedgerow and found a place to sit at the water's edge, by the footpath to Banbury. It was a weekday afternoon. There were boats on the river, people strolling; small children. She took a painted smokes tin out of her backpack – same shabby, tapestry compendium she'd been using in the summer before Dissolution – lit a spliff and handed it to him.

'Did it bother you?'

Neither of them had talked to her about that aspect of the Islamic Campaign. Walked out of the soldier-business and shut the door behind them: she'd supposed it was best.

'Not as much as it should have done. There was one occasion, when I had to fight my way . . .' The skull grimaced. 'Well, never you mind. One occasion was seriously unpleasant. Otherwise, nah. It was contact sport. We had to *be there*, couldn't stay back at HQ keeping our hands clean, so—' He shrugged. 'I'm not a pacifist by nature—'

'No!' Fiorinda gasped and stretched her eyes. 'Gosh, really not?'

'Fuck off. Ax bloody is, though. He has no objection to taking insane risks with his life, or committing awesome damage to property. But he hated the killing. *Hated it.* Don't know how he hacked it. Went on hacking it, day after day . . . It was horrible to watch.'

'Well,' said Fiorinda. 'I know about one of his brilliant coping strategies.'

'He told you about that?'

'The smack, yeah. And he told me how you harassed him into seeing the error of his ways. Thank you.'

'De nada.'

Fiorinda had found a cache of curling swan feathers in the rough grass beside her. She started lining them up and setting them on the water, one by one. Would some of the swans belong to Ax, she wondered, when he was President? Or did they still belong to the *ci-devant* Royals, absentee swan-lords. But Ax wasn't going to be President. He preferred a different title, and was holding out for it.

'Is he still saying they have to call him dictator?'

She nodded. 'The suits are convinced he's joking, but he isn't. I think he sees insisting on the brutal truth as making up for the crime of getting democratically elected.'

'Hahaha . . . *That* didn't feature on any of the lists.'

'Absolutely not. Ax doesn't think much of democracy.'

'Nor do I. It's just a word the masters of the universe like us to use . . . But trust Ax. Fuck, why does he keep *doing these things* to himself?' Sage considered, and rejected, an itemised list. Might contain some nasty anxieties Fiorinda hadn't thought of. The company that did Ax's implant had gone bust while they were in Yorkshire. Ax had said, casually, *there go my updates*; and Sage didn't want to ask how much he knew about the unpleasant possibilities. He was tired of hearing about *dislocated risk perception*, and generally getting out-Aoxomoxoaed by a soft-spoken introspective guitar-man. 'I dunno how he gets away with this Mr Sensible tag. I think he's the most perfectly reckless person I have ever met: and that's counting me and you, brat.'

'So naturally you adore him.'

The skull did a mix of its *you beyond belief* grin. 'So naturally I adore him.'

Another feather down the stream, with a freight of silvered water drops.

'Sage, what'll I do with my money? I don't want to give all of it away, I am not that noble.'

'You could hand it over to me an' George, let us play the markets for you.'

'No.'

'Then cash it. That's a better idea, mess the finance world is in. Buy real estate.'

'No thanks. I never want to own anywhere. I hate the idea of being pinned down like that . . . *You* don't have any property, except your hovel and the van.'

'If ever you have an irate ex after your hide, come to me. I will tell you what to do.'

'She's not still after you, though, is she?'

'Don't think so. But I've found out that this is the way I like to live. I *like* my hovel. You could buy yourself a decent piano.'

'Oh.'

'Sounds good? Then you'd need somewhere to put it.'

'I'm going to move in with Ax.'

'Oh yeah. I knew that.'

Ax was buying a place in Brixton, having refused all the suits' preferred candidates for the Presidential residence. They sat in silence for a while, listening to the plash of oars; birdsong from the trees on the other bank. Sage turned to her. 'While you're here,' he said, skull doing something like *cautious speculation*, 'could I look at something?' He picked up the tapestry bag, hefted it and shook his head sadly. 'God. Still luggin' your pet rock collection around?'

'Lay off, it's my bag, do I ever ask you to carry it? What are you looking for?'

'This.' He held the birchwood saltbox in his masked hand. 'I've been thinking, it just came to me, the other day . . . do you ever need to refill it?'

She stared at him, and the fallow gold was mantled in carmine: Fiorinda blushing, a rare and lovely sight. 'Leave me alone, Sage. It's none of your business.'

'So that would be a no, I take it.'

'What are you planning to do? *Blackmail* me?'

'Now don't get excited, I'm not going to tell anyone anything you don't want me to tell . . . I just wondered if there was any connection — between a girl who can do strange things with fire, a saltbox that never needs refilling . . . and the way you were after the May concert?'

The lovely blush had faded. She took the box from his hand, smiling, and stowed it away. 'Oh, is that what's worrying you? Well, there's no connection at all. The saltbox is innocent, and so's the fire thing. Honestly. Trust me.'

He nodded. 'Okay, fine. But I still think you ought to tell Ax—'

'About my party tricks?' Fiorinda picked at the threadbare, unravelling hem of her green dress. 'Well I don't want to, not at the moment. Maybe sometime. Please lay off, Sage. I don't want to be investigated as a weird phenomenon.' She looked up, scowling. 'Hey, I lost the plot for a few hours. I had a panic attack. Is that such a crime?'

'Okay, okay. We drop the subject.'

'Some day soon, you're going to go diving into one of *your* black holes, and Ax won't like that at all. He does not have the rockstar tantrum gene, and he won't understand.'

'What black holes? Don't know what you're talking about.'

The skull and Fiorinda pulled horrible faces at each other, and laughed: white water fishes, kindred spirits of extreme experience. Then Fiorinda sighed. 'Oh, Sage, how did we get into this situation? I do what Ax puts in front of me because I love him: but *I don't like any of it*. I don't believe anyone can change the world, or save it.'

'I don't know,' he said, drawing up his knees and resting his chin on his folded arms. 'I've been thinking about that. I've decided I was looking for trouble. Some way to cut loose, go into the desert, find out what I'm made of, and this glorious opportunity came along—'

'Are you serious?'

'Yeah, why not?'

'Oh, please. One of you with a mystical mission is bad enough. Take it back. Tell me going to that fatal seminar was just Sage being wilfully bizarre as usual.'

'Of course, now I remember. It was just Sage being wilfully bizarre . . . Fiorinda, *I really hate it* when you do that to me. Why the fuck do you do it?'

'I'm sorry—' she said, dismayed. 'It's a silly game. I'll try to stop. It's because I like to hear you tell me *everything's going to be all right*. Especially when we both know it's nonsense.'

She ducked her head, hiding behind the brim of the donkey-eaten straw, not knowing how to recover, how to say it without trespassing: *I'm going to live with Ax, and I'm not your brat anymore, but I can't bear it if we're not best friends* . . .

'Everything's going to be all right.'

She risked a glance around. The skull was looking at her very kindly.

Fiorinda smiled. They got up and walked on towards Reading town, talking about the houses on the other side of the river, which were being squatted now, and dismantled. Some cases, it couldn't happen to a nicer bijou riverside residence. Others it was a real shame.

Well, I go this way. She left Sage at the gate to the Travellers' Meadow and wandered (catching the occasional nudge and glance, *hey, there's Fiorinda*: but not much of that, mostly she could have been invisible). Thinking about Ax Preston and early days. Was it the fourth or fifth time they were together, when he read her the lecture on safe sex? Said lecture received by Fiorinda with sixteen-year-old indifference and dumb insolence, but she'd had to agree that if they gave up his precious condoms she'd always use protection with anyone else. *Oh, all right.* I'll get some of the spray-on stuff Sage uses, that you don't have to think about. One size fits all, hahaha . . . (But Ax would be a durex man until his dying day: such a *fogey*). Took her weeks to realise that he'd finessed her into going steady.

He's a sneaky bastard.

Oh, it's never been simple. It's a relationship full of twists and turns, dead ends and winding passages, some of them going right back to that twisty, blocked beginning when I thought he was someone else. *Involved* is a good word: I can feel it. I'm *involved*, by all those twists and turns, in something different from and more vital, more permanent than being in love . . . Even the sex wasn't simple. It could be horribly frustrating, when she held him in her arms and knew he was off on another plane, making love to the perfect, china-fragile Fiorinda-of-the-mind. All the more wonderful though, when it worked right. Fiorinda being a rock chick in the front row at one of the crisis management gigs, Ax Preston with the Chosen in some tiny West Country venue: stage only a metre-high platform, he looks at her out of complete *mastery* of his playing, such a flash of pure, arrogant, besotted lust. I ought to yell at you, I'M NOT A GUITAR, but I can't. Knees are too weak, know what you plan to be doing minutes, nay *seconds*, after you get off that stage, and I can't wait . . .

She walked through the fair: Titania wearing a reminiscent grin of ravishing sweetness, that turned the coolest heads; counting the changes and the survivals. The wildflowers, seed sown everywhere and some of it thriving, tough pretty weeds in clumps and skeins, right up to the beaten earth in front of Red Sage. *Anansi's Jamaica Kitchen*, the van where she and the Heads used to buy breakfast, gone from its pitch. Rupert the White Van Man must be on tour. There was a new climbing wall in Violet Alley, where the Megazone Circus lived, but the karaoke and amateur-night tents (Bands of the Highly Improbable Future) had vanished. And my hut's gone, she thought, the one where I lived when I was fighting with Ax last summer. When Luke was dying, and Sage was so miserable, and I got that letter from Carly—

She stood watching the kids on the climbing wall, but the beautiful smile had faded.

She was twelve years old again, and there was something terrible growing inside her. Is it worse at the first shock, or is it worse when it seems as if nothing's happening, and you try to pretend nothing's happening, but you know it's still in there, still *growing* . . .

Beyond Violet Alley rose the eau-de-nil geodesic of the Zen Self tent.

What if she let herself be investigated? Would a brainscan find anything unusual, any underlying reason for the spectacular panic attacks? Olwen Devi had been trying hard to get hold of Fiorinda again since Fio took part in that gut-bacteria pilot scheme. Did that mean the guru had already somehow picked up on something strange? Trust Olwen? She didn't know whether she was frightened, or tempted, by that idea. At least she could be certain that Sage would *never* tell. Never trust Sage when he backs down easily, on any subject; but he'd still never tell. No, she decided. Better not. I'm in control. I did what Sage told me to do. I took over. If ever, even for a *moment*, I feel that I'm not in control, I'll tell Ax and Sage and Olwen Devi at once . . .

Maybe it was nonsense, anyway. Maybe what had happened on the night of the Mayday concert had simply been a nightmare, a babystar fit of hysterics. In fact, that was probably it.

She turned and quickly walked away.

The two weeks after the Mayday concert had been incredibly busy. Ax had established that nobody had dibs on *Oltech* as a domain name or a trademark, and they were pursuing that development: operation making Olwen Devi's fortune. Ax's old lady friend Laura Preston had told him about a scheme she remembered, where manufacturers and distributors handed over surplus goods – food, clothes, furniture, consumer-stuff of all kinds – and if you were a worthy cause you could go along to the warehouse and take anything you could use, for a nominal price. They were pursuing that idea too, as a means of supplying the drop-out hordes. They sent Fiorinda out with a business plan she'd devised, on personal approaches. Since the May concert, rich CCM fellow-travellers all wanted to meet the Rock and Roll Reich's wild-cat glamour puss. They met her, encountered that *glacial* intelligence, and it was a killer combination.

Allie hit on the idea of having banners at the gates of the Insanitude: tall Japanese-style banners, bearing the names and insignia of the Few and friends – DARK's eclipsed sun; the white-on-black cross of Cornwall for the Heads; Zen Self's gold infinity-strip figure of eight; Snake Eyes on three pair of dice, held in the loving-cup of two dark hands; the stone axe which had been the Chosen's logo since their first album. Chip and Ver's favourite molecule. That sort of thing. The other bands and popular artists, who were now flocking to get in on the act, could earn the right to have a banner up there, *if they proved themselves useful*. It looked good, and the element of competition did no harm.

Ax was planning for Zen Self daughter cells to be set up in other campgrounds. He thought this would be safe. As long as Oltech developments affected only humans, and were kind to the environment, he reckoned most of the CCM could be won over. The anti-science hardcore would be left in peace, denied the oxygen of argument.

Spinning stuff like ATP for the general public was a more difficult project.

'Whyn't we tell them it's a cure for obesity,' said Fiorinda, who'd never taken the treatment, and never would. 'We'd be addressing a problem people really care about.'

'Huh?'

'Use ATP, and you can be svelte as the next hyperactive anorexic giant rockstar, without compromising your couch potato lifestyle. They'll love it.'

'Oh yeah,' said Ax. Who hadn't taken the treatment either, on the grounds that his implant (which no one out there knew about), and his being a Muslim, was enough already, and though he opposed them, he had to keep the anti-science tendency sweet . . . Good excuses, *fogey.* 'You know, that might work.'

Everyone laughed. There was a lot of relief-from-strain and escape-from-panic-laughter at these Office meetings. Fiorinda giggled to herself, head down and doodling hard as usual. Her bodyguards looked at each other across her shoulders and shared a rueful grin. She's holding up amazingly: bounced right back from that night of fugue. The babe is magic.

So they were putting up hippie decorations and scrounging – how Countercultural can you get? – but there was another side to things. The guys who ran the protection business for London's clubs and venues came knocking, letting it be known that the Insanitude needed to think about its security. Ax told 'em to fuck off. After a couple of rounds, this negotiation ended in a meeting of bizarre formality, in the Ballroom late one night, barmy army officers in attendance, the bad guys frisked of their weapons, but most of them disguised in digital-mask fancy dress; Sage and the Heads for once looking mild and reasonable in their demeanour; Ax explaining gently that he was committed to non-violence but, on the other hand, he had an army at his back . . . The big fellas were thrilled, they loved it, they swore allegiance. And how long will that last? How long will their taste for pantomime outweigh their taste for violence, and *fucking hell, what are we getting ourselves into?*

Shouldn't really be driving the car alone. But he reckoned he could afford a little personal transport hypocrisy, for the rural rides. Here we are at a miserable barracks for multi-drug-resistant TB treatment, in Shaftesbury. The apparatchiks welcome him (webcam, live global transmission on the cheap, no actual camera people today); and he's a rockstar for this part. Then he becomes a paramedic volunteer, changing bedlinen, administering drugs, cleaning up limp and withered bodies. They are prisoners, but it isn't a big issue. If they ever manage to get non-infectious, many of them are incapable of coping with the world outside.

Here's a guy blind all his life, decades on the road. Touring, crusty-style, doing a lot of drugs: picked up one day and dumped in here like a sick old dog. The man has to be cleaned, and his bed changed. They chat while this gets done: he's very docile, very apologetic about the stink of piss and the wet sheets.

'No worries. Happens to friends of mine all the time, hazard of getting smashed, innit.'

'But I've not had a drink . . . You use yer hands a lot, don't you. What d'you do wif 'em?'

'I play guitar.'

'Oh right. In yer spare time, eh? Will yer let us touch yer face, lad?'

The face proffered. 'Where d'you come from?'

'Taunton.'

'But you're coloured, aren't you?'

'Yes.' Wondering how the blind fingers worked that out.

'I c'n 'ear it in yer voice,' said the old man proudly. 'Just very slight. So where d'you come from origerenally?'

'Oh, *originally*.' Touching, reflexively, the place where they cut open his skull. Lift the slack bag of bones, insert arm into fresh pyjama jacket. 'Originally I'm not human.' Insert other arm, smooth jacket down, lay him back on the pillow. 'My people came here from a dying world . . .'

He stayed a quarter of an hour, sitting on the end of the narrow bed, making up answers to the old man's questions about his home planet. Took out a cigarette at one point and was detected instantly. *You can't smoke that in 'ere, lad* . . . Sat rolling it between his fingers, thinking about that meeting with the Yardies. Ax in his best suit – not flash, but luckily impressive enough for the occasion. His friends ranged around him, including Fiorinda and the power babes. Some of the women have to be present. That's a vital signal. Thinking of Muhammad's diwan, that day in Yorkshire, and the future that terrifies Fiorinda. Talking smooth and hard, praying to God he can make her understand that he *has to do this*, he has no choice . . .

Straight up, being good to others is the light relief. It's a fucking rest cure.

Though not, of course, if you do it forty hours a week for shit money with no respite.

After his shift he sat in the compulsory-stay-clinic staff lounge with other volunteers and the regular screws (everyone enjoying telling him he couldn't smoke his cigarette) and was asked *How long is the volunteer thing going to last?* I don't know, he said. As long as you all want it to go on. *But is there still a crisis?* Is there? he asked them. And refused to say more.

After Luke's birthday, the Heads moved in on the Office computer network. They'd been shocked at the state of affairs they had discovered when they got involved in organising the May concert, and had decided they'd better sort it, before some awful catastrophe occurred. Three days into this operation Sage was in the Insanitude canteen, alone, untouched cup of coffee in front of him. Just smoking a cigarette, drifting, thinking about the software he'd been installing, Allie Marlowe's attitude problem. The tender, gravity-defying undercurve of Fiorinda's breast, held in green silk, as she stood up beside him in the boneyard—

Benny Preminder came along and said, 'Ah, Sage, I was looking for someone to consult. Could I have a word with you?'

Benny Prem, the suit that wouldn't die. They were planning to get rid of him, but Ax said, ominously, that it might not be easy. On the public record Benny had been innocent of any involvement in the Pigsty coup. He was an efficient paper-shifter, and he had friends. So here he was, with one of those rambling, post-Dissolution government job-titles: something like *Parliamentary Secretary With Responsibility For Countercultural Liaison*. Maybe it was easier to work around him than to force open a can of worms. He'd reinvented his appearance: lost the flab, grown out that thick, shiny black hair and had it styled, got himself some sharp threads. Goodlooking dude, in principle, but repellent.

Sure, anything I can do. Except I was about to leave.

'It's a little problem of etiquette,' Benny explained chattily. 'How to get rid of Albert.'

This was strange enough to be followed up.

So they crossed the Quadrangle and passed into the State Apartments, the night club venue, that gilded bordello staircase opposite the Grand Hall looking ugly by daylight. It was mid-afternoon, the place was empty. They stood in front of the statue of Albert, Queen Victoria's consort, with bare legs and what looks like a marble *nappy*; seemingly they had an interesting private life, those two. It was about the only objet d'art left behind by the Royals: a replica; they had the original. Some people wanted it thrown out.

Benny Prem felt it wasn't cool to dump Albert on a skip . . . and there were alternative suggestions, and somehow the conversation came round to the way Ax keeps giving Worthy Farm the cold shoulder. What has Ax got against Glastonbury?

'Ancient Britons.'

'But that wouldn't be a problem for you, would it, Sage? Being a Celt yourself.'

'Yes, it would,' said Sage, cheerfully. 'I hate 'em, crystal-swinging faggots, neo-fucking Bronze Age dykey matriarchs with their fuckwit psychic powers. Sooner they get wiped out by that organic mutant-cholera epidemic they are asking for, the better I will be pleased.'

Benny laughed uneasily, just the same as in the old Think Tank days.

The Ancient British Tendency were aggressively anti-science and covertly white supremacist. They wanted a bigger piece of the action and they couldn't be allowed to have it. But Benny Prem knew all that. So what was going on here?

'I gather you don't like the idea of power-sharing?'

'Nah,' sez Sage. 'Got to have it all, me, or I'm not fucking interested.'

They left Albert to his fate and strolled, Sage still wondering what was up: *but beginning to get an idea.* The former owners had been good about leaving fixtures and fittings. There were carpets and curtains; even some furniture here from the old days, when the summer tourists used to pay a tenner to trot around. In the Throne Room, Prem decided they would stop. He sat on the steps to the dais, where two frumpy embroidered chairs were still standing in front of a swag of red curtain.

Sage folded down beside him. Prem started to play, only in fun of course, with this idea of Sage being a Celt, and having such charisma, such a great populist following; and generally being, amusingly enough, so much more like the *natural* leader of the CCM. So they went a few rounds with that, and how would Sage like to be the Duke of Cornwall hahaha, until at last Prem came out far as he was likely to come, with the remark that if anything were to happen, there'd be no need to worry about the government. They'd always turn a blind eye to a little power-shifting within the funky parallel establishment, long as the CCM was happy.

So now I'm Pigsty, thought Sage. Well, well, well.

The skull doing cautious, guilty speculation, with a touch of naïvely impressed.

Prem (not very flattering, this) seeming readily convinced.

'Uh, this is a good game, Benny. I'm enjoying it. But you've missed out something. You've missed out . . . yeah, got it: there has to be a reason *why I would do this.* Why would I want to be the leader of the CCM? I'm rich an' famous already, an' I don't need the aggravation. You'll have to think of something that would turn me on. What would be the *inducement?* I mean, not that it's a serious option.'

'You get Fiorinda.'

'Oooh. And you're saying you could, er, deliver Fiorinda?'

'Well, all in jest: but I'd say that wouldn't be a problem. I think she'd fall into your hands, if you were in power. The little lady is a realist. Remember those murdered children? Frankly, I admire her for it: but the first thing she saw in that affair was an opportunity for her boyfriend.'

'It's a point of view.'

'But if she didn't want you, that could be fixed.'

'Really.'

'Hypothetically,' said Benny, coy smile twitching at his well-cut lips.

Sage began to laugh. Laughed uproariously, overcome with merriment. Prem sat there, nonplussed, looking absurdly *offended*. 'Nah,' said Sage, when he could speak. 'I'm sorry, but it doesn't appeal.' He leaned forward. 'A piece of advice: you'll have to look further afield. You won't get anywhere with the Few. It's not that we're incorruptible, everybody has a price. It's to do with what happened one night, and I don't believe you're going to get past it.'

Prem didn't catch the reference. He'd been nowhere near the action on massacre night. He didn't understand what had happened in those grey hours of intense, shared experience, in a committee room in Whitehall.

'I think I've been misunderstood.'

'I think you haven't. Forget it, Benny. Attractive as your offer might otherwise seem, someone I have to trust has warned me never to trust *you*.'

'Sage, you're taking this far too seriously.' Benny was still smiling, keeping his temper. 'It was a joke, nothing more. But I'd like to know, who told you not to trust me? In all fairness, I think you should tell me that.'

'It was Paul Javert. Remember him? Guy who got his head shot off by your last protégé.'

Everyone was out in the gardens. Dilip came into the practically empty canteen and found Sage there, looking very down. He helped himself to a bowl of salad and some camomile tea; sat himself opposite.

'Hey, Sage. What's wrong?'

'I think I just made an enemy.'

'Oh, come on. Who could be *your* enemy around here? Aside from Allie,' he grinned.

'Benny Prem.'

'Oh? What did you do?'

'Laughed at him. Over a ridiculous proposal he made to me.'

He recounted the pitch Benny had made: oh, purely in jest. Suppressing the Fiorinda part.

'You think it's serious?'

'Why would he talk to me like that for fun? Yes, I think it's serious; and I think I shouldn't have called him on it. Unfortunately the fucker made me lose my temper.'

'What did you say?' said Dilip, stirring the salad for which he now had no appetite.

Sage sighed, rubbing the skull's brow with his masked fingers. 'I told him I already have a life, and he should look for another struggling instrumentalist in need of a part-time job . . . But he might do that. There's no shortage of them around here. And Prem's right, our friends in the suits can't be trusted. Offer them a more malleable leader for the CCM, some of the idiot bastards would jump at the chance.'

Gangsters flirting with Utopia, was how Ax described the current administration.

'Fuck. Are you going to tell Ax?'

'Of course I am.'

'I hope he pays attention.'

They both knew Ax would not pay attention. Ax would continue to come and go as he pleased, drive around alone in that instantly recognisable black Volvo, park it wherever he liked. Unarmed. No bodyguards, no entourage. He would go on treating Benny Prem like a difficult sessions musician, sadly prevented by his unlovely personality from becoming anything more. Go on living his fearfully public life in this fearfully changed world as if he were a private person with no enemies, and the date some mythical year in the nineteen sixties.

Fiorinda needed a new publishing strategy. She'd decided she hated the idea of being a solo artist (the rock-*chanteuse*, costume-changes, yuck, disgusting). Playing with DARK at the May concert had reminded her how much she missed the band; and somehow the aftermath of that night had made her realise, *it was possible*. All she had to do was accept that the band would always belong to Charm, and convince Charm to take her on as an associate, a songwriter and vocalist. No control-struggle, no more fist-fights, just sometimes I play with DARK, sometimes I don't . . . However, this meant she'd have to detach herself from lambtonworm.com, the north-east artists' co-op that had brought out both *No Reason*, the DARK debut album, and Fiorinda's album, *Friction*. There was nothing wrong with lambtonworm, they were brilliant and it was a shame to leave. But the co-op was run by Charm Dudley's best mates, and that wasn't going to work. Charm must have space. Fiorinda must be an independent power. She'd have to have a different outlet.

Production, publishing, management, all of that, oh God. How do you begin?

Life goes on. Career decisions have to be made, no matter what.

On the night of the twenty-fourth of May she was alone in the new place in Brixton. It was late. Ax was off playing with the band. She was in the first-floor flat (they had two floors, the ground floor was going to be studio and offices. There were two more floors above, flats belonging to other folk), with a spliff and a bottle of red wine, surrounded by unpacking debris, secretly plotting; checking her friends' download sites on the tv screen. What, me set up my own cyberspace company? Before she'd tackled the Volunteer Initiative she wouldn't have dreamed of such a thing, but she was more confident with information technology now. She'd had to learn to handle it, at least the front end of things.

There were plenty of Fiorinda sites by this time (most of them best ignored), but she'd never had a website of her own, business or personal. Never wanted one. Actually, she still didn't want one. She knew that internet music publishing was a wonderful thing: and without the web they'd all be either corporate slaves or nowhere. She'd had that lecture. The Heads, needless to say, had been in this business since it was wild cowboy territory. They knew everything. But without exactly yearning to be one of those dreadful pampered slaves (perish the thought), she couldn't help thinking, *surely all this part is somebody else's job?*

Those old-fashioned reflexes again.

I'm a child of capitalism. I don't want to be Renaissance Girl.

So, find another co-op . . . But that seemed kind of a wussy option.

She clicked around, looking at *SweetTrack* (the Chosen); and *Tone*, the Somerset artists' outfit started up by the Preston brothers, now run by other people. *Whitemusic.com*, which was the Heads, and *Tide* (Sage) . . . amused by the different personalities, thinking, *I could talk to Chip and Verlaine, or even Shane Preston . . . get some advice.* NOT Sage. Nor any of the Heads. Couldn't have those heavyweights taking charge, handling it all for her. That would never do. Pity there were no girls she could ask. But the only girl-nethead in the Countercultural Think Tank had been killed on massacre night.

Tiring of the investigation, she sneaked a guilty look at some of the stranger Fiorinda stuff, and at the rather unbalanced DARK/Fiorinda fanpages on *lambtonworm* . . . state of affairs there a bit unfortunate for the project of disarming Charm Dudley's resentment.

Well, I can't help it, she thought. I didn't *plan* to be the fucking CCM Crisis Sweetheart.

Today at the San, Benny Prem had come sidling up to her and asked, 'Fiorinda, what does PoMo mean? Does that stand for *post modern*?'

Prem was testing the water, wanting to see if his rash approach to Sage was going to have repercussions. She'd returned his trademark uneasy smile as blandly as she could. 'It stands for Post-Motown.' His eyes had stayed on hers, without a flicker. 'Black music, lot of people on the stage, lot of melody. I'm sure you've asked me that before, Benny.'

'I find it difficult to keep all the jargon terms straight.'

'Don't worry about it,' said Fiorinda. 'No one expects you to understand.'

No, Benny. You're not in trouble. You just make my flesh creep, same as you always did.

Ax had displayed complete lack of interest in Prem's intrigue. This casual attitude, my darling Ax, will bear further discussion . . . But now Fiorinda had crashed.

She wasn't surprised. It was a stupid time, prime gridlock time, to be surfing. She wasn't alarmed, only annoyed, when she found she couldn't shut the screen down. Shook the remote control, considered throwing it against a wall or dropping it hard onto the uncarpeted floor. Better not . . . Finally switched off, unplugged and booted up again. Same screen, still frozen. A message in gothic font slowly appeared.

GOD MUST BE A MUSCOVITE.

Fiorinda sighed in disgust. She decided to call the Heads, in Battersea. Chances were they'd know about GOD MUST BE A MUSCOVITE, how bad it was and how to fix it. Unfortunately, her phone wasn't working. Typical! The maisonette didn't have a landline phone connection yet, so that was about it . . . She tried a couple of terrestrial channels, to make sure the tv reception wasn't buggered. Normal rubbish. Went to bed and read a book.

One of the two viruses involved in what happened on the night of the 24th came out of the Polish Counterculture. Its name was Ivan, it was supposed to attack Russian sites, as an act of solidarity with the underdogs in an ongoing Russian-satellites civil war. The other was English, she was called Lara, and she meant no harm to anyone, she was just expert at getting around and exploring places. On the night of the 24th, Lara accidentally escaped from a private hackers' meet, and she and Ivan got together. Within minutes, Ivan/Lara3g had wreaked havoc throughout Euronet leisure-and-reference access: had destroyed huge swathes of big science, research and academia net, had been downloaded into the cellphone system, and was doing scary things like crashing air traffic control, power-station and water-pumping software. A few years previously, the effect would have gone global that night. The post-modern internet, or nets, had been re-engineered and retrofixed with exactly this situation in mind. Between the virtual boundaries of the signatories of the World Internet Commission, there were complex, fractal bulkheads, designed (among other policing functions) to contain infection. The people of Europe, from Belarus to Portugal, from Sicily to the Baltic, were the ones who woke up with a real problem.

Ironically, Ivan apparently never made it into Russian cyberspace.

The hardliners were thrilled, and eagerly claimed responsibility for the fuck-up on Gaia's behalf. The English public didn't panic. There'd been so many demon viruses that fizzled out; and so often in the last few years a cataclysm that had turned out to be not so bad (such as the Tour). Emergency preparations went into gear, but most people assumed it would be over soon: merely another modern telecoms traffic accident.

On the afternoon of the fifth day, Ax went to check on how Sage was getting on.

Ax had been helping to nail the myriad ways Ivan/Lara could fuck the infrastructure of civilisation, getting to some of them in time, others not. Thank God the Internet Commission had forced its signatories to maintain a worst-case scenario drill. At least they had a plan, even if it was full of holes . . . Nothing had been said, but he was sure the high-powered bureaucrats he was dealing with must know he had a warehouse implant. He couldn't remember if it mattered or why, couldn't think about that at the moment.

Sage had been drafted onto the assault team – an eclectic network of legendary amateurs, academic and state security cryptographers, robotics experts, even rockstars. Ax knew very little about this gruelling effort, but some nethead had said on tv that Ivan/Lara would either be defeated within ten days, or it would be beyond control. The limit seemed arbitrary, but it stuck in the mind. So this was halfway.

The Heads' studio was a converted warehouse, right by the river. George answered the entryphone. Peter and Bill were off doing good deeds, crisis-management shifts: the show must go on. Ax went up to the impossibly cluttered room with the wide windows overlooking Battersea Reach, where Sage was working on his piece of the puzzle: Sage with a wireless wrap around his eyes, lying in a big, heavily designed-looking padded chair, a bank of monitor screens in front of him, his masked hands moving over the boards. He'd been at it for ten hours this session, George had said: catheter-job, as they called it. But Sage was like that when he got stuck into something. Incapable of taking a break. It wasn't a *bad* sign.

Ax stood and watched. First time he'd realised there had to be something more than a giant drunken toddler behind the skull-mask had been when he noticed (ignorant as he was of the craft) the complexity of those immersions. That flood of weirdly sensual, brain-battering sound and light was *built*: bit by fucking bit. Listening to Sage and Peter Stannen talking about what they did: shooting strings of ten and twelve digit hue-codes at each other, computing the rainbow, could be chilling. It made you think that this was how the mask handled its repertoire of emotions: shuffling telephone numbers. But it was impressive.

Maybe the netheads will sort it, he thought. We could get lucky.

'Hi, rockstar.'

'Hi.'

'How's it going?'

'Have a look.' Masked little finger of the right hand moved a slide: a dizzying landscape of strange hills and valleys appeared on the centre screen, in faux-3d: a cratered plain, an array of glassy smooth volcanic cones, the impression of immeasurable vastness.

'You any the wiser?' inquired the skull, malignly.

'I suppose it has something to do with probabilities, statistically preferred solutions.'

'Well done.'

Ax came over and peered at another monitor screen. 'Who's Theodosius the Dacian?'

'Romanian bloke. We met 'im when we did the East Bloc tour. Computer artist, good one. He's bonded labour to some division of World Entertainment: they bought him, they own everything he does, and they do nothing, just sit on it . . . Is he bitter? Yeah, he's bitter. He ripped us off . . . can't remember. Tickets? Venues that didn't exist?' Sage's hands kept tapping keys, shifting slides and toggles, but the landscape didn't change, that Ax could see. 'George doesn't like him much. I got into a correspondence with him, never sure whether it was friendly, always, you can fuck off rich lucky crass no-talent, I'm better than you . . . which you endure because, you know why . . . And . . . here we are, talking about how to fuck Ivan. He's my cellmate, him and Arek. You know Arek Wojnar?'

'Music publisher? Shit, yes I do.'

'Also hacker . . . Small world.'

'You're working in a virtual reality?' Ax looked closer at the dizzying landscape. 'In there?'

'Nah . . .' The skull kept staring ahead, the wrap around its eyesockets looking very weird. 'I never had much time for frolicking around in cyberspace dressed as the Easter Bunny, if we could spare the bandwidth. I wear my mask on the outside. The machine I'm using is standalone. What you see there is an image of what my cellmates and I are trying to do, but we're working separately. I prefer to have the chat come up as lines of type, it's less irritating. But I can talk to them, and I can send them updates in plain code by cable . . . For a little while longer,' he added grimly.

There was a tiny glowing ball rolling up one of the slopes. As Ax watched, it slipped back.

'Can you tell me anything I'll understand?'

'Oooh, okay. Look, this is part of a reconstruction of the original Ivan.'

The strange landscape on the centre screen vanished, replaced by a lot of code.

'Ivan is . . . slow. Polish anti-Russian comment. That's where GOD MUST BE A MUSCOVITE comes from, in whatever language you're using. Apparently it's a quote from a letter of Chopin's . . . meaning, God's always on the side of the bastards. Ivan slows things up a tiny amount, but over a few billion iterations, it clogs the works. That's what Ivan *does*. Very simple. What Ivan is, is *fucking outrageously complicated*. This is not some plug-the-modules late-capitalist-slacker conceptual art. This is a class act. The shits who put Ivan together could have got a fucking *Nobel Prize* for this kind of coding. But no, they are hippies. They prefer to tear things apart. And that's why I'm in on this, by the way . . . there.'

Sage pointed at a section of teeming code, at random for all Ax could tell, with a virtual finger. 'That's from *Morpho*. I wrote that.'

The Heads' first album, which had burst on the world like a solar flare, a new dimension: telling a retro-handicraft guitarist he might as well pack it in. If Ax had been prepared to listen.

'Oh. So . . . if you wrote it, then you must be able to unwrite it?'

'No such fucking luck. I was a lot cleverer when I was seventeen, and . . . the *Morpho* code is way back at the dawn of time by now. Precambrian. I haven't a clue.'

'What about Lara? What does she do?'

'Oh, Lara. Bless her.' Sage laughed. 'What d'you think she does? She wanders around looking for things. She jumps, she runs, she can get into the most impregnable strongholds, and she is . . . strangely attractive. But you knew that. Lara is also seriously overdetermined, extremely complicated: a labour of love. You should be proud of these people, Ax.' The hands moved with bitter precision, doing something that made the ball hop around in a wistful way, like a bored toddler . . . 'They are genuine post-futuristic *artisans*. We have the guys who wrote Lara on the team, as you probably heard: couldn't turn themselves in quick enough, and they are very sorry. But they can't help much. She's back at the dawn of time too. Trouble is, nothing we already thought of works. This is like, *chaotic alien molecular biology*. Oh, someone will work it out. Someday. But it is not going to be me. Other problem, worse than the weirdness of Ivan/ Lara, is the revolution. Trying to contain a really smart virus, never mind zap it, under pan-European CCM Crisis conditions . . . is fucking impossible.'

'So the Lara part sneaks itself into different systems, then the Ivan part slows things down, and this causes all hell to break loose.'

'You got it.'

The question that Ax had wanted to ask was answered by the skull's bleak expression, and the tired, angry sound of his friend's voice. He sat down anyway, clearing a stack of immersion storyboard notebooks from a chair: thinking of Yap Moss, and the great comfort of having Sage by his side through that whole ordeal. Wishing he could do something, bewildered that he could not, hoping that by *being here* he could offer some support.

After a very few minutes, the astronaut couch swivelled round. Sage pulled off the eyewrap. The skull wasn't looking friendly. 'Ax, I had a visit this morning from the powerbabes. I spent an hour trying to explain quantum cryptography to them. I don't know why I did that, I am weak and vulnerable . . . Would you kindly *fuck off*. I'm busy.'

'Okay, sorry. I'm leaving. Just one more question.'

'*What?*'

'Are we winning?'

'No.'

By the seventh day, people were beginning to get worried. It had even dawned on the Few that their livelihoods were at stake. Bill came up to the studio to tell him that Sayyid Muhammad had called for special Friday prayers from all the Faithful. Huh. Muslims don't argue with God. Think I don't know that? Christian and Hindu leaders followed suit, not to be outdone. Did no good. Gaia obviously had the divine intervention angle well closed down.

On the ninth day, they knew they had to give up.

'Hey, Arek . . . Theo . . . Reckon it's time to call Mission Control?'

. . . Way past time, dear Sage. But convince our team leaders. Who likes to admit defeat?

Theo had stopped talking. He sent a poem. The poem said, everything is fucked, the only thing left is to die with dignity. It didn't seem to Sage like an overreaction.

The team-leaders decided to quit about six in the evening.

The morning after the virus-cracking team surrendered, four skull-masked Heads turned up at the Insanitude together. Most of the Few had been there all night. Ax had been waiting for a call from the Prime Minister, telling him what the Internet Commission had decided to do. The PM had called at midnight to say he had no news yet. Nothing since. Everyone was in the Office, drinking dishwater coffee and staring at the fly-eye screen. Nearly all the cells were blank. Two were playing kiddie programmes; there was one black and white movie, and a single French station, reporting with very bad sound from Lyons on some fearsome street-fighting riots. Radio news had nothing, either.

'This is ridiculous,' said Verlaine. 'How are we supposed to find out what happened?'

'Go out and buy a paper?' suggested Chip.

'It's an idea,' said Dilip. 'Are you going to call the suits, Ax?'

He shook his head. 'I don't think that would be appropriate.'

It felt like another day, different troubles, but this time the problem wasn't one poor crazy murdering bastard. The monster they were shackled to this morning had killed hundreds of people, directly or indirectly, left millions more stranded without power or water, destroyed European e-commerce, slashed billions from the finance markets, triggered new CCM violence, and was still wreaking apocalyptic havoc—

George said, 'This network's been offline since well before Ivan/Lara struck. We're clean. Let's power up and log on, see if we can get out.'

'We can't log on,' protested Allie. 'We'll catch the virus. What do you mean? Get out of where?'

'Someone hasn't been paying attention,' said Bill Trevor.

'Fucking bizarre,' said Peter. 'And yet she's a whizz with a spreadsheet.'

Sage sat at one of the office-work keyboards, powered up and (with a sour grin for the Heads) ran the new virus-checker they'd installed. After taking Allie so severely to task for her appalling, wilful ignorance of anything behind the front end, the Heads and Sage had both been wiped out within an hour of the strike. Fiorinda must have been among the last hitters to see them alive. There was no defence against Ivan/Lara.

'Might as well,' said Bill. 'Why not.'

Everyone stood around, praying they wouldn't see GOD MUST BE A MUSCOVITE.

'Okay,' said Sage. 'I'm going to Australia. Straight from our gate, no changing planes.'

No.

'Well, fine. I don't like Australia anyhow. Too many huge blond guys, getting hammered and falling over things . . . crap like that. I think I'll go to India.'

No.

'Let's go to Russia, watch some war movie—'

No.

'What about China?'

No way into China, or Japan . . . Africa South . . . West African Union . . . United Islamic Republics . . . Israel . . . ASEAN . . . 'Shit, this is boring. Let's go an' ask the masters of the universe, what the fuck? What kind of way is this to run a communications business—?'

No entry to North America.

It was the charnel look today, dry and yellow, with the clinging slivers of flesh, upper joints of the virtual fingerbones on his right hand stained nicotine brown, sly touch. He went on trying and failing, cheerily rattling in the codes, seeming to take a mordant pleasure in it, until he had covered the whole wide world. Pushed himself away from the desktop.

'That's it. Meltdown. We do not exist.'

'Maybe they just upped the barriers,' suggested Bill.

'You wish.'

'Maybe it's a solar flare,' said Chip. 'It would be like our luck—'

'Not at this latitude,' said Verlaine wisely.

'Maybe it's World War Three—'

'Oh, *excellent idea*.' The skull turned on her with such a vicious snarl, poor Allie actually jumped backwards. They all stared at each other, and involuntarily also moved back.

Sage tapped his wrist. 'Olwen . . . Hi, Olwen. How's Serendip? . . . Thank God for that . . . Well, I am *feeling* superstitious. Yeah, we just found out . . .' Silence, Sage listening, sombrely attentive. At last he said, 'Thanks. Yeah, you too. Later.'

The Office, with its stacks of flyers and demo acetates, documents and big fat reference files, everything neater than usual because of the computer network overhaul, seemed to watch them as they waited for him to explain. On the wall above the desktop where he was sitting, there was a cork noticeboard stuck with map pins and messages. A cartoon clipped and put up by Fiorinda: guitarist bends vampiric over his girlfriend's lovely throat. Think bubble says: *Why! She's got a neck just like my Stratocaster.*

A distant dance beat thumped from the club venue, where life was going on. The San was established now; it had its deadpan entry in London Listings: Great system, no dress code, very mixed crowd. Resident DJ is classic IMMixer DK; if you really want your brains burned, *must catch* Aoxomoxoa and George.

'This time yesterday,' said Sage, 'we thought we could see Ivan/Lara starting to downscale. We couldn't prove it, and we couldn't take the risk. Today, Olwen says someone's proved that the virus *will* fade, soon. But it's too late. Ivan/Lara sneaked into the US somehow and flared up there yesterday afternoon, Eastern Time. They'll be okay, it's contained, but this made up the Commission's minds to proceed with the most extreme of the sanctions options. They're building clear water firewalls around Europe, to remain until we have replaced the infected networks *from scratch*. Which is not going to happen, the state things are in. So that's it. We are fucked. The dark ages begin here.'

He stood up, and put his arms around Allie Marlowe. 'Sorry. Shouldn't have yelled at you.'

This unprecedented move did not last long. Sage backed off at once, Allie just nodded, hurriedly, still looking scared. But it seemed to confirm the grim awe of the situation.

'What does *clear water* mean, exactly,' said Chip, cautiously, 'in this context?'

'Sudden death. Physical exclusion, besides the software barriers and signal jamming. Cut the undersea cables, fry the earth stations, police the ionosphere. They've had two years to watch what's been happening in Europe and plan for this kind of disaster. They were ready to go. They've already cut the transatlantic cables, and zapped Goonhilly.'

'Jee-sus . . .' breathed George. 'Can they do that?'

'I just said, they've done it. They're the firemen. They can do whatever shit they like. And since Ivan/Lara is capable of *destroying modern civilisation*, for a while at least, wherever it strikes, I don't fucking see how we can blame them.'

'I can't believe it,' whispered Felice, the senior powerbabe. 'How could things get *so bad, so quickly*?'

'It was one of the losses I was expecting,' said Ax, wearily. 'One of the top probabilities.'

When he spoke they realised that he hadn't spoken before, and that their cyborg was standing out of the group, watching them across what suddenly seemed an abyss. Fiorinda crossed it instantly, put her arms round him. Ax's head went down, face hidden against her shoulder for a moment. He looked up.

'Welcome to my world, folks. Remember when you wouldn't let me tell you the details?'

They went on staring, some of them looking very weirdly concerned.

'Oh, don't be stupid. What d'you think I'm going to do? Stick a modem jack in my eye-socket? I will not catch Ivan/Lara. True. Fuck's sake, let's get this in proportion. It's something that was more or less bound to happen, it's not *new* bad news; and we'll deal with it.'

The phone did ring at last. Ax went off to Whitehall, and was gone for hours. Rob and the Eyes went back to Lambeth Road, to touch flesh with their people, bring the household up to speed on the state of the calamity. The others stayed behind, hanging round the Insanitude. The world seemed in suspension. It was like a metaphysical power-cut, a loss so formless it felt like a physical symptom: a dull headache, a hangover, a bereavement.

Some time in the afternoon, after the last clubbers had gone home, Fiorinda went looking for Sage. He was in the ballroom. How strange, if they'd just been bombed back into the Stone Age, that he was still able to search the fx index and plant this huge, ivory-white carved column of coherent light in the middle of the floor.

He was standing staring at it, arms folded.

'What is that?'

'Trajan's column,' he said, without looking round. 'Scanned from the plaster cast in the V&A. Amazing, isn't it. Did you know, the Romans had military technology that wasn't reinvented in the West for fifteen hundred years? Battlefield medics as good as anything until World War Two. Brock used to be full of shit like that. Pub quiz answers.'

'Brock?'

'Reenactment nut, up in Yorkshire. He'll be a happy man today. Those guys are Dacians. Romanians. I think my friend Theo killed himself last night. Not sure, but I think he did.'

She could feel the pain and anger and darkness that welled out and surrounded him, pulling him into the dreadful spiral where nothing is any good. 'Sage, is there anything I can do?'

'Fiorinda.' The skull turned on her a look of cold, final distaste. 'Leave me alone.'

That evening the club was closed. The door police, catering and bar-staff either didn't turn up or were sent home. The Few and friends gathered in the Bow Room, a nightclub chill-out lounge opening onto the gardens. No one wanted to be up in the Office, with those Sunspark monitor screens staring like the eyes of dead animals. Rob and the babes had returned with a stack of takeaway. A random feast in cartons was scattered around, none of it very appealing, but people were eating anyway. It was something to do. Everybody was longing for Aoxomoxoa to jump up, saying, 'Ah, this is no good!' and make it all right, take them on the town. But not this time. Sage was sitting in bleak silence, the avatar mask doing *fuck off: this is a time out*; the other Heads grouped around him like a defensive guard.

'We should cut a collaboration,' said Dora, the middle powerbabe. She was huddled by the windows to the terrace, propped against one of the Bow Room's sleek marble columns. It was summer evening daylight out there, but so cold you looked for frost on the grass. 'Call it *Dead In The Water.*'

'What fucks me up,' said Cherry, the youngest babe, 'is the way it goes on, and on, and on, and on. One *damn* thing after another, one *damn* thing after another.' She was near to tears. 'It's never going to stop, never going to let up, and then when I'm old I'm still going to have to spend *ten fucking years dying of cancer.*'

'It's a tough way to spend the last days of my youth,' said Roxane, wryly. S/he was looking very tired. 'At my age, catastrophic disasters show up far too clearly in the mirror.'

'You probably won't die of cancer,' Ax told Cherry. 'It was an epidemic, we brought it on ourselves, a lot of it's on the way out. One thing the green movement has been good for.'

'Gee, thanks, Ax. That really helps.'

'Who needs cancer,' said Sage, bitterly, out of his dark distance, 'when we have about fifteen hundred strains of viral pneumonia, and no drugs for any of them.'

Ax had come back from his hours with the suits looking haggard. The news he'd brought was, in one sense, reassuring. They were not in trouble.

Of course they were not in trouble. This for certain was not the moment for the government to be picking a fight with Ax Preston. Otherwise, everything was as bad as it had looked this morning. The Ivan/Lara devastation went on, and they had been dumped out of the world.

Apart from grey areas in South East Asia and Africa, that didn't count because they were in worse disarray than Western Europe; the only protests against the WIC action had come from South America, where certain nation-states were asserting that they would maintain public-access data relations with the Rock and Roll Reich. How they would manage this, in defiance of the Commission and across the firebreaks, remained to be seen, but it was comforting, in a depressing way, to know that they'd like to. Ax Preston and the Chosen had always been mysteriously big in Brazil.

The status of Ireland (where some of the Commissioners had been gathered, in Dublin, since the Ivan/Lara emergency had begun) was under discussion. Scotland and Wales were with England, deep in shit.

'Losing the cables is a fuck of a thing,' said Ax, after a long silence. 'But we have short-wave radio. Olwen was able to pick up the news from the US quite easily, this morning—'

'Whatever "policing the ionosphere" turns out to mean—'

'Look, *it isn't so bad*. The finance markets have survived so far, they're well protected, they'll come through: and there will be the Commission's quarantined satellite link, which we can access; and the multinationals aren't going to give up and go away—'

'Those that haven't quit Europe already. Along with our US ambassador.'

'This isn't anti-virus hygiene,' said Rob, 'it's *punitive*.'

'Yeah. And well fucking deserved.'

'Sage,' said Ax, getting tired of this, 'can't you think of anything positive to say?'

'No.'

No one is going to say it, but several people are thinking: the reason Aoxomoxoa is so gutted is because *he's* the global rockstar and internet megabuck earner. Which is grossly unfair, and that's why nobody's saying it: but it hangs in the air.

'What really fucks me off,' he says now, 'is how many hippie idiots are *triumphant* tonight.'

'You're exaggerating. It was an accident, or not an accident, a helpless consequence of monoculture and system overload. Nobody wanted this.'

'No? Then Gaia is some fucking ace virus author.'

'Don't say that, Sage. Grow up. Conspiracy theory is the *last* thing we need.'

'Oh, please tell me what I'm supposed to think, Ax. What's the spin? What's your fucking happy little fantasy this time?'

'I'm not going to pursue this conversation. If you haven't the brains to know when you're burned out, I can't fucking help you. Go away and get some sleep.'

The skull and Ax glared at each other. Everyone else kept quiet.

'Hmm,' said Sage. 'George.'

'Yeah, boss?' said George, uneasily.

'You remember, few years ago, we discussed having a manager?'

'Uh, yeah.'

'An' we talked it around, an' we decided we don't need any no-talent parasite scum telling us what to do. We can run our own lives.'

'Yeah,' said Bill, looking hard at the floor.

'Then let's go.'

Up on his feet in one lithe movement. Aoxomoxoa stalks out of the room, the band following, glancing at Ax apologetically.

'Shit,' said Ax, after a shocked pause.

'Don't go after him,' said Fiorinda. 'It won't do any good.'

'I'm not going to chase after him, I just want to—'

He stood up. They all followed him, in a flurried procession, upstairs and through to the East Wing, to the first windows that looked down on the Victoria Monument. Then they saw what Ax had wanted to know. The Heads were cutting down their banner. George stripped it from its pole, rolled it up and stuffed it under his arm. There was no one else about, no sign of the nightwatchmen. Four skull-headed idiots walked off, towards Buckingham Palace Road.

'I hoped he wouldn't do that,' said Ax. 'Fucking childish. Well, I suppose he means it.'

The netheads of England decided to hold a wake. They hired the McAlpine Stadium in Huddersfield, and of course invited the Heads. That was the way things happened in those days: people wanted to do something and they did it, no bureaucracy, no delay. The Heads came on. Their frontman lasted ten minutes on stage, walked off and did not come back. Aoxomoxoa, in various states of consciousness, had subjected his band to many kinds of mayhem: totalled expensive equipment, their own and other people's (never on purpose); knocked himself out, broken a wrist, a foot; cracked ribs, dislocated his shoulder, temporarily blinded himself; sliced open his scalp and played the rest of a set with the skull mask bathed in blood. But this was a first. An appalling breach of the Ideology. The Wake was not a Crisis Management gig, but Sage's behaviour was taken by many to mean that the split was permanent.

The Heads returned to Reading. Stayed there, incommunicado.

The Chosen stayed in London. Ax took his brother Jordan out, to see if they could resolve the trouble Ax was having with the band. The problem was the same as always. They wanted Ax back, and life to be like before. The way it expressed itself was hard to take in the present situation: *You're our brother, why aren't we more important?* The brothers ate together and went to a bar. By eleven o'clock Ax was heading back to Brixton, drained and angry and miserable, Sage's absence walking beside him like a horrible ghost.

Fiorinda had been on at the Academy with Snake Eyes. They'd been running free concerts there with nightly guests, all through Ivan/Lara. She came in at two, heard the guitar as she plodded upstairs, and knew from the way he was playing that he was alone. She wasn't surprised. She hadn't expected the alcohol therapy to work. He put the guitar aside when she walked in.

'Oh well,' he said. 'I hope your show was better than mine.'

Fiorinda shrugged. 'I turned in a performance. Nothing special.'

They sat up in the bedroom, talking, Fiorinda in her midnight blue taffeta, with the emerald sparkles (from the Sue Ryder shop in Belgravia, long ago), curled on the bed; Ax on the floor by her feet. There was no other furniture in the room. Not much else in the flat, besides a newly delivered piano, Ax's guitars, and some partly unpacked boxes. They'd had neither the time nor the heart to think about interior décor.

'I hated my childhood,' said Ax. 'My dad's not violent, have to give him that, but he *battens* on people. We'd be penniless, literally, and he'd be down the pub spending the child benefit. I wanted *not to be like him*, the way other aspiring rockstars want the private jet. As blind desperately, probably as stupidly. I remember it from when I was about six years old. The idea of being the man with the guitar: someone with pride, dignity, a code, righteous standards—'

'The Chosen One,' said Fiorinda, gently.

After that Ballroom parley with the bad guys, she'd had him crying in her arms half the night, *I can't help what's happening to me, I know you hate this, please don't leave me.* And she'd comforted him, promised him she'd always be there. She lay back, thinking how trapped they both were, how miserable and lonely her future—

'Yeah, right. That's where the megalomania comes from. Getting away from my slimeball of a father, being that guitar-man, taking Jordan and Shane with me, that's where it all started. Now I look at Jordan, and I see my dad. He looks at me, he sees a celebrity, and he wants a bigger piece of the perks . . . Did I tell you Milly's pregnant?'

Oooh. 'How pregnant?'

' 'bout four months.'

Ax had never talked about his ex, or how he felt about being traded-in for his hunky no-brain brother. But this was bound to sting. 'Well, it's no use whining to me,' she said, bracingly. 'I think you're mad to expect anything different.'

'All blood-relationships being rotten to the core, by definition. I know. God, yes. *Your* next of kin would frighten the Borgias.' He leaned back and kissed her bare foot. 'I'm not expecting sympathy, I just feel like whining. You wait 'til I get onto racism in the school playgrounds of the rural South West. Another spliff?'

'Yes please.'

No use whining to Sage, either, thought Ax. Fucker used to slide away from the topic: *we drop the subject*. Ax had treated his band like kids, so they behaved like kids. They saw Ax purely as big daddy the meal-ticket, and he had only himself to blame . . . Sage knew it, but he would never say it. But thinking about Sage's forbearance brought him back to that night in the Bow Room. Aoxomoxoa baffled, defeated, up against the wall.

God. I could have given him one kind word.

'That's something I always admired about Sage,' he said. 'Even when he was plaguing the life out of me, the bastard. The way he refused to behave like a celebrity. Something Chrissie Hynde said in an interview once, *if you can't sit on a doorstep in a crowded street eating a slice of pizza, you have lost the game of life*. Sage won't let anyone kick him off that doorstep. Does his circus act, an' drops right back into the crowd: and I know he doesn't find it as easy as he makes out, either.'

'He claims he loves being famous,' said Fiorinda. 'But he wears a mask.'

'Yeah. I spotted that . . . Ah, shit. How the fuck could he *walk out on me*, Fio?'

'He didn't mean to hurt you. He'd just had enough. He gets like that. Did you know, last time he went to Cwm Gared, after Yorkshire, Mary threatened to ban him from ever coming back? She says he's made Marlon into a terrorist target, getting in so deep with us.'

'*God.*' Sage's relationship with his ex-girlfriend and their son was difficult enough at the best of times. 'Why didn't he tell me?'

'I suppose because he didn't want you to know. I'll be in trouble if he finds out I told. If he ever speaks to me again, that is.'

'Well, at least he's got Olwen.'

She went on staring at the ceiling. 'That day we were all moping around at the Insanitude, George said to me he thinks the fling is over. Very good friends, better friends than ever, but it wasn't going to be long term, was it? She and Ellis are very married, in their peculiar Welsh way. And Sage is no breaker-up of happy homes.'

'But if he isn't with Olwen, why's he at Reading? Why hasn't he fucked off somewhere?'

'I don't suppose he cares where he is.'

It was nearly daylight. The naked bulb overhead had faded to sickly yellow. In the unpacking litter on the floor lay a flash American magazine a month old, with Fiorinda on the cover: *Cool Britannia?* said the copy. *They don't come cooler, but please don't use the 'B' word!* Ax stared at it with eyes too tired to look away. Cinders and ashes. There'd be no more covers like that. The internet was *over*, he told himself. Permanent gridlock, stupid. A couple of years down the line, we'll have something new and better. Look on this as an opportunity . . . Cinders and ashes.

'Ah, sod it,' he said. 'This is ridiculous. Let's go and dig him out.'

Sage was lying on his bed in the back of the van, which was more or less what he'd been doing since the Huddersfield gig, chewing on the humiliation of having walked off stage (please tell me I didn't do that); thinking about stupid things. Why do I have crippled hands? Why do I have a kid whose existence ties me *for life* to the corpse of a rotten, evil, destructive relationship? Why do I have to be in love with my best friend's girl? Does Ax know about the *Flowers for Algernon* scenario? Round and round, down and down, getting nowhere, scraping bone, the tedium of it worse than failing to crack Ivan. I don't know what to do with the rest of my life. I *just don't know*. Thinking of Theo, and the millions of people who had *really* been fucked over by what had happened to the world, and despising himself.

He heard people arriving, voices, George saying, 'Come to see the Creature From The Black Lagoon?'; he didn't move. Fiorinda and Ax walked in.

'Hallo,' said Fiorinda. 'Are you feeling any better?'

'No.'

'Luckily you don't have to do anything except sit in the car,' said Ax. 'Come on, get up. You're taking us to Cornwall.'

The avatar mask stayed blank, Sage's long body sunken flat into the silver grey quilt; not a spark of interest. 'You can't go anywhere. You have to help the government sort the crisis.'

'Fuck 'em,' said Ax. 'They'll have to get by. "εις τουτον 'εγω καθιζιμι τον θρονον 'ευ ωι πλεον ουδεν 'εξουζιν οι φιλοι παρ'εμοι των 'αλλοτριων." '

'What?' said the mask, barely moving.

'It's ancient Greek,' explained Ax, sitting on the end of the bed. 'Means something like *I didn't get into this shit so I could let down my friends*. It's what Themistocles said to the Athenians, when they were accusing him of cronyism one time in the Persian Wars.'

'*Themistocles?*' Sage sat up, abruptly. '*What have you been doing to yourself, Ax?*'

'What's the matter? I've been looking at the freebies that came with my datastack. I never bothered before, I naturally assumed it was a pile of junk. But it's good. There's a whole lot of the Greek and Roman stuff, God knows what else. I've hardly started.'

'You're completely mad,' said Fiorinda. 'Your head will explode.'

'And when you've opened these files,' said Sage, looking at Ax intently, 'they stay instantly available, in your memory, yes? Have you tried closing them again?'

'Well, no, because the only way I know how to do it is with Delete, and I don't know how well Undelete works. I'd hate to lose something I might need. There's stuff about it in the manual, but it's in gibberish, and anyway, who reads manuals?'

'Some people do. You can download, can't you? Would you download a copy for me?'

Ax shook his head. 'No,' he said firmly. 'Sorry, but no. This is mine.'

'Okay,' said Sage, reckoning he could surely find what he wanted somewhere on the nets – should have thought of it long ago—

But not now—

Ax laughed. It was wonderful to see the mask come alive, mobile and transparent as ever. 'Better get him out of here. He's just thought of something else that he can't do.'

'Well, I'll have to talk to George.'

'You don't need to talk to George. Just get in the car.'

'Let him talk to George,' said Fiorinda, resignedly. 'It's quicker in the long run.'

Ax and Fiorinda had started their day very early, but arranging an impromptu flight responsibly (Allie had not been pleased) had taken time, and the drive was slower than it had been before the Tour, owing to ripped-up motorways. It was twilight when they reached Bodmin Moor. Ax pulled up in the middle of nowhere. They all three got out of the car, the road at this point an unfenced single track; the rising land stretched out, vast and wild in its small compass, to every horizon. They listened again to what Ax had heard. A few sheep went on cropping the summer turf, unperturbed.

'That is a wolf, isn't it?'

Sage nodded.

'How many are there?'

'Eleven. Used to be thirteen. One got killed, one decided she was a care in the community case and kept hustling for scraps round Bodmin. Had to go back to the reservation.'

'Aren't you afraid they'll kill the panthers, pumas or whatever they are?' said Fiorinda.

'All those pumas are Labradors. The world can spare a few stupid Labradors.'

He walked away, into the landscape. After a few minutes they realised they'd better follow him. When they caught up he'd found a hut circle, the Stone Age debris half-buried in green bracken. They sat on either side of him, leaning against the stones. Fiorinda looked at the nameless small flowers growing around her feet: a moss covered with tiny red-capped stalks; the lichens on the boulders like thick slow spiderwebs. She thought the moor was like Sage's art: bare and stark on the wide scale, nit-pickingly complex in detail.

'Ax,' said Sage, at last, 'you've got to do something about Benny Prem.'

'Problem with that,' said Ax. 'I don't want to get involved in politics . . . All right, very funny, both of you: go on, laugh. I mean *conventional* politics.'

'Oh yeah. Like assassination, that kind of conventional.'

'It won't come to that. I'd rather leave him alone until I know more.'

'I can't stand him,' said Fiorinda. 'There's a kind of bloke who, the first time they look at you, their only thought is *she wouldn't fuck me*, and probably they are right, but where do they get off—? But they instantly hate you for it, and will feel justified in doing you down, forever afterwards, any way they possibly can . . . Bastards. Huh. All men are scum.' She noticed that they were staring at her. 'What? What's wrong?'

'Except us?' said Sage, anxiously.

'Fiorinda, could we have a truce on the battle of the sexes? Just a *temporary* truce?'

She sighed. 'Ah, okay. Truce while the woods are burning. You're right, Ax; sorry.'

They sat together, not talking, listening for wolves, but failing to see or hear any further sign of them, until the stars began to show, in a chill sky of robin's egg blue. Then they drove on.

The cottage was cold. It had been empty since they were down in March. They'd eaten before they reached the moor (Ax had eaten; Sage and Fiorinda had stared at some food), so they didn't have to worry about cooking. Fiorinda lit the fire that had been set in the living room by Sage's housekeeper, weeks ago. The kindling was damp, but she used her tinderbox and it caught instantly. She sat back on her heels, the apple-shape of the box cupped in her palm thinking, *now it's serious*. The last time they'd been here, the situation had been like a game in comparison. The relief at being friends with Sage again was intense, it turned everything around: and changed nothing. She stared at the young fire, fear crisping her nerves, a thought coming to her unbidden, like a premonition . . . *in the end, there will be nowhere I can hide.* Ax had taken their bags upstairs. He came back and headed for the cupboard where the jigsaws lived, touching her hair as he passed. Sage was reviewing the archive of black vinyl and other dead media in the high-stacked cabinets against the back wall.

'Any requests?'

'Better be nice to him,' said Ax. 'He's having a nervous breakdown, remember. How about one of those wonderful four hour reel-to-reel Dead concert bootlegs, circa 1972?'

'Any more insolence, I'll make you sit through *From Anthem To Beauty* again.'

They been forced to watch *From Anthem To Beauty*, the video record of the Grateful Dead's early years, a sacred scripture of the Ideology, when they were here in March. 'That would be fine,' said Ax. 'I have no problem with the fiction. It's the music I can't stand.' He brought the puzzle he'd selected over to the hearth, set it on the jigsaw board and began sorting out edges. 'I can take the feedback shit. And even some of the songs. But that endless futile impro on over-sugared melody—'

'Like yards and yards and yards of pink fondant icing,' agreed Fiorinda. 'Makes you wonder what kind of acid they had in those days. Must have been sickly stuff.'

'Why don't you put on *Aoxomoxoa*, Aoxomoxoa? You must have a copy. Very Crappest Dead album, against some tough fucking competition. Did he ever play that for you, Fio?'

'Yes, he did. Well, he put it on.'

'What'd'you do?'

'I howled like a dog.'

'You two are sleeping with the slugs.'

'But I always wondered, with the name: do you really *admire* that unbelievable shit?'

'That's it. You're under the hedge. I'm gonna put both of you out in the garden.'

'I think it's the first track of side one that counts,' said Fiorinda. 'Saint Stephen.'

Stephen was Sage's original name. He stalked out of the room, the skull giving them a blistering glare; returned with a bottle of red wine in each hand. 'Get some glasses, Fee.'

'Hahaha. Sainthood, what a touching aspiration. We all have our little fantasies.'

'Don't we, Oh Chosen One. You can stop being nice to me now, thanks. I feel much better.' He set down the bottles, returned to the dead media wall. Something warm and steely and classical began to play, reproduction in stunning contrast to the age of the vinyl.

'What's this?'

'Beethoven, cello and piano. Okay?'

It was a very old jigsaw, a three-masted ship under a lot of complex canvas, the subtle difference between the sails and a faded, cream and golden rack of sunset clouds going to be a challenge. They worked on it together for an hour or so, drinking the wine, Sage and Ax continuing to snipe at each other gently; softly barbed play-fighting . . . Fiorinda sat back to get a better look at the pieces and suddenly, in the lamplight and the fireglow, she saw them as two animals – as if she'd taken one of those jungle drugs from South America. Sage stretched out at lazy length, uttering harmless threats. That growling sound is really the big guy purring. Ax crouched on one knee, the other leg folded under him, eyes fixed in alert, relaxed calculation on the prey. This pasteboard world, which he will patiently subdue into order: sort it, seize it, run it to the ground . . .

My tiger and my wolf. I wonder what I am to them. Not an animal, I think. More like some vital element, like water or fire.

Or meat.

The next day was still cold, as if the May heatwave had never been.

They spent it as they'd spent their time in March, bickering pleasantly over the chores, playing computer games in Sage's studio, watching the birds in the garden. They ventured outdoors once, late in the day, to walk up and down the little river Chy from the waterfall pool to the stepping stones, but did not leave the twelve acres of Tyller Pystri, the magic place. Came back to the house to cook together in that defiantly inconvenient little kitchen: smoking grass, drinking wine, Fiorinda making chapati dough, Ax chopping vegetables (not from Sage's garden: Mrs Maynor, his housekeeper, had brought them from her husband's allotment); Sage rooting out a tin of chickpeas. 'Fuck, an actual sealed tin, no ring pull . . . Oh, Ax, reminds me. Remember the bottle of wine we drank in the van, that night with Fiorinda?'

'No.'

'I'm not surprised,' said Fiorinda. 'You were *severely* out of it, Ax.'

'Look who's talking . . . Well, it turns out that was a bottle of wildly expensive irreplaceable Montrachet, given to George by Laurel last Christmas. (Laurel was George's wife, the potter.) He thought it was safe from me because he knows I hate trying to use a corkscrew. I told him it was nectar of the gods, and he's reasonably happy with that, so you will back me up? Hey, isn't anyone going to open this for me?'

'Nectar of the gods. Sage, last time we were here I recall trying to take an antedeluvian tin-opener task away from you and you were at my throat. Said you *fucking come here to get away from being treated like a fucking toddler.*'

'Yeah. Sometimes I feel like that . . . sometimes I don't.'

'And we have to guess,' said Fiorinda. 'Like Russian roulette.'

'Thas' right.'

They ate and cleared away and settled to a round of Risk, the world domination game. The usual pattern swiftly emerged: Ax and Fiorinda stockpiling their plastic soldiers and plotting; Sage playing *go for it until you got no armies left*. To Ax's annoyance, this idiotic strategy swept the board as often as any other plan. Honours in the tournament were even.

'Do you wear the masks when no one else is around?' asked Ax. 'Often wondered.'

'Yeah, we do.'

'Can you tell whether it's on or not? Are you conscious of it?'

'If I think about it. Not usually.'

'So when *do* you take it off? Are there Head Ideology rules about that? I'm gonna seize China. Two dice.'

'Well, I have to take it off to sleep, but otherwise, lessee, what else? To shave—'

'Right. Brings us up to about twice a year—'

'Fuck off. As a gesture of respect or to make a point, sometimes; and to fuck. But even then,' the mask switched, grinning evilly, to the freshly rotted version, with tiny crawling maggots, '—not always.'

'You don't scare me,' said Fiorinda. 'Do the sicking-up worms. See how Ax likes it.'

'Ha, the Red Army stands firm. Another throw?'

'Yeah. Why d'you have to take it off to sleep?'

'Because if I don't it gives me nightmares.'

'Really?' said Ax. 'That's interesting. My implant gave me horrible nightmares when I first had it done. Literally indescribable. It's a very unpleasant feeling, waking up terrified from an experience for which you have no words, no images. Went on for weeks. Okay, now we're getting somewhere. Again . . . And once more.'

'The things you do to yourselves,' said Fiorinda. 'You're both insane. You must be dead clever, Sage, if you can make a mask that will lift your expressions and copy them in the avatar in realtime. Which we always assume is what it does . . . at least, when you want it to.'

'Nah. Building an avatar mask is simple, just obsessive. I could teach you. Either of you.'

Teach, Ax heard. Now there's an idea. 'China is mine. I'm stopping there, give me a card.'

'It was my hands that I wanted to hide,' said Sage, unexpectedly. 'Call it childish if you like, Ax, but I don't enjoy looking at them. The skull was a natural extension, and then we all had to have one; and it became . . . a game, an addiction. Couldn't give it up now, for business. Punters would never forgive me. But I won't wear it any more when I'm with you two, if you don't want.' And his natural face was there with them: eyes lowered, smiling faintly, white skin still wheat-coloured from two weeks of NDog sunscreen.

'Oh, but I *love* the mask,' said Fiorinda.

'Hm.' He grinned. 'Well, I always thought it was an improvement, myself.'

'I know it's not a mask, I know it's you.'

'I don't mind either way,' said Ax. 'It's all Sage's face to me.'

'Fiorinda, I'm attacking Iceland.'

'Hey, I thought we had a pact of non-aggression.'

'We do, we do. I just have to recover my continent. Look at you two, divvying up the world between you. C'mon, let me have one miserable continent.'

About midnight, Fiorinda said, 'Are we going back tomorrow?'

They were back in the living room. When she spoke they all looked at the landline phone on the table by Sage's bed. Allie had the number, and permission to call them if she really needed to. At least it'd kept quiet.

They'd had two days of escape. Couldn't really ask for more.

'I suppose we'd better,' said Ax, slowly. 'You okay for that, Sage?'

'Oh yeah,' he said, 'since we must.' He sounded surprised. 'Why wouldn't I be?'

'Er . . . you were having a nervous breakdown two days ago.'

'His tantrums are horrible,' said Fiorinda, 'but they vanish. You'll get used to it.'

Sage went to change the record, giving her topnotes of withering scorn and dire warning, mixed with tender affection; remembered that he was unmasked and started to laugh. No remote controls, only about four tracks to a side: listening to black vinyl entailed a lot of getting up and down, kind of like a religious ceremony. He came back and lay on the couch. Fiorinda and Ax kept on working at the sailing ship jigsaw, although they weren't going to finish it. Fiorinda in her venerable green dress, her hair aglow, Ax's guitar-man hands problem-solving as if with their own inbuilt intelligence . . . Suppose this is it, Sage thought, watching them. She's mortally afraid of things she can't tell. Ax is in despair at what's happening to him, but he can't quit. I'm no better off, in my trivial personal way. And the world out there is fucked to scary shit. What if there's no way out, and the situation only gets worse? What if this, now, is all we have? After a while Fiorinda looked up, and then Ax. Nothing was spoken.

Fiorinda returned to the jigsaw; Ax decided to go and look at the stacks of vinyl. The lamplit room was filled with a strange and painful tranquillity. Very bitter, very sweet.

EIGHT

Rock The Boat

Strange how much remains unchanged, although the world ended (again) ten days ago. The tv studio, late night and live: very simple, no fx being layered over what you see here – the comfy chairs, the presenter, Fiorinda, Aoxomoxoa and the Heads, and Roxane Smith. Quite a line up. This is a date that was scheduled before Ivan/Lara, and postponed. More than half the country still has no tv reception, but they've decided to go ahead: might be a while before the proverbial normal service gets resumed. The presenter is a young woman (only a few years older than Fiorinda) called Dian Buckley. Thrilled at having the Heads – who so rarely do this sort of thing – on her programme, she's unwisely decided to talk about the big break. Did you have any idea that *Morpho* was going to be so successful?

'No,' says Aoxomoxoa, unhelpfully.

'So, how did you feel? Suddenly, you were eighteen and famous.'

'Very surprised.'

'What about the rest of you, were you surprised? That was a *stunningly* successful debut album.'

'Oh, we knew,' says George Merrick. 'We kept tellin' 'im, but he wouldn't believe us. He thought the record company would dump us in six months.'

'Whereas what happened was that you decided to dump them . . . and it turned out to be hard work. Do you now think that was a mistake?'

'We're a live band,' said Sage, ignoring this. 'For what we do, do it best, you need a space you can saturate and manipulate, and a couple of hundred sweaty punters. I can't never really see taking our stuff home and sitting there with a wrap round your head—'

'They shouldn't be *able* to dance . . . The club IMMix stuff you get now is nothing like what we started off with—'

'Uncontrollable vomiting and defecation is okay—'

'Much less doing the show in a fucking great huge *field*,' puts in Peter. 'People are weird.'

'But we don't mind taking their money—'

Moving on to the current anomalous situation vis à vis Ax Preston and friends . . . Fiorinda, now you're the one who's eighteen and famous. Before the virus, you'd bumped the Heads from the top of the European album charts, *and* you were keeping Ax Preston and the Chosen out of the English singles spot (it's such a cliché isn't it, teenage girl beats the heavyweights?). How d'you feel about people saying it's only the Ax effect?

Huh. *Stonecold* is not exactly a babystar popsong—

'Gutted,' said Fiorinda, and answered some more fairly patronising questions in the vein of *how does it feel to be the kid sister in the gang?* with good humour. She had a nerve-free indifference to this sort of event that came of having started in when she was fourteen and so wrapped up in her own little world she 'did tv' without a thought.

'It's her aerobics video what worries us,' said Aoxomoxoa, leaning back to grin at the teenage star. 'Once she gets that out, the rest of us are totally fucked.'

Okay, but how long can this go on? Admitted we can't talk about figures at the moment, but there's been an Ax effect in England since the Deconstruction Tour. Snake Eyes and the Adjuvants and DK have been seeing their sales rocketing, and the associate bands, to a lesser extent. Isn't this getting to be like a totalitarian state, where everyone has to, um, buy Chairman Mao's Little Red Book?

'I don't think you can shoot us for being the latest over-exposed media sensation,' said Fiorinda cheerfully. 'It'll pass. We'll be last year's things soon enough.'

'No one's beating 'em into the record stores with clubs,' Peter Stannen pointed out.

'But isn't there this *atmosphere*? Ever since the Tour? You have to have a banner up at the Insanitude gates? Conformity or else—'

'You might have a point,' said Roxane, 'if we were talking ideological anthems, or if the artists were of a different class. But when some of the best musicians in the country—'

'It's the B list that goes for charity work,' Bill reminded everyone dryly. 'Ask anyone. Either crap artists, or flagging-career stadium rockers. Not sure which we are—'

'I'd rather be the crap,' growled Sage.

'Kiss of death,' sighed Fiorinda, 'for a kid like me. Now I'll never be taken seriously—'

'Let me *finish*, children . . .' boomed Rox. 'I repeat, some of the best rock musicians in the country, having given an enormous amount of work and energy for free, start to sell some records simply doing what they do . . . And even then, most of the money goes back—'

But here s/he was vehemently shouted down. The Heads and Fiorinda don't want to talk about where the money goes, none of that. In all their dealings with the media-people of their own industry, tonight and always, the Few will insist on being treated as Indie rockstars, futuristic artisans – who *happen, for the moment*, to be involved in something else besides their music . . . The presenter sat smiling in this lively cage of lions: helpless, excited, glad things were getting more relaxed. Moving on. Roxane, as a male-to-female transsexual, with a bisexual boyfriend, is changing sex the way we change our clothes still glamorous, still radical—?

'I'm not female.' The doyen of rock critique was wearing a long gown of teal green velvet, under a draped, crimson lined jacket, with a sort of flattened, tasselled turban in the same colour scheme: like Dante in opera make-up. Crossing one long leg over the other, folding much beringed, sadly aged hands around one knee, s/he fixed Dian with a look of stern reproof. 'Whatever gave you that idea, young lady?'

'Oh, well, er—'

'I'm an ex-man. That doesn't make me a woman. It's a long time ago, but I'm sure I never intended to become a woman. That wasn't, for me, the object of the exercise.'

'So, how would you define your sexual identity?'

'I *believe* the object of the exercise was to escape from definition. If memory serves.'

'And d'you think you've achieved that?'

'I think sexual identity is a convention that always breaks down – behind closed doors, among the rich, among the poor, among artists and their camp-followers. It's a paranoid, master and wage-slave phenomenon that disappears in any natural society, moral or immoral. Whenever it gets the chance the great divide vanishes, collapses into a fractal mosaic.'

'And do you wish you'd known that—?'

'Thirty years ago? Not at all! I made a personal, innate decision. I'd do it again now.'

'Your particular shape in the mosaic . . . But isn't this just old-fashioned decadence—?'

'It is the way the cards always fall. I think that should tell us something.'

'What about you, Sage? You've been the king of the lads, you've said

233

you hate gays, now here you are in this post-futuristic supergroup, have your opinions mellowed?'

'I don't hate *the idea* of blokes fucking blokes. It's the gay nation. If it's not fascist uniforms, it's a shitload of bitchy misogynist wannabes pretendin' they are girls. Can't stand 'em.'

'*Sage!* That is so crass!'

'And dykes are as bad. I mean, perpetuating the very structures of oppressive gender determinism. Why make a secret society of who you fuck?'

'This would be completely different, of course,' mused Fiorinda, 'from four close male friends habitually going around together dressed up as Hallowe'en decorations?'

The Heads cheered. 'Let Fio interview 'im, Dian,' shouted George. 'She's up to 'is weight.'

'You should ask 'im why he calls hisself a Palindrome, if he don't go both ways—'

'I don't like sex,' said Peter firmly. 'I've tried it, I don't like it. Sage c'n have my share.'

'Fiorinda, do you have a—?'

'Oh, me? I'm a phallus-worshipping lesbian. You can get those. I read about it.'

'So about those masks,' says Dian, after the laughter. 'Do you ever feel trapped by them? Stuck with something that was a novelty ten years ago?'

'Wouldn't do it now,' agreed George, 'but ten years is a long time. We're set in our ways.'

'It's true, you see a lot of masks around these days. Insects, daleks, any fucking thing—'

'We only like the skull'eads. We think the rest are crap.'

'But Sage, yours is different. Now that's something many people would find far more controversial than unorthodox sex . . . a non-medical implant. Isn't that unnatural and scary?'

'Nah. It's a harmless little thing. Look.' Aoxomoxoa popped the masked fifth finger of his right hand into his mouth, sucked it, held his masked right eye stretched wide with the left index finger and thumb, deftly inserted the sucked fingertip into the corner of his eye and—

'Auwk!' squawks Dian, recoiling.

—reaching far *inside* the eyesocket, brings out a bright, tiny button resting on the now unmasked fingertip: offers it to the pretty media person. 'There you go. Don't drop it.'

She can't take it, can't even look at it—

The other skulls have vanished too. This is quite an occasion, the Heads *au naturel* on tv: George Merrick looking splendidly piratical, Bill Trevor splendidly cadaverous, with that elegant hatchet nose (and that's why Bill's skull looks too big, the mask having to accommodate the nose), Peter solemn and rosy and bucolic, and wearing his glasses for a treat. He hates contact lenses, but the others usually veto hornrims on a skull in public. They reckon it isn't the right message.

'That's why we've never let 'im make us avatar masks,' explains Bill, entirely sympathising with Dian's reaction. 'Too fuckin' intimate. And *gross*. But him, he'll try anything weird—'

It has been obvious from the outset that Dian Buckley would not be at all averse to a twenty-second dancefloor courtship. Aoxomoxoa unmasked, right next to her, all blue-eyed, oversized animal magnetism, puts her in a complete tizz . . . a situation the bad lad clearly finds most entertaining. (Dian seems to have been forgiven for daring to talk about *Morpho*.) Now, mask button carefully laid on the table, he's showing her the wrist implant, letting her feel the other little button set into the bone behind his ear. Not weird at all, no no no: rockstars are always having to stick different beans in their ears, it gets annoying, this you can programme, makes life much simpler—

So then Dian tries on George's digital mask – the Countercultural market stall kind, that can be worn in a piercing stud, lapel badge, a cufflink, an earring; on a wristband. No, it doesn't need a battery. Works on ambient. 'You know,' she says, skull-masked, intrigued, turning her head this way and that as she looked off the set into a monitor screen, 'I can see this! I can see going down the supermarket like this, after a heavy night . . .'

'Skull'ead nation welcomes you,' sez George.

Moving on to the newest of the Heads' rockstar toys, something called ATP, and that's what the goldfish bowl full of water on the table in front of the Heads is for, it is to be used for a demonstration. George takes off his jacket; Sage is already wearing only a singlet. Bare arms, nothing up their sleeves, they touch the water for a few seconds and sit back. Dian, gamely playing her Blue Peter part, confirms the water was cold and is now hot. Wow, it's really hot! Within seconds it bubbles: it boils.

Can't prove anything on television, but that is amazing!

At the moment, says Sage, that's a party trick. Doesn't really make sense to use ATP to boil an egg, not yet. But we're getting there. He's been in disgrace with Olwen Devi and with Ax for inciting the weird-science tendency among Reading staybehinds to pump their weedy hippie systems full of creatine supplement and grape sugar so they can do tricks like this one. Tonight he restrains himself, leaves George to say a few words about metabolic energy amplification, and the fun of being your own powerhouse.

Then Sage picks up the mask button on his fingertip, licks it and casually tucks it back into place. With all the skulls restored (before Heads fans watching this start to panic) the discussion becomes general: Rox providing intellectual comment, Fiorinda deflating the excesses. How near to cost-free these futuristic tricks can be, in production and in use, in terms of pressure on the environment. The lives that could have been saved when Ivan/Lara struck, by radically decentralised ATP power supply . . .

Hope you're enjoying this, dear manager.

Not too little, not too much. Soon they were back on interview territory, are you going to tell us any new cheats to get at the secret stuff on *Bleeding Heart*? No! says Sage, laughing. If we told you, it wouldn't be secret, would it, explains Peter patiently. You got to use your initiative. Improve your IT skills . . . Fiorinda, do *you* do this? Is, um, the Guinness Book Of Records since 1989 inclusive hidden on *Friction* anywhere? Not that I know of, says Fiorinda. Whatever shape I am in the mosaic, I definitely do not have the anorak gene—

Curled up on her comfy chair with her boots off, bare toes hidden under opaline organza skirts, she was thinking: life used to be so simple. No nerves, no doubts, no question. Every day, even before she met the man who was her father, either a step towards, or a setback on the way to *a particular kind of fame* . . . The wild-card success that wins all the prizes, without patronage, without corporate backing, just by being the best. Now that's gone. All gone. And the stupid, arrogant little girl who was so obsessed, must see her life from now on in terms of the people she loves, because there is nothing else left. So here she sits in Gulag Europe, playing Ax's game, taking her cues and contemplating this strange new gestalt (the people I love).

She caught Roxane smiling at her, with such understanding she felt frightened.

The Insanitude internal network was running again, Allie's staff picking up the pieces of their empire, with Sage on hand on the first day to troubleshoot. Fiorinda and Anne-Marie Wing were there too, working; plus Chip and Verlaine allegedly helping out, in fact pestering Sage. The triumvirate-soap-watching pair were most intrigued by the flight to Cornwall. It was a great relief to everyone that the three had returned reunited: but what was behind these tantalising references to slugs, and jigsaws—?

'What d'you *do* when you're there?' asked Verlaine.

'Get a little peace,' said Sage, standing up from the board where he'd been sorting out a problem for one of Allie's people. 'Okay, try that.'

'Thanks, Sage,' said the young man nervously. It's an alarming privilege having Aoxomoxoa for technical back-up. He's so big. You pray to God you won't fuck up.

'And war. Ask him what happened in Venezuela,' suggested Fiorinda from across the room.

'Vicious brat shafted me,' said Sage, 'that's what happened.' He left the nervous kid and went over to watch Allie Marlowe's screen.

The tour of the north, promised by Ax and Sage at the end of the Islamic Campaign, was soon due to kick off. They'd decided it had to go ahead, and damn the torpedoes. The whole roadshow circus, the Few and friends, illustrious guests, local support, would be zooming around Yorkshire, Lancashire, Cumbria and the North East for a month, through the start of the Festival season; and then straight back into rehearsal for Ax's inauguration concert at Reading – inauguration or accession, or whatever it was. The suits had capitulated to his weird terms and now wanted this to go ahead as soon as possible.

Nightmare to organise. But by this time Allie felt she was *addicted* to nightmare conditions.

'Is that the big date?' asked Sage.

'So far,' she said, wishing people wouldn't peer over her shoulder, something she hated. 'It works for the suits, haven't had a chance to ask Ax yet—'

'You're gonna have to change it. That's the middle of Ramadan.'

'Is Ax really going to observe Ramadan?' asked Chip, coming over.

'Yeah,' called Fiorinda. 'No food or drink from sunrise to dark, plus he plans to take no drugs at all. It's going to be rough. You're all going to meet that nice Ax Preston's evil twin.' No sex either, apparently, but she didn't think the kids needed to know that.

'Shit,' muttered Allie. 'Well, in July you'll all be touring. It'll have to be September.'

'You don't have to move it far. Just past Eid il Fitri.'

'Oh, but we have to have the full moon,' protested Allie, unexpectedly sentimental—

'Got to have that fat old moon coming up behind Red Stage—' agreed Verlaine.

'Does it? Oh yeah, suppose it must—'

Now they were all breathing down her neck, Chip and Ver and Sage and Fiorinda and Anne-Marie Wing, all getting into the game— 'You couldn't have done it on the August full moon anyway,' said Anne-Marie. 'That's Hungry Ghosts, I'm sure it's inauspicious—'

'I hope you're not going to clash with the Last Night of the Proms,' said Chip worriedly.

'Can't have it in October, that's getting too near Samhain, very much the wrong message.'

'But, ooh, mid-September, isn't Yom Kippur around there? What's the feng-shui on that?'

'That's *not helpful*, Sage. And Yom Kippur is not at the full moon, thank you very much.'

What to do about Benny Prem? At the end of a Whitehall meeting – at which, conveniently, none of his friends had been present – Ax attached himself to the Parliamentary Secretary and strolled with him towards his private office. They were in the building that had been the original home of the Countercultural Think Tank. The meeting had brought up news from France about Alain Jupette and his cadre: seemed as if Alain had decided to stop fanning the flames and was trying his version of the Ax effect: pop-culture icons for social stability. So, what d'you think, Benny? Can Mr Miniskirt swing it?

'You mean the Marquis de Corlay?'

'If he insists.' Ax grinned. 'Alain always did have terrible taste in stage names.'

'I can't get over the way you all know each other,' said Benny wistfully. 'All you rockstars.'

His office was a nice big room, tastefully furnished. He had looked after himself, the treacherous slimeball. Ax sat down by the desk. Benny hovered, clearly very uneasy about this tête-à-tête, but seeing no way to escape. 'We don't. It's the way you and Paul Javert picked out your Think Tank. English rock musicians who'd come to a seminar like that would be likely to have run into Alain.'

'The natural leaders of the Movement.'

Ax laughed. 'Benny, the natural leaders of the CCM were gunned down on massacre night. Except for the ones still lurking in the woodwork, resenting me deeply. The Movement is a political thing. What we are is something different. Lissen—'

Thus invited, Benny – not daring to put himself behind his own desk – sat on another chair.

'We're not their political leaders. We're more like their gods. That's what rockstars are to their public, Countercultural or otherwise. Objects of superstitious devotion. And most of them are clueless, impotent, docile cashcows, getting well fed and making the priests rich, same as most of all the other gods you ever heard of . . . except for the ones who are also criminally insane. It's fair enough. People don't expect any better. They're only as fooled as they want to be. But I'm not like that, Benny. Sage isn't like that. Or Fiorinda, or any of the Few.'

He took out a cigarette and offered the packet. Benny shook his head.

'So that's what you're up against,' said Ax, easily. 'A handful of minor deities, turned out to be real and effective; and walking among the mortals. It's a strange situation. Be careful how you mess with it.'

Held the guy's gaze for a good long moment of calm, smiling silence.

'I see,' said Benny.

Ax had been more worried than he'd liked to admit by that approach to Sage, but he was convinced it was better to leave Prem in place until he knew what lay behind it. He knew he could romance this guy, poor Benny with his irrational longing to be one of the gang . . . Sucker him with a charisma punch, get him to talk: quite possibly turn him, temporarily at least.

Celebrity culture's got to be good for something.

Benny's secretary put his head round the office door, said he had some urgent information from the Internet Commission link, arrived by courier from GCHQ. Benny took the disc, put it into his new Ivan/Lara checker-box, fed it into his machine only when it had come up clean; decrypted it and stared at the text. Ax waited, wondering what now.

'Ax,' said Benny, chummily, looking a little bit thrilled (it must be bad). 'You said losing the internet was something expected . . . What would be *new* bad news?'

Ax shrugged. 'The Black Death?'

'Mmm. I'm to pass this on to you. And the PM will want a meeting, urgently.'

One of the constants of the last few years had been the problem of displaced persons – refugees from war, economic meltdown, climate failure – on the move through Continental Europe. Some were wilful vagabonds, the equivalent of England's drop-out hordes and festival-ground staybehinds. Some were displaced within the EU. Others were from Africa, from Central Asia, Russian satellites, Turkey and beyond.

Some had been deported back, some were settled in camps. A stream of them had kept going, up the Rhône corridor from the Mediterranean, down the Rhine valley from the east. The news from the satellite link was that a mass of refugees were preparing, on their own initiative, to cross the North Sea.

Challenged by virus-free landline, the German and Netherlands national authorities confirmed the news. They pleaded CCM crisis conditions and Ivan/Lara, and said they had no control over the situation. Scandinavia was chocka, Ireland had its own problems. The European Parliament was planning to hold an Assizes On Displaced Persons, real soon now. (Thanks a lot.) So there was no escape. The three nations of mainland Britain were going to have to deal with this, somehow.

Getting down to numbers, the numbers were big. An armada of over a hundred vessels was involved – idle passenger ferries, bulk freighters and car transports that had been lying empty in Rotterdam and Hamburg, stranded by the collapse of world trade. If it couldn't be halted, the refugee population of mainland Britain (currently around three hundred thousand) stood to be more than doubled in a single month. Approximately three-quarters of these people would be at least nominally Muslim. If they were turned back, there would be hell to pay with the English Islamic community.

If they were allowed to land, dealing with *that* would be a different hell.

The gentle people, the genuine radicals of the Countercultural Movement, came out on the streets at once, insisting that the Boat People must not be turned away. Ax decided to join them, and the Few went with him. By this time nobody in the country would have expected anything else. Sayyid Muhammad Zayid came out too, along with other church leaders. It was strange, and touching, to be with the sensible-shoes wing of the CCM, the middle-class civil disobediencers, the do-gooders, aid-workers, persons of goodwill; to see them out in such strength. But there was a lot of anger on the streets too, directed at these peaceful demonstrators: there were ugly scenes. Better hope the governments of the three nations, in urgent consultation with their continental partners, managed to secure a compromise.

Emergency preparations got underway, construction workers putting up instant reception centres. The army had to move into the ports, to protect them.

*

On the eve of the tour the Few met around those schoolroom tables one last time. There wasn't much to discuss. There would be volunteers from the Volunteer Initiative joining the government aid-workers, but that was all fixed. The barmy army was ready to be mobilised if it had to be, but everyone was wary of that option. Campground councils, somewhat reluctant about offering space, were offering instead to share their sterling expertise on lo-impact living—

'I really don't think so,' said Sage. 'Can't believe these DPs are going to be desperate to know how to swing a crystal, chew their own comfrey leaves—'

'My grandfather's name was Markowitz,' remarked Allie, wearily. 'My mother's from Hungary. I suppose even Sage's family must have come over with the – the Beaker People, or something, and displaced someone else—'

'Just nature taking its course,' agreed Dilip. '*My God*, I am tired of all this. Why did that bastard Javert have to pick on me?'

'He didn't,' said Fiorinda.

'Huh?'

'Paul Javert didn't pick anyone, except Pigsty.' She looked around, surprised at their surprise. 'But you know he didn't. Paul knew sod-all about rock music. We used to joke about it, remember: how he should have gone for a team of soap-opera stars, or conceptual artists, that he could talk to on his own level and they wouldn't always be giving him an argument.' (Her grasp of the demotic, thought Sage, has come on wonderful.) 'Nah, Paul bought himself a big fat gun. It was Allie who told him who else. She recruited us.'

Everyone stared at Allie.

'Oh yeah,' said Sage. 'Shit, you are right. I never thought of it.'

'I suppose it's true,' said Allie, biting her lip, eyes down. 'I'm sorry, everyone.'

'Hey, don't apologise! Never had such a glorious time in my life!' Sage cackled horribly, skull doing a delighted oafish leer. 'I'm so immensely flattered! I had no idea!'

Allie, olive cheeks aflame, was not finding this funny.

'Lay off, Sage,' snapped Fiorinda. 'God, you can be a bastard. Leave her alone.'

'But whatever his weight in pounds, shillings and ounces,' murmured Chip the irrepressible, 'he always seems bigger because of his bounces—'

'Please forgive me, Allie,' said Sage, dead sober. 'Warped sense of humour.'

'I'm sorry too,' said Fiorinda. 'I don't know why I said that. I wasn't thinking.'

'S' all right,' said Allie. She sniffed, wiping her eyes. 'I don't know why I'm upset—'

They were all on edge, all of them worn out.

Fiorinda had taken down the vampire guitarist and put up a page she'd pulled from a history textbook in the network library. It showed what had really been going on, invisible to the people on the ground, in the fifth century CE, when a civilisation was falling apart. The broad arrows of violently displaced population, sweeping across Europe, bringing on the end of a world. Thanks, Fiorinda. Most helpful. Ax stared at this cold-equations diagram, from across the room. What did that? Climate change. Yeah, always the major factor, no matter how it comes about. Anaerobic bacteria, dinosaurs, the Roman Empire, us.

Dead ironic that this global-warming summer continued to be dismal as November.

So they were back to the original hapless plan, staving off anarchy with free rock concerts. At least they'd be on the spot. Apparently the Boat People were convinced they would be turned away from the south of England. They were refusing to communicate by radio, but helicopter observers, tracking the ships as closely as the bad weather allowed, reported that they were heading for the Humber, and Teesside and the Tyne – as close as they could get to the Yorkshire heartland of the Islamic separatists, who had been in a shooting war with the rest of the country until Ax made peace six months ago.

Great. Just great.

'Okay,' he said, 'tomorrow we're going to have Oltech phones for everyone, our own virus-free network. They have ATP batteries, new development, so treatment virgins will be okay, and the base stations will be driving around with us. Voice and text only: but we'll be able to stay in touch with each other. Rule is, you keep your phone with you always and you *keep it switched on*. This means you, Fiorinda.'

The telecoms-allergic babe, sitting between her bodyguards as usual, ducked her head and muttered something. Sage poked her in the ribs. 'What was that? Didn't hear you, brat.'

'I said *all right*. Okay?'

Ax sighed. 'It's probably going to be fine. Immigration happens, it's natural, we need it. The numbers'll turn out to be wildly exaggerated and the panic is for nothing. Let's hope so.'

'And pray,' said Dilip.

That too.

On the twenty-third of June, the circus rolled north. The first gig, in
Sheffield, had its share of disasters. Aoxomoxoa and the Heads found
themselves facing a packed stadium with no power at all on stage. They
coped handsomely, Sage seeming glad of the chance to wipe his awful
crime at the Internet Wake off the record. Incidents like this were bound
to be commonplace, in current conditions, but they would soon be
regarded as minor indeed. Already, on that first night, they noticed the
extraordinary mix in the audience: people of all ages, all classes, all dress-
codes, all shades of green and otherwise politics. This could have seemed
like a compliment, but it did not. Seemed like a deeply, deeply mistaken
confidence.

Sheffield, Doncaster, Leeds, Bradford, York, Hull . . .

On the twenty-eighth the first ships arrived on Humberside: inade-
quately crewed, overcrowded, poorly provisioned, battered by heavy seas.
Turning them away would have been a humanitarian disaster. The
government chose this moment to announce that negotiations had broken
down, and the whole armada would have to be accommodated, at least
temporarily. Rumour carried this news to the wide areas where there'd
been no internet, no tv or radio, no newsprint for weeks (not to mention
no mains power), and made it sound much worse. A lot of people were
sincerely convinced that the refugees were plague carriers, any contact with
them deadly. The east coast of England erupted in panic.

The circus had split into two at York, one line-up staying east of the
Pennines, the other heading west, to be reunited at Gateshead Festival,
fourth weekend in July. When things got rough, the eastern tour split
again. Ax and the Chosen stayed on in Humberside (at the local
authorities' request) for a week of extra gigs. Fiorinda and DARK, and
the Snake Eyes big band, headed north. Fiorinda's plan for a negotiated
peace with Charm Dudley, DARK's frontwoman, had been interrupted
by Ivan/Lara, but Charm had agreed on a reunion, at least for the
duration of this emergency. On the seventh of July, DARK rolled into
Newcastle-upon-Tyne, with a police escort, through shouting crowds.
They'd left Snake Eyes behind in Middlesborough, owing to the same
sort of situation as on Humberside.

Fiorinda was playing Pictionary in the back of the tourbus with Tom
and Cafren and Gauri, and Fil Slattery the drummer. She sat up, listening
grimly to the sound of her own name. *Fiorinda. Fiorinda. Fiorinda.* Charm,
drinking and yarning with a couple of music-press types who had hitched

a ride, glanced over, narrow-eyed. Idiot woman, thought Fiorinda. That's not *for me*. It's just an angry, frightened noise.

The whole area around the Arena was swarming. There were big screens up in the Life museum concourse and under the Redheugh Bridge, for the crowds who hadn't been able to get inside. The Boat People had reached the Tyne yesterday. There'd been clashes between soldiers and protestors at the docks, looting and arson all through Tyne and Wear . . . The situation was not good at all, and this concert had become a focus, nobody knew quite why: maybe some kind of refuge, maybe a theatre of violence. The illustrious non-Few guest band supposed to be headlining had pulled out on safety grounds. The police didn't want anyone to go on. They wanted to send all these people home.

But that was obviously nonsense.

Charm, aggressively *non-star* in an eclipsed-sun teeshirt and baggy jeans, mud-brown dreads tied back with string, stood propping up the dressing room wall, while Fiorinda was buttoned into the silver and white cowgirl dress (which had recovered from its experience on the night of the Mayday concert) and had her hair brushed out. First time Fio'd had a personal minder on tour, but her two dear bodyguards, backed by Allie Marlowe, had insisted. She suspected the woman was chiefly there to prevent her from thumping Charm.

'Your boyfriend's going to get us all killed.'

'He didn't know it would be like this. Anyway, I don't know what you're complaining about. We're headlining now, *and* we'll be on the telly. Such as there is. Sounds good to me.'

One of their own security guys put his head round the door and said, 'We're ready to take you down.' The opened door let in a blurred, thunderous rush of noise: massed bodies charging the police horses, a rattle of gunfire. At least it sounded as if it was back towards the station somewhere. Cafren's breath hissed through her teeth. Tom Okopie mopped his brow. Sweat was dripping from under the rim of the Potemkin cap.

'Jesus, Lenin and Trotsky,' he muttered. 'Is this *England*?'

Maybe they were being naïve. But surely even the Deconstruction Tour had been nothing like this, nothing like so bad and festering and dangerous—

'This is England,' said Fiorinda. 'This is how it feels. Hey, Tom. Freedom to flail?'

They slapped hands, the six of them, united in scared, sweaty defiance. Freedom to flail.

'Aw reet hinnies,' said Charm, grinning hard. 'Aw reet, *princess*. Let's go.'

Fiorinda walked on stage, picked up her Strat from the piano stool and stood there. She couldn't see much, but the atmosphere was thick with tension. They'd made the crowd wait. Now she was making them wait again, and she could feel the band getting uneasy. Ax not here, Sage not here. Rob and the powerbabes not here. Well, moral authority isn't something you can argue about. If they decide you've got it, you've got it.

She walked to the front, taking a mic from a stand, the guitar clutched by the neck. (She looked, on the big screens, like a little girl dangling her favourite doll by the hair.)

Thank God, at least no technical meltdowns tonight.

The yelling had stopped. There was almost silence, out in that seething, spinning void—

'Hey,' shouted Fiorinda. 'I wasn't born here. I can't hardly speak your language, Geordies. But it's a small world. I think I'm at least partly human. So do I stay or do I go, and DO YOU GET THE MESSAGE?'

Without waiting for them to answer (don't tempt fate), she swung around, donning the guitar, grinned at Charm, and they plunged together into the opening chords of 'Wholesale'.

And DARK delivered it—

Newcastle Arena (and thereabouts), 7th July: NME reports from the Edge of DARKness— She made us wait, but we don't care. She came up front and gave us a sound telling-off, and we loved it. She leaps into action, and the crowd explodes in sheer relief because it's bad and nasty and violent out there, but we're going to be ALL RIGHT NOW. We're in the engine room right next to the fire and we are fine, we are ecstatic, we are wonderful, and she's hauling this whole fucking Titanic of a national emergency around by sheer blackhole radiating female energy. Damn the torpedoes, damn the giant berg of human flesh that just rammed our island. DARK are brilliant and inspired, all power to DARK, but Fiorinda is magic tonight, and I'm going to fucking belt the next person that tries to tell me it's the Ax effect. This girl is the music . . . She shrieks, she wails, she whispers. She leaps, she whirls, she loses the plot and we don't care, we know she'll find it again. She even, for a brief aberration, lets us know how gorgeous *that voice* can be. Fiorinda for God! howls the mosh pit, Fiorinda for God! we all join them. She laughs like a hyena and goes *flying* into the crowd, caught in a hundred arms, the airborne-cams following her, she's dancing with us, if you've got tv that works you can see her doing it in your living room: down in our dirt, absolutely without fear, that hair on fire, flashing piston arms and legs, nothing can harm us now. I swear to God we'd die for her, all fifty thousand of us here tonight. We'd die for her.

Joe Muldur. On the road with DARK

Ax was called back south. A huge old roro ferry had struggled into Southampton Water with cholera aboard, in pretty rough conditions. He had to walk around looking reassuring about that situation; and see how many could be taken in at the campgrounds, because the government settlement provision down here was seriously overbooked.

It was the eighteenth of July, and he hadn't managed to catch up with Fiorinda. Things kept happening too fast. The Rock the Boat Tour (formerly The Peace Tour) had fragmented, so many calls on them, travel so difficult, weather abominable. They were managing to put on *some* kind of gig wherever a gig was demanded, or had been promised, best they could do. He could only talk to her rarely, and catch the reports from afar, awed and terrified by the stunts she was pulling. Sage, meanwhile, was zooming around being a morale booster for the barmy army and the real military: which meant zooming, unarmed, into deadly dangerous fucked-up confrontations. So those two were both giving him sleepless nights, as well as the rest.

The next day he was in London, where the camp in the Park (which had been dismantled after Pigsty died) was being put back together. The armada's numbers were up to the worst estimates: it was a case of packing them in anyhow. He found himself yelling furiously at Dilip, who had been ordered home from the western tour with nervous exhaustion, but had now decided he was fit enough to dig latrines and run a concert party—

'I lived in the Park all Dissolution Summer,' the mixmaster protested, angrily.

'Yeah. Most of the time SO FAR OUT OF YOUR TREE you knew not where you were. When you're half sober I expect you to have more sense. Give me credit, I know you won't endanger anyone. I don't want *you* getting sick—'

'I've been seropositive for fifteen years, Ax. It's my problem. I have never made it anyone else's problem. Just BACK OFF—'

Rain drummed on the canvas overhead, barmies tramped to and fro humping stuff and banging up partitions; pointless argument was the last thing Ax needed.

'Fuck's sake, give me a break. I am not insulting you! I'm begging you. Please. Be my Fiorinda substitute. I can't protect her. Let me try to keep *someone* I love safe—'

He collapsed, head in his hands, on a roll of heavy-duty bubble wrap.

Dilip sighed, sat down next to him and put an arm round his shoulders.

'Ax, you are a sneaky bastard. Okay, okay, you win. As always.'

The suits had wanted Ax's advice on whether they should keep quiet about the cholera. He thought it hardly mattered. Too late now. They should have kept quiet weeks ago, and let the country discover the size of the problem ship by ship. People will stand amazing pressure if you increase it *gradually.*

The whole fucking situation almost made him wish he was a war lord again.

But in a week more, ten days at most, all the ships should be in. They would have made it through to the other side without utter disaster, and they could start to shake down.

There was a flexible screen taped up on the canvas wall of the marquee, showing crisis coverage. (Everyone who had access to working tv watched the coverage, obsessively.) Dilip and Ax sat staring, blank with exhaustion, at Aoxomoxoa in a studio somewhere, in biker leathers and a black iridescent shirt, looking like some great oil-mired seabird. A settlement centre on fire, bodies being carried. Fiorinda on the stage at Newcastle, doing 'Sparrow Child', the new single from *Friction* that Worm (formerly, lambtonworm.com) had defiantly managed to release this week. Haunting melody, insistent catch, Fiorinda's truly beautiful voice, different as possible from anything else on the album: something for the silent majority. In a moment she'll leap into thrash again, she'll dive into that terrifying pit, giving herself to the crowd with utter, *don't care if I live or die* abandon. Something for the desperate. The kid is being amazing. She's performing miracles.

Sleeping in doorways, I have been a sparrow child
I was hiding in your city, because your world out there's so wild—

Ax hated that song. Couldn't hear it without seeing a thirteen-year-old kid adrift on the streets of London, a dead baby in her arms . . . But no question it worked on the punters.

If we can just get through this part.

*

Fiorinda got mislaid after a gig DARK did in Scarborough. It was an accident waiting to happen, so much confusion, someone was bound to get left behind some time. When she extricated herself from the crowd, hours after the show, the circus had left without her; and her Oltech phone was on the bus. She teamed up with a German band called Königen, from Munich. They had signed for the tour expecting something very different from this experience. They'd had the idea that Ax's England was peace and love man, hippies with beads, but 'this is just like home,' they said happily. 'This is so familiar!' They'd come over with Médecins Sans Frontières, part of the Boat People camp-following: aid workers, rock bands, disaster-tourists, media folk – some of them sharing the conditions on the ships, some using virus-free light aircraft. She drove north with them, drinking hard, singing 'Bohemian Rhapsody' and swapping CCM crisis stories while the sun came up in bruised glory over the sea. They stopped in Whitby, where the vampires come from, and couldn't get anything to eat; went on drinking instead. Fiorinda was speaking German quite well by the time they reached Redcar, where the gallant Bavarians had business at a reception camp.

They were acquiring hashish (excellent hashish as it turned out). Fiorinda walked about in her rainjacket, between rows of instant prefabs huddled in a stark grey field, looking at the little families in their strange clothes, lot of hard-faced women, lot of skinny children; thinking, *So it's you.*

Blowing in here like thistledown—

She had been on a PR visit to one of these places. She hadn't paid much attention, the celeb visitor role was too horrible. Now she was thinking silent majority thoughts, neither paranoid nor compassionate, just stupid: *why on earth do you want to come and live here? You must be out of your minds.* But they had come from places where things were much, much worse. Who's going to drive them home? No one. They are home. This is home.

Before long one of the aid workers came up and said, er, are you Fiorinda?

She admitted she was because it seemed daft to lie about it, and got them to try and contact the tour. They couldn't get through, and she couldn't remember where DARK was supposed to end up tonight. The Bavarians were no use, they'd given up the mobile telecoms habit as a thing of the past. She decided she'd better go straight to Gateshead. Königen were happy to drive her, but it took time: what with getting lost, and trying to find a callbox that worked, running out of alco fuel (for the van, not for themselves), and the roads being potholed by Deconstruction Tour damage, and a couple of detours around trouble.

They reached the circus's camp in Beggar's Wood about seven in the evening. Königen took off to visit the Angel of the North. Fiorinda found DARK, reclaimed her phone, had a stand-up fight (verbal) with Charm about whose fault that had been, and sat outdoors of the catering tent, dazed and miserable, wondering why Ax didn't call her. The Festival hadn't kicked off yet, but there were a lot of familiar faces and vans around: techies, road crews, Anansi's Jamaica Kitchen. She'd told everyone to *leave her the fuck alone*, so everyone was doing that, and everyone was busy anyway—

She was trying to summon up the energy to go and get a shower and change when a motorbike roared up. Sage jumped off, grabbed her, shook her down for the phone, *switched it on*, and started yelling at her furiously. Fiorinda hadn't realised the phone was switched off, but she was too shattered to respond any way except by yelling back. She *did* know how fucking serious things were, she *was not* crazy, she *knew what she was doing*—

'You DO NOT! I only found out you were here because Rob called me, why the fuck couldn't you call people yourself? You've been out of touch for *eighteen hours*. You take off without telling anyone, you won't listen to anyone. Supposing you run into a firefight on one of these impromptu walkabouts? Supposing next time you do one of those *fucking* stage dives, some overwrought bastard decides he's going to do Fiorinda, how cool, gets you down and rapes you? *Suppose he starts a fashion*—? How are you going to stop them, who's going to be able to reach you to haul you out—'

'Doesn't sound like a bad idea!' shrieked Fiorinda. 'What else am I good for? I'm a valuable piece of meat, fair game unless I'm locked away. Obviously you're thinking the same way as this *overwrought bastard*, and if that's all you think I am, what do I care who else—'

At this point Rob Nelson managed to get between them – literally holding them apart, one hand reaching up and planted on Sage's chest, the other hauling on Fiorinda's shoulder—

'Hey, hey, *hey*! Stop this! Sage, you are being unbelievably tactless! And *you* . . .'

The right words failed him. 'You need to eat something. Come on indoors.'

When Sage followed them into the tent, a few minutes later, Rob had a plate of chicken, rice and peas in front of her. His arm was around her (all bones, shaking with fatigue, felt like an exhausted little bird he was holding); while Rupert the White Van Man tried to get her to eat.

Sage came and sat at the table, big and awkward, skull looking very contrite indeed.

'I'm sorry, Fee. That was horrible. I've just been *so scared.*'

She turned on him. 'You and Ax,' she said, balefully, 'were in Yorkshire for three months. I was as scared as you've been today, *every fucking moment.* It's not nice, is it?'

'No, it's not nice.'

His barmy army pager started to bleep. He took it out, read the message.

'Shit. Have to go.'

It seemed as if Fiorinda was angry enough to let him zoom off unforgiven. But no, she got up with him, biting her lip, saucer-shadowed eyes brimming with tears, and hugged him fiercely. They stood, locked tight, Sage stooping so the skull's grin was buried in her red curls, while their friends compassionately looked elsewhere.

Sage left. Rupert took Fiorinda's spoon and divided the rice and peas into two portions. 'Now you eat your food, girl. You eat up that part.'

'I can leave the rest?'

'We'll see.'

Felice came up with a glass of warm milk.

'*Rupert,*' she said, contemptuously. 'You don' know the first thing. She can't eat rice, her stomach is all closed up. Here you are, baby. Sip this, I put honey in it. And then I'm gonna take you, sponge you down and put you to bed. No argument.'

Gateshead Festival kicked off the next day, daytrippers and weekenders streaming in to join a small, hardy contingent of Tyne and Wear stay-behinds. An atmosphere of beleagured triumph prevailed, and a certain North East smugness. Down south Festival-goers were celebrating Rock the Boat in contemptible bourgeois comfort, nowhere near the action; and *they* didn't have the Few. And it wasn't even raining. The western tour arrived; Aoxomoxoa turned up again. The only name missing was Ax himself, and he was due any time.

About six in the evening Sage was called to the main entrance, where he found a tall, thirtysomething, upmarket Mrs Leisurewear waiting for him, firmly on the outside of the gates. It was Kay, the younger of his two older sisters.

'Hello, Stephen. Don't panic, no one's dead. I'm here because I brought someone—'

An eleven-year-old boy stepped out from behind her: not very tall, glossy black hair combed from a centre parting into two short, silver-bound braids behind his ears, intricate Celtic embroidery blue-inked around his left eye—

'I thought he ought to see you making history. I convinced Mary you'd have a platoon of heavily armed bodyguards to keep off the terrorists, so you'll back me up on that, if she asks. I'll collect him tomorrow evening. No piercings, no more tattoos, and you'd better be around when I turn up, and both of you reasonably sober.'

'I don't take drugs!' said the child.

'I—'

'You know I won't talk to that fucking mask. You owe me one. See you tomorrow.'

Kay walked off. Marlon came through the gate, offering his wristie to be tugged with a worldly air. They looked each other over.

The skull grinned sheepishly.

Marlon jumped into his dad's arms.

Gateshead Festival, Saltwell Park, Still Rocking the Boat, stardate 23rd July text Joe Muldur; photography Jeff Scully

The weird thing about the far north is it doesn't get dark. The other weird thing is that, apparently and somewhat eccentrically, none of the most famous native rock musicians at this festival is going up on stage, they're all too tired or some pathetic excuse, and can think of nothing better to do than wander around aimlessly, rubbernecking the crowd like a bunch of poncy journalists. Well, we're tired too, but that's not going to stop us waylaying England's darlings, asking them stupid questions and name-dropping about it. We are not fucking quitters. Encountering Aoxomoxoa in the backstage carpark, we took him severely to task over the lack of any Few input: but (levitating about three metres into the air and gently settling, cross-legged, on the shining bonnet of our rival organ's Arctic safari jeep) he would do nothing but *kvetch* about the price of some item of personal décor that a certain Marlon Williams has been trying to chisel out of his unspeakably stingy and puritanical dad. Fully expecting to be killed, skinned and eaten, in no particular order, by big-biceped dykey DARK fans tanked up on Newkie brown and that bad old cannabis resin, we ventured into the arena, where we signally failed to score any of the legendary solids, but ran into Ax, and very politely asked him when we could expect the Chosen to perform. 'I'm not talking to you fuckers,' sez the great man. 'You think I've forgotten the way you wankers always took the part of that shite Aoxomoxoa and printed his bastard disgusting puerile letters, well I have not and you can go and fuck yourselves.' We pointed out, taking editorial responsibility, that 'we' would have been happy to print Mr Preston's disgusting letters, were he not above such things. 'Didn't you hear me,' he replied, 'I said fuck off and fuck yourselves. Oh, and have you seen Sage anywhere. I need him to hold Fiorinda down, so I can brush her hair. She hasn't let anyone touch it for a week and it is a disgrace.' Holding the nation's glamour puss down while her boyfriend makes her scream and bite sounded like a good gig to us, but we're a bit scared of Fiorinda, so we directed him to the carpark and off he wended, clutching his little black Denman* (*a kind of hairbrush). About ten p.m. the sun was still coyly refusing to go down on the horizon. Netherlander ladies Dalkon Shield (or something?) offered matronising congratulations from the stage, in embarrassingly good English, on us not having massacred too many Boat People, and got soundly canned for their insolence. We gave up on the line up and repaired to the dance tent, where we discovered Fiorinda, lying around doing nothing in the company of some strange Bavarians, and asked her does she think Ax will ever, *ever* forgive us for calling him Captain Sensible that time. 'I shouldn't think so,' was her callous response. 'But you could try giving him a whole lot of money. That sometimes works.'

'Hi rockstar.'
'Hi, other rockstar. Where's Marlon?'
'Asleep in the van. Where's Fio?'
'Asleep . . . They've got no stamina, the youth of today.'
It was about three a.m. The arena was still gently hopping, the cool northern darkness laced with music and light, smoke and flame, colour and moving bodies. They fell into step together. 'How was the western front?'
'Oooh, quiet. Dunno why you're asking me. I was hardly there, spent the whole time schmoozing with the generals back at the château. You'll have to ask my shadow.'
'Where are you heading now?'
'Nowhere special. You?'
'Somewhere where I don't have to talk fucking Desperanto no more.'
'They all speak English, Ax. It is *de rigeur.*'

'I know, but I am too proud to let 'em. I have to give them my useless rocktour German, and worse Dutch, and have them be embarrassingly polite about it. Let's see if the backstage bar's still open.'

The next day the weather cut up rough again. Two ancient car transporters failed to make the mouth of the Tyne, and spent the day wallowing out at sea. Attempts to helicopter-lift the most vulnerable passengers had to be abandoned. The ships were foundering. It was decided (they'd given up their radio silence) that they would try to beach themselves at South Shields.

Ax got a call from the Tyne and Wear police. They believed that the British Resistance Movement was planning some last-ditch violent protest against the last of the Boat People. So Ax went with the cops to a house in Gateshead, a brick terraced house painted all over with Union Jacks, arriving casually and unannounced for a chat with a bunch of suspected terrorists. He didn't suppose this would achieve anything, but it is always good to do the police a favour. The terrorists were a couple of defeated-looking middle-aged blokes and three male teenagers, likewise. He sat with them in an upstairs room, a boy's bedroom full of football posters, instant food cartons, model kits, smelling of socks and damp. They were thrilled, in their *but I'm as good as you, mind* northern way, to meet Ax Preston. But he could hardly understand their accent, and getting them to talk would take a fuck of a lot more than one surprise celebrity visit. He knew afterwards he'd seen something in the room that bothered him, but he didn't know what.

Gateshead Festival fought bravely to its conclusion, through the foul weather. The circus took off south, leaving Ax and the Chosen, Fiorinda and DARK behind. They'd meet up again on Humberside, where the big final Rock the Boat event was due to be held in a few days' time. The car transporters had managed to beach themselves, with the help of the coastguard. DARK were booked to go down in the morning with government aid workers and greet the refugees, for the media folk.

Everyone was staying in the Copthorne in Newcastle, clogging up the bathtub drains with Gateshead mud and a month's accumulated general filth. The band ate breakfast together in the restaurant at an early hour, Fiorinda back into her DARK mode, having left Ax warm and sleepy and just-fucked in that big soft bed. It had been very *odd* over the weekend, being with Ax and having DARK around at the same time.

Tom Okopie the bassist, sleek black Tom, inveterately rounded, was getting teased because he had managed to put on weight over the last weeks. Anxiety, said Tom. Nah, Tom, said the band. Admit it, you *like* foetid ancient butties and coagulated pizza. You are a tour-food pervert. Cafren Free, rhythm guitar, with the limp blonde hair and milky skin, our English rose. Gauri the keyboards queen, Filomena the drummer. Tom and Cafren, Gauri and Fil (this raw, rebel band is ludicrously domestic); Fiorinda and Charm . . . er, the odd couple. Cafren had confessed, over the weekend, that she thought she was pregnant. Charm was determined that Cafren simply had an upset stomach; Fiorinda said why don't you do a test?

'I don't want to,' said Cafren, blushing. 'I *want* to be pregnant, but . . . I don't want to know.'

Well, this makes perfect sense.

Their drivers arrived. They crossed the estuary; reached the Boat People welfare circus on the seafront at South Shields, and did some talking there for camera. The storm had blown itself out. The sun was bright, the sea glittering under a clear sky. The white strand looked magically empty, only missing the coconut palms, hohoho. But for a change it was genuinely *warm* today. Cafren and Fiorinda got in the front of their vehicle, the coats and a heap of medical supplies in the back. Tom was in the next jeep with a couple of reporters, Charm and Gauri and Fil coming along behind. They bounced along a track laid over the sand to the car transporters, lying there like two vast dead whales, pinned down by taut strands of cable.

The regular army driver, ethnic Asian with a Midlands accent, was not very sympathetic towards Boat People. He said he didn't mind protecting them and he didn't think they should have been turned away, but . . . 'they're not *immigrants*, Fiorinda. Immigrants are different. These muckers don't want to be here, they have no ties here, no plans, they're just after—'

'Any port in a storm,' said Cafren, peeling windblown hair out of her mouth. It was warm, but breezy for an open-topped jeep ride.

'Yeah, I hear you. They reckoned they got no choice. But—'

The Chosen and their manager, the crews and media folk, ate a later breakfast in the Copthorne restaurant, majestic view of the Tyne through the big windows (which, being at the back of the building, had escaped street-fighting damage). Ax, sitting with Kit Minnitt and the lovely Dian Buckley, noticed that he had a definite, sizeable *entourage* here. Should make Jordan happy, he thought, without rancour. The brothers were getting on much better since Ax had been forced to depend on Jordan to get the Chosen through this tour, scratch up a guitarist when Ax was called away; generally run the band.

'What's your proudest achievement of the Rock the Boat Tour?'

Ax did not approve of media folk at mealtimes, but it couldn't be helped—

'I'm very proud of having come through without having my drummer vomit on me—'

'That's unjustified, Ax,' shouted Milly, from the next table. 'I haven't thrown up for weeks. It was your fucking nephew's fault anyway, not mine—'

What had they achieved? A month ago disaster had seemed hideously likely. Militarised Islam on one side, British Resistance on the other, in evil alliance with the Counterculture's nihilists. The whole north country awash with leftover armaments from the Islamic Campaign, and a mass of have-nots, genuinely threatened by the invasion, *right on the spot*. Had the country been about to split in two, collapse into civil war, until the situation was saved by rock and roll? This morning the idea seemed absurd. We will never know, he thought. Maybe we made a difference, maybe we didn't.

It didn't hurt for the future, however, that a heavy proportion of the forty million seemed quite convinced that the Rock and Roll Reich had saved everyone's bacon. Again.

But who was financing the British Resistance? Ax and Mohammad Zayid were near to proving that certain Islamic Yorkshire businessmen were involved – men who had access to those leftover armaments, and no desire for a massive influx of destitute co-religionists. Who had hoped to make things so ugly Europe would *have to* find another way. What to do about that investigation? Pursue it? Drop it? Sometimes the truth is going to do no one any good.

He poured himself another cup of coffee and looked over at the tv screen that was showing DARK on the beach. Thinking about those defeated blokes in their back bedroom, pawns in the game . . . Suddenly he saw, the image jumping at him like a shape in a nightmare, *that room again, and the thing that had worried him*. A cracked plastic sports bag, jutting out from under the bed, glimpse of camo-cased hardware inside, one of the blokes pokes the bag out of sight with his foot, hopeless little tidying-up gesture . . . Mouth dry, heart thumping, he tried to convince himself he was mistaken. Okay, they're idiots and they didn't know the police were coming but how could they be so insane as to have that gear in plain sight?

But he knew—

'Oh my God,' he whispered. Dropped the cup, coffee everywhere. Grabbed his phone from his pocket—

'Ax!' cried Kit. 'What's the matter?'

'They've mined the beach.'

Fuck's sake, *Fiorinda, answer me—*

The rest of the circus was at Easton Friars, the derelict country house near Harrogate that had become barmy army HQ during the Islamic Campaign. They were eating breakfast too, in a shabby salon overlooking the rose gardens and the deer park. Rugrats all over the place. The western tour had been infested with children. Roxane by herself in a corner, talking copy down the line: *the insistent 'you' in 'Sparrow Child'* . . . *'your city'; 'your wind', 'your walls', clearly stands for her father, Rufus O'Niall, as the man who owns the world, but also for world capitalism* . . . Boat People prefabs forming a vista with the fake Gothic ruins, the beach at South Shields on the tv; Fiorinda getting into a jeep, tired and hollow-eyed but smiling—

'What was your *best* bit?' Chip asked Verlaine—

They knew how serious things were. But the sun was shining and (okay, only on the local, High Street scale of the post-internet), their album *Correspondances* was selling brilliantly.

'Carlisle for weirdness,' decided Verlaine. 'The climber-technos in the welding masks—'

'Yeah, but what about Sage and the Irish persons at Platt Fields?'

In spite of the presence of Anne-Marie and Smelly Hugh, the western tour had clearly been the one for the intelligentsia: Sage and the Heads (and Dilip before he crashed out) able to let their hair down for once, talking about Baudelaire and Brecht . . . Prowling the curfewed streets of Lancaster and Preston with Aoxomoxoa in barmy army officer mode, how cool. The thunderstorms for the two big outdoor gigs in Manchester. Pearl, Anne-Marie's six-year-old, dumping her baby brother Jet in the pig pen on Heaton Park urban farm (to see if pigs really eat humans). Two hundred addled punters in Liverpool, getting the cortex-burn-out concentrated version of *Bleeding Heart*. Smelly Hugh and Anne-Marie debuting their new alt.folk band Rover at the other, massive, Liverpool gig—

Sage and George were playing with Sage's shadow, to annoy Pearl Wing. The real Aoxomoxoa was eating toast, the hologram matching every gesture, mirror-image.

'I don't like it,' said the horrible child uncertainly; glowering. 'It's *stupid*.'

'Oh well,' said Sage. 'If Pearl doesn't like him, we'll have to scrumple him up and throw him away. George, Sistine—'

The shadow got up, did a very elegant twirl and dropped into his Adam pose, reaching out a hand to the origin of his existence. Sage extended a masked finger, godlike: the shadow doubled over, writhing like a punctured balloon, and withered into nothing—

'I DON'T LIKE THAT!' yelled Ruby the toddler.

Pearl gave Sage a glare of disgust and ran off through the open French windows—

'*Sage*,' said Anne-Marie, 'if you bastards frighten my kids into nightmares again—'

'Hahaha—'

'How much do lemons cost?' wondered Silver Wing, the eight-year-old.

'I don't think you can buy them up here, sweetheart,' said her mother.

'Why?'

'I'm going to make traditional English lemonade and sell it to the refus.'

'Silver, you can't sell things to them.' Chip was shocked. 'One *gives* things to refugees.'

'*Why not?* They've got money. They've sold tons of Nepalese and Afghani shit.'

On the tv, three jeeps rolled across the sand—

BLAM!

Everyone jumped up, instantly—

Cafren was saying, lots of places in the United States are worse than this has been, more violent, more guns: and that's the heart of empire, that's where everything still works—

Fiorinda was saying, Caf, can you reach my jacket, I think I can hear my—

Then she was flying through the air, in an envelope of violent sound.

She was tumbling, head over heels, sand driving into her eyes, in a ringing, singing whiteness. Landing, winded, something warm and sticky falling, spattering her, in her mouth, tasted like raw meat—

She was lying at the foot of a grassy sand dune. The jeep she'd been in was on its side; the one behind it was in smoking pieces. Cafren and the driver were sprawled right out in the open. She jumped up and ran back to them, painful stitch in her side. She had not grasped, in her spinning head, what was going on. She thought they were under attack from the air. She grabbed Cafren and yelled, Can you get up! Caf's mouth working without a sound, the driver trying to yell something, but no sound from him either. Cafren was able to stand. The driver had a big slice out of his leg which was bleeding like mad, but they could have helped him between them if only he would stop struggling. Finally she got it. Oh, we hit a mine. Big mine, maybe there's more. Well, okay, we'll do it on physical, back the way I came in. I didn't blow up. *Stop thinking, do it on physical,* what Ax and Sage said, in circumstances that would often sound mad and scary unless you were in the habit of performing on stage—

So they got back to the grassy part. A roaring in her ears, she crouched in the brilliant sunshine with Cafren in her arms, staring at the wrecked jeeps, the third one behind, stranded out there motionless, with the rest of DARK; but *where's Tom???* Cafren sobbing without a sound, people come running, what *is* this foul sticky goop all over us?

Oh shit, she thought. This is bad. We fucked up, we didn't make it.

Then she was in a trailer hospital, in a cot bed in a little room with metal walls. She'd had her bruises dressed, and the bits of Tom washed off. It hurt to breathe; she'd cracked some ribs. She was wearing a hateful hospital gown, wishing she could pass out, but the sedative they'd given her wasn't working. Ax was there, she was telling him (it weighed on her terribly) about the times she'd fucked Tom, back at the beginning with DARK; because it was her policy not to make a fuss, she would do it with anyone that saw the ribbon and still wanted sex . . . and she hadn't known Cafren would mind. Why would anyone mind, it was only Fiorinda, stupid worthless kid. But Cafren *had* minded, and it had been a little bit between them ever since. Oh, why can't I go back and not have done that? And where's Sage? *Why isn't he here?* She couldn't understand why Ax wasn't talking to her, not that she cared, she was too dizzy and confused to care, as long as he would hold her.

The driver of the second jeep, and one of the reporters, had been thrown clear and had survived, badly hurt.

Bits of Tom in my mouth, oh dear, oh dear, can't get rid of that—

'Sage.'

'*Ax!* Is she okay?'

'She's okay. She's hurt, but she's okay. Tom Okopie's dead—'

'Yeah, and that reporter. We saw.'

'Sage, I have to go to fucking Cleethorpes, right now. Got to leave her. Can you get back up here, soon as humanly possible—'

'Ax, *what is it you're not telling me?*'

'*Nothing*. Nothing serious.'

'Can I talk to her—?'

'She . . . she can't hear you, temporarily deafened by the blast. She's sleeping. Just be here when she wakes up. *Don't leave her alone*. She's not in a good state—'

Gone. Sage had walked away from the table where barmy army officers were urgently discussing what had happened. He stared out through mullioned windows: relief still mixed with terror. He'd been waiting for Richard Kent to show up, ex-British infantry major who was the barmies' Chief of Staff. No way he was waiting any longer—

Someone knocked on the Victorian-gothic door: a timid sound, almost like one of the kids. Except that any of the kids in this circus would have marched straight in, knocking on doors a lost, archaic concept, Sanskrit to the lot of them. Along with the words *no*, and *bedtime*, and all stuff like that. Someone went to open it. Smelly Hugh stood there, diffident.

''Scuse me fer interrupting. Has any of you guys seen Silver?'

They established that she'd been missing for four hours. Forced to give up the lemonade idea, she'd taken advantage of the upset this morning, half-inched a litre of vodka and a shot glass, and set out to sell tots in the prefab village. The village was supposed to be out of bounds, but some other tour kids, who'd been playing with refugee kids on sanctioned, neutral territory, had seen her over there. The vodka story they extracted from Pearl, Silver's usual business partner . . . but Pearl had come back alone.

When Fiorinda woke up she was in a different bed. Charm Dudley was there, red-eyed, looking furious. But fury, in Charm, had to stand in for several other emotions somehow permanently missing from the repertoire. To get on with her *at all* you had to accept that—

She sat up, ribs twingeing hard. 'Where's Ax?'

Charm picked up a notepad from the bed table, and scrawled on it, He's gone to Cleethorpes.

'Oh . . . Oh yeah, I remember, I'm deaf . . . Hey, me Beethoven.'

'You fucking self-obsessed little prima donna! The fucking country is about to explode, Ax has gone off to get himself killed by the mob and TOM IS DEAD! You're unbelievable! How can you think of yourself at a time like this?'

'You're wasting your breath,' said Fiorinda (getting most of this from context, as Charm was not remembering to write it down). 'I'm not kidding, Charm. I *really* can't hear you, and I don't know how to lipread. Oh, I suppose I'll have to learn . . . What about Caf? Is she okay?'

She's not pregnant any more, Charm wrote. And her lover is dead. Otherwise fine.

'What about me getting out of here? Where is here? Is this a hospital?'

You're under guard. Sage was supposed to come back and babysit, but he got held up.

Fiorinda stared ahead of her, thinking what to do. Every breath she took was painful—

'Where's Ingrid? I need some clothes. Oh, and I need to talk to a doctor . . . Hey, this is the North East, isn't it? You're from around here. Get me someone who deals with extreme sports.'

There were two hundred and fifty-odd Boat People housed in Easton Friars deerpark, about two thousand more in emergency-requisitioned caravan parks and tourist campsites in the area. The Easton Friars spokesperson insisted no one in the prefabs had seen Silver, or her vodka bottle. The refugees' social workers were understandably on the defensive, but if this wasn't an infuriating prank (which it still might be), the worst conclusion was probably the right one. Easton Friars was a sink estate, in Boat People terms, quietly arranged that way with the idea that the barmy army could handle any trouble. And obviously, now this had happened, a stupid place to bring lawless, fearless Countercultural infants. There were some very bad bastards from very bad places lurking among the dispossessed.

They had found her dress and cardigan stuffed in a hole in a wall in the mock monastic ruins. No shoes (Silver rarely wore shoes); no underwear. Her Oltech tag was in her dress. Was that smart kidnappers, or rapists, or Silver being wild and free? The search of the grounds continued. Sage and others moved out to the satellite camps.

He'd talked to Ax and to the people at the hospital, got some reassurance about Fiorinda, and left messages for her. Best he could do. In the grey dawn of the day after Silver had disappeared he was completing a circuit around Easton Friars, looking for a beaten-up white panel van, that possibly didn't have a number plate. Pearl had eventually confessed she'd seen her sister *getting into a van*, and the social workers had reluctantly agreed, they knew a vehicle like the one the kid described. Gate control was not tight, refugees went in and out, some of them had wheels, van could be anywhere by now. What do we do if we cannot put a cap on this thing? Shall we try to make light of it? Hey, one little rockstar hippie kid, we have several more, no worries, see, we're smiling . . .

Another caravan park, government Boat People Welfare trailers at the entrance. It was a rundown looking place, weird idea of a holiday spot, next to a breaker's yard; Ilkley moor off to the west, with Yap Moss somewhere beyond. He left the bike a few hundred metres up the road and headed back. No dogs about, thank God. Spoke quietly to the night security; went to have a look around. Alone. They were trying very hard to be discreet. The van was on the grass by one of the permanent trailers. It had an unreadable licence plate, hammed by gunfire. There was also a large dark BMW, with a hire-firm sticker in the back window. He touched his wrist. 'George. Think I have something.'

Walking softly, he went right up to the trailer and looked in. The interior was brightly lit. There were six men around a small table, drinking. Four of them were better dressed than the average Boat Person, the two others younger, no more than teenagers, *maybe* he'd seen them at Easton Friars, hard to be sure. The little girl was tied to a chair: she was naked. There were three handguns lying on the table, two well-used assault rifles propped against a wall. If there was another weapon, it was out of sight. As he watched, the six men took cards from a pack, each turning up his choice among muttering and uneasy laughter.

It looked as if they were drawing lots.

He turned away. 'She's here. There are six of them, armed. Get to me soon as you can.'

The light was changing as the red limb of the sun rose over the Vale of York. Should he wait for reinforcements? A few minutes could mean a lot to Silver Wing. Many times in the past few weeks being big, weird and welcome to at least some of the crowd had allowed him to get away with non-violence. But he did not think there were any Aoxomoxoa fans in that trailer. Better just go for it.

The door shattered like matchwood. The kidnappers jumped to their feet and he piled in, making best use of the confined space. Had them too busy to go for the guns, but *he should have immobilised their transport*: what Ax would have done, but Ax had two good hands and a fucking unholy knowledge of how to make a motor go or not go. Sage would just have to make sure no one here got the slightest chance to grab the kid and escape. This thought, along with the memories of Pigsty's video diaries, instilling a ruthless and brutal determination *not to fuck up* . . . he was surprised how quickly it was all over. Three of them down and out, the fourth nursing a broken arm, two of them out the door. The sound of the van's engine: too bad. He cut the child free with his pocket knife, stripped off his jacket and his shirt, dressed her in the shirt. Silver hadn't made a sound through the action.

'Well, kid, did you get raped?'

There were wheels and engines outside, doors slamming, footsteps. She shook her head violently.

'What *the fuck* have you been doing, Sage?'

George and Bill were standing in the broken doorway.

Surveying the wreckage, skull masks grinning in disbelief.

'Um . . . I was in a hurry.'

The North Yorks police, who had been discreetly supporting the search, took over. Sage had not killed any of the bad guys, and the teenagers who had caught Silver and sold her on were picked up without further mayhem. But too many people had been involved. The story of the child's abduction was out, on the air and in newsprint, forming a vicious symmetry with the explosion on South Shields beach. Angry crowds gathered again. The final gig of the Rock the Boat Tour suddenly looked like a ready-made flashpoint.

They'd originally planned to hold the grand finale of the northern tour in Bradford Civic Centre. Before setting out they'd switched the venue to Humberside, the date to coincide with the estimated arrival of the final ships, and left Allie's team to fix it all up. The site they'd chosen was at Cleethorpes: a former amusement park called Pleasure Island, where a CCM festival had come into being in Dissolution Year.

The 'Festival' had been a local affair, little more than a few permanent campers' tents planted among the rides, and the karaoke bar turned into a Countercultural rock venue. All that had changed. The boating lake in the middle of the site, which had been drained as a health hazard when the park fell into disrepair, was now the centre of the arena. Marquees and pavilions stood around. Big screens had been erected; and a towered stage. Some of the white knuckle rides had been fixed up and set running by the engineers (irresistible, but NOT A GOOD IDEA). On the morning of the concert, with the crowds already pouring in, ready to ignite, Fiorinda and DARK were in the Olde England section of the theme park, in conference with Doug Hutton, chief of tour security, in an impromptu dressing room decorated with fragments of defunct kiddie-rides – a giant teacup, the huge head of a plastic caterpillar with a very sinister grin – when Ax arrived.

Fiorinda and Cafren had discharged themselves from hospital,, re-grouped with DARK, and persuaded Fiorinda's guards to escort them down to Humberside overnight in the good old tourbus. Everyone had been drinking hard, and they were determined to go on.

'What the fuck are you doing here!' yelled Ax.

'We have a gig,' said Fiorinda. 'Like it says in the programme.'

Doug and his lieutenants, caught between two awesome fires, muttered excuses and left—

'Fiorinda, I'm still in two minds whether to *cancel*! This place is a fucking *death trap*, I wish I'd seen it before . . . Don't you understand what's *happened*, the past two days?'

'Yes, I do. That's why I'm here.'

'Shit. Are you crazy? Listen, they meant to kill you. We don't know when those mines were planted, *but we know when the bastards switched them on*. They were watching the tv, they saw you on the beach, and *then* they sent the signal—'

Fiorinda shrugged. 'Ouch. Yes, I spotted that. But it isn't relevant, Ax. What's relevant is that the punters need a big shot of theatre, *now*, before anything else bad happens and shifts the balance further. And we're the ones to give it to them, because we got blown up—'

'In football terms,' said Gauri, earnestly, 'suddenly wor side's a goal down. We have to regain possession. We canna let the sad bastards take the advantage off us—'

'I want to play,' said Cafren Free, speaking low. 'I want to do this, for Tom.'

'It's not your decision, Ax,' said Charm, belligerently. 'We've made up our minds.'

'*What* minds? You're fucking out of your heads—'

'You could be right,' agreed Fiorinda, grinning fiercely. 'So WHAT?'

'We've talked to Doug,' said Fil, attempting to sound rational. 'He reckons the risk is rickable, I mean manangerable.'

'Yeah, he says that, because Fiorinda has the security crew hypnotised. The site is full of dangerous lunatics, real bad guys, a lot of them planning to be in the mosh . . . Fuck, I don't believe this. How can you fucking sing with broken ribs—'

'They're not *broken*. Anyway, I've got that sorted. Miracles of modern medicine—'

Suddenly he was distracted, staring at her. 'You can hear me.'

'Er, yeah.'

'Then why didn't you CALL me, TELL me about this plan—'

'It comes and goes. I think the alcohol helps. *Darling* Ax, trust me. I know what I'm doing. Me, cynical manipulative crowd pleaser.'

She saw him weaken, and held out her arms. He hugged her carefully, kissing her hair, her bruised face. 'My lovely girl, you'll drive me crazy, okay, go ahead, not that I could stop you.'

'There's one other thing,' said Fiorinda, smiling up at him sweetly, pissed as a pickled pack rat. 'Charm can be Tom. She's an okay bassist. But then we need a lead guitar.'

'Doesn't have to be any good,' said Cafren, reassuringly. 'Anyone can be wor Charmain. Three chords and a horrible attitude: that's all you need.'

Fiorinda and Ax on stage together. It made sense, if anything was going to work. But he couldn't believe DARK's frontwoman would stand for it. He turned to her, cautiously—

'Is that okay with you, Charm?'

Charm glared at him. 'Don't fucking take it as a precedent.'

Fiorinda and Cafren went back to the bus to rest. When they came out again (having spent their time drinking instead of resting) the Olde English Theme Park street that had become the backstage of this thing was a mill of strangers – mainly male, many of them openly carrying weapons. Fiorinda, walking among her guards, saw Ax with a couple of barmy army officers, talking to some big guys in digital masks, Ax in that rather wonderful dark red suit, with the Nehru jacket, smiling easily. He was unarmed, of course, but he had a guitar slung over his shoulder (his Flying Vee, *not* the Les Paul) – none too subtle reminder of a different sign of mastery: the British Army assault rifle Ax Preston had used in the Islamic Campaign. The guitar-man as warlord. Follow me. Keep the peace. Or take on me and my army.

Their eyes met.

So this is where we're at. This is your role, and this is mine . . . 'Better get on, Fio,' said one of the security men, respectful but uneasy: not happy about her being out in the open.

In a hotel suite in York, Allie present only as a wandering voice, the Few had discussed the stage effects for this gig, which they'd decided to call the Armada Concert. Verlaine had been distressed about the lack of logic: Elizabethan Armada *bad thing*, about *bad invasion of foreigners*. Surely that was exactly the wrong, exactly the opposite—

'No, no, Ver,' Fiorinda had explained to him, 'Armada *good* because we won, and romantic historical thing. This Armada therefore also *good*. Get the message?'

'But we, er, whoever "we" was, I'm a Papist myself, we *didn't* win. They got blown off course by a storm and ended up wrecked in Ireland and places—'

'This is the British-I'm-sorry-I-mean-English public,' said Sage. 'Logic? You are kidding.'

'A lot of the punters at home won't get off on Elizabeth the First,' pointed out Anne-Marie worriedly. 'Do they know who she is? They're not re-enactment nuts—'

'Doesn't matter. A lot of silent majority folks *will* get off; and feel included.'

'There'll be big screens live in the Park,' said Allie's voice. 'And at Leeds, and at Reading. We're still working on the rest, but we should have reasonable coverage—'

And Fiorinda, the CCM crisis sweetheart, will be dressed up as the Virgin Queen.

The red and gold dress, long tight sleeves and small waist, full skirts below the knee. The square neck was cut high enough to hide most of the bruises; the boned bodice would keep her back straight, and help her breathing . . . The sporting-injuries doctor had injected some weird jelly stuff into her back, that would float around her cracked and bruised bones and render them more or less innocuous. He'd warned her it would have to be *sucked out again*, or the ribs wouldn't heal, and this would be very painful: but fuck tomorrow. Fiorinda sat in front of the dressing table mirror, drinking tequila and thinking of her lovely moonstone, opaline organza, spattered with blood and human flesh. Definitely an ex-dress, that one. 'Oh' she said, 'ouch. *Now* I know why you're here, Ingrid. There's no way I could have dressed myself tonight. But is there anything you can do about my face?'

Ingrid slipped a make-up bandeau around her hair. 'It's gonna to hurt a bit.'

'Hahaha. Never mind. I will try not to squeal.'

She waited for the band to get settled: Cafren wearing the Battleship Potemkin sailor cap at a jaunty angle, Charm looking furiously out of it, scaring the stage crew . . . I guarantee we're going to screw up, hope we don't wreck everything. Such a hissing and whooshing in her ears, wish that would go away. My God, what a lot of faces. So many people, here and in the Park, and at Leeds, at Reading, at Wembley, wherever else anyone had tv. She'd reached the stage where she didn't feel drunk; she could just barely remember that there was something called normal and this was different. Borne up, shattered, spread like a thin Fiorinda-film over all those screens . . . She walked on stage, took a mic from a stand and went right to the front. The huge triumphant roar that had greeted DARK's appearance died away. Calm little grin—

The Fiorinda Appreciation Society had convened, with additions. Allie was there, and Roxane; all of the Chosen, most of the Few—

'She's *smashed*,' murmured Dilip anxiously. He'd just arrived from London.

''Fraid so,' agreed Ax. 'They all are. Completed hammered. It's okay, they've, er, reached a plateau. I wouldn't care to try it myself, but DARK have done this before, you know.'

'All too often,' muttered one of the music-press types, insinuating pair, who'd been adopted by DARK over the tour. 'True fanatics reckon they can tell the difference—'

The onstage screens were showing the Spanish galleons and the Virgin Queen, blown up and intercut with the people-stuffed hulks of the present and the refugees coming ashore from the grey thankless waters of that bad old North Sea. No laser beams, no fabulous fx. If they'd been available, it wouldn't have been the right message.

'History lesson,' shouted Fiorinda. 'Listen. 'Bout four hundred and thirty years ago, another Armada set out to invade our country. They never made it. It was a stormy summer, like this one, and they got blown away. The weather's not going to save us now. We have to save ourselves, and four hundred thousand desperate neighbours of ours. But we can do it. We can face the challenge, and this Armada will not destroy us either—'

She broke off, and stared at the crowd for a long moment. The Fiorinda Appreciation Society held its breath. Has she dried? What shall we do, why doesn't she—

'You know, *that* summer, people told the queen of England she should stay indoors, hide behind bodyguards, for fear of the mob. People have been saying the same to me. I think you know why. Well, I'm not the queen of England, I'm just a singer with a rock and roll band. But I feel the same way as she did. *Fuck* that . . . Hey, *Let tyrants fear*. I have always so behaved myself that under God I have placed my chiefest strength in the goodwill of my faithful and loving people—'

'She's quoting. What's she quoting?' demanded the other music-press type, wide-eyed.

'She's taking a riff from Elizabeth the First's speech to the troops at Tilbury,' said Roxane Smith, 'if I remember rightly. You might want to note the date, Joe. It was the fifth of August 1588. Ax, was this planned? Did you know about this?'

Ax shook his head. 'Not until just now.'

Smelly Hugh looked bemused. 'Uh, is it bad? Is there a copyright issue?'

Fiorinda, on stage, was yelling (more or less in the words of that other consummate performer, great lady), that she would rather be dead than distrust the crowd, that she was here to live or die with them, to lay down her honour and her blood, even in the dust—

'Don't worry about it, Hugh,' said Ax. 'Fiorinda can get away with anything.'

'And I THINK FOUL SCORN that any prince of Europe should dare to imagine we can't hack this thing because we can. Without violence, without shame. *We shall come through.*'

She had to wait, grinning, a long time before they'd let her speak again.

'Hey, I forgot. There was something about being a weak and feeble woman—'

Renewed shouting, louder than ever – Fiorinda! *Fiorinda!*

'Okay, okay, I'll get on with it. Well, as you know, we're missing a guitarist. I've asked someone to help us out. Be nice to him. He hasn't had much chance to rehearse.'

' 'Scuse me,' said Ax, 'think I'm on.'

A few days after the Armada concert the barmy army was winding down, getting ready to leave the remaining problems (the British Resistance and their land mines, residual crowd control) to the conventional authorities. Sage went to say goodbye to Richard and found him in the operations room with his long-time partner, another ex-regular army officer Cornelius Samson, presiding over a barmy debriefing. His entrance caused a stir, something new and different from the usual, *hey, look, it's Aoxomoxoa!* It was going to take him a while to live down that stunt in the trailer park.

'We're off, Richard, okay? I mean, permission to quit, Sah!'

'Of course,' said Richard. 'Oh, Sage, wait a moment, there is just one thing.'

The vision in biker leathers turned back, that fearsomely beautiful mask frowning a little.

'What?'

'We think you look lovely in your fascist uniform.'

DARK returned to Teesside; the tour circus headed for London. Ax and Fiorinda stayed behind, in the campground that had developed around Pleasure Island. Continentals, and Boat People Counterculturals from as far away as Central Asia and the Sub-Sahara, had converged on the last concert site, all wanting to talk to Ax . . . about dam-busting, coastal erosion, volcanoes going off in the Ring of Fire; what this year without a summer would mean to CCM crisis Europe. Fiorinda didn't take much part in these conversations. Desperation control, she would do. Foreign policy, no. On the fifth night after the concert, just as the last ships were trying to dock at Immingham, another storm arrived. It was short but fierce. There wasn't much lo-impact accommodation left standing. They spent the day visiting the afflicted and helping out at hippie soup-kitchens – ended up bivouacked in an army-surplus ridge tent, in a field back from the shore, on the other side of a ruined caravan park.

Ax was fast asleep. Fiorinda sat beside him, leaning against a slippery, prickly straw bale, wrapped in a blanket. She'd had the jelly sucked out and her ribs were aching madly; she couldn't get comfortable lying down. Humped recumbent bodies lay around her, dimly lit by ATP patches taped to the canvas walls. She could hear the sea, sullenly roaring. She was thinking of the last Boat People, in their Friday-afternoon-job prefabs. (The first batches of instant housing had been wonderful, but things had gone steadily downhill.)

'Hey, brat.'

She must have closed her eyes for a moment. A tall shadow stood in front of her.

'Sage!' She turned to Ax.

'Nah, don't wake him. I don't suppose he's slept much over the past month.'

'How did you find us? I didn't think anyone knew where we were.'

'Oltech.' He folded down beside her. 'Oooh, I shouldn't have said that, should I? Trust me, Fiorinda. You are not revealing your whereabouts to the Russkies, or the NSA, or anyone else you might not want to know it. Only to your friends.'

It was the first time they'd been together since they had their fight outside the catering tent at Gateshead. They smiled at each other, peacefully and happily. Hold the thought of that embrace. Don't think about the implications, just be glad. It will always be there.

'What have you been doing with yourself all this time?'

'Ha. My life among the bib people. Directing traffic, rescuing kittens. Nothing compared to *your* stunts, you crazy mixed-up kid. How was the hangover?'

'Not too bad, considering. I heard about the kitten. How are your hands?'

'Fine,' he said crossly.

'Give.'

Reluctantly he unearthed the hands, which were burrowed deep in his jacket pockets. The masks gave nothing away, but she could feel the two lumpy real fingers on the right seized-up and locked against his palm. She rubbed them until she'd transferred a little warmth. 'You're such an idiot. How can you ride a motorbike with only one hand working?'

'Fuck off. God, I am tired.'

'You can go to sleep here if you like. I'm afraid this is it, for rockstar luxury.'

'Seems okay to me.'

Stretched full length, head pillowed on one arm, he looked up at her in the dim light, skull doing *lop-sided grin*, and somehow conjuring a sleepy sparkle around its eyesockets.

'Hey, Fiorinda. Are we through to the next level? What d'you think?'

'*Maybe* we are through to the next level.'

'Good. G'night.' His hand slipped from hers and he was gone. Instantly, like switching off a light: nothing left but this warm, breathing rock. Amazing. How does he do that?

Ah, Sage.

She drew up her knees and laid her head on her folded arms. Sage. We never thought, did we, what might happen if the brat grew up? Or maybe you did think. Maybe you realised the risk you were taking, and gave me all that unconditional love anyway . . . She watched him for a while, then settled back against her straw bale. She wished she still smoked, because it was one of those occasions when she didn't mind being awake, but she'd have loved the little comfort-hit of a cigarette. She decided that Sage's Anandas didn't count, frisked him, found a pack, and had just sparked up when another shadow came looming urgently towards her.

'I'm sorry, Fiorinda you can't smoke in here.'

'Oh. Oh, of course not. Sorry.'

'You could come outside. We got a fire. Got a brew on, too.'

She left the two of them sleeping and went out.

The field was very dark. There was no moon, and only a few faint stars struggled through the overcast. The nightwatchmen had a fire in a ring of

269

heavy chunks of driftwood; it smelled of iodine and gave out blue salt flashes amidst the orange veils of flame. Shadowy figures clustered around it, men and women of the Counterculture, drawn by the warmth. They made room for her. She smoked her cigarette, listening to the talk and thinking about the world that was gone; and how outrageously smashed the band had been that night; and how it had felt to be on stage without Tom. That was why they'd had to be smashed, of course. Had to play, but they'd known how horrible it was going to be, up there without him. Knowing they would never see him again, not even to lay him in his grave . . . Couldn't remember anything about it, really. When she'd seen herself on the tv afterwards, God, how excruciating. But it had worked. Or something had worked. So here we are, she thought. Not a looting and a shooting . . . much. Not collapsed into anarchy. Not beaten yet. Me and the people I love.

'D'you take sugar, Fiorinda?'

'If there's no milk, yeah, please. Two.'

She should have known better. The tea was good old Rosie Lee, but the sugar was beet molasses. The brew was undrinkable.

Ah, well.

NINE

Rivermead

Five Years? Is That All We've Got?
They are both twenty-eight years old. Ax Preston was brought up on a
council estate in Taunton, the son of an unemployed baker; his mother
worked (and still does, from choice, although she's no longer the financial
support of the family) as a care assistant in a geriatric nursing home. Sage
Pender's father is Joss Pender of eks.photonics; his mother is the novelist
Beth Loern – but in Sage's childhood, the future software baron and his
partner were living out the lo-impact, self-sufficiency dream in an oddly
similar council house in Padstow. Until three years ago, Ax was fronting a
West Country guitar band called the Chosen Few. He had a formidable
personal reputation in music circles, but the band was not well known. In
the summer of Dissolution Year, this soft-spoken instrumentalist was
recruited by the then Home Secretary, Paul Javert, to join a half-baked
conception called the Countercultural Think Tank. After the sixth of
December Massacre in Hyde Park, Ax took control of that terrifying
cascade of events now universally known as the Deconstruction Tour . . .
and the rest, as they say, is history.

Sage Pender of course was and is Aoxomoxoa, of Aoxomoxoa and the
Heads. Rumoured to be one of pop music's few eurobillionaires, the
techno-wizard with the bad-boy reputation, idolised by his global fans, was
also recruited by Paul Javert. While it's hard to unearth even a slightly
grubby rumour about Ax Preston's private life, Sage has missed few of the
pitfalls of rock success: former heroin addict with a record of public and
domestic violence, an ugly legal battle over custody of his son; more messy
litigation with a major entertainment group. But that's all in the past. Now
he's Ax Preston's right-hand man, and behind the deliberate weirdness of
that digital mask, we find we have a genuine hero. 'They're both very brave
men and very good officers,' says Richard Kent, ex-regular CCM army

commander, with whom they served in that little English pocket-war in Yorkshire last year. 'And that's what counts today: leadership and compassion. I don't know where the rock music comes in.'

The vision and integrity, the will and sheer energy of these two young men are, beyond doubt, at the core of the phenomenon – part supergroup, part alternative government – we call 'the Few and friends'. Yet the third member of the triumvirate is perhaps the most extraordinary. A rock and roll princess by birth (her father is Rufus O'Niall of the Wild Geese, her mother was Suzy Slater, legendary music journalist), at thirteen she was lost on the streets of London, after family problems around a tragic early pregnancy. But Fiorinda's talent won out. She was sixteen when she joined the Countercultural Think Tank as a rising star; she's the brains behind the Volunteer Initiative, she became our national sweetheart and our inspiration; and after the astonishing courage of her Rock the Boat Tour performances (not all of them on stage), she's something very like our uncrowned queen.

You have to seek a long way back in English history to find any parallel to the events of the last three years. It's appropriate that the title Ax has insisted upon is older still. The office of dictator was instituted around 501BC to meet a crisis in the state of Ancient Rome that was beyond the control of the two consuls: a short-term extraconstitutional appointment, primarily military; and populist. Modern usage finds the name tarnished and sinister. We all wish that he'd let us call him something *nice*, something anodyne and comfortable, like 'President'. But these are not anodyne, nice or comfortable times. Ax is right to make us face the reality of our situation. We've come much closer to the brink of anarchy than the other nations of Britain. We're in trouble, and we need to remember that. But we also have the right to congratulate ourselves. We've held our ground (history will say, thanks in very great part to Ax and the Few); and the Boat People crisis has earned us the gratitude and the respect of our Mainland Britain partners. We even have the makings of a mini-Utopian revolution somewhere under the debris, like spring flowers hidden under snow. Truly the only bad thing about that 'dictator' word is that Ax seems to be telling us he regards his appointment as temporary. Without any idea of perpetuating the crisis, and with every hope for the long-term future of this young country, we think he may be much mistaken.

'Family problems around a tragic early pregnancy,' remarked Fiorinda. 'Very tactful. Why do journos always obsess about how old people are? It is creepy.'

'I don't mind being a junkie what beats up half-starved refugees,' said Aoxomoxoa. 'But do I have to be a billionaire?'

'Long as my obscure little band gets a namecheck,' said Ax, 'I suppose I must be grateful . . . I don't like the expression "alternative govern-ment". Could we cut that?'

'Cheesy headline. D'you think they know what the Bowie song is about?'

'Doubt it.'

'I like the "spring flowers under the snow",' put in Rob, kindly. 'That's nice.'

'Shit,' said Allie Marlowe, scowling at the triumvirate across that irregular circle of tables. 'Fucking *artists*. No one you know will read this. It's only a leader for a newsstand broadsheet. Just say yes and forget about it, why can't you?'

'Ah, okay.'

Yeah, yeah. Go ahead. Vetting deferential-yet-patronising newspaper articles was a minor irritation. They'd come back from Rock the Boat feeling they needed to lie down and die. Instead, it was straight into preparations for Ax's inauguration, including the big gig at Reading. Last thing anyone felt like thinking about, but it had to be done. The Counterculture must have its celebration, couldn't let the suits take over.

'But will the punters behave themselves?' Fiorinda wanted to know. The ribs were healing, the bruises on her face had faded, but she was still looking drained. 'Dear manager, I don't want to be the awkward bugger, but *I have had it* with fascist rallies.'

'Don't worry,' said the Minister for Gigs. 'These will be tame punters; it will be fine.'

The Zen Selfers at Reading had never stopped, through the Pigsty crisis, the collapse of the internet and the turmoil of the Boat People disaster. They were still adding to the mysterious and bizarre repertoire of activities in the geodesic tent. One morning in August, in a small lab partitioned off from the main space, Sage was the guinea pig for a new game. Dilip and the Heads, with Chip and Verlaine, were the audience. Sage lay on a cot, taped to a cardiograph, other monitoring stuff, his head in a scanner; emergency resuscitation was standing by. The body lay there, lax and still. Its double – looking like a free-standing hologram, familiar tech for a decade – stood in the middle of a clear patch of polymer floor. It was dressed the same as the body on the cot, in white cotton drawstring trousers, barefoot – and semi-transparent. The Selfers, who treated all their experiments with religious intensity, were very keyed-up. Sage's friends kept quiet. Olwen stood at a desk of control toggles and winking telltales. The shadow looked around, blue eyes very wide.

'Sage?'

'I'm here.'

The voice came from a speaker on the control desk, but the shadow's lips had moved.

'What's it feel like?' said Chip.

'Very, very weird.'

'What can you do?'

'Just a moment. Lemme see . . .' The shadow slowly raised one arm, turned the wrist; let it fall, tried the other. The movements were strangely dislocated, awkward and slow. 'Hmm. Like drawing in a mirror . . . Wooo. God, this is weird. This feels so—'

His voice faded. The Zen Selfer who was watching the body monitors looked less than happy. 'Twenty seconds,' said Olwen, watching her own telltales. 'Time to stop—'

'No, no, no. I'm getting useder to it by the moment . . . Gimme longer . . .'

What they were looking at was the legendary yogi trick, bilocation technologically mediated: Sage as a mirror site, copied in real time. It took, at present, some heavy brain-chemistry medication to achieve coherence – without which the body image projected in this way would revert to the one held by the somatosensory cortex; an extremely grotesque apparition. What Olwen and the Zen Selfers feared was loss of coherence, which would not be good for the real (the physical? the material?) subject. This was the longest trip so far and trouble a hairsbreadth away. Bill and George weren't clear on the dangers, but they picked up serious anxiety from the Zen team; and because they knew Sage. They also knew that Sage could twist Olwen Devi around his little finger. So to speak.

'Lissen to what the doctor says, boss,' said George. 'Back in the box, right now.'

'No, no, it's good, really good. Not yet . . . I'm fine, I'm . . . *Augh!*'

'Sage! What is it?'

The shadow had been experimenting, moving more smoothly, freeing shoulders, twisting at the waist; like a dancer warming up. Now it had its arms wrapped round itself, as if terrified—

'Augh! I just realised! I have no mask! Everybody will be able to see what I'm thinking!'

'Quit clowning,' said Bill. 'We always know what you're thinking, you poor sap.'

'Yeah, but I've never been quite this transparent before, hahaha—'

One of the Zen Selfers murmured urgently. Sage's mouth and (weirdly, this wasn't in the manual) his *eyes*, had started to swell. The perfect, naked gymnast's shoulders were shrinking and twisting. 'Shit,' muttered Olwen. 'Sage, I'm stopping this *now.*'

The doppelgänger vanished. The Zen Selfers checked that their guinea pig seemed to have come to no harm, slid him out and proceeded to unhook him. Dilip, Chip and Ver began to interrogate Olwen Devi, wanting to know what real-world applications she saw for the mirroring, what did it mean in Zen Self terms, how long before both mirror and original could be functioning at once . . . and what would that feel like? Their eyes were shining. The question each really wanted to ask, middle-aged mixmaster as eager as the kids, was, *when can I have a turn?* 'The obvious applications would be medical,' said Olwen. 'If we could make the procedure safe enough—'

Three skull-headed idiots went into a huddle, off in a geodesic corner.

'I don't like it,' said George. 'Did you see his hands?'

'Sage fucking did,' said Bill. 'And didn't say a word. I don't like that.'

'We got to watch this. Something here smells like a shit of an addictive drug.'

Silence, while they thought up psycho-Luddite contingency plans. George had the answer.

'Okay, if it gets bad we play the smack card. Tell him fucking with this stuff makes 'im behave unpleasant.'

'Tell 'im it's makin' him be unpleasant to *Fiorinda!*' Peter added triumphantly.

George and Bill looked at him, forbearance for the afflicted. He can't help it. Peter, although he never really deserved to be called Cack, is, in fact, an alien lifeform. 'Nah,' said Bill. 'I couldn't do that to the boss. Not the way things stand.'

They were absorbed, like this: the Heads in their concern for Sage, Dilip and Chip and Ver in their longing for that eternal one step beyond, when something entered the lab – which was still permeated by the field that had contained the mirroring. It entered the space and entered them all: an astonishing sweetness – without limit, inclusive, penetrating, bathing all perception and every memory, every facet of time and being . . . Dilip saw that Sage was sitting up on the cot, still unmasked, eyes deeply intent and lips a little parted—

Then it was gone, it had passed.

'Wow!' breathed Chip. '*What was that?*'

The Zen Selfers kept their cool. They knew about these rare, tantalising visitations. Sage and his friends stared at each other, grinning in open amazement and delight. And these seven, Olwen Devi noticed, had passed the first test without even realising that it was there.

'That was the Zen Self,' she said, smiling faintly. 'So now you know.'

The weather changed; the sun began to shine. Reading Festival site, more crowded than ever with the extra campers from far away, dried out and started to have a Summer of Love: non-stop partying, radiantly drug-fuelled political discussions, random acts of senseless beauty. The Heads were back in residence in the Travellers' Meadow. Anne-Marie Wing – devoted to Sage since he had rescued Silver Wing from the bad guy refugees – moved to Reading and set up house with her kids in a bender in the hospitality area (having failed, to the Heads' intense relief, to get a pitch in the Meadow). Sage commandeered the Blue Lagoon and had all the Few down to try something he was planning for the concert. This turned out to be a very long day's work – and a convincing demonstration of why the Heads called their giant toddler genius *the boss*, suppose anyone had still been wondering.

'Again, again,' grumbled Chip bitterly. 'Who does he think we are? Fucking Teletubbies?'

'I am disillusioned,' said Ver. 'Surely slavedriving is totally against the Ideology.'

Bill Trevor, working in the wings with the Heads' tech crew, was not sympathetic. 'Hard fun *is* the Ideology, dickless. You thought our stage act was *innate* or somethin'? The boss works us like shit so we can get out there and do it, chainsaws an' all, whatever state we are in.' (And deal with whatever hideous fuckups he throws at us, he might have added. But never let the truth get in the way of a good wind-up.)

Back on the tiered seats, Allie was going over merchandising orders with Ax. The red *It's The Ecology, Stupid* singlet, a favourite because Ax often wore it, was causing problems. 'It'd help if you'd wear something else . . .'

'I don't want to. I will not do that kind of crap. Thin end of the wedge. Why'n't you get them to do a faded one. Then you'd have two versions.'

'That wouldn't help. What we need is for you to be seen around in public in one, or maybe a couple, of the other shirts—'

'Okay, pretend we discussed it, and *then* I said no. Let's move on.'

Sigh. Ramadan was not exactly making Ax unreasonable, not yet. Just tetchy.

They both looked up to watch Fiorinda as she hooked up her safety harness and launched herself into a swallow dive from the scaffolding – caught by Sage and held, effortlessly, arm's length above his head. 'Shit,' he said, spinning her around. 'Hollow bones . . . she must have!'

'She shouldn't be doing that,' muttered Allie. 'Her ribs—'

'Hey, George! Catch!'

Allie gave a yelp. 'Ax! *Stop* them!'

'You break my girlfriend, maestro,' called Ax, unperturbed, 'you buy me a new one.'

'Understood! Sah!'

'Sage, we really don't get this. Is it Oltech—'

'Or is it some kind of secret, old-techno-geezers' code? Where's the transporter room?'

'Is it going to be under the stage?'

'We don't mind being dissolved into subatomic particles. We just want to be *told*.'

Chip and Verlaine were back at the stage, aggrieved and determined. Sage set Fiorinda on her feet and came to the front. 'What the fuck are you talking about? Pass me your notes.' The scribbled-over Sellotaped sheets of printout were handed up. Sage looked at them and the skull mask got seriously mean. 'I don't see any problem. Hey, if you two don't want to play, it's very simple. You can piss off and stop wasting my time. Nothing is compulsory.'

'It's after "Under My Thumb",' Chip persisted bravely, 'and Allie and Fiorinda with the firehoses. Where we get beamed up—'

'*What?*'

Chip and Verlaine backed off, looking scared. Sage walked away, all intimidating bigness and dangerously tested self-control. People on stage retreated out of his path. '*Ah!*' he said: jumped down, held up a masked left hand. 'Pen? Anybody?' Took the pen, and added a few swift lines to the musical notation.

'There. You see these things called quavers? I wasn't sure how I wanted them joined up in beats here. Which we called beamed up. Now it's done, fuck it. You happy?'

'Er, yeah,' said Verlaine. 'Yeah,' agreed Chip, faintly.

'Good.' The boss levitated himself back onto the stage. 'Serves you right for being able to read my writing, what insolence. Allie, c'mon. Your turn.'

'When I first met him,' said Ax, grinning, 'he had me convinced he couldn't read music.'

'When I first met him,' said Allie, ruefully, 'he had me convinced he couldn't read.'

'Well, you better get up there. We'll finish this later.'

At dusk he let them go. They changed their clothes, took picnic food and walked out together towards the campground boneyard, following the same path as Fiorinda and Sage had taken on the day of Luke's memorial service: over the stile, through the hedge, into the other world. The south bank of the Thames was common ground, amicably (for the most part) shared by townsfolk and Counterculturals. There was very little artificial light – the town itself was much darker than it would have been three years ago; the festival site's lo-impact twinkling lost in the deep blue twilight. They strolled downstream, to where the bank was wide and settled around a big poplar tree. Passers-by glanced at them, and studiously paid no attention. Stone Age Fame. Ax watched Fiorinda and Silver Wing having a crabwalking competition, the littler kids trying to copy them, flopping about like stranded mudskippers. George and Sage joined him.

'Did you guys teach her to do this stuff?'

'Nah,' said Sage.

'We taught 'er a spot of tumbling,' said George. 'She could walk on her hands and shit when we met her, says she always could.'

'She's a fuckin' *dream* compared to most of this shower,' said Sage. 'But a few more sessions of vicious bullying should do it. How's Ramadan going?'

'Slowly,' said Ax.

It was the sixth night of the holy month and the white young moon was high in the sky. Something had come up at Reading. They'd been offered the Leisure Centre buildings. Some green-is-good business persons had agreed to bankroll a new facility for the townspeople. On a brownfield site, of course. Only problem was the Few would have to find some money, without robbing the Volunteer Initiative or any of their other concerns.

'What we could do,' said Anne-Marie, grinning shyly at her hero, 'is we could bottle Sage an' Ax's come and sell it to rich Americans, by mail order, for designer babies.'

'Don't think they'd be impressed. There's nothin' in it.'

'Same here,' said Ax. 'I'm not an active member of the gene pool.'

'What about cheek-scrapings? They don't need sperms, all they need is DNA, isn't it?'

Neither of the favoured candidates had any answer to this, except to look disgusted.

'We'll stick with teeshirts,' said Allie. 'Think of the lawsuits.'

'Yeah, imagine if the customer got a normal-sized, quiet and retiring Sage clone—'

'We could git Anne-Marie to cast a spell,' suggested Smelly Hugh. Hugh wasn't allowed to share Anne-Marie's bender; he wasn't house-trained for such close quarters. But he'd come down for a conjugal, in the funky tourbus belonging to their new band. 'To fetch the money.'

'Do you really think you could do that, AM?' asked Milly, curiously . . . 'I mean, *really*?'

Anne-Marie Wing, Merseyside Chinese-Irish, dedicated Counter-cultural, seemed to believe in everything, from daoist-tantric ritual to crustified-anarcho-syndicalism; a source of fascination to the others – how did she keep *track*? At this she looked wise and superior. 'Maybe I could, but I don't do that stuff. I never would. It turns on you.'

'But she *'as* got the gift,' insisted Hugh. 'She can see auras. She's bin teaching me, but I 'avn't quite got it yet—'

'So tell us all our auras,' suggested Allie. 'Sage ought to be red. All that aggression.'

'I *am not* aggressive. Just watch it, you—'

'Oh no,' said Anne-Marie seriously, 'Sage is mainly blue. *Ax* is red—'

That got a laugh. No prizes for spotting Ax's favourite colour. Or knowing that lazy-dressing Aoxomoxoa, if he strayed from the black or white he wore on stage (for obvious reasons), never got further than grey, or occasionally blue. 'What about Fiorinda?' wondered Verlaine. 'Let me guess. She's green, huh?' They all looked at Fiorinda, sitting there by the water, the green silk of her dress (that beloved dress, a collection of tatters over her yellow choli blouse and yellow underskirt) darkly shadowed in the twilight.

'Oh, *Fiorinda*—' said Anne-Marie – and then for some reason broke off in confusion. 'Doesn't need me to tell her,' she finished, dropping her eyes.

It was here, thought Fiorinda, letting the talk drift away: just here, the day I arrived from the Festival of Dissolution. I took off my boots and heard the three witches talking, about the man who would be king. And now this is where we're at. Back where it all began, another battle won. We're still in a disaster movie, things still getting worse (the refugee crisis was nothing like *solved*; it had simply joined the rest of the ongoing crises). But we reach pools of equilibrium and this is one . . . Suddenly her heart thumped. *Where's Ax?* Where is the master of all this, the rock-lord enthroned?

But if there was a centre to the group, it was in the roots of the poplar tree, where someone had planted an Oltech campers' lantern. Silver Wing and her sister Pearl sat there giggling, grabbing at the insects that blundered into the light. Ax was out on the margins with Rob, collecting the kids' picnic debris, and trying to stay clear of the cannabis and tobacco smoke. Poor Ax, it was nicotine starvation that hit him worst. She went and slipped her arm around him, leaned her head on his shoulder.

'What's the matter? Something wrong, little cat?'

'Nothing's wrong. Nothing at all.'

Always be my Ax. If I dared to wish for anything, that would be my wish.

Strange how things you thought would last forever can slip away while you are too occupied to notice; and you don't know what you've got 'til it's gone. In the van, one warm evening, George and Aoxomoxoa sat at that cluttered kitchen table. Bill and Peter separately off on their own business – Sage having come back after spending the night and day elsewhere on site to find George in a morose and valedictory mood, shot glass and a whisky bottle in front of him. They were both masked, of course.

'I always knew,' said George, 'that one day you'd be over Mary, and then I'd lose you, some way. I never thought, *never*, it would be to another guy.'

For more than a decade they'd been playing this elaborate game together, since the boss was seventeen and George Merrick twenty-one years old. How many hours of fun is that?

'Can't you both be my best mate?' said the giant toddler, bewildered. Then (commonsense kicking in), '*George*, what is this? What the fuck are you on about?'

'Ah, nothin', boss. Getting maudlin.'

'Thas' from drinking alone. C'mon, on your feet. Let's go find some company.'

Dilip, in his tower block eyrie, was preparing artwork for the concert, 'Let It Bleed' on the sound system very loud. He'd moved out of the Insanitude after Allie left, chiefly because he was buggered if he was going to be the only member of the Few on permanent call there. No fixed abode since. The life he'd left behind, when he came down to London for Dissolution Summer, felt like old clothes. He'd tried to go back and he couldn't do it. Ax would not let him camp in the Park, so here he was camping out in a room walled in windows, St Paul's and all the City spread below, in a flat that belonged to a woman who'd been a lover long, long ago.

Good to be so high up. Dilip loved being high.

He worked in gouache on board; always painted his pictures before scanning them and applying the digital arts. Three faces rose from the sweeping curves of the *trimurti* . . . Can't let those broadsheet assholes steal our babies, we must have eclectic, exotic, beads-and-sitars Counter-cultural hagiography. Now which is which of this she and he and he? No prizes for assigning the patronage of the Lord Protector. He bent to the board, applying his own Vaisnavite mark to Aoxomoxoa's skull. He'd have liked to depict Sage without the mask, but that would not be true to life. 'Ram, Ram, Ram Ram . . . and not afraid of the sight of blood, either,' he murmured (thinking of goats with their throats cut, in the heat of Madurai). 'A trait that may yet be useful again.' Sage's sign is Capricorn, stonefish, goatfish. His birthday is the eighth of January, his elements are water and earth, his patron deity is Visnu . . .

Fiorinda's element is fire, she was born on the fifth of April, and now I realise her patron is obviously Lord Shiva. If you insist on a female aspect, that should be Kali, but I see no necessity. Gender in a god is symbolic: and then, for all her girlishness, she is one of those girls who is little different from a supple boy. She does not bleed, for instance. Of course many young women in the normal world do not bleed nowadays, and mean nothing by it. But among our powerbabes and earthmothers and rockchicks this singles her out as one who secretly disdains the great divide. The ancient music jiving him around as he added the caste-mark to her pure brow, astrological signs of the ram (stubborn, daring, sure-footed) to the green shawl cast lightly over her hair, and the flame-tongued wheel of Shiva—

And now for Ax. Who is an Aquarian (surprise!). Born on the eighteenth of February, in the same year as Sage, which, interestingly, makes Aoxomoxoa the older, and by the way makes Ax a Dragon whereas the Beast of Bodmin is a Rabbit (but what do those Chinese know?). Ax's element is air, the breath. His patron is Brahma, tainted with monotheism, the deity we Hindus neglect and quite right too, God is in all things, there is no god of the gods; but for this purpose he suits. See how it all fits in . . . And you are the waterbearer, *bhisti*, the singer not the song, the teacher not the lesson, lover of the world, and you are al-Amin, the trusted one, though no way am I putting anything Islamic into this painted image, I have more sense than that. He added the appropriate symbols to Ax's portrait and stepped back.

Very good. Like a classic movie poster, the apotheosis of a movie poster, exactly to rights, just what the spindoctor (that means Allie) ordered. *I've had them both, and they were both marvellous* . . . He cocked a wry eye at the skull. But not you, my lord (in his mind he was speaking in Hindu, so *my lord* didn't sound too weird). I don't believe that's because of the virus, my brave friend. Is it true that you never, ever have sexual feeling for another guy? How strange, but maybe so. So there they are, our royal family. He grinned, envisaging Sage as the big strong mother of the tribe, Ax the father of his people, Fiorinda their shining prince. But any permutation of the roles would be equally valid . . . Where do we go from here? Who knows? The world is our oyster. How extraordinary it is, this second Spring, the flame rekindled, and how many second Springs does that make, so far? How many times have I come back to life? Ah, who cares. Let them roll. The hard times and the good.

The full moon of August passed, with a massive homegrown line up on Red Stage, and revelry in the arena. There were reports of another group of storms, coming in from the South-West this time. One of the stranger losses of Ivan/Lara had been accurate weather forecasting. Information was being gathered in old-fashioned ways: radio messages from ships at sea, watching to see if the cows were lying down, that sort of thing. But people took any storm warnings seriously. In Reading town the sandbags came out. On the Festival site the camp council laid more chicken wire track, and staybehinds in the worst boggy bits were exhorted to move into shelter in the Leisure Centre. Some of the vans in Travellers' Meadow (the only place where live-in wheels were allowed, except for the hospitality area) left for higher ground. On the morning of the twenty-sixth, Sage stood looking at the sky and chewing the stump of his right thumb. The weather was definitely changing. The barometer had dropped hard. There was an overcast and a gusting breeze, tugging at the walls of the ramshackle canvas annexe, sending one of those black polythene bundles, spooks of the campgrounds, flapping into the branches of the oak tree in the hedge.

'Think we should move the van, boss?' said George.

'I think we should move the camp,' said Sage. 'In a perfect world.'

A water meadow would have been a stupid place to put a permanent neo-mediaeval Third World township, even in what was formerly the normal English climate. But these temporary, fucked-up things happen, and set down roots, and you get attached to them.

'Nah, we'll stay. We've seen storms before.' He looked up at the oak again, and temporised. 'Maybe we'll move the van across the field. And take down the annexe.'

So they did that. It was a sad moment. The annexe had been left standing all the times they'd been away; it had been up since the very beginning. Fiorinda used to sleep in there.

The twenty-sixth was dance night in the Blue Lagoon, an event traditionally held the weekend after the full moon, and open to the favoured public, with invitation tickets like gold dust. It was bigger than the full moon fest itself this month because Aoxomoxoa and George were going to do a set, and everyone knew the Few would be around.

Sage met Ax and Fiorinda at the station. They walked through town together.

'How's it going?'

'Fine. Could you stop asking me that? The fast would be no fucking trouble, it's not meant to be penitential. It would be *good*, if I could share it with people doing the same thing.'

'Then why don't you?' said Fiorinda, without rancour, but clearly not for the first time.

'I can't because *that's not my situation*. I can't disappear into the Islamic community, totally the wrong message. I have to face it, I'm on my own and I always will be, things like this.'

The two of them rolled their eyes and sighed. Ax set his teeth and changed the subject.

'So, did you get your shirt?'

'Nah,' said Sage, 'I think I've given up. Every time I ask her she has some new ridiculous excuse. I bet the kids have sold it.' This was the black iridescent shirt Sage had lent to Silver Wing when he rescued her, a favourite of his, which had never come back.

'Either that,' said Fiorinda, grinning, 'or AM's been using it as a fertility charm. She looked very worried, I noticed, when you told her you don't make babies.'

They'd arrived at Blue Gate. There was a mill of people, mainly wannabe guests trying to finesse themselves into the party. Someone came up to Ax and said, 'Hey, Ax, you got a moment to get me past your fuckin' private police force? For old times' sake?'

'Yeah, okay,' said Ax.

Ax talked to site security, and they passed on.

'Who's that?' asked Sage, without much interest.

'Does he come from Taunton?' wondered Fiorinda. 'Sounded like it.'

'No, he's from Bridgwater. A much hipper burg. You didn't recognise him?'

They shook their heads.

'Fuck. Another nail in my coffin. That was Faz Hassim.'

'Oh yeah, now you mention it, maybe I vaguely did recognise him—'

'Who's Faz Hassim?' asked Fiorinda.

'Fronts a no-talent guitar band called the Assassins. Woolly-anarchist persuasion Counterculturals, useter get some media attention, before your time, babe.'

'That's one way of looking at it,' said Ax gloomily. 'I wonder why he's here. He hates the Few. Oh well, it's a free country. Whatever that stupid expression is supposed to mean—'

The Assassins had been hard to miss in the West Country when the Chosen Few were starting out. At first there'd been a bond, both bands basically non-white, rare enough in the west, and because of Ax's politics. But the Chosen had got successful, in their modest way, while Islam's original Countercultural rockers had stayed hungry. It was the usual thing. Any kind of success means you've sold out, and people who claim they've no fucking interest in being commercial still manage to hate you for it. Sad, but inevitable.

'Assassins means the crusties are in town,' mused Sage. 'Could mean trouble with our lot.'

'Not necessarily. There's plenty of crusty-tendencies among the Reading staybehinds.'

A hippie is a Countercultural with political rationale. A crusty is an aggressively or else helplessly unhygienic ditto: with extra righteousness or extra nuisance value, depending on your point of view. Fiorinda thought her own thoughts while they went a few rounds on crusty versus hippie rock bands, behaviour of, relative derangement and combustibility; swopped sides a couple of times . . . A pleasant background noise, but slightly irritating that they knew so much.

In the Blue Lagoon Anne-Marie and Smelly Hugh, with a group of distinguished staybehinds, were supervising the inauguration of a huge chunk of quartz, before the partygoers were let in. It was being hoisted into the apex of the marquee, roped like a calf.

'It's gonna soak up all the negative ions and protons and stuff,' explained Hugh.

'Vibes, Hugh,' said Sage, 'the scientific term is vibes.'

'Oh, right. We had it in the bus with us last night, it give us some weird dreams, I'm telling you. Like visions. No fuckin' word of a lie. And the dogs wouldn't shut up.'

'I have a vision in which I see that bastard dropping on someone's head,' said Ax.

'What is a bastard?' asked Silver Wing, toying idly with a Stanley knife she'd lifted from a hoister's gadget belt. 'Exactly . . . in this context?'

'Useter mean, someone whose parents weren't married,' Sage explained. 'That's become obsolete. Nowadays, means any shit you don't like. Give the guy his knife back.'

'Oh, I see. Like fucker doesn't mean sex. No, I *need* this knife.'

'I wouldn't do that if I was you,' said Fiorinda, apparently referring to the quartz getting hoisted, and walked away before anyone could ask her to explain.

Allie wasn't coming, neither was Roxane. Everyone else was in the backstage bar. Shane and Jordan and Milly had heard that the Assassins planned on being here, and were full of this bad news. Jordan was very unhappy indeed when he found out what Ax had done. He wanted Faz and his compadres chucked off the site.

'For crimes they might commit?' said Ax. 'Oh fuck off, Jordan. They'd have got in anyway, they're not exactly outsiders. He did that door-police number to wind me up.'

'It's the fasting month, though,' said Chip wisely. 'So they won't make trouble.'

'Not so,' Ax told him. 'Better the day, better the deed, is the Islamic attitude on that. Not that Faz was ever, er, conventionally devout. But I don't think it'll come to anything.'

Party night at the Blue Lagoon, the traditional shakedown for weapons slowing the queue to get in as outside guests got argumentative; brisk traffic at the drugs-testing. By now there were about a hundred licensed brands of mild hallucinogens, serotonin-boosters, cannabis cigarettes and rolling grass available at any off-licence. Not to mention the doom-warning, sultry-packaged hard stuffs. Naturally the Counterculturals preferred dodgy contraband, but they loved getting their gear checked for contaminates. Made them feel all sensible.

George was setting up in the DJs' box. The Few and friends had moved onto the stage.

'Hey, Silver, wanna mind Sage's boards for me?'

'Oh yay!' squealed the little girl, leaping to her feet.

'George!' yelled Anne-Marie, 'don't you DARE! She's eight years old, what the fuck do you think you're doing, she can't handle Sage's stuff—!'

'Yeah,' sez George, unmoved. 'Kid ought to be in bed, couldn't agree more. I blame the parents myself. Since she's not she may as well make 'erself useful.'

Head fans staking claim to space at the front were regaled by the sight of a little girl wearing a patchwork smock and butterfly wings perched up behind Aoxomoxoa's desk, a wrap around her head and every appearance of being in charge – until Sage came along from his shift on former-Class A testing and lifted her down.

'Hard drugs are the kind that make you hard-hearted,' remarked the child.

'You should be in bed. Go away.'

'You never take any of those sort of drugs anymore, do you Sage?'

'Maybe not. What's it to you?' Her black Chinese eyes gazed up at him: dead inscrutable. 'Hmm. No need go shouting about that to my public, Silver.'

'Your secret is safe with me,' said the imp, and darted away. Leaving him to consider, until the set began and performance took over, his personal situation and the demands it was making on him: *hard fun* indeed, and maybe never going to get any easier, and yet he would stay with this thing. Follow it through, wherever it might lead. That was certain.

Fiorinda was on the floor, right next to the trouble when it began. She'd been talking to a big leather-clad woman with a tattooed face, a staybehind poet, hoping to fill in some gaps on the Assassins thing. She found the expression *before your time, babe*, extremely annoying. Instead, she'd had an earful about Glastonbury getting massively fake, and truly political people realising LONG before the crusty shits that better the openly meaningless populist rock vibe of Reading, like your stuff

286

Fiorinda . . . It was not an easy conversation to follow, in the midst of Aoxomoxoa and George. She'd suggested they dance, and then suddenly there was a stumbling wave, barging into them: another wave, more violent, and they could see the fight, lurching through Sage's visuals, spreading fast. The big staybehind grabbed Fiorinda and started shoving her way to the stage. She was built like a brick outhouse; she had no trouble getting through: planted a kiss on Fio's lips and boosted her up there into safety; turned back and plunged into the affray.

'Where the fuck have you been?' demanded Ax—

'Dancing,' said Fiorinda, putting on her dark glasses, and losing the huge sound and wild illusions too abruptly for comfort. 'What's the use of coming to a party and not dancing?'

Everyone was wearing IMMix blocking glasses up here, and very silly they looked too, like vampires' night out. But the fight on the floor was rapidly turning not funny.

'It's the wind,' said Anne-Marie. 'It always makes my kids crazy—'

Finally even the demon DJs noticed something, put on a relatively soothing loop and came down to examine the situation. It shouldn't have been the Few's business, whatever went on. But from their vantage point they could see that the resident peacekeepers were not doing much peacekeeping. Many site security persons, in their lilac- and yellow-flashed teeshirts, were getting very unprofessionally involved. The lights came up; the IMMix system cut out. The Lagoon's current manager, a skinny thirtysomething from Brighton with ginger dreadlocks, appeared, and stood there looking depressed.

'Shit,' said Felice, senior powerbabe: disgusted. 'They're anarchists, aren't they? This is their idea of fun; we should just leave.'

'But if there're women and kids, guys too, that don't want to be fighting—' protested Dora, who tended to be the respectable citizen of the three.

'It's pissing with rain outside,' Dilip pointed out. 'Roll up the walls. That'll do it.'

'Try rolling up the walls in this wind, the whole fucking thing probly' go,' said the manager. 'Anyway, how're you gonna? There's no button you can press, we're lo-tech, got to crank them up mechanically. We gotta difficult situation, Ax. Don't know what's got into 'em.'

'I do,' growled Jordan. 'I told you Ax, but you wouldn't fucking listen, would you?'

'So much for our tame punters,' someone sighed.

'Why not blast them with some really heavy IMMix. Blow their fuses?'

George and Bill's masks didn't do natural expressions, but they managed to look alarmed. 'Better not, Fio.'

'The effect of that could be unpredictable,' said Peter.

The rain drummed and the wind howled over the sounds of battle. The Few stood together, this disparate little group of rockstar folk, suddenly head-on with the bare-knuckle violence of the drop-out hordes. It was so *petty*, after what they'd been through, yet they seemed to be completely defeated. Before they could resign themselves to a tactical retreat, the frenzied mass parted and four bearded, wild-haired figures came out of it. Then the guy Ax and Fiorinda and Sage had met at Blue Gate emerged, wearing a bloodstained white scarf as a dishevelled turban, his eyes huge and crazy. He stood there swaying.

An uneasy quiet spread.

'I'm Faud Hassim,' he bellowed. 'I'm here for you, Ax. You're gonna fight me. You son of a pig, you uncut blashempous faker. Show us who's the boss. Like you did in Yorkshire.'

His four companions started a ragged slow hand-clap.

The crowd waited to see what would happen, nearly all of it quieted now.

Ax just shook his head, and turned away.

Faz Hassim roared with laughter, launched himself at the nearest staybehind: grabbed the guy's shoulders, nutted him savagely, and kicked him in the balls as he recoiled. All five Assassins leapt back into the crowd, and the mêlée recommenced, more rabid than ever—

Jordan glared at his brother. 'I'm getting Milly out of this.'

Milly Kettle, by now visibly pregnant, said, 'Lay off, Jor.' But she looked worried.

'We should call Thames Valley,' announced Dora, 'call the cops. This is out of control.'

'She's right,' said the manager. 'We could rack up a lot of casualties.'

'Those wankers!' snapped Ax. 'They'll either not turn up at all, or they'll arrive with a fleet of Apaches tomorrow morning and strafe the site . . . Shit, I suppose they do their best. But they don't want to mess with us, and I don't blame them—'

'Who's us?' muttered Verlaine. 'Do we even belong here? Did we ever?'

Aoxomoxoa had not expressed an opinion. He was leaning against a partition, hands in his pockets, skull gazing mildly into space. Ax glanced at him with annoyance, took a turn up and down the stage; looked at Fiorinda. Apparently these three were in conference.

Fiorinda shrugged. 'I think it's just that kind of night, Ax.'

Aoxomoxoa went on silently looking as if he was waiting for someone to press the on switch. 'Oh, *okay*,' said Ax. 'You could be right. Go on, my recovering gunslinger. Sort 'em.'

The skull produced a malign and beautiful grin. 'DK, you're on. Give us a happy beat—'

The manager gave them some sound back, Dilip took over the desks. The Heads and their chief came off the stage in one smooth predatory rush and went into the ruck like tigers, irresistible and glorious. Dora and Milly stayed back. Fiorinda and Felice and Cherry, shameless hussies, stood up front, dodging random missiles, and cheered.

'Are *you* going down there?' Rob asked Ax, in a tone that made it clear Rob was not.

'Not unless it's a matter of life and death,' said Ax firmly. 'Which it won't be.'

Four Heads, plus another four skull-masked Heads crew members, moved through the crowd, peacekeepers rallying to them: breaking up fistfights, disarming bottle wielders, treating the home team and the aggressors with impartial ferocity. The obvious thing was to open the place up, give folks a chance to disperse. Sage reached the marquee wall. Another skull-headed idiot, couldn't tell who, had shinned up a scaffold pole to signal he was at the opposite side. They needed a through draught, or the tent would rip itself apart. He struggled with tackle, fending off a large and trolleyed black Assassin fan who wouldn't give up—

'I saw you on that tv without the mask!' shrieked the overwrought black guy, pummelling wildly. 'Hey, you an albino African, innit?'

'That . . . would be going a long time back. Knock it off, huh, I'm trying to—'

'If you' not a brother, how come you got that nose? How come you got that nappy hair?'

'Lost tribes of Israel. Shit, STOP that—'

The wall-section came free; the storm came bursting in, full of icy rain. Overwrought black guy grabbed some scaffold. A mass of heavy marquee fabric slammed into them with such violence both men went flying, black guy still hanging on. Sage, crashing onto his back, drenched as if he'd fallen in the river, saw that lump of quartz, flailing in the shadows up in the apex like a huge, blunt bolas weight: swinging, catching, hauling on the shifted frame, propelled by the force of the wind . . . ah, shit . . .

'SHIT, FUCK. I am trying to *give up* doing stuff like this—'

'Don't blame yourself man,' said the black guy, as everything around them went sideways, into wet, howling, roc-wing flapping chaos. 'These things happen.'

Ax left the wreckage of the Festival site early in the morning. He had a gig he couldn't miss. He took the train as far as London, but had to drive to Hastings, storm damage having disrupted the railways. Got back late in the afternoon, and went straight to a tv studio to record for the *Laylat al Qadr* broadcast. The spiel more polished than it had been two years ago in the Garden Room at Pigsty's hotel, but sounding to him even less convincing.

Stick together, be good to each other. If we can just get through this part—

Fiorinda had stayed at Reading. That was okay, he'd always planned to spend this night alone. *Laylat al Qadr*, night of power, commemorates the night the Qur'an descended into the soul of the Prophet: an occasion for wakeful prayer and meditation. The scholars say no one can tell exactly when it should fall in Ramadan. Traditionally it was celebrated on the twenty-seventh night, which was when Ax's recorded spiel would be broadcast. But he'd decided to make his own private vigil also, and this had seemed like the time. He cooked for himself and ate, sitting on the floor in the living room of the Brixton flat, watching tv; Elsie the cat in turn watching him attentively, ready to sneak onto his lap soon as she saw half a chance.

He was thinking it was a pity he disliked dates; it took the romance out of breaking the fast on this desert-arab food, when his phone rang. It was the nursing home. Laura Preston, the old lady he'd visited faithfully – except when utterly prevented – since he came back from the Deconstruction Tour, had died about two hours after he'd left. Not unexpected. She always took an interest and had a smile for him, but she'd been saying she was very tired; and she'd kept getting these chest infections. She'd been just on a hundred years old.

Yeah, he told himself, responding politely to the matron. Yeah, it was time, she was ready. That was a good thing, and it's over . . . But the loss shook him. A sad omen.

The smell of a geriatric home was one of his early memories. Must have been somewhere his mother had been working. Shrunken creatures lying under knitted blankets, a little boy stares in through the half-open door. Maybe I learned compassion there. Or maybe I just learned about trying to hold back the tide. That some people instinctively do this, and you fail in the end, whatever you do: but somehow it seems worthwhile.

Making the best of things, my mum would say.

He switched off the tv. Cleared away his meal, put Op 130 on the sound system, took out his india stone and brought it back to the rug which he seemed to have adopted as the locus for his meditations. Fingernails on the left, and on the thumb and index finger of the right hand, kept invisibly short. The nails on the other three fingers must be exactly square and buffed smooth to perfection . . . Thinking about the government's plan to hand over the Upper House to the CCM. Which was still moving along, and which he couldn't openly resist. Pack the former House of Lords with mouthy, quarrelsome green nazis, and make Ax accountable to them. Oh, terrific . . . Benny Prem wanted watching, though any idea of a conspiracy against Ax was pretty fucking toothless at the moment . . .

Hadn't yet thought of a way to get the punters on mass to take the ATP treatment. More seriously, there were the ATP 'batteries'. A killer-app, and difficult to resist, but they were just more of the same. Green power, that gets made in a factory and you buy it from a shop or a service provider. The radical change was lost. Ax was having megalomaniac thoughts about suppressing the fucking things (because the market never will). But that was stupid.

There ought to be a saying, to match *if you're in a hole stop digging*. If the engine's turning over, stop pushing. It's time to jump on board and let yourself be carried; you're no longer the motive force. Horrible feeling, though. That was why he loved the Volvo. The fact that it had a stick and gears, and a mechanical engine; and he felt in charge. Ah well. As the music biz teaches us, lack of control is the chief misery of the struggle; and the first price of success.

Unless your name's Aoxomoxoa.

Poor Faz. Unrecognised in the crowd. Something so heartbreaking about the way he'd stood there, crazy drunk, uttering his ridiculous challenge. Yet though the incident seemed nothing now, completely upstaged by the weather, it had been dangerous – the gap between Ax and his friends and the 'real' Counterculture suddenly, horribly visible. Better keep an eye on that. Lucky that Sage and Fiorinda had known how to turn it around. Yeah, there's such a thing as good violence, exhilarating, face-saving, cathartic: but Ax would never understand that code. He paused in his finicky work with the oilstone, thinking of his brilliant ally. So fucking wise, sometimes. Yet still capable of insisting you come and admire the impressively large turd he has just laid. When this boy decided he wasn't going to grow up, he was *serious*.

And Fiorinda: stubborn, secretive little cat. It was strange to look back, from this long perspective, and see how quickly the alliance had been formed. Almost from the first meeting of the Countercultural Think Tank they'd been working together, running rings round Paul Javert, their friends only occasionally catching up with the plot. Ax Preston and Aoxomoxoa, and that extraordinary little girl, exercising faculties the music biz had left to atrophy. None of them, not even Ax, having any idea where this was heading. Sage at those sessions frequently so hammered you wondered how he could see straight, but it never shut him up; while Fiorinda was quietly stealing Ax's heart away . . .

Like something out a fairytale. I fucked her when I didn't know I loved her, and now look at my darling. Her beautiful smile, her graceful little body, so different from the fishbone waif he'd taken to his bed. Glimpses of Fiorinda, rising through the frost and snow. He could almost wish to have that time back, only to know how much he was going to love her; though God knows it hadn't been easy. To touch her hair again, as on that first night. To hold her naked in his arms, and kiss her little breasts, for the first time again.

Perhaps he shouldn't be sitting here thinking about his girlfriend's breasts. Even if it was with pure affection and no carnality . . . much. Theoretically he should be praying.

Keep me on the straight path.

But he could not recover the mindset of Ax-in-Yorkshire, struggling towards Islam. Things had happened so thick and fast, acceptance seemed like just a word. He had never prayed for the success of his enterprise, and that still didn't seem right. *Insha'llah*. In the end he just sat, feeling numb; listening to the Beethoven and wishing he could have his nice life back, a pretty-good guitarist with a pretty-good, noncommercial little band. The cat on his lap curled tight and purring hard. Oh well, he thought. I have two best friends who don't never stand no shit. As long as they'll put up with me, I'll know I haven't turned into a complete monster.

Later, he went and fetched the Qur'an and began to recite. He didn't need the printed Arabic, had it all in memory, but he took comfort in the ritual.

When he got back to Reading he left the car up the road, to avoid the inevitable flak. On the south bank, at Caversham Bridge, people were miserably watching fallen trees getting hauled out of the water; that lovely big poplar among them. But the flood had already subsided. Every storm is different. This one seemed to have had a vindictive interest in one short stretch of the Thames Valley – as if it had been planning revenge while Ax and his friends were off on the east coast, scoring points against its buddies. He walked into the site through the main entrance, Storm Damage PA coming to meet him across the devastated camping fields: Fiorinda singing, in duet with someone, that they came across a child of God, he was walking along the road . . . Interrupts herself to respond to remarks that can't be made out; rueful laughter, messages (is Evan Curran of California on site? Evan, if you come over here, someone wants to wish you a happy birthday). Who's that harmonising with her? It's not Sage. Oh, it's George. Good work getting the PA functional again so quickly.

Stardust, golden . . .

PLEASE, no more wet gear to the Leisure Centre, FUCK IT. We've run out of space.

On the fence at the gates to the arena, someone had created an installation of dead birds: glittering speckled starlings, chaffinches, a blackbird, a pitiful yellow and slate smear that had been a bluetit; and here's a swan, huge wings outspread, like a murdered angel.

Lot of damage. Only the eau de nil geodesic of the Zen Self tent seemed untouched. Red Stage was okay, but looking strangely lopsided, oh, one of the towers gone. Near the site of the Blue Lagoon, where Storm Damage PA had its outdoor headquarters, he found Dilip, Chip and Verlaine and the Heads. They were sitting around a bonfire with some Zen Selfers and others. He sat down just as George and Fiorinda arrived back from their PA slot, and joined the atmosphere – of shocked, bereft and weary people whose own home has been wrecked this time; who have finally become victims, not defenders.

'Oh well,' said Chip. 'I guess we'll have to put on the show right here in the barn.'

Even Chip the impervious sounded as if he knew that was a bad joke.

Ax glanced around. Something felt wrong, besides the obvious. He knew that Rob and the babes had gone back to London, and the Chosen were back in Taunton. Anne-Marie and Hugh and the children were probably somewhere about . . . 'Where's Sage?'

Dilip shrugged glumly. Chip and Ver kind of winced at each other. 'Sage has fucked up his hands again,' said Fiorinda, 'humping things, and punching heads the other night—'

'Fucked up—? Oh yeah, I know.'

Sage's ruined hands could give him hell sometimes, Ax'd found out about that in Yorkshire. Though you would never, ever know it from the way he behaved, or from that stage act.

'So he's gone away by himself,' Fiorinda went on, the cut-glass vowels very apparent, 'to think about how *utterly stupid and unreasonable he is*, not to use normal painkillers.'

'There's no use getting pissed off with 'im Fio,' said George. 'It never does no good.'

'Doesn't he have any NDogs?'

'They were in the van,' explained Bill.

Sage's van had been in a sorry state after the storm. It had escaped the fall of the oak tree, but the Heads had left it to be used as an emergency shelter, while they were busy elsewhere, and it had taken a battering from unscrupulous campers—

'Peter tracked down most of the nicked stuff and got it back—'

'But Sage had gone off. An' he won't have anyone going after him, when he's like this.'

Oh, he's got you well trained, thought Ax. All four of you. The stupid bugger.

'Gimme the gear,' he said. 'I'll find him.'

A film crew came and filmed the destruction, and wanted to know if this was the end of the staybehind dream. Dogs, usually excluded from the arena, trotted aimlessly. The Few took it in turns with homegrown, staybehind rockstars to go over and do live spots on the PA. A passionate, highly articulate naked hippie turned up and ranted. He'd worn nothing but mud since Dissolution Summer, and if others would follow his example, the hole in the ozone layer would heal up. A couple of hours before sunset, the Dictator-elect and his Minister appeared, coming slowly over the littered waste. What are they talking about? The heat death of the universe. Why worry about a few pretty trees? It'll all be the same in fifty billion years' time.

'Was that fifty billion, or five hundred billion?'

'Don't know as it makes much odds to you an' me, Ax.'

As they sat down with her, Fiorinda muttered *sorry*, from behind a barricade of red corkscrew curls. Sage gently tugged one of them, smiling. 'Thas' okay.'

Some councillors came along to see Ax. 'You going to yell at us about the fire?'

Fires, like dogs, were strictly forbidden in the sacred precinct.

'I'm amazed you got it started,' said one of the tribal elders, looking suspiciously at Aoxomoxoa. 'With everything fucking totally soaked. You haven't been using *chemicals?*'

'Mmm, not for firelighting,' said Sage, dreamily.

'Oh, that was Fiorinda,' explained Verlaine. 'With her brilliant little tinderbox.'

The councillors reported on the structural damage to Red Stage, and said the things such people have to say in the circumstances: everything's fixable, we're not beaten, our game plan allows for disasters, we're staybehinds, we'll stay. But they were hurt deep and it showed, and the Few (their own tower of strength lost to them, sitting there wrapped in spooky, synthetic-neurochemical-induced calm) didn't have much comfort to offer. Not right now.

'We were plannin' to start a nature studies school,' said Peter Stannen sadly. 'We found out, on the western tour, none of these Counterculture kiddies knows ash from oak.'

'Yeah, weird. AM's kids know absolutely fuck.'

'We'll have to educate them for the future instead,' said Chip. 'Like Ax says: the natural environment of people, is people.'

'ISpy Rock Festivals,' murmured Verlaine. 'Five points for a comatose crusty—'

'Five points for a naked hippy, ten for naked hippy wearing mud—'

'Septic piercing, ten.'

'Alfresco sex, five. Fifteen if involving vegetables, or pets.'

'How many of these kinds of vomit can you spot?'

'Ax Preston committing Personal Transport Hypocrisy, *nul points*—'

And so on, while the sky grew dark and the bonfire crackled.

But now reality of the inauguration loomed horribly close. The publicity was everywhere, especially that Trimurti poster; and everywhere, in every relevant or irrelevant context; in advertising, in soaps, the catchphrases lifted from Ax's speeches: *Be good to each other, It's the ecology, stupid. Positive interference, start from where we are, the natural environment of people is people, if we can just get through this part* . . . Allie had nothing to do with the latter phenomenon, but Ax began to hate her for all of it. He knew he wasn't going to be able to protect his friends from any of the horrors of the civil ceremony (that ride down the Mall, oh God); and though reports from Reading were optimistic, the Countercultural celebration plans were a mess. Nothing had been done, nothing had been decided.

They had a meeting at the Office, just before the Eid, when he came along armed with a checklist, determined to *get through to them* that this was a bad situation. The day was fine, golden sunlight pouring through the balcony windows, gleaming on all the insufferably gaudy décor. Ax sat with Allie for a change and powered his agenda along, trying not to be sidetracked by people making difficulties, about ridiculous stuff like the catering.

They didn't like the winelist. *Sage*, who couldn't tell Beaune from alcoholic Ribena—

'But Ax, even I know English red wine is filthy. Surely you're not going to let the suits offload their marketing-freebie junk on our guests, who will hold us responsible.'

'Well, obviously it'll go on being filthy if nobody drinks it. There's no reason why it shouldn't be good. We have the same climate, same chalk, same vines, just less experience—'

'Okay,' says Aoxomoxoa sweetly, 'fine.' Exchanging a glance with George Merrick that spelled, as Ax of course knew, an agreement to sabotage—

'This would be the Sage "okay", meaning, *I'm going to do what the fuck I like anyway?*'

'Thas' right.'

'Shit,' muttered Ax, but took it no further: it wasn't the moment. 'Now, the concert. Look, I don't quite understand why we haven't agreed on any kind of order in this line-up, except for Sage's extravaganza being last.'

'We didn't know if DARK were coming down,' said Fiorinda.

'Yeah, but you know that now. You've known since Monday.'

'And we've had trouble getting hold of one other person, who's supposed to be involved.'

In spite of his protestations, Ax *had* been drawn away into the Islamic community during the fasting month. It was true he hadn't been available all the time.

'Oh. Well, okay. I'm here. So tell me what I've been missing.'

'Will he be able to handle your bit?' Fiorinda asked Sage. 'He hasn't rehearsed much.'

'Oh yeah. I'm not asking for any backflips, an' he's a lot fitter than he was.'

'That's good. These wussy, non-camping, indoor-plant types—'

'Think it was the constant humiliation, up in Yorkshire, got him down the gym.'

The others, already unhappy about the unnatural configuration, the triumvirate divided, flashed nervous glances. Ax stared at his list, muscles knotting at his jaw. 'Can we move on?'

'Have you decided whether or not you're going to play "Jerusalem"?'

'No. I mean, no I am not going to play "Jerusalem". It's not appropriate. This is an overcrowded liferaft, not the City of God.'

'If Ax isn't doing "Jerusalem",' said Fiorinda. 'I'm not doing "Sparrow Child".'

'But Fio, you have to!' protested Cherry. 'It's *your song*.'

'Yeah, but I hate the fucking thing and I wish I'd never written it. I won't do it.'

'Children, children—' sighed Roxane.

Dilip leaned back in his chair and stared at the ceiling.

'We're all feeling the strain,' said Rob diplomatically. 'Look, it's lunchtime, why don't we leave this, we've been working hard, let's get something to eat.'

'Go ahead,' snapped Ax. 'I'll wait here.'

'Okay. Ax isn't doing "Jerusalem", and the nation's sweetheart isn't doing her loss-of-habitat number. Do we have a supergroup decision on "Oats and Beans"?'

'NO!' yelled several people. Everyone detested the no-brain barmy army marching song.

'So that's unanimous, is it? Well done. But too bad, we're doing it. Can't hurt the army's feelings, remember we may need them again. This brings us to the "Ode to Joy".'

'What about the "Ode to Joy"?' said Ax suspiciously. 'That's not a problem on my list.'

'There's no *problem*, Ax,' said Fiorinda. 'We just need to tell you we won't sing it.'

'What are you talking about? You have to sing the anthem, this is a state occasion, we'll have EU guests. What's wrong with the "Ode to Joy"? Good tune.'

'I think what's wrong,' said Rob, slowly, 'is that those dipped-in-shit bastards aspiring to be the European government didn't do a *fucking thing* to help us or anyone with the Boat People. They haven't achieved a *fucking thing*, over any crisis issue.'

'I can't sing,' said Allie. 'I'm only going on stage to please the rest of you, but I won't *pretend* to sing that.' There was a general murmur of assent.

Ax stared around the ring of tables, robbed of speech. His friends stared back, obdurate.

'What do you want instead, then?' he snarled. '*Fucking Rule Britannia?*'

'Nah,' said Sage calmly. 'The national anthem will be fine.'

'My God. What a bunch of fucking self-centred Little England FASCISTS—'

Slammed his chair back. Jumped up. Stormed out of the room.

Silence. 'Aren't you going after him?' asked Allie at last.

Fiorinda shook her head.

'No. We're going to let him alone,' said Sage, skull mask doing between tough love and callous amusement. 'It may seem cruel, but sometimes it's the only way.'

They broke up and reconvened in the gardens, with food and wine from the canteen: Roxane in a canvas director's chair Verlaine had carried out for hir, the rest of them lying about on the grass. Sun burnished the late summer foliage, waterbirds cackled on the lake; the occasional rumble of some passing vehicle reached them from Grosvenor Place. They hadn't been there long before Ax came up, looking ashamed of himself, and sat down between Sage and Fiorinda. The tale of legendary rock-bad-behaviour that Roxane was telling halted; and went smoothly on. George Merrick, who was rolling fat joints of resin and tobacco for the company, glanced at the triumvirate, and maybe sighed. A little later, when there was a gap in the conversation, he said, 'Hey, boss. Remember Near Miss year?'

'The summer we got rich and famous?' said Bill. ''Course 'e does. Some of it, anyhow.'

'We were on the Lizard,' said George. 'In Bill's auntie's field, hopin' to get vaporised or some such thrill. Not involved in that Rock Festival. Weren't you on there, Ax?'

'Yeah,' said the Dictator-elect, 'that was before the Chosen. When I was with Mulan.'

'D'jever get paid?'

'Can't remember. As I recall, the punters stayed away in droves.'

'Yeah. Anyway, 'course the so-called Near Miss was a washout. But that night . . . Sky had cleared, load of stars, comet like whacking big frame-freezed firework. We were sitting around drinking, me and Bill and Cack and Eval Jackson, this was before Luke's time. Sage'd wandered off to commune with mother nature.'

'Or anythin' else female he could lay his hands on.'

'He'd got involved wif one of those pretty Jerseys in the next field,' Peter recalled.

'Yeah, we was worried for her. But it was just a fling. She came to 'er senses.'

'Realised she was too good for him—'

'So anyway, he'd gone off—'

'Whatever happened to Mulan?' inquired Sage. Who had spotted where this anecdote was heading, but couldn't quite believe such utter perfidy—

'I could tell you, but it's boring,' said Ax, intrigued by his Minister's evident unease. 'Go on, George. What happened then?'

'Boss comes back, all excited. On yer feet, he says, c'mon, you gotta hear this. This guy from Taunton, playing out the back of a panel van, best guitarist you ever heard in your—'

'YOUR DEAD!'

Sage erupted, and came flying through the air. Everyone scattered as best they could, laughing and shrieking, grabbing wine bottles, too bad about that hashish, out of the way of the ferocious wrestling match which ensued, outcome by no means a sure thing. Sage had the advantage in height, and flexibility (and outrage). But George Merrick was a big guy too, with a lot of broad, full-grown muscle and two good hands—

It ended, before Dora felt impelled to call the cops, with them both lying on their backs, laughing and gasping. 'Who won?' asked Fiorinda, bending over them.

'He did,' said Sage, coming effortlessly to his feet and reaching a hand for his brother Head, 'Always does, unless I can punch him out.'

'You gotta *plan ahead*, boss. I've told you a fuckin' million times—'

'Shit,' said Ax, looking at his watch. 'I have to go. Lissen, folks, I'm *sorry*.'

'For what?' said Sage. 'For yelling at us? That was nothing.'

'For everything,' he said helplessly. 'For dragging you into this shit.'

'As I remember,' said Fiorinda, 'we were volunteers. Don't worry, Ax. Everything's going to be fine.' She grinned with sweet malice. 'If we can *just get through this part*—'

Chip and Verlaine had handed everyone a plastic cup or a bottle. Silently, they toasted him. Ax tried to laugh, choked up, and quickly walked away.

DARK came down to Reading, where they were booked in at the Holiday Inn (for old sakes' sake). Fiorinda went and stayed with them. They rehearsed: their loss still raw, sober by unspoken agreement; a guy from one of the Few associate bands acting as temporary bassist. It would be a while before they could think about replacing Tom. Charm and Fiorinda didn't have a single fight.

Sage disappeared for two days just before it, and refused to say where he'd gone or why. The civil ceremony otherwise passed off without incident.

How typical of their career, and how fitting, that they would spend most of their own celebration either waiting to go on or else up there. 'Reminds me of my mum, washing the kitchen floor last thing on Christmas Eve,' said Kevin Hanlon, aka Verlaine. And yes, it was a lot like Christmas, or Diwali or something, one of those hybrid traditional events, half party, half excruciating familial obligation (much like life in Ax's idea of the Good State), because everyone's mum had a backstage pass for this. Including Sayyid Muhammad Zayid and his entourage, Ax's family, Sage's family and Marlon Williams (Mary Williams had decided to stay away, thank God). Plus assorted VIP suits, celebs and illustrious Counterculturals from Westminster, the Celtic nations and the continent. Exhausting stuff.

Fiorinda stared at herself in the mirror. No dresser tonight. She really didn't need anyone fussing around like that, except *possibly* on tour. She'd just escaped from Alain de Corlay, the artist formerly known as Alain Jupette, who was here with Tamagotchi, the musclebound kooky-girl from Alain's band Movie Sucré. Alain in *white tie and tails*, Tam in fishscale silver from head to toe, looking like a big scary Joan of Arc, with her Dauphin on her arm. Talking like suits. God, is this where we're at? Are we doomed to become suits?

She had a moment's vertigo: saw Allie Marlowe coming towards her, in the arena at twilight, a world's end ago. *Is politics really the new rock and roll then?*

'Alain's getting very grown-up,' she complained. 'Have you seen him in his white tie? If he gets any growner-upper, I'm not going to like him anymore.'

'Don't worry,' said Sage, reaching over to take the spliff she held out. 'I have a plan, for after this. I'll have old Smash-The-State Alain dressing in girl's clothes and acting like a six-year-old again in no time.'

They were alone in the dressing room, a welcome interlude of calm. Sage was basically ready, in slick black trousers and a white singlet. Fiorinda was wearing the silver and white lace cowgirl dress. She would change, after DARK's set, for the athletic part of the show.

'You never used to wear make-up on stage.'

'Only because I was sure I'd mess it up. Didn't want to end up looking like Courtney Love, yecch.' She applied eyeliner and grinned at the skull in her mirror. 'Go on, tell me I look better without. I dare you.'

'To me you look wonderful either way, baby. As you well know.'

She wondered where remarks of that kind were leading. Not to anything that would hurt Ax, she was certain. 'At least I'm trying to look wonderful, rather than scaring people. I'm sure poor Chip has nightmares about you, after those rehearsals. Verlaine too.'

'Hahaha—' said the skull, acting tough, but looking worried. 'Nah . . . I wasn't that bad?'

'Hideous wake-up sweating nightmares about were-skulled giants biting their throats out. You were horrible to those poor kids. And Bill was really winding them up too.'

'Fuck off. I was not . . . Chip is five years older than you, Fee. And Ver is twenty-one—'

'I know. How do they do it? I don't think I was *ever* that young. Another spliff?'

'Yeah.'

They were silent for a moment, Fiorinda looking for her smokes tin. Sage was occupying several palsied plastic chairs (backstage not very palatial in these regions), long legs stretched out over three of them, leaning on the back of another, the skull's cheekbone propped on a skeletal hand, the mask's blank gaze passing idly over the dressing room clutter.

'What d'you think of Ax's Dad? D'you like him?'

'Er. Since you ask—' Fiorinda pulled a guilty face at the mirror. 'Well, sort of yes.'

'Funny you should say that. So do I.'

Ax's father was a disgrace. Untrustworthy and shiftless, and a dead weight on Ax's gentle mother. But alas, he had that flashing smile, that gleam in his eye—

'Ax must never know,' said Fiorinda solemnly: and they laughed together.

'I'm fucking glad Ramadan is over,' she went on, sparking up the new spliff. 'I now see why fasting is such a popular sport in many hard-nosed traditional cultures. It concentrated his ideas wonderful. I tell you, if he does that again next year, he's going to invade Poland—'

'Maybe we should do it with him. So he doesn't feel so alone and misunderstood.'

'I practically have been . . . But you could be right. Only we'd have to get equally as narky, or we'd just make things worse.'

He wanted to ask her about the magic. Fiorinda and the saltbox that never needs to be refilled. Fiorinda and the tinderbox, in the other half of that polished birchwood apple, that never fails, even if everything is soaking wet. Maybe he should warn her that Anne-Marie was onto her. Salt and fire . . . Well, the world is getting stranger. But why is that a *bad* thing, Fee? Why does it have to be a deadly secret?

Why does the girl who can command those pretty tricks have stark fear in the back of her eyes when Ax is getting teased about the dawning of the Age of Aquarius, the unstoppable rise of irrational beliefs in his kingdom; and she's laughing merrily along with the rest of us—?

But no, it was not the moment. Wait until there's a good time. Wait until you can deliver some protection, before you ask her to trust you.

And what, Sage wondered, watching her paint her lovely face, would be the mentality of someone who could decide, at this point, *I've had enough of this. It hurts. I'm gonna jump ship and go and live in Venezuela.* So much mystery, so much trouble and danger and promise. The adventure has only just begun.

Someone knocked on the door. Peter Stannen put his skull-head around it, gave them the thumbs-up. 'Right,' said Fiorinda, 'just a minute—'

The others, including Ax, were lurking in a bar upstairs, normally the sanctum of off-duty site security, a dartboard and gruesome calendar haven, which no one had prettified for the celebrations. In the home straight now, and everyone at last beginning to get high. As Fiorinda came in, Verlaine was saying, 'We can mint our own money, with Ax's head on it!'

'Bring back sacred measure, pounds, shillings and pence.'

'And get hated forever,' said Ax, 'by anyone who has to make change—'

Fiorinda went to Ax and hugged him. 'No one makes change anymore,' she said. 'They press buttons. Only an esoteric minor clan of Counterculturals can count. Shouldn't you be out there collecting autographs, Mr Dictator, Sir?'

'Oh God, I suppose you're right—'

Ax stood up. But when he made for the door, he found Sage in his way.

'Not so fast. Go and sit down again. We've got something to say to you.'

Ax went and sat down on a palsied plastic chair. He looked worried.

'What's going on?'

'Ssh. Just sit quietly.'

The Few gathered in a semicircle around him, DK, Roxane Smith, Chip and Verlaine, Rob and the babes; Allie, Fiorinda and three skull-headed idiots. Anne-Marie and Smelly Hugh, Jordan and Shane and Milly hanging back a little. All of them dressed in their best: a rainbow of silks and velvets, lace and leather, tech-infused polymers. Sage was inside the arc they made, holding something wrapped in peat-brown homespun. He went down on one knee and put this parcel in Ax's hands.

'Open it,' said Fiorinda. 'It's a present. From us.'

Ax unfolded the cloth and found a perfect, slender, unpolished blade of greenish stone; about the length of a man's hand, the cutting edge unblemished, as if it had never been used—

'What's this?'

'It's an axe, Ax.'

'*I know what it is*. This is the Sweet Track Jade. There aren't two ceremonial stone axes same as this in the country. What, is it a replica?'

'No, it's the original. I had to go to Cambridge to find it. It belongs, belonged, to the university because they funded the dig that turned it up.'

'A jadeite axe of uncommon perfection,' said Roxane, 'found by an archaeology student beside the causewayed road called The Sweet Track that leads from Taunton to Glastonbury. Where someone dropped it, or possibly placed it as a sacrifice, more than five thousand years ago.'

'We asked Jordan,' said Fiorinda, 'what we could get for you. He said the stone axe that's the Chosen's logo was because of the Sweet Track Jade; and you loved it, you used to take him to see the replica in Taunton museum, and drool over it—'

Tough guy Jordan shrugged, grimaced, and tried to look as if he couldn't remember this conversation. Ax stared in amazement at his brother, and then in wonder at the ancient treasure.

'Hey. *How did you get hold of this?*'

Everyone laughed.

'Oooh, my reputation,' said Sage, the skull doing its *you beyond belief* grin. 'I asked. Told them who it was for, and they reckoned that was okay. There's a letter goes with it, I'll give it to you later, which you may want to frame.'

DARK and Fiorinda went on first, with their already-legendary Rock the Boat set; and the crowd went crazy. In 'Stonecold', that rageous, paradoxical anthem, (*singalong with this and we'll kill you*—) Fiorinda felt the huge response coming back at her, caught Charm's eye and saw her on the edge of panic. Oh no, she thought. You don't run scared on me now, we're for the Big Time: and then the vertigo as she remembered, that's not what it's about anymore. Then it was the end of the set, and they were singing 'Dark-Eyed Sailor', but differently tonight: holding down the jangly guitars, pulling out the melody and the lyrics, unashamed tears on their faces, *sometimes a cloudy morning, a cloudy morning, brings on a sunshine day*—

Traditional music, immemorial loss: but we go on.

Then DARK were joined by Snake Eyes, the whole big band: short set of this unlikely fusion, and next the Heads come on, Aoxomoxoa dueting with Rob, singing Bob Marley, the way they did at Gateshead, brilliant, segueing into a NO HORRID BITS sound and vision set from the techno-wizards. Thence to the Adjuvants with DK guesting, lending his turbodrive to the kids' fragile, clever ideas; and Anne-Marie and Smelly Hugh's Rover joins *them*. PoMo thrash techno-IMMix-funk folk-punk; and last but not least, a classic little guitar band. Sage had said he was looking for *positive interference*: amazingly, or not so amazingly, they did have a fairly sympathetic crowd, it all seemed to work. At the end of the Chosen's set, they took a break. Nearly at the end of the break, Fiorinda had to scoot off in a panic to change.

She scurried back in time to knock back another glass of vintage champagne, flowing in industrial quantities and damn the crisis (Ax better never find out what George and Sage spent on this lot). Allie Marlowe rushed up to plonk a wreath of traveller's joy on her head, pinned it down, grinned at her sweetly, muttering shit, what a lot of hair; gave her a hug and a kiss. Then they're walking on stage together, Fiorinda and her bodyguards. She in a green gym tunic and footless dance tights, missing her skirts *terribly*, flowers of the wayside for her crown: hardly daring to meet their glances full of love and pride, her tiger and her wolf; and *isn't this great? Isn't this our life's blood?*

They face that roaring ocean and launch into 'Wonderwall', close harmony, a capella.

The secret of the Battle of the Sexes masque had been kept so well, most of us delirious masses really genuinely didn't know what was going on, at the end of that storming set by the three rulers of the Rock and Roll Reich, when Ax and Sage apparently unilaterally decided to do 'Under My Thumb', and Fiorinda went ballistic. Could have been a nasty stage invasion by barmy army commandos in defence of our queen, but luckily the firehoses and the foam made things clear: and who'd have thought the big bruiser had such a hidden talent for family entertainment? Well, he always was a crowd pleaser. We didn't really like the masque, it wasn't to our taste, and if you're going to take off Andrew Lloyd Webber you have to be slicker than that, Sage. But who that saw it will ever forget Aoxomoxoa as the Don, hitting on Fiorinda with that Mozart? Or Allie Marlowe, Queenpin of the Countercultural Administration, as Polly Peachum in the Beggar's Opera riff? Or Mr Dictator Preston as the Pirate King? None too soon, however, Ax doffed the fake 'tache and donned a guitar, walked over to Sage and said something – exactly what will be fuel for endless speculation. Then he started to play, and everything went quiet. We have to admit that we went quiet too: it's not exactly a new idea but we think a country's national anthem has never been given such a spine-tingling epiphany of rock-redemption since Jimi Hendrix played. Maybe not then. We forgot to breathe, we hardened hacks in the media corral. And everybody on stage, by this time a cast of thousands: bands, crews, techies, hangers on, rock-muppets, infants in arms, listened as if they were hearing it for the first time too:

> I vow to thee my country all earthly things above
> Entire and whole and perfect, the service of my love

Whole arena teary-eyed, when he started over and it was time to sing. We were frankly sobbing into our organic recycled backstage serviettes. Forgive us if this sounds mawkish. It's been a long, strange, three years on the winding road that lead us here.
Joe Mulder and Jeff Scully

What Ax said was '*I still resent this—*' and then into the solo, completely unplanned, that no one had ever heard before; which Sage thought he might actually be playing *for the first time*. He had that air of casual intuitive grace, Ax improvising: maybe having given the chords a few moments' thought, while he was pissing around being a Pirate King. Nice one, Ax.

The cast of thousands, caught off balance, recovered and formed up, tall folks at the back, Sage next to Roxane Smith. 'Reminds me of Tolstoy,' s/he muttered. 'Something he says in *War and Peace*. You may go to war like a duellist with a rapier. But when you're massively outgunned and the situation's desperate you throw away the rules, forget good taste and pick up any brutal blunt instrument . . . We're going to regret this. We're invoking demons here—'

In the dawn of this day, Sage and George had flown down to Helston to the Air Marine base, and been taken on a helicopter trip to Lizard

Point, to light the first beacon. As they sailed over Goonhilly Down they'd seen the great dish aerials of the earth station, Arthur and Uther, Guinevere and Lancelot, Geraint and Merlin, staring up at them, mute and dead. Signs of that global consciousness, the brief peak of civilisation which *for us is in the past*. They had looked at each other, unmasked in respect. My God, my God. The nav marks on the Lizard's flank painted up bright, after years of disuse. Hard times, hard times, and it's going to get worse, no doubt of that. So that's how we hepcats end up on stage, at what was formerly the site of a carefree global capitalism yoof culture annual knees-up, singing the fucking *national anthem*, with tears in our eyes. Sorry Rox, but this is an emergency—

> The love that asks no questions, the love that pays the price
> That lays upon the altar the final sacrifice—

I've seen him do that. I've seen Ax lay down his life, no joke, unreservedly, not once but over and over, to get us all out of a jam. Still don't know what makes him do it. He's just the Ax.

'You talking to me? Do I look as if I read Tolstoy? Shut up and sing.'

Some time after the show, Ax and Sage came across each other in the mêlée. Later, they were holed up in a disabled toilet in the Leisure Centre, for reasons already lost in the mists. Sage was sitting on the cistern, Ax was on the floor, propped against the wall, rolling spliffs: both of them very relaxed. Running water, sanitation, dry underfoot, nice roomy cubicle. Light's too bright, but by rock festival standards, an excellent gaff. Quite likely they were hiding from the barmy army – who were milling around in large numbers, getting emotional; and having Ax and Sage in sight only encouraged them—

'What are you going to do,' sez Ax, 'when your fans finally work out that the drug-addled drunken oaf they adore, is actually a very fuckin' clever bloke who works very fuckin' hard—'

'No problem. They all think that is what they are secretly like themselves.'

'Modest, too.'

Sage stared dreamily at the tiles on the wall. 'Ax. I made, still making, absolute shitload of money out of *Bleeding Heart*. Me personally I mean, not talking of the band. Do you want it?'

I'm happier than I have ever been in my life, thought Ax. God, this is perfect, completely perfect, this is paradise. There's nothing else I could possibly want. 'Ah, but can you get at it? In't your financial empire tied up in knots since Ivan/Lara?'

'I can get at plenty. I *said*, Do you want it?'

Perhaps he'd been a tad ungracious. 'Uh, yeah. Yes I want it. Thank you very much.'

Sage laughed, but the skull's blank sockets were considering Ax's pinned pupils with disapproval. 'Then it's yours. An' I'll tell you what all else, my dear. You ever touch that stuff again, I'm going to beat the fuckin' shit out of you.'

Suddenly the mask had vanished. It penetrated Ax's happy world that Sage had a right to be angry, meant what he said: and Ax was going to get seriously hurt—

'Hey, don't panic, come back to the party. I said *if*. And you're not going to, are you?'

'I won't,' said Ax, drug clean left him. 'I'm a fool. I will not do smack again. Not ever.'

He was looking up at Sage's natural face, and somehow kept on looking, seeing as if never before the blue eyes and golden brows, the wide cheekbones and blunt, wedge-shaped, almost animal muzzle, all centred on that overblown mouth . . . Verging on grotesque, yeah. But in some lights, and if you're in the mood, the guy can look like several billion dollars—

Sage looking back at him, with a little smile—

Someone thumped on the door. Fiorinda came in and stepped over Ax's legs.

'Ah, the lovebirds. I knew I'd find you two tucked away together somewhere romantic.'

Sage clambered precariously to the floor, lost his footing, sat down beside Ax and held out his arms. Fiorinda settled herself against his chest, sighed deeply in contentment, and gave her boyfriend a dirty look. She knew what he'd been up to.

'I'm not speaking to you.'

'Ah, don't be hard on him Fee,' said Sage, kissing her hair. 'Not tonight.'

'He's already given me a bollocking—'

'Oh all right. Come here.' She tugged at him until he was arranged to her liking, and the three of them settled together, Ax with his head on her lap, Sage's arms around them both. Wrong again, Ax thought. I was not perfectly happy, but now I am, and if I had the power this is where I would make time stop, this is where I'd stay forever.

This is it, this moment. This, now.

END OF PART ONE

The story continues in

Castles Made of Sand